A FAT

Tall Willow was inconsolable. For three days she cried and wailed as only a grieving Indian mother can. Then she went into shock and retreated from the world altogether.

The tragedy which had visited the DeGeers moved Major Pease to pity and sympathy, something he wouldn't have extended to Renee under ordinary circumstances. Pease even offered Renee a hand as Renee balanced the load on his packhorse and bound it securely.

"You'll never get her back, you know," Pease said solemnly. "You'll have to ride straight into the heart of the Lakota lands and they will be waiting for you, Renee. It's what they want you to do. You'll be dead before you ever get to her."

"I'm dead now," Renee answered brusquely.

"No you're not," Pease shouted. He grabbed Renee by the shoulders, spun him around, and shook him. "You are alive. Willow is alive. Hell, your daughter is alive. They won't kill her. She's more valuable to them whole and healthy. And like it or not, she's a wife now. She's . . . Lakota."

Renee pushed the agent from him as if Pease were an infectious carrier of the Black Plague. "She is my little girl!" he raged. I will bring her home where she will be safe and her mother will be well again. *Adieu.*"

Renee mounted, accepted the reins of his pack animal from Pease and kicked his horse into a canter.

Books by Mardi Oakley Medawar

The Glory Days of Buffalo Egbert
a.k.a. People of the Whistling Waters

Remembering the Osage Kid

Rainwater on the White Road
a.k.a. Misty Hills of Home

**For more information
visit:** www.SpeakingVolumes.us

The Glory Days
of Buffalo Egbert

Mardi Oakley
Medawar

SPEAKING VOLUMES, LLC
NAPLES, FLORIDA
2018

The Glory Days of Buffalo Egbert
a.k.a. People of the Whistling Waters

ISBN 978-1-61232-769-3

This book is dedicated to the nicest
man I have ever known:
My dad.
In loving memory from
an eternally grateful daughter.

CHAPTER ONE

In the 1830s, two brothers ventured into southern Montana and established a trade center. Crude at first, what would become a town started life as a trade-fort, a good portion of it dug out from the side of a foothill. The front and two sides were log-walled. The large cavelike room was not only the trading floor, it was the storeroom and primary living accommodation for both brothers. In a storm, it also housed the ten horses owned by the duo. True, with the horses inside, life was a tad bit cramped and gamey, but the brothers, Enois and Jaccob Webb, didn't mind the temporary discomfort, as comfort in these first wild days was not high on their list of priorities. Their trading goods and their pack horses were their only considerations. Their own personal comforts were an afterthought.

Their rough and hardy existence slowly evolved, as did

their attitudes toward their creature comforts. In time, both brothers married Crow women and moved into separate, more commodious households. Their trading fort, too, cultivated the air of an actual fort. More white men trickled into the territory and, for various reasons, many settled in with the brothers. More and more of the men choosing to put down stakes with the brothers had women with them, many of these women being white, or "damn near."

In 1838, behind the erected palisade walls of "Fourt Absarokey," there were a livery and smithy, corrals, log homes, trading center and bath house/tonsorial parlor, the proprietor of the latter eager, for the sum of one dollar, payable either in coin or trade, to relieve any and all of "uncommon smells—body hair—& troublesome vermines."

In the autumn of 1851, a pair of newlyweds, Jeffery and Adell Higgins, arrived on the brothers Webbs' doorstep, as had many more newcomers. During the past thirteen years of steady growth, "Fourt Absarokey" had slipped its bonds and had doubled its size both inside and all around the demarcation walls. The Webb brothers had a real town on their hands. Timber was desperately needed to supply the newly constructed mill, and Indians were becoming more and more peevish about the felling of trees. So, log by log, the high walls of the "Fourt" came down and were converted into planks, the product sold or bartered off to meet building needs.

Adell Higgins was a doll of a human being, barely sixteen years old, standing exactly five feet, weighing less than a hundred pounds, and owning the largest pair of blue eyes ever set in a human face. Her lanky six-foot-three husband was a mild natured fellow, good looking and twenty three years old. Following the wedding ceremony, Jeffery packed up himself and his new bride and headed toward Montana. This was Jeffery's second trip to the territory. The first had been as a bachelor. After working for the Webbs a full year, Jeffery returned to his native Colorado and married his sweetheart. Armed with promised employment and Adell's dowry of seventy dollars, life seemed long and full of prosperity for the dewy-eyed pair.

Shortly after their arrival, Jeffery plunked down the asking price—nearly all of the seventy dollars—on lumber which would become the small salt-box house in which his only son would be born on June 5, 1854. The money given over was the last bit of real currency he would ever see in his lifetime, as his employers had recently implemented a payment scheme they called "earned credits," which meant they paid in goods from their store, said goods worth so many credits, credits worth so many hours. These credits were transferable to the other businesses in town. The idea caught on so well that it lasted until the late 1860s.

Jeffery and Adell's long-legged infant weighed in just under seven pounds. Adell's labor lasted thirty six hours. She remained frail and sickly for the rest of her life. But on his birth, the young couple was overjoyed, naming the baby for Adell's father. The midwife, Mrs. Cooksey, wife to the owner of the livery business, was a little disgruntled that such a lusty man-babe would be saddled with the name of Egbert.

"I'd have named him Sam," she muttered as she scurried away from the home of the new and happy parents. "Sam's a good strong name. A name that sounds like trust. Anybody'd trust a man what looks ya straight in the eye, offers out a firm hand an' says, 'Hello thar. The name's Sam.' "

Never once was Mrs. Cooksey bothered by the notion that her personal preference in names sprang from the fact that her husband and eldest son were both named Sam. Nor did it niggle a brain cell that as a direct result of her midwifery, a goodly number of the boy babies safely delivered into her hands during the last five years had been duly dubbed Sam.

In that same month, on the dawn of June 23, 1854, and sixty miles away, in a large Crow summer camp, another male child entered the world. The Canadian-French father, Renee DeGeer, held his freshly birthed firstborn child in his two beefy hands. Tears choking his voice, in a barely audible whisper, he thanked the elderly woman who had presented him his son. In a rush of jubilation, Renee thrust the child aloft, holding the baby over his head as he let go his medicine holler. The newborn half-caste, who would subsequently be named Jacques, screamed and writhed in his father's strong hands as he was so alarmingly presented in the early morning air, cold and afraid, to his cheering throng of relatives known as the Whistling Waters Clan. Inside the birth lodge, thirty yards from where the proud father loudly rejoiced in his son, the infant's mother, a seventeen year old Crow girl by the name of Tall Willow, and the only daughter of principal chief Sits-In-The-Middle-Of-The-Ground, turned an annoyed face toward her birth attendants.

"Someone rescue my baby before his idiot father kills him."

The two boys did not meet until the summer of 1860. Both were six years old. Jacques was a Crow prince. Egbert was a town boy. Jacques wore only a doeskin breechcloth and finely sewn moccasins with multi-colored dyed quills, cut into varying sizes, used like beads and sewn into an elaborate design. His hair trailed past his shoulders, fastidiously brushed, and shining with oil, a rich deep black/auburn.

Egbert's spriggy hair was bowl cut, almost non-existent around the sides, the longer length topping his head and springing directly from his crown, the nut brown color fanning out in all directions as if he had just received a severe shock or had been struck by lightning. He wore faded overalls, which had known one or two other boys before coming into his possession. As it was summer, Egbert was naked beneath the overalls, the bib and straps touching his chest and crossing his bare back. The trouser legs were rolled up several inches above his ankles. He wore no shoes. His feet were wide, well able to support his rangy body. And his enormous blue eyes could not take themselves off the Crow boy as the young princeling stood next to his frontiersman father in the Webb Brothers' store.

Egbert, looking like a squirrel with a nut stored in its cheek, rolled the piece of hard peppermint to one side of

4

his jaw. The piece of candy was his salary, collected every Saturday for a week's work of continually sweeping the wood flooring free of tracked in dirt and the occasional dog droppings. The work kept the boy busy. Webbs' Trading had come a long way from the original hole in the side of a hill. Their new trading store (over ten years old but still referred to as the "new" store) measured five thousand square feet. Human (many of them accompanied by their dogs) traffic was always brisk.

There was a loading dock in the back where wagons were regularly coming and going, either bringing in supplies or packing out trade goods, primarily furs and hides sold by both Indians and frontiersmen. The building had a storage basement the same size as the trading area. There was an upper floor; this equal-sized space divided off into separate offices for the partner brothers. The opened area remaining between their offices was used as a game room and was equipped with a billiard table and a large poker table. Only very important men and special friends were invited up the stairs to share a game and a whiskey with the brothers. Egbert's father, a long-standing employee, was not counted in this number. Egbert was allowed in only to sweep up, empty ashtrays overflowing with ash and stubbed out cigars, and to clear away whiskey glasses, the typical debris left each and every Saturday night.

Jacques, feeling the stare of the town boy boring into his back, turned his head, his chin almost lining up with his right shoulder, his eyes slewing to the corners. Egbert in that moment crunched down hard on his bit of candy, loudly cracking it in half, and in an exaggerated wallowing motion, rolled both pieces in his mouth.

Jacques frowned at the town boy, his brows colliding over the bridge of his nose as he tugged hard on the hanging fringe of his father's buckskin shirt. Having gained Renee's attention, father and son whispered hissingly back and forth, Jacques jerking his head in the direction of Egbert.

Egbert craned over the thick handle of the broom, perking his ears, as he tried to understand the words passing between distant father and son. The words were odd, completely unfamiliar to the boy's ear. He had no way of knowing the Indian boy and his father were conversing in French. Egbert kept waiting to hear a familiar word or phrase, anything to reward his blatant eavesdropping.

Egbert knew a lot of Crow words. Crow was essentially the second language of the town. Constructed as it was on the verge of expansive Crow country, the ever-sprawling town belonged as much to the Crow Nation as it did to the whites dominating and steadily building it. Then, too, frontiersmen wafting in and out of the town typically spoke half English, half Crow. It was impossible to grow up in this town, the name of which had dwindled from "Fourt Absarokey" to "Absarokey" or Absarokee," depending on how much paint was available to various businessmen setting a sign above their establishments or how keen they were on getting the misspelling of the real name of the Crow (actually spelled "Absaroka") anywhere near anyone else's misspelling of it.

All businesses were required to preface their advertisements with the town's name. Signs blared Absarokey Hotel, Absarok Claims Office, Absarokee Bed & Board, etc. This wasn't, as it might appear, to suck up to the Crow. They couldn't read the signs. It was done to maintain agreements with the middle aged Webb brothers who had either sold the land the business stood on, or cannily leased it. The Webbs insisted on the name as another form of genuflection to the Crow people, ever aware that what the Crow gave they could easily reclaim. Then too, the displayed homage added to the queenly aura the Webbs' Crow wives radiated as they trod the streets among their forelock-tugging peasants.

This superiority wasn't restricted to the Webbs' wives. All the visiting Crow affected this pose, and, because at this time Indians still outnumbered the whites, this attitude was given back to them. Which was why when the Crow child indicated he wanted candy, all five employees of the store, Egbert's father included, fell all over themselves to give it (free of charge) to the demanding lad.

Egbert watched as the Indian boy popped a single piece into his mouth. The Crow boy dropped all four other pieces, one at a time, into the small carry pouch dangling

by its drawstrings from the fancy belt covering his breech-
string. Burning envy fired Egbert's little heart. His own
dwindling piece of candy lost its joy, turning sour and
acidic in his mouth.

Egbert propped the work broom against a counter and
silently, pushing his way around long barricading adult
male legs, made his way outside. Stepping into the bright
light, his own tanned golden hue radiated the attention.
But the disheartened boy neither felt the warmth of the
sun nor recognized his own honeyed response inside its
brilliance. Going to the end of the wide porch, Egbert sat
down on the top step and propped his elbows against his
knees, resting his face against the knuckles of his fisted
hands.

He sat there, feeling alone, totally absorbed in his own
self-pity. His torment was intense, almost exquisite. In the
way a child feels the passage of time, the fifteen minutes of
his self-imposed isolation seemed an hour. Then the large
group of Crow began pouring out of the opened double
doorway. They ignored him as they passed, talking loudly,
laughing easily as they descended the three steps, mounted
their tethered horses and sat waiting, carrying on with
their easy banter as they waited.

Egbert scooted over to the nearest squared column of
the porch and huddled against it, his blue eyes concealed
by his frowning hooded brows, glaring at the warriors.

He felt a tap on his shoulder. Head swiveling on his
neck, he looked up and into the face of the young prince
standing over him. The Indian boy's face looked just as
glum. Behind the Crow boy stood his gigantic father. The
Crow boy bucked forward, encouraged by a nudge his
father gave him. On this cue Jacques grudgingly stuck a
hand out, shoving it under Egbert's nose. A white chunk
of peppermint, drifting its tempting aroma, rested in the
palm of the privileged boy. Egbert's eyes went from the
offered rock candy to the offerer.

"Thank you," Egbert said in Crow as he snatched the
candy and popped it into his mouth before the other boy
was able to change his mind.

"You welcome," the Crow boy's father answered in
disjointed English. Then the pair bounded down the steps,

Egbert watching as Renee mounted, then bending in the saddle at his waist, extended his arm. The son used his father's arm like a rope, climbing his father, scrambling up behind Renee onto the horse, his hands locking onto the material of Renee's buckskin shirt. The group en masse kneed their horses and left the town, riding out of it like ruling lords.

Egbert sucked his new piece of candy and watched them until the dust cloud they raised obliterated them from his view. "Lucky," he said in a flat, discouraged voice. "That boy is real lucky."

The children didn't see one another again for two years. During that time Renee and his entourage of Crow warriors appeared in the trading store on official business regularly, but Egbert did not see them all that often as the town now had an informal school at Mrs. Clara's. Classes lasted half a day and were held three days a week. The school seriously cut into Egbert's entrepreneurial activities. But on one of the occasions when he happened to be in the store earning his ration of peppermint candy, Egbert learned a rather startling fact. And this knowledge came to him as he watched his father and Renee DeGeer inspect a bundle of furs the Crow offered in trade.

The two men were glaringly different. Although both men stood approximately the same height, Renee, because of his superior bulk, appeared larger. And Renee was dark, as dark as the Indians he lived with. He had long brown/black hair which, when he stood to the front of a viewer, looked extremely short because it was pulled tightly back into a single pony tail. Jeffery's hair was deep brown and home-barbered. Jeffery, having little body hair, was always smooth shaven. He tried to grow a moustache once but it was so pitiful and he was teased so vigorously, that he abandoned the effort. Conversely, Renee had a full thick beard. And it was red. Vividly red. As red as, what one ill-fated individual some years back had made the mistake of jokingly announcing as being, ". . . redder than the dick on a dawg."

Egbert never really learned what had happened to this fabled person, but he did understand that since that day, no one ever teased Renee about his beard or, for that matter, anything else. And as Egbert grew, he realized that there was always an undercurrent of fear emanating from others when in the presence of Renee DeGeer.

Everyone except, Egbert was astonished to notice, his father. Jeffery laughed good naturedly as Renee loudly bantered in his garbled English. But this easy presence dwindled as the Webbs came bounding down the stairs of their private sanctum. Using their arrival as a diversion, Egbert helped himself to a soda cracker from the nearby cracker barrel. Hidden from view as he enjoyed his stolen snack, Egbert continued his observations.

After lumbering down the stairs and greeting the frontiersman heartily, the hefty Webbs dismissed Jeffery, personally attending Renee, making a show of inspecting his bale of furs, their bawling voices sounding like a pair of argumentative bulls. Both traders, using the bulk of their combined backsides, pushed Jeffery Higgins into the background, where the latter stood, assuming a lesser's pose.

Egbert had seen his father stand aside for the Webbs many times. Jeffery's secondary status didn't embarrass his son or make him ashamed in any way. It was a fact of life that when the Webbs ventured down from their upstairs domain, they, and they alone, were the masters of the trading floor. Anyone having a problem with that did not stay long in the Webbs' employ. But Jeffery's being pushed out just when he and Renee were coming to an agreement on the furs rankled Renee.

"I don't know," Renee drawled. Folding his arms across his fulsome chest and rocking back on the heels of his squarely planted moccasined feet, he yelled over the heads of the Webbs, hailing Jeffery, and rousing him from silence. "What you think Jeffy? These two old bandits tryin' to rob Renee, eh?"

Before considering the right or wrongness of his

response, Jeffery called back, "It's a fair offer, Renny. I would have made it."

"*Bon,*" Renee grunted. With a smile stretching his face Renee extended a hand to the nearest gobsmacked Webb for a concluding shake. "Jeffy say it fair price. I take it." Then, pushing between the two Webbs, Renee laughed, "Jeffy, you gotta help me find pretty things for my womans. Willow got the mad-on with me. So mad maybe I gotta use all these credits to buy her happy again."

They were shoulder to shoulder walking toward the shelf-lined walls, all of the shelves dangerously burdened with goods guaranteed to turn a woman's head, when "Jeffy" was heard to laugh, "What have you done now?"

Off together, the two polar opposites absorbed in their own business were indifferent to the round-eyed stares sent to them by the two store owners, four clerks, assorted customers and one open-mouthed boy. Nor did the two seem to notice that other than the sound of their own voices the air inside the enormous store had become so still and so quiet that an ant's fart would have produced the same jarring effect as a double barreled shotgun unexpectedly going off.

At six that evening, after the store was locked for the night, Jeffery and his son walked toward their small home a mile across and on the edge of the town. They wore light coats as the spring evening air still held winter's tenacious chill.

"Pa," Egbert said, slipping his hand into his father's, "I didn't know you and Renee were bestest friends."

"He's Mister DeGeer to you," Jeffery gently, but firmly corrected.

"But you call him 'Renny.' "

"Yes I do," Jeffery replied. "I call him that because I am an adult, his equal, and most importantly because he invited me to."

Egbert did not respond. His mind was concentrating on his father's statement that he was Renee DeGeer's equal. Renee was an important man. Egbert's heart fluttered realizing that his father, too, must be an important man. Egbert couldn't understand, observant as he was, how he had come to miss such a momentous piece of information.

Egbert's good feelings weren't to last. As they approached their house, he felt his father stiffen. Then both father and son stopped, standing silent and still as they stared at their house. There in the fading light stood Mrs. Cooksey on their front stoop, wiping her hands into the body of the apron tied around her ample waist. Egbert feared his father would squeeze the bones of his hands into powder. Jeffery Higgins might appear to be slightly built, but his strength was unbelievable. Working for the Webbs involved hard physical labor of lifting boxes and barrels. Under his oversized shirts, Jeffery had muscles Egbert, never having seen his father naked or even partially clad, had never suspected. But he felt them, crying for his father to let go of his hand.

This brought Jeffery out of his daze. In a voice Egbert had to strain to hear, Jeffery said, "Go to Mrs. Cooksey's house. Be on your best behavior and wait in her kitchen until word comes that you can come home." That barely said, Jeffery bolted from his son's side, running toward their home.

"She ain't good," Mrs. Cooksey said. Her voice choked back sobs; her eyes were red-rimmed and teary. "An' the babe's gone."

Jeffery staggered away from the stoop and stood with his back turned to the woman. His shoulders were hunched, his hands set deep in his pockets as he struggled with his emotions. He was crushed. Adell's miscarriage was her third in two years, and had come in the middle of her fifth month. The length of this pregnancy had filled Jeffery with such joy, such hope that this time she would carry the child full term.

"What was it?" he asked in a rasping whisper.

"T'were a girl-babe." Mrs. Cooksey did not add that the baby had looked like a porcelain doll complete with a shock of dark curly hair and rosy cheeks. Nor did she say that it had been the most beautiful premature baby she had ever seen, or that in her learned opinion, if the child had come to term, it would have looked like an angel incarnate.

11

"She suffered bad with this slip," Mrs. Cooksey did volunteer.

She pulled the door closed on the off chance that Adell, sleeping in the front bedroom, might overhear the conversation taking place on the stoop. "The babe was too early but even so, it was a good weight. Your woman had to go through a full labor to pass it out. Not like the last times when they just sorta fell out, the whole thing bein' over with higgle-de-jig. No," the woman clucked her tongue, shaking her head sadly, "this time was a torment. She was already bad off when I come to do my regular check on her. I found her flat out on the floor an' bleedin' bad. I did ever'thing I know to keep her from passin' that babe, but I was already too late when I found her."

"Can I," Jeffery put a hand to his brow, shielding his eyes, hiding his tears which sounded in his voice. "Can I see the baby? I've never gotten to see any of the babies." Mrs. Cooksey went to him, folding her arms around him, allowing him to weep uncontrollably. "There have been so many of them," he sobbed. "We've buried so many."

"They're with God," Mrs. Cooksey said softly. "You just rest now," she said guiding him into the house. "You just sit yourself down an' rest. Trust God an' me to tend that baby. Poor li'l mite is in safe an' caring hands."

Life inside the small house changed radically after that day. Adell remained poorly. And in, as Mrs. Cooksey termed it, "a woman's way," which meant she was menstruating on a frequent basis, so frequently that Jeffery was obliged to sleep on a pallet on the floor of his son's small bedroom located to the rear of the kitchen. Egbert was no longer allowed to accompany his father to the trading store. His new responsibility was to the caring of his steadily weakening mother.

"I don't need my son to pamper me!" Adell sobbed.

"We got no choice," Jeffery yelled down at his distraught wife. "You're not fit to take care of this house and yourself. You have to rest and build back your strength. And Bertie's all we got to count on. Mrs. Cooksey's kind, but we can't have her here day and night. We're beholdin' to her too much as it is." Jeffery did not add that he could not abide the woman and her meddlesome ways. After all Mrs. Cooksey's kindness, he felt guilty simply thinking it.

"She doesn't mind."

"I mind," Jeffery shouted. "I mind very much!"

Adell never fully recovered her health. Jeffery's self-imposed celibacy, meant only as a temporary measure, stretched into months, Jeffery finally moving a cot into his son's room along with all of his clothing. The marital bedroom became Adell's private sickroom.

The altered morning routine began sharply at 5:30 each and every morning, Jeffery and Egbert rising and wordlessly making their beds before moving into the kitchen where Egbert tended the stove while Jeffery readied the coffee pot. While Jeffery washed and dressed behind the curtained off "lavvy," Egbert sliced bread and pan-fried it. This form of toast and a cup of coffee served as breakfast, and was taken to Adell on a tray by her son. She smiled painfully each morning Egbert appeared with the tray, but as often as not, later in the morning when Egbert removed the tray, nothing had been touched. The coffee with its heavy lashing of cream had congealed, the toast shiny with grease, had turned as hard as a board. Jeffery kissed Adell's cheek as he set out for work, leaving his son solely responsible for the running of the house and the tending of the ailing Adell. This was not a good system, and Jeffery agonized silently as his wife drifted into a steady decline, but there was nothing else he could think of to do.

Had there been a doctor closer than Bozeman, Adell might have been saved, for she was suffering from the insidious ailment, pernicious anemia, made worse each time she endured an untimely menstrual flow, the loss of valuable iron going unreplaced as her dietary supplement plummeted due to her lack of appetite and the family's habit of frugality with fresh meats. They were not vegetarians. They were simply poor. Meat always went into the stew or soup pot and was stretched with water to last a full week. Soda bread and coffee were the staples.

Owing to all of this, Adell was in serious trouble.

Over the months Adell worsened. She lost weight daily

along with wads of hair and skin elasticity. She began to resemble a cruel caricature of her former self. Her front teeth, once thought of as charming over bite, bucked out from under a drawn-back bloodless lip, the lip permanently fixed against receding gums. Her cheekbones, never a strong feature, dominated her face as her eyes sank farther into her skull. And as her liver failed, Adell radiated the orange hue of a ripening pumpkin.

Mrs. Cooksey was with Adell more often than not, practically a live-in. Egbert was an invaluable help, but Mrs. Cooksey was appalled by the idea of the child attending a dying woman or washing out menstrual rags. There were just some things a little boy had to be spared. Jeffery finally relented his pride and Egbert was bustled out of the house. Jeffery would not take the boy back to the store with him because he wanted Egbert close should Mrs. Cooksey need to send for him. But outside of tending the vegetable garden, there wasn't really a lot for Egbert to do.

It was a hot August day. Egbert wandered, his overalls pant legs rolled up to his knees, his feet bare as he plodded along the dusty road that led into the town as well as out of it. The sun beat down on his head and shirtless shoulders as he slapped his feet against the road, and watched tiny dust clouds puff out from between his toes. Dragging a stick behind him, leaving a lightly furrowed trail, he hummed, "Shall We Gather At The River," a song Mrs. Cooksey forever lent full voice to, and in its own way comforting to both mother and son forced to hear it over and over again as it was the only song Mrs. Cooksey knew all the way through. He heard hoofbeats in the distance behind him and subconsciously responded, moving to the far right side of the road, continuing on with his walk in the same self-absorbed manner.

The horse and rider eventually caught up with him, Egbert still paying little attention. It was only when the horse reined up that Egbert's head jerked up, his eyes squinting against the sun at the shadowed rider.

Awed that the lone rider was none other than Renee DeGeer, Egbert respectfully backed onto the verge of the road, swallowing hard as Renee spoke to him in garbled English.

"Ain't you Jeffy's boy?"

"Yessir, Mr. DeGeer."

"I understand you mama be sick."

"Yessir."

"You leavin' her all alone?"

"No sir. Mrs. Cooksey's with her an' Mrs. Cooksey don't like me in the house no more. She tells me to go off an' play." The boy lifted both shoulders, his palms skyward as he shrugged, "I got no place to go play."

Renee barked a short laugh. "You ain't got you'self no play friends?"

"No sir."

"Well that ain't no good," Renee snorted. The saddle squeaked as Renee moved around in it, balancing his crossed arms on the saddle horn as he leaned toward Egbert. "I got me an idee. I know where there be play friends for you. You come with me, an' you have you'self a good day." Renee leaned farther forward extending his arm. Egbert looked at the strong masculine forearm as if it were a snake. "Come on boy," Renee urged. "You be safe with me. You papa my strong friend."

"I—I can't stay away from home for too long," Egbert stammered. "My pa won't know where I am."

"Yes, he will. After I take you to my camp I ride back to the store an' I'll told Jeffy where you be. Is gonna be all right. I promise."

Egbert clasped hold of Renee's hand, as the frontiersman hauled him up from the ground. The single motion, ordinary in function, was, as Egbert would realize in his declining years, thoroughly and explicitly symbolic.

Egbert, having never in his life been on a horse, bounced like a badly synchronized rubber ball behind Renee. The horse started to snort and jerk its head. Only a mile's ride down the road Renee halted, turning in the saddle, looking his small passenger directly in the eye.

"Boy!" Renee boomed. "You ain't no good on a horse. You makin' this horse mad with all you hoppin' around. You keep doin' that an' this horse throw our butts on the ground."

"I'm sorry," Egbert whimpered. "I'm doin' my best."

"That ain't no best," Renee scoffed. "Thata worst. Now, you just sit there an' do like I'm toldin' you. You know my shoulders, yeah? Well you keep you shoulders right square with mine. When I lean, you lean. Always with my shoulders, you understand? An' you keep them little skinny hips right even with mine. If I'm sittin' down you ass ain't suppose to be in the air. That's wrong son. Can you do like all this?"

"Yessir," Egbert managed in a small voice.

"Oh *mon Dieu,* I hope you can. Otherwise this ole horse gonna throw us both away an' run off laughin'."

Thankfully the small village was only another four miles away. Renee's horse continued to threaten with each jog but saw them safely home.

That began Egbert's first day in the autumn camp of the Whistling Waters Clan. This small camp, containing only a few of the families of the larger clan, had just recently broken off from the large summer camp, and was recouping from the demanding summer activities before moving on to the site of the winter camp where they would join the rest of the clan as well as several other clans.

High Plains Indians, typically nomadic, rarely moved more than the four acknowledged times within a well calculated year, each move timed by the seasons. The first move was the spring move, and made by separate clans or families breaking away from the winter camp. The winter camp was comprised of bands, these bands broken down into individual family clans. Counting only the heads of the warriors, each clan could contain as many as one hundred males, accompanied by wives, children, herds of horses, and an incalculable number of dogs.

In order to meet the needs of so many people wintering for as long as five months in a single area, the winter site had to be large enough to accommodate everyone comfortably. But even so, the protracted length of time spent in one spot with families in such close proximity tested the patience and good will of everyone involved. It was with a sense of relief that smaller groups split away at the first sign of spring. The time spent in the smaller spring camps was used to repair lodges, fatten horses on new grass, while the people readied themselves for the strenuous summer work season.

As the spring days lengthened and the night air lost its chill, with all the migratory instincts of the animals they were to hunt, families readied themselves for what was considered the most important move in their calendar.

In this second move, all of the bands united for the summer, setting up a huge hunting camp, tepees stretching for mile upon mile, snaking rivers, dotting valleys. But before the weeks of hunting officially began, old friends savored joyous reunions, newborns were celebrated and named, and new marriages were agreed to. The first weeks in the summer camp were also spent observing religious ceremonies.

When the summer hunting time ended, typically the last weeks of June, smaller family clans splintered off in this the considered autumn move, the third phase of Crow life. This camp was the most relaxing of all the camps in that there was plenty of food available, the weather, barring the seasonal thunderstorms, pleasant. Families enjoyed a more leisurely pace of life, recuperating from the hectic days of summer. As was their wont, Renee's family and select relatives moved close to the town of Absaroke. But their choice in autumn campsites had nothing to do with the town. This valley that many of the Whistling Waters returned to year after year was traditional ground, and it was into this same valley that a lifetime ago, two brothers known as Webb slogged their way with the idea of setting up competition (on a very small scale) against the northwest fur companies. This site was also chosen because of the nearby Fort Ellis. The brothers had not simply blundered into their prosperity. Everything, right down to the marrying of Crow wives, had all been carefully orchestrated.

And year after year, in this same peaceful valley, women labored tanning the green hides, product of the summer hunt, while the men did just about whatever pleased them. Which meant long days of storytelling and gambling, their summer work of raiding and hunting behind them for another year.

When the leaves began to change their color, the clans moved for the last time, going to the winter place chosen beforehand and voted on by the principal chiefs. This land was selected for its pastures, good water and wood sources, and even more importantly, its many trees. Thick stands of trees were needed as winter lodges were set well within the tree lines, the tall conifers and pines acting as natural windbreaks. And there in that place, the gathered clans would stay until the worst of winter was solidly behind them, ending for another year the natural cycle of the Crow life pattern.

Egbert did not know any of this, nor did he know that the camp he began to consider his second home was in truth a short-term addition to his daily life. All of it had the feel of permanence. Daily, following Mrs. Cooksey's early morning arrival, Mr. DeGeer would appear at the door and Egbert willingly clambered up behind him, excited by the expectation of yet another day in the Crow camp and in Jacques's company.

For the first time in his memory, Egbert was enjoying himself as a boy should, carefree and with a horde of free-roaming playmates. While he footraced in teams of sprinting boys, or learned to ride a pony and shoot an arrow through a rolling hoop, Egbert did not consider that the reason he was barred from his mother's room was because she was dying. And dying brutally.

But on one afternoon a small alarm bell did sound inside Egbert's skull when Mr. DeGeer informed him, and in an unusually thick and husky voice, that a sleeping place was being provided for him inside the DeGeers' large family tepee. His father, it seemed, had given Egbert permission to spend his nights as well as his days in the Crow camp. Jacques whooped with joy, while Egbert, a smile frozen on his face, struggled against a worry busily worming inside him like a writhing maggot.

During the last days of Adell Higgins's time on earth, her son found himself easing into the DeGeer household, toting baby Marie on his hip, helping Willow fetch water, rolling with Jacques as they wrestled like a pair of puppies, and squealing delightedly as he and Jacques dangled in the air, each of them hanging on to Renee's flexed arms. Renee raised and lowered the boys as if they weighed nothing at all.

A week later, Renee rode into the family camp. He looked drained. After dismounting, reins in hand, he solemnly approached the two staring boys. Egbert flinched as Willow, baby Marie on her hip, came up from behind and placed a protective hand on his shoulder.

Over the heads of the two boys, husband and wife conversed with each other in French. During the brief time in their company, Egbert had come to know this as the DeGeers' private family language. This personal language excluded outsiders, even clan members from the DeGeer confidential business. While Egbert had been in residence, the family had conversed mainly in Crow, for politeness, while Renee translated the lion's share of the conversations. Gradually Egbert had picked up more of the Crow language as well as being able to say good morning and good night in French.

The conversation flying thick and fast over his head, he knew by instinct he wasn't suppose to understand, and that worry worm, the one Egbert had lulled to sleep, instantly woke up with a whipping twitch.

"She died," Renee gruffed.

"How is the man?"

"He's bad. How do you expect him to be? The woman he loved just died. He wants me to bring his son back."

Willow exhaled deeply through her nose. Absently, she adjusted the toddler on her hip. "I don't think the boy should go there. It's too soon."

"That's not for us to decide. We are not his parents."

"Then you should talk to the man, Renee. Make him see reason. The child should stay with us. At least until the man has finished his grieving."

Renee's head snapped back as he let go a soft mocking laugh. "You're not fooling me, Woman. I see your heart in your eyes. You like this boy. You've gotten it into your head to keep him."

"He's a good boy," Willow sniffed, tossing her long, loose hair haughtily. "He's not afraid of us and he adds a special life to this family. Only an idiot would throw him away."

"Am I an idiot!?" Renee yelled.

"When you go giving perfectly good boys away," Willow retorted hotly, "yes you are."

Renee scrubbed his clean-shaven face with one hand. That was another thing Egbert had learned about the DeGeers. Renee was only allowed to wear his famous beard when he was so far from Willow that she couldn't get her hands on him and shave him.

"Woman," he tried in a voice straining to keep its patience, "we are Crow. We are not Lakota. We cannot kidnap white children. We have peace with the whites. We cannot break that peace for the sake of one male child."

"I remember a time," she said, "when you didn't care very much how the whites felt about anything. In that time you would have kept this boy if I said I wanted him."

"That was in a time when I was young, desperately in love, and a little bit crazy," Renee responded evenly. "*And*, there weren't so many whites around, so who cared what they thought about anything. Now that more and more of them live here, I have to care what they think. I don't like it, but I can't ignore them anymore. Our people are surrounded by the Blackfeet, the Lakota, the Arapaho, the Shoshone, and the Cheyenne. We don't need another enemy. But what we do need are the guns the whites give us to protect ourselves against our traditional enemies. Besides, Jeffery is my friend and he is suffering because of his dead wife. Am I to add to his misery by betraying his trust and stealing his son?"

Willow frowned, pouting as she turned her face partially away from him. Renee fought hard at the smile tormenting his lips. He knew she hated it whenever he won an argument. Willow did not know how to accept defeat graciously. This was why he wasn't surprised by her stubborn rebuttal.

"I protest sending him back to that backward culture. I protest this waste of a perfectly good child. And the next time you bring a child into my home, know this, Renee DeGeer. I'm keeping it."

After heart-wrenching, tearful goodbyes, Renee, in the company of a party of seven Crow warriors, galloped Egbert home. Less than fifty yards from the Higgins' front door, the party stopped. With one arm, Renee lowered Egbert to the ground. Before sending the child off and turning to leave, Renee said in his garbled English, "Don' be afraid of nothin'. If you ever need me, I will know an' I will come."

A fat tear rolled down the curve of the child's cheek as Renee and his Crow departed, the hooves of their horses throwing back chunks of soil and grass as they hastened away from the house of grief. Ineffectually, he cried after them, running as hard as his legs would pump, waving his arms, screaming as loudly as he could, "Wait! Wait!" But they did not hear him. He ran and ran until he dropped to the ground, paralyzed from exhaustion. Lying there, helpless and alone, he wept himself to sleep. He did not feel his father's strong arms lifting him, carrying him home, laying him down on his own bed. Nor was he conscious of Jeffery lying down beside him, holding onto him as Jeffery wept copiously, grieving for his woman and the life they had known together.

CHAPTER TWO

Shortly following his wife's death and subsequent funeral, Jeffery Higgins changed. It was not for the better, nor was it gradual. One day Egbert had an affectionate father. The next, he simply did not. And it was all down to a slip of Mrs. Cooksey's lips. Had the good lady considered the grieving husband might overhear her, she would, as an act of decency, have kept her opinions to herself until a more appropriate moment. But as Mrs. Cooksey had been a second mother to Adell, she felt that as such she was more than entitled to her full bout of grief, which she thoroughly vented, sobbing uncontrollably, wailing as the coffin was lowered into the earth.

It was at the reception in the Higgins' home, the small sitting room filled with respectful mourners, all of them enjoying the potluck meal provided by the good ladies of the town, that Mrs. Cooksey let go her remarks to her surround of attentive listeners. The few words, innocently said and never meant to be overheard by any male, much less the newly departed's own husband, would forever play on Jeffery's mind, warping it, fatalistically discoloring the rest of his life.

"Over-birthing's what killed that poor little mite. But if there was a penny in this town, not already trapped deep inside a Webb's pockets, then a proper doctor could have saved her. But like I said, proper doctors cost cash money. An' that really fires me up. Them two squaw wives of the Webbs get their precious selves hauled over to Bozeman whenever a piss-ant bites 'em, but here was this poor baby left to die like a whelpin' bitch-dog jest because her man is heavy debted to the Webbs. I'm tellin' you, bein' poor is a sin. An evil sin!"

"Just give him time," was the collective comment of the concerned citizenry as Jeffery's lack luster attitude was noted. "He's young and strong. He'll bounce back." And after three months, Jeffery did seem to be bouncing, perhaps not quite as high as he once had, but there was a hopeful glimmer of his gaining momentum. Concerned townfolk returning to their own business, breathed a unified sigh of relief.

It was noted, but brushed aside, that Jeffery ambled about in the store. This was a nuisance in that he was more times than not merely in the way of others, including customers and clerks alike, who were involved in actual business. He seemed to be active, but precious little action resulted. In greeting patrons, his smile no longer reached his eyes, his laugh was forced, hollow, his clerking services steadily devolving into more of a nuisance than a help. In true ostrich fashion, his long-standing friends chose to ignore these warning signs.

His son Egbert appeared to be the polar opposite, sprinting about the town like a dervish, all of his furious activity as intent as his father's was lax. Egbert had landed a new job, one a ten year old could really get his teeth into. Egbert was the butcher's boy, and the delivery job paid in meat. In all weathers Egbert dogtrotted the town, thick

23

buffalo steaks impaled on a pole, the combined weight of pole and load digging into his shoulder. It scarcely mattered to anyone that the raw steaks were exposed to every germ and bacteria known to God as Egbert scuttled about on his deliveries. The product he was in charge of was wrapped in nothing other than brisk Montana air. Butcher paper was an unheard of commodity. It was not on the order list from the East because it was too expensive and too wasteful. Besides which, butcher paper could only be used once. A good stout pole was a thing forever.

Shopping housewives picked out cuts of meat and then returned to their homes waiting for the butcher's boy to do the messy bit, handling the blood-weeping goods, delivering it safely to their kitchen doors. As a result of this hard work, Egbert and Jeffery ate better than at any time in their memories. The irony being that Adell had died of pernicious anemia. The steady diet of steaks her husband and son were currently appreciating would have saved her. But as neither were aware of that fact, they ate their meals with gusto, which filled Egbert with a special pride as these mealtimes were the only moments in his life as a widower that Jeffery actually seemed to enjoy.

And then everything changed again.

Jeffery's attention had been sparked. Within the past week, the news of gold strikes became the buzz of the town. Already the town was emptying of men heading off toward the rumored strike area, a place in northern Montana called Gold Creek, presently being mined by two brothers, James and Granville Stuart.

The thought of gold further warped Jeffery's already confused mind. In a dauntless bid to disembroil himself from the oppressive hold of the Webb brothers, he leaped from pan to fire, into the ensnaring clutches of the brothers Stuart.

In his haste to grab some of the fabled riches in this the first gold rush of Montana, Jeffery was blind to the impending jeopardy. He only heard Mrs. Cooksey's voice. "It's a sin to be poor. An evil sin," and he was as convinced as she that it had been his penniless bondage to the Webbs, more than her insidious ailment that had killed Adell.

THE GLORY DAYS OF BUFFALO EGBERT

Astounded that his father was actually leaving him, Egbert stood wide-eyed and silent as Jeffery packed up his few articles of clothing, stuffing them into shoulder carry bags.

Jeffery spoke as hurriedly as he packed. "I thought I was gonna be walkin' most of the journey, but Sam Cooksey decided to go at the last minute so a crowd of us are going with Sam in his buckboard."

He threw the bags across his shoulder, then straightened, looking down on his son. Egbert was so deeply dismayed he couldn't take his eyes off the quilt covering his father's bed. Jeffery placed a hand on his son's shoulder, the first physical contact between the two since Adell's passing.

"Now Mrs. Cooksey says you're welcome to sleep in with her an' her brood, but if you want to stay in your own home and have her just look in on you, she'll understand. I told her you were a big boy able to look after yourself. An' anyway," Jeffery managed a lame smile which Egbert, looking up at his father, did not return. "I'll be back by Christmas an' we'll be rich as kings. Then we'll go someplace nice, like, New York City. I hear a lot of good things about New York City. They have fine restaurants, and schools. An' only rich people are allowed to live there. So once we're rich, we can live there too."

"I like it here," Egbert replied quietly.

Angered, Jeffery jerked his hand away, turned his back on his son, and proceeded to march stormily through the small house. "You'll live in New York City and you'll like that!"

Egbert jumped as the door slammed hard behind his father. In the silence of the house Egbert imagined he heard his father's boots crunching the hard ground as Jeffery walked purposefully away. Sobbing, Egbert ran to the sitting room, pulled back the calico curtain draping the window, and watched his father's back as Jeffery walked forever out of Egbert's life.

Mrs. Cooksey couldn't control him. She tried but she had five children of her own. Egbert was turning out to be

25

more work and worry than all of her own combined. The child did not seem natural. He did not play. He worked. And he worked every hour God sent. What he did not take in trade he stockpiled in credits with the Webbs. All of this Mrs. Cooksey tried to believe was bearable, until Egbert found part time employment in Absaroke's newest and most infamous establishment, a whorehouse-cum-saloon known as the War Shield. Working for "Mother Irene" was, for Mrs. Cooksey, Egbert's final rip in the cloth. She stopped wasting her valuable breath on Egbert, saving it instead for Jeffery's return.

Mother Irene has a special place among The Notorious Women Of The West. The one photograph taken of her smiles out at the unsuspecting in horrific sepia, her dark eyes glittering, explicitly alive with obscene notions, apparent even across the decades. Edentulous (because of an over-fondness for anything sweet which caused her to lose every tooth in her head), her chin meets her nose. She wears a slashing smile and thick lips, heavily rouged, looking black, which seem to wrap around her head. Her hair, in a matronly bun, adorns the top of her skull like a crown. Her clothing is a dance-hall nightmare, hanging rather than decorating her shriveled body. Looking more like a gnome in drag than a human being, it is an impossibility to equate this image with the amorous legend living on after her. But impossible to believe or not, the fact remains that this person was, in her day, the most sought after woman in the Montana Territory.

Her looks had nothing to do with her popularity. Conversely, her edentulous state had everything to do with it. Just as the sign behind the bar reading, "Better head served here," had nothing to do with the beer on tap. And for a nominal fee, Mother Irene willingly made a believer out of any man crossing the threshold of her establishment.

Enois Webb became an ardent admirer of the odious woman. There were some things a man simply did not impose on his wife, and this particular said "indignity" was extremely close to Enois Webb's heart. So much so that in no time at all, Mother Irene's War Shield Saloon boasted a pool table, said table formerly of the Webb brothers' game room.

Although Mother Irene looked old enough to be everyone's mother, the truth was that when the lady passed away, some eight years after establishing the War Shield, she was only thirty seven years old.

Mother Irene's "daughters" (three of them) were as profane and as homely as their adoptive mother. Sometimes their risque antics were more than just a little off-putting even to their more hardbitten clients. On the day the pool table arrived, two excited patrons of the saloon paid a high price, traded to Mother in furs, for a try at the table. As the game progressed, the winning opponent, cue stick in hand, craned over the table, lining up an important shot. It was then that Christine hiked her leg up, planted her foot over the corner pocket, and lifted her skirt, revealing the threadbare material of the aged knickers straining to cover the darkened and thoroughly quarried cavern of her crotch, all the while hooting a laugh and shouting, "Shoot it in!"

The poor man's concentration went out the window, he lost the match and reportedly never again touched a pool cue during the remainder of his long life.

And it was in this atmosphere that an appalled Renee located Egbert a year later.

He almost didn't recognize the boy. Egbert had grown, but Renee, expecting that type of change had come prepared for it. What he had not expected, and nothing could have prepared him for, was the jaded and worldly attitude the boy displayed.

It was a given that simply being around Mother Irene could wear down an angel, but she wasn't a cruel person. If anything, she had a tendency to be too generous. Egbert had not suffered in her company—seen and heard too much, yes—but he had not been abused. Egbert's problems went deeper than that.

But when Renee clamped a hand on Egbert's arm, he wasn't interested in the boy's problems. His mind was set on a fatherly solution. Fighting against same, Egbert bucked and hollered as Renee lifted the boy by the back of his trousers and hauled the lad outside where, stretched out across his knee, Renee proceeded to apply open palm to raised buttocks, each delivered blow cracking the air like an exploding cherry bomb.

"I did the best I could with him," Mrs. Cooksey assured, following Renee around the Higgins' house. "He's just contrary. The minute you say 'don't,' he's gonna do." Easing in closer to Renee as he bundled up Egbert's personal items, Mrs. Cooksey noisily whispered in Renee's ear. "How did you say Mr. Jeffery died?"

Renee scowled darkly at the woman. His black eyes flitted toward Egbert sitting stonily in a cushioned chair, staring out of the window. The child acted as if he hadn't heard. Renee knew that he had and cursed the meddlesome woman nipping at his heels. Instead of satisfying her curiosity he said instead, "You man say for me to tell you he ain't comin' home. He say to tell you that maybe he come home after the next cold season."

Mrs. Cooksey clicked her tongue loudly. "I heard that same message last fall. I'll look for that man when I see him comin' an' not a minute sooner, but thanks for your trouble anyway." She leaned in again; this time she didn't bother whispering. "What's gonna happen about this house?"

For the first time since entering, Egbert in tow, Mrs. Cooksey flapping behind him, Renee took stock of his surroundings. The house was immaculate. Mistakenly, Renee likened its condition to Mrs. Cooksey, never once considering the child may have maintained the home solely and alone.

"He ain't goin' to need it no more. When his papa say for me to take the boy, I say to him, 'Jeffy, I live with the Crow,' an' he say, 'Then that's where my Bertie live too.' He didn't say nothin' about this house, so, if you want it, I give it to you."

Two pair of eyes slewed toward Egbert's direction. Neither adult breathed, waiting for some sort of protest from the orphaned child. When none was forthcoming,

Mrs. Cooksey accepted ownership with a nod of her head.

Egbert rode behind Renee, his arms knotted around Renee's waist, the horse running at a comfortable speed. Bitterly, the ride reminded Egbert of happier days. The days when he had felt secure, had two living and caring parents, and a childhood. He hadn't felt or had either in such a long time. He had even given up on Renee, believing Renee's last words to him, "If you need me, I'll know and I will come," to be, according to the clients of the War Shield, a load of buffalo muffins.

A spark of joy ignited inside Egbert when Renee had first sauntered into the saloon. But the joy quickly died as Egbert felt the blast of fury radiating from Renee. Just as Egbert hoped Renee felt his fury for the public whipping Egbert had suffered. But if Renee felt it, he didn't seem to care as neither had spoken more than two words since the humbling incident.

Before sunset, Renee reined in not far from a small stand of trees. After dismounting he pulled the petulant child down. Egbert jerkily came to stand on his own two feet.

"Gather wood," Renee barked.

Like mortal enemies trapped on the same desert island, each went about setting up a night camp with as little contact with the other as could be managed. It wasn't until the night surrounded them, its negativity threatening to encroach on the small pocket of light battling back the rim of blackness, that Renee finally broke the flinty silence.

He cleared his throat noisily while poking a long stick at the fire. His naturally spirited voice in its halting, broken English, cut through the still air, silencing the chorus of ground crickets and the twitterings of night birds roosting in the treetops.

"You want to hear about you papa or no?"

"I don't really care," Egbert muffled.

Renee studied the small face of the boy sitting opposite the fire. The dancing light colored the child in oranges and purples. He was a handsome boy. But his attitude was driving Renee over the brink.

"Well I gonna tell you," Renee growled. "He was a brave man, you papa. He died well. A boy should be proud of a papa like that."

Egbert leaped to his feet and with the same motion threw a stone into the fire, sending up a showering spray of sparks as he screamed furiously, "I don't give a damn about him! Just like he didn't give a damn about me! I'm glad he's dead. I hope some Injun scalped him an'—"

"You got you wish," Renee interrupted, his voice thunderous.

Egbert's tantrum stopped abruptly. For a long moment he stood, staring stupidly at the man sitting cross-legged on the other side of the fire.

Renee locked eyes with the boy and, without breaking the contact, continued, "You papa, he diggin' for gold, yeah? He tell me he diggin' it for you, so you be rich. So you be safe. Only he the one ain't safe. He went diggin' around where he not suppose to be. An' he do that because them two Stuart brothers, they got the other places all claimed up. An' you papa, he owe 'em big money. He got he'self trapped workin' for them an' they were workin' him like a mule-slave. So he go away from them. He go to a dangerous place, a place what belong to the Lakota. An' the Lakota don' like that so they get him. They get him, but they don't kill him dead like they thought they do.

"Jeffey, he turn out to be harder to kill than that." Renee pretended not to notice Egbert's knees wobble, then give out, the boy's bottom colliding with the earth in a solid thump. Renee untied his long ponytail and with both hands scratched at the base of his skull, his long dark hair flying like a wing. Renee tossed his head, his freed hair swirling around him. More relaxed and satisfied now that he had an attentive audience, he continued his story in a casual tone, as if the story had nothing to do with either the teller or the listener.

"When them Lakota leave, Jeffey wake up. He got no hair, but he awake. An' hurtin'. The first thing he know he gotta do is get off that mountain an' get he'self some help.

30

THE GLORY DAYS OF BUFFALO EGBERT

"Now me and my brothers, we ridin' home. An' we takin' our time. Ain't in no hurry 'cause we goin' home to some hoppin' mad womens. We been out longer than we told 'em an' wives get a little funny when they mens be late. One time my brother Twisted Foot got beat over the head with a stick he woman so mad with him. None of us laugh at him because maybe some day we get hit on the head with a stick. An angry woman is fearful. Don't you never forget that.

"Anyway, we takin' our time because we all rememberin' Twisted Foot an' we not in any big hurry to have what happen to him happen to us. One brother say if we stay out even longer maybe our womens think we dead and maybe after a long time we come home, they be so glad we alive they give us kisses instead of hits on the heads. That sound like a good idea, so we turn north.

"That was a good thing for us to do. Two day, maybe three day later, we find Jeffy."

Renee leaned in the fire, threatening his thick beard, as he spoke in (for Renee) hushed tones. "He walkin' but he look like a dead man. An' we couldn't get him to stop walking. We kept puttin' our horses in his way but he walk around 'em. Finally I jump him an' bring him down. That was the only way to stop him walkin'.

"We make a camp an' we try to fix him up. The first day, he look like he gonna make it. He eat good, an' he talk to me steady, tellin' me ever'thing that done happen to him since you mama die. Then he start talkin' about you, about bein' rich, puttin' you in fancy school, makin' you a somebody. Then he cry, sayin' ever'body rob him, keepin' him down, keepin' you poor. An' he don't quit cryin'. He cry for the whole next day, an' he hot, he whole body burnin' up. That when I know he gonna die.

"Just before he pass, he make me promise to take you. Make you my son. I say for you to be my son you gotta be Crow. Jeffey say, 'What the hell,' an' then he died dead. I take that to mean you bein' Crow is all right by him.

"After I bury you papa, I go home an' have a talk to my woman Willow, who by the way was so interested in the story about you papa she forgot to be mad with me. Which was good because all my other brothers were in big

31

trouble with they womans. Willow say, you go get that
boy an' you brought him here to me. But I told her that if I
found you happy with another family I was gonna leave
you there. She say for me to go look, so I go.".

Renee shook his head sadly, breathing heavily through
both nostrils. "I didn't find you happy with no damn
family, did I?"

Defensive, remembering all the lonely days and nights
he had endured, all the hard work he had done to earn the
credits and nice things for the house just given away
without being asked, Egbert stuck out his chin. "I didn't
need you to come. I was doin' all right."

"Ha!" Renee bellowed. "In that mess! Bein' around
them filthy womans? I shoulda took the skin off'n you
backside boy! But when I beatin' you butt I make big a
decision. You MY"—with his index finger Renee pointed
emphatically at his chest as he roared the word—"boy!
Mon fils! An' MY boy don't be around no damn whores.
You ever do that again an' you better run fast an' you
better run far 'cause I'm gonna find you an' you ain't
gonna like that. Now you lay you'self down, my young
son an' get you'self some sleep 'cause tomorrow we gonna
go home. From this time on if you don't do exactly like I
told you to do, I'm tellin' you mama on you about them
damn whores, an' Willow she take a stick to you head an'
I'm gonna laugh all the time she hittin' you."

Egbert went immediately to sleep, but his dreams were
fitful. Renee watched over him, re-covering him with the
heavy sleeping robe each time Egbert kicked it off.

At daybreak, a groggy Egbert pulled himself into the
sitting position, the heavy blanket falling away as he vigorously rubbed his eyes. The strong aroma of boiling coffee
filled his senses. Blinking his gritty eyes, he focused on
Renee.

Renee squatted beside the fire, impaling strips of fresh
meat on sharpened sticks. " 'Bout time you wake up," he
grunted. "I already hunt down a deer for breakfast, tend the
fire, an' make coffee. An' you, you lazy, you just lay there
an' let me do it. You got no respect for you new papa . . ."
Renee's teasing voice trailed off. Setting the sticks securely

in the ground, the meat dangling over the flames, Renee concentrated his attention on the distant boy.

"I been meanin' to ask you," he began guardedly, "you like the name you got? I mean, you got a special feelin' for it?"

"No," the boy answered after a pause for thought. "Not especially." Then with a lift of his shoulders, "It's just a name I guess."

Renee, deep in thought, twisted his wide mouth to the side. "It ain't a bad name, but it don't fit with DeGeer. An' that who you be now. You a DeGeer."

"Really?"

Renee smiled expansively. With a short laugh Renee barked, "What the hell we been talkin' about for the last two or one day? That's what I been tellin' you boy! You a DeGeer now!"

"What does Jacques say?" Egbert asked, remembering Jacques as the prince regent and himself as the lowly spittoon scrubber.

"Jacques say what I tell him to say," Renee snorted. He threw wide a sweeping hand. "ALL my children say what I tell 'em to say. An' that 'ALL' includin' you."

Renee pursed his lips as he scratched the underside of his beard. "But I gotta tell you the truth. I don' want no son of mine bein' named an Egberts. That be one ugly name. Got no music in it." Renee became thoughtful once again, his gaze flittering over the boy. "I tell you the name I like. Is a name I pick for Marie before I find out she a girl an' we name her Marie. I been savin' this name for my next son. Since you be him, I give you that name."

Renee clapped his large hands together, popping the air, rubbing them together as he offered, "How you like 'Nicolas'?"

Egbert-cum-Nicolas greeted the suggestion with a non-committal tilt of his head and another indifferent lift of his shoulders.

"*Tres bon!*" Renee cried. "Nicolas. That's you name. Now get you little ass outta that bed if you want to share food with you *pere*."

CHAPTER THREE

Renee and his new son packed up their light camp. The morning was brightening, the sky an azure blue, cloudless, limitless. The boundless landscape rolled, like a gentle ocean in its expanse. The newly-dubbed Nicolas rotated slowly, ignoring Renee as he viewed the unbroken panorama. A town boy, he was now out of his element, small, insignificant, in comparison to the enormous prairie stretching uninterrupted toward the sky. Suddenly, all of the emotions he had held in check, pretended didn't exist, overwhelmed him. Fear, anger, confusion, loneliness—all of these had little to do with grief, because for all intents and purposes, his natural father, Jeffery, had been lost to him for well over a year.

Slumping to his knees, the desperately frightened child began to weep, the salty tears burning the lids of his eyes.

Renee hurried to him, coming in beside him on his

knees, taking the boy's limp arms and forcing them around his neck as he hugged the weeping boy tightly against him, his voice thick with emotion croaking, "You let it go my son. You let it all go. Don't you be ashamed. You pere is here. An' he ain't never gonna leave you."

In response, the child folded into Renee, yielding to the superior strength, resting in the security Renee offered. And with relief, the newly-christened Nicolas let go of his pain, let go of his former life. Reborn in that moment as Nicolas DeGeer, he would not think of the person named Egbert Higgins again for a long, long time. This land of light blotted out all of the dark memories of a lost child.

The boy was growing confident, not hanging on so tightly as he rode behind his adoptive father. He held on to Renee's buckskin shirt with one hand, while the other hand held a strip of hard-jerked meat to his mouth, his teeth tearing at the meal as they pushed northeast toward the Crow encampment.

Renee ate the same light meal as he drove the horse at a steady pace but, unlike his new son, Renee didn't concentrate on the portion of food. Renee was on the constant alert. The area they had just entered was a section of land hotly contested by the Crow and the Lakota (Sioux). The Hunkpapa band of the Lakota declared it their ground. The Crow knew it to be their rightful territory. And right was on the side of the Crow. All tribes of the Lakota were the newcomers to the plains. They refused to admit it, but their refusal to acknowledge the truth did not make it any less of a fact. Twice during separate Seven Fires councils, the Hunkpapa were forced to face this truth, as they presented their case for claim of this area. And typical of the hardheaded Hunkpapa, when they realized they were losing the argument, they became even more abusive.

The Crow were strong believers in tit for tat. After each Hunkpapa sortie, the Crow invariably gave back full measure in whatever they had received. And so this sparsely treed tract of high-grassed landscape gradually became known to all the tribes as the Dark and Bloody Ground, because the ownership of it was questionable (dark) and there had been too many battles for it.

Were it possible, considering the safety of the child riding trustingly behind him, Renee would have avoided this area. But it was necessary to cross this strip because the Valley of the Shields, a favored camp area large enough to support the lifestyles of several gathered clans, lay directly across this mean section. Before leaving camp to fetch the child home, Renee made arrangements with a group of his brothers to meet him on the return to act as escort for himself and the child. As yet there was no sign of them. There should have been. Renee was worried.

He had a right to be. He had been less than truthful about Jeffery's death. He and his warriors had not simply found Jeffery wandering alone. They had actually found him in time to fight the Lakota bent on killing him and running them off. In the battle, Renee had killed two warriors. Warriors belonging to war chief Bear Ribs. Since leaving the Lakota, Renee and Bear Ribs had sparred like a pair of wary boxers. Renee was determined not to give Bear Ribs an opening and for years, by keeping his guard up, had managed to keep peace, of sorts, with his former brother. Now at last, Bear Ribs had been handed a cause to declare war on Renee. And Renee knew Bear Ribs well enough to know he would use this incident to his full advantage to pay Renee back for what Bear Ribs had always seen as Renee's betrayal of the Lakota.

True to his nature, Renee hid his concern behind an easy humor. In a low conversational voice Renee said, "I never did tell you all about you *mere*, did I?"

"My what?"

"*Mere*," Renee repeated, elongating the term. "It mean you mother. I am *Pere*, you father. Willow is *Mere*, you mother. You understand, eh?"

"Yes."

"*Oui*, Nicky. You say '*oui*.' You must begin to learn the language of you family."

"*Oui, Pere*."

Renee grunted approval, then continued with his story.

"I meet her when I ride with the Lakota." Nicolas made a disbelieving noise causing Renee to chuckle. "Ah, *oui*. I rode with the Lakota for many seasons. My first country is Canada. I begin my ride with them there. You see, my mama an' my papa, they make a lot of babies. Eight babies, but only three boys. Too many girls, eh?" Renee laughed. "Me an' my two brothers, we think so too. But they run to Montreal, an' me . . . I run to the Lakota. I don't like cities.

"When I was still a young warrior with the Lakota, we ride to meet with our southern brothers the Hunkpapa. I like this place, so I stay, always gonna go home to Canada after just one more season. But in the third season, I was with a small hunting party an' we get lost in a storm. A bad storm. Lightning, hail, rain, wind. We lost our horses an' almost our lives. After the storm was over, we had to walk, an' we walk right into Crow land. Like big fools we just wander in like we sayin' 'Kill me, kill me! Easy coup here!' "

Nicolas didn't have any idea what a coup was but obviously it was funny, so he laughed along with Renee.

"We were lost but we weren't stupid. When we finally know where we were, we throw away our weapons. That way we look like we come in peace. An' the Crow scouts finding us felt sorry for us because we lookin' half dead. So they take us to their camp and give us food and shelter. I know it sound strange to hear this kind a story. Peoples don't think of enemy tribes helpin' each other out. But that's because maybe they ain't never lived with the Indians. You got to live with Indians to know what they all about. An' what I'm telling you now is a strong custom, you understand? Indians don't never, never turn away anyone comin' into their camps askin' for help. That would be very bad manners. If the unwanted company is a big enemy, Indians always wait until their guests leave an' are far away from the camp before the warriors go after them. Is like a game, Nicky. A dangerous game, ah *oui*, but still, a game.

"When I was in that Crow camp with my Lakota brothers gettin' fat on Crow food, I was figuring all the time how we gonna get home without the Crow killin' us.

37

It was always on my mind ... until I see Tall Willow. Then I couldn't think of nothin' but her.

"Then my Nicky, I had me two problems. *Un,* I was in a place where ever'body wanted to hurt me, an' *deux,* I was in love with a girl who had a papa twice as big as me an' as ugly as dirt." Renee looked over his shoulder at the laughing boy. A wide grin on his face, Renee jokingly scolded, "Don't you be laughin' at you granpapa. He can't help bein' big an' scary.

"He name is Sits-In-The-Middle-Of-The-Ground. He need that name 'cause he fat an' need lotsa room to sit down in. An' he hated me Nicky," Renee made small noises ending with "*OOOH My!* He wanted to kill me right then, bad manners or not. But Tall Willow, his only daughter is liking me, an' I'm busy likin' her right back."

Renee reined in, turning in the saddle to view his earnest listener, and typically French, gesturing with his hands, Renee said with a deep sincerity, "You *mere,* when she a young girl, she had a walk that could make a man crazy. She be tall, slender like a willow tree bending in all the right places when the wind blow.

"My son, I tell you this most honest, when you grown up an' you find you'self a womans with a walk like that, you grab her with both you hands 'cause you ain't never gonna hold her if you don't. Now where was I?"

"Sits-In-The-Middle-Of-The-Ground hated you."

"That's right! He did. An' I offered him ever'thing I ever hoped to own in my whole life for that girl of his, an' he kept sayin' no. He was makin' me crazy an' his daughter was makin' me crazy. Because of them two I couldn't think of no how for my Lakota brothers to escape from them Crow, 'cause I was out of my head.

"Finally I just asked him, what do you want for her, an' he say, 'Nothing a Lakota can ever give.' That's when I know."

"Knew what!?"

"You ain't payin' attention," Renee sighed impatiently. "I know ever'thing that's what I know. I know how to save my Lakota brothers an' have Willow at the same time. The answer was all the time right in front of my face. I had to trade MYSELF for all of them. That's what that old man wanted. No horses. No guns. No blankets. He wanted a husband who wouldn't take his precious daughter away from him. He wanted a son-in-law to stay with his family. That's why he couldn't give her to anyone outside the Crow Nation. To be with her, I had to be Crow. Nothing else would work. So that's what I did. I agree to live forever with the Crow. In return, my Lakota brothers were allowed to leave in full peace, an' I married Willow."

Nicolas was given time to digest the story of his adopted heritage, the horse beneath him moving again as he replayed Renee's story in his mind. Shortly, his thoughts were interrupted.

"Course it wasn't easy to be a Crow."

Nicolas's attention was instantly perked.

"The Crow were happy to get me," Renee hastily added, "I was young, strong, an' a proven warrior. After Sits-In-The-Middle-Of-The-Ground give Willow over to me as a bride I put a baby in her quick, which proved I was a good breeder. All of these things are very important to the Indian, my Nicky. But even with all that, I was not thought of as a true Crow. That because I was still on the outside all of the warrior societies. I couldn't get in 'cause I had no relatives to recommend me an' a man with no brothers, no matter how many horses he own, is a poor man. In the Crow world, it's how many brothers you got that make you rich. Bein' rich got nothing to do with what you own. So I had to get myself adopted by a clan before I could join a society of warriors and sit in their company."

"But I thought you were in the Whistling Waters."

"I ain't in the Whistling Waters!" Renee jeered. "That you *mere's* clan. If I belong to that clan then I would be her brother. Can't marry her, eh? No, Willow is Whistling Waters. I am Greasy In The Mouth Clan. But you, as the son of Tall Willow, you, Jacques, an' Marie, you all three Whistling Waters. Children take from they mother, not they father. Ole Sits-In-The-Middle-Of-The-Ground, he in Greasy Mouth, he take me into that clan—after Jacques is born—he decide he like me pretty good. But he only decide that *after* I put a grandson in his arms. It was after Jacques born that I become full Crow."

39

Renee pulled the horse to a gradual stop. Turning slightly at the waist and looking at Nicolas he said, "You full Crow now. You mama done decide that when she say for me to get you. Chiefs got to look you over, but that ain't no trouble. Willow already done talk to 'em." Renee snapped back forward as a distant sound broke the quietude. "Look at that my Nicky."

Renee stretched forth an arm like a lance. Nicolas's anxious eyes followed its direction. Nicolas tensed as cresting a distant knoll and riding hard in their direction was a large party of warriors all of them whooping and kiyiing at the top of their voices.

Renee felt the child's grip strengthen and calming his fears Renee laughed, "Here my Nicky, here come the proof of who you are. Here come the only wealth a man can ever know. Here come you brothers of the Whistling Waters."

Renee's laugh was booming, which helped the boy's frayed nerves only slightly. The Indians surrounding them, whooping, shaking lances over their heads, were frightening. The child remembered a few of their faces having seen them before in Renee's company. At those times they had been quiet, elegant in their demeanor, but still just as frightening. When Nicolas had visited the DeGeer family, seemingly a lifetime ago, he had always managed to stay out of the way of grown males. Now they were all around him. Nicolas pressed against Renee's spine, trying desperately to hide.

Renee felt the pressure as well as the boy's fear. Turning in the saddle, he grabbed hold of the boy's arm and pried him loose, Nicolas madly fighting to hang on as if he were a cloying multi-legged caterpillar.

Nicolas felt his breath leave him as he suddenly flew through the air. The dazed condition lasted only a second but inside the stunned boy's head, time slow-motioned. His breath left him and time resumed its normal pulse as a strong arm gripped his waist, pulling him in tightly. When he smelled a new odor, a new musk buried inside the natural odors of leather, wood smoke, male essence, and horse sweat, he realized he had changed hands. With fear-widened eyes he looked up into the face of the young warrior holding him, formally meeting for the first time the man who would be his lifetime friend and brother. Vaguely he heard Renee's barking introduction.

"Nicky! Say hello to you brother Medicine Crow."

Indians rarely need an excuse to eat. Sharing food is one of the five primary pleasures of life. So when the Crow escort located Renee, and found him alive, it was cause for an immediate celebration. A quick picnic camp was established and a packed meal produced. Dried buffalo chips for the fire were collected and once the fire was established, blankets were arranged around it for the men to sit on. While all of this was being done, Medicine Crow kept the boy with him, instructing, by rough and wordless gesture, for Nicolas to hold onto the ornate wide belt covering the warrior's thin breech string. Like a caboose coupled to an engine, Nicolas followed Medicine Crow unquestioningly, Renee ignoring the boy's pleading, soulful looks for help.

He breathed a sigh of relief when Medicine Crow released him, shoving Nicolas into the sitting position between himself and Renee. The mealtime conversation, conducted in the Crow language, flowed over and around the boy as he enjoyed the sweet, ripe plums given to him by Medicine Crow. Nicolas understood a few words of the guttural language but not enough to follow the gist. Through non-use, he had lost a great deal of the language and now, to his untrained ear, some words in the Crow language sounded like a disjointed series of grunts and coughs, as if the speakers were strangling. Then too, he couldn't be bothered with listening because he was starving. Any piece of food Medicine Crow passed his way, he quickly snatched at.

"He's a good eater," Medicine Crow grinned to Renee over the boy's head.

"He's healthy," Renee grunted. "He's still very nervous, but given time he'll settle in. Being around Jacques will help him."

"It is good of you to adopt him."

MARDI OAKLEY MEDAWAR

"No," Renee disagreed, "it's selfish. His father was a brave man. The son is as brave. When I found this child, he was taking care of himself. Not in a way Willow would appreciate, but he was fit and he was clean. And he has cried only one time in my presence. He's an emotionally sound boy. Willow always said he was too good for the white world. She's right."

"My sister usually is," Medicine Crow chuckled.

Reaching around Nicolas's intent form, Renee clapped Medicine Crow's back. "Well, now she will be a satisfied woman. She has two sons and a beautiful daughter. With those three to fill up her days she'll stop pestering me about giving her more babies and will allow me to go out with my brothers."

Medicine Crow shook his head dolefully, a wistful curve to his full mouth as he said softly, "You've always been a hopeful person, Renee."

Renee responded to his younger brother's understated wit with a loud booming laugh.

Nicolas rode in the front and in the saddle of Medicine Crow's horse. Medicine Crow, taking the less comfortable seat on the horse, guided the animal, his arms protectively around Nicolas as they rode. Now that Nicolas's fear of the young warrior was slowly evaporating, he continually wormed around to view the Indian. All of the Crow were dressed alike—breechcloths, leggings, plain moccasins, soft leather vests over shirtless chests, and bone and bead chokers around their necks. Their hair was their principal finery. Crow men were especially vain about their hair, wearing the body of it straight and smooth, while the crown, or bangs, jutted upwards, stiff and tinted an un- natural gray as if an attempt had been made at bleaching this small section of hair. The discoloration was due to the wood ash and mud paste mixed into the hair to give it the stiff body it needed to defy gravity in such a manner. Inside the length of the hair dangled beads and tufts of feathers.

Studying his face, Nicolas decided the warrior known as Medicine Crow was extremely handsome. He was young, no more than an adolescent. He had a Roman nose—long, arched and narrow. His cheek bones were high and pronounced, as if the handiwork of a sculptor with an eye to extremes. The mouth was wide, his lips full, the center of his upper lip meeting in a pronounced cupid's peak.

"He's staring at me again," Medicine Crow yelled to Renee. "Tell him staring at a person is impolite."

Renee maneuvered his cantering horse next to Medicine Crow's, the animals moving in cadence.

"Nicky! You makin' you brother crazy. Turn around an' quit lookin' at him. He don't like it. I want you to be friends with him. Of all you brothers this one got the big spirit. When I ain't with you I want you to always stay close to him. You understand?"

"*Oui, Pere.*"

Chuckling, Renee lightly clipped the boy's ear. "You damn good, you know that?"

In the fading light of late afternoon, the journey came to an end. The returning warriors signaled their presence to the camp which, being over the next hill, was hidden from view, by firing their rifles in the air and hollering shrill ear-splitting caws. As they cleared the top of the rise and paused momentarily on the hill, Nicolas saw down into the Valley of the Shields.

The view was spectacular. A sight beyond his imaginings. The Crow encampments he had previously seen were the private family camps when they set up outside the town of Absaroke. Those camps were camps of about thirty tepees, sometimes less, but never more. The Valley of the Shields hosted three hundred tepees, stretching to fill out the wide floor of the valley. And in the surrounding meadows were several large individually picketed grazing horse herds, their numbers too vast for Nicolas to count.

The enormous village churned with people. The villagers, having heard the rifle fire and the cries of the warriors, ran toward the outskirts of the village; heading toward the hill, the riders on top of it lined in a spread-out file. The villagers howled to the riders and the riders whooped back. And while the air split with the sound of human voices, Renee retrieved from Medicine Crow his new son. With Nicolas safely aboard, safely in front of him so that everyone could plainly see the child, Renee nudged his horse and proceeded down the hill heading for the cheering throng.

Medicine Crow and the other warriors became separated from Renee as the descent was made. The waiting crowd overwhelmed them, isolating each rider as Renee's horse was culled from the group. Nicolas's heart trip-hammered in his chest as extended hands reached up at him.

"Smile," Renee yelled in his ear.

Terrified yet obeying, the child stretched his mouth widely until his taut skin threatened to crack. "I want to go home," he whimpered behind his gritted teeth.

"You are home," Renee grunted, the sound reverberating in his chest. "You be brave boy a little bit longer my Nicky, then you *mere,* she take care of you. You can do that, eh? Otherwise you gonna embarrass you poor old *pere* Renee. An' I don't like for to be embarrassed, Nicky."

The boy took the last statement as the warning it was intended to be, suddenly feeling uncomfortable in the possession of the man he had, until that moment, trusted implicitly. The threat of tears was relieved by Jacques's sudden appearance. The other boy was given a leg up by two pedestrians. Jacques, after successfully clambering aboard his father's slow-moving horse, planting himself firmly on the horse's rump, raised one fist to the heavens and let go a shrill victorious cry. His yell set the ocean of people moving around them off again, their combined noise vibrating inside Nicolas's skull. By the time the procession entered the center of the village where five principal chiefs stood awaiting them, Nicolas was holding onto his frayed nerves with every ounce of strength at his command.

Renee pulled up the reins, bringing his walking horse to a complete stop. The people all around the animal gradually became very quiet awaiting Renee's address to the chiefs. When Renee was certain he had everyone's complete attention, he stood in the stirrups and, in a loud voice that seemed to echo off the enclosing foothills, announced,

"This is an orphan child. His dead mother was a woman of high virtue. His dead father a man of acknowledged bravery. I request permission to adopt this parentless man-child, giving him as a gift of my esteem to my lady wife and her noble family the Whistling Waters People. I ask permission to do this of my principal chiefs, men of reputed honor and wisdom."

Without preamble, the chiefs in question moved forward, villagers moving away from Renee's horse, making room for the approaching honorables. As soon as the chiefs neared the horse, Nicolas felt himself being pulled down and carried off. His eyes distended, his face bloodless with fear, Nicolas looked back toward Renee. Renee sent him a darkly meaningful look. Nicolas did not fight the men carrying him, nor did he utter a protesting sound.

Set on his feet, he bit down hard on his lower lip as the five older men pulled him about and freely ran their hands all over him, inspecting him as if he were a colt being offered in a trade, which is precisely how they thought of him. Life was hard. Only the fit survived. A cripple or a weakling was therefore, and out of protective self-interest, not an eligible candidate for adoption.

Finished with their rough handling, the chiefs pushed the boy forward positioning him to stand before their semi-circled body. He almost ran back to Renee, but Renee raised a staying hand, and the child froze. From behind him Nicolas heard one of the old chiefs bark the recognizable name of Tall Willow. The boy closed his eyes, nearly fainting with relief when she appeared almost magically beside him, placing a warm hand on his shoulder, bringing him in gently against the side of her long leg. Instinctively reaching out for her familiar comfort, the child wrapped his arms as far as they would go around her hips. Trying violently hard not to give in to the tears that brimmed in his eyes, he clung to her.

"Tall Willow," her aged father Sits-In-The-Middle-Of-The-Ground demanded in his most authoritative voice, "do you accept this child your husband presents to you?"

Touching the back of his head softly she said in a clear, ringing voice, "Yes, I do."

Sits-In-The-Middle-Of-The-Ground humphed approvingly. "He's a strong boy. He has a brave heart. I pinched him hard and he made no sound. He will make you a proud mother."

A roaring cheer went up as the verdict was declared. Renee dismounted, dragging Jacques with him. Before the rest of the villagers could reach his wife and his new son, carrying Jacques, Renee raced toward them. By the time the well-wishers reached the new boy to touch him for luck, the little family sheltered him like a human tepee. As the crowd pressed in threateningly, Jacques laughed into the new family member's face. "Welcome home, Brother! I have waited for you for a long time. We're going to have a lot of fun now."

Decades later, even in the softening light of Nicolas's memory, his first three months in his new home could be described as anything except fun. His feelings about his new life vacillated daily, sometimes hourly. Renee had stopped translating, and because of this refusal, Nicolas suffered moments of such sheer frustration when he was being addressed, depending on the speaker, in either French or Crow, that he would have gladly offered his soul for a moment's sound of Renee's butchered English. In those moments, knowing Renee's stubborn nature, he all but loathed and despised his new father.

And he fought with Jacques. Physically.

Jacques was not one of life's greatest sharers. Thoroughly spoiled, Jacques had to be forced to be generous, just as Nicolas had to be forced to be grateful. All of this unnatural sharing and gratitude led to in-family squabbling. The arguments between the two boys would have been even more heated if either had a clue as to the names being hurled against one another.

Marie was a special problem. A sweet-faced little girl with a ready smile, it was hard for him to ignore her. But on the other hand he did not like playing dolls with her, either. After all the rough edges he had known in life, it was almost an impossibility to revert to the innocent. And besides, he was a boy; he had boy things to learn. He just felt it was a terrible pity he had to learn them with Jacques.

But he did learn, slowly, painfully, and in high competition with his brother. Both boys attended a form of warrior school. At first Jacques had the edge because he was an experienced rider. Renee closed the gap between them when he presented Nicolas with his own horse and Nicolas, devoting himself to the animal's care and well-being, was soon as masterful as Jacques.

During the days of lessons which the older men tried to present as games to their young pupils, the DeGeer brothers, along with a horde of youths their age, learned to catch hold of a warrior's arm as said warrior on horseback thundered toward them and, with the aid of the galloping rider's extended arm, to leap onto the running horse's back. This one vital lesson, as it was repeated again and again until the boys were able to do it with ease, caused a lot of bruising and sore bones, the results of many nasty falls.

All of this happened during the summer encampment. When summer waned and the time came to make for the fall campsite, Nicolas moved with his new family, riding his horse confidently, the thick band securing the quiver of arrows crossing his bare and deeply tanned chest, the quiver itself resting against his spine. His bow was within easy reach, dangling from the carved saddlehorn. After just these few weeks, he was able to speak halting French and even more halting Crow. For survival he had learned to employ sign language during the trickier bits of spoken conversation. He was no longer a frustrated communicator. And he was, (grudgingly) beginning to like Renee again.

The one rub in his new life was that he and Jacques still hadn't settled into a working truce. The more fluent Nicolas became, the more combative their squabbling, because they were finally figuring out what the names they had been calling each other actually meant. And when they went for one another, Renee was heard to bawl, "Outside!" Still locked in mortal grips they tumbled out the doorway, proceeding to tear each other apart outside the boundaries of the family tepee. With his two sons

47

wrestling each other to the ground like a pair of snapping dogs, Renee, safely inside, watched the contest through the opened door and enjoyed his meal in comfort, rooting for one, then the other, safe from the threat of flailing arms and legs.

Willow was never allowed to intervene and separate her battling sons. Despite the Crow matriarchal system, women knew better than to intrude on the training of their sons, no matter how their agony wrenched a mother's heart. And the two brothers bloodying one another was, in its way, a form of training. Oddly enough, their physical contests bonded them, as Renee knew it would.

The next year, Jacques and Nicolas were finally at peace. Nicolas, in the company of his family, a family he was now completely comfortable and secure with, traveled to make their summer camp.

He had changed again through the winter and spring. He and Jacques were taller, their budding masculinity apparent. Nicolas's hair was longer, reaching his shoulders. And the blossoming adolescents were riding new horses—not ponies—but full man-sized horses, presented to them by a glum faced Renee who snarled, "The next time you two need new horses so that your feet don't drag the ground, I expect you to do the honorable thing. Steal them yourselves."

During this first summer, Nicolas became so fluent in Crow and French he could barely remember English; his bonding to this special people became complete. He, of his own choosing, mentally as well as physically, adopted the Crow as his people, embracing their way of life, religion, and form of thinking. In short, Nicolas DeGeer forgot he was white.

The Crow forgot it too.

Another year passed. The DeGeer family in the company of many Whistling Waters families and families of two other clans made their way to the appointed winter camp on the Bighorn. Both Nicolas and Jacques were fifteen. Both were leggy, a joy to their mother, a trial to their sister and a festering sore to their father. They had become a brotherly team, and between them they worked Renee over like a dispirited bear, following him around, delighting in the fact that together they could make him crazy. They were also in the grip of puberty, lust for anything in a dress sending them into a frenzy.

Willow constantly fretted over Nicolas. He was thinner than Jacques. Jacques was developing muscle. Nicolas only appeared to be developing more bones.

His rattling physique wasn't due to poor diet. Willow shoveled food down Nicolas's throat whenever she laid hands on him, as did the other women of his clan, whom he addressed as "Mother" or "Sister" depending on the woman's age and marital status. His physical condition greatly worried the women of the Whistling Waters. Women were always ultimately held responsible for the outcome of a child. If the boy grew into a great warrior, his myriad of mothers was given all of the credit. Conversely the same was true if the child grew up to be a "no-good." All of the mothers suffered dual shame. And so Nicolas's mothers took to crying after him as he clattered around going his noisy, bony way, "Food only goes to his legs! He eats more than three men! It takes all of us to feed him!"

Jacques was tall, as it went against basic Crow nature and genetics to be anything but long and lean. He was exactly the same height as Nicolas, but his fuller body made him appear the taller of the two. Both boys were proud of their height, but they were clumsy with it, as if their brains hadn't yet caught onto managing their lengthening frames.

Nicolas had achieved some fame among his people because, with his long legs, he could outrun almost everyone in the tribe. Before beginning the move to the winter camp on the Bighorn, those in the autumn camp, days before disbanding, held a great cross-country race. Nicolas stretched out his legs and put yards between himself and his closest competitor. As the winner, he was the guest of honor at a feast held later that night. During the feast, an old couple whose own children were married with families of their own, quickly laid claim to the victorious Nicolas. Being adopted by more than one family was a common practice, especially when the adopted child could add prestige to the adopting family.

"This is my son," Buffalo Wallowing announced during the festivities as he held Nicolas in a tight bear hug. "His name from this day forward is 'Wind Runner,' for on this day, he outran the breath of the Creator Himself." Grasping Nicolas's shoulders, Buffalo Wallowing whirled Nicolas around. "Wind Runner! Behold your mother." And to his anxious wife, Buffalo Wallowing said solemnly, "Woman, behold your son."

The corpulent woman knocked the wind out of the runner as she threw her arms around Nicolas, squeezing him tight and lifting him off his feet, his toes inches above the ground. His face turning blue, Nicolas espied Jacques, bending over double, laughing soundlessly, as he disappeared into the gathered crowd.

His new parents presented Nicolas with a fine shirt heavily embroidered with dyed porcupine quills. The workmanship was without par. A century later, protected under glass and on display in the Smithsonian Institution for the world to view, the artistry of designs, the textures of natural materials and the hues of the berry and root dyes used, would stand as homage to the artist long dead, though the simple sign beneath the shirt would merely read:

Crow shirt—Male—Circa 1870s

When the Crow people tried to use Nicolas's new name, Wind Runner, Renee protested vehemently. "I named him Nicolas. In my lodge he is only Nicolas DeGeer. That is my word."

Renee's edict would have been far more impressive if Nicolas actually still lived in Renee's lodge. But as it happened, two weeks before the race, Renee had booted both of his sons out of the family domicile.

The ouster hadn't been due to family feuding. Far from it. Apart from their games of teasing him blind, the boys got on extremely well with their father. At least as well as anyone could get along with the irascible Renee. The time had simply come, Renee decided, for his sons to take up lodging with other boys their own age and begin the hard process of weaning them away from their mother.

But the underlying reason was that with teenage sons constantly lurking, smirking and nodding knowing heads to one another whenever Renee showed signs of affection toward Willow, their adolescent presence made life under one tepee roof much too crowded.

So it happened that the brothers had come home one afternoon, after a full day of being meddlesome teenage boys, to find their things neatly bundled and stacked outside their parents' lodge. As they weren't ready to make it on their own, they protested loudly about being thrown out of their secure family lodge. Like clamoring baby eagles they screamed for their mother.

Undaunted, Renee fetched their belongings and headed for the tepee he had selected for his sons. By purposeful design it was located on the other side of the wide village. Nicolas and Jacques tagged after him, yelling their heads off, as Renee led them through the village toward their new abode. Willow was hardly Renee's staunch ally. She brought up the rear of the streaming parade her menfolk created, wringing her hands, sobbing loudly over her sons' premature eviction. Marie trod the heels of her mother, waving a royal airy hand at the staring spectators the unruly family bisected.

The DeGeers were an entertaining lot.

By the time of the footrace, the boys found that they were actually quite happy with their new arrangement. They shared a lodge with two other displaced adolescent friends, all three fathers sharing in the expense of their sons' new bachelor lifestyle. The boys were supposed to hunt to fill their bellies, but their mothers, not ready to chance their sons' skills, bootlegged food into the young men's lodge. The four boys soon realized that they had an easy life. They were young bachelors, free to come and go as they wished, yet they were still young enough to accept the hot meals smuggled in to them by a steady procession of well-meaning mothers.

Jacques and Nicolas adored Willow, but in truth were

more strongly attached to their father. Both boys worshipped their father and (to his frustration) continued to pop into his life on a daily basis, eating his food, crowding in inconveniently—still managing to kill the odd romantic moment.

Even though Renee loudly protested their daily visits, Willow knew her husband was secretly pleased that his sons were so unyieldingly loyal to him. When Renee slapped his thighs and lamented, "I'll never be rid of those two," everyone hearing him knew it was more of a boast than a complaint.

Two days after establishing his family camp in the winter encampment, Renee awoke before dawn. Stepping from his lodge, he bumped squarely into Nicolas, who stood just outside, huddling under the heavy winter robe, protection from the dark and frigid air, waiting in ambush for his father.

"I have to talk with you, *Pere,*" Nicolas hissed in a loud whisper.

Renee, naked under the hoodless robe he wore, grumbled a mild curse, walking away from the lodge, Nicolas in hot pursuit. Yards away from the large family lodge and smaller storage tepees, Renee urinated onto the thin layer of snow covering the ground. Emitting a sleepy laugh, Renee said, "Remember what I always told you about yellow snow Nicky?"

"I don't have time for jokes, *Pere.* I have to talk to you seriously."

Irritated that his old joke was ruined, Renee barked, "Then talk!"

"I can't talk to you here!" Nicolas gasped as if offended. "What I have to say is too personal."

"Ha!" Renee snorted. "I can pass my water here, but you can't speak to me here?"

"Please, *Pere?*" Nicolas begged in an urgent whining tone.

Sighing heavily, his breath frosting the air, Renee rolled his eyes in his head. Another morning ruined. He had planned on snuggling the day away in Willow's warm arms, but one more time one of his sons had killed the romance in his soul. "All right," he frowned. "Wait for me to get dressed."

Both of them burdened down with their winter robes and hoods looked like dark bears moving awkwardly through a misty hoarfrosted forest. When they were a good distance from the multitude of tepees, the permanently blackened tops curling smoke high into the wintry morning sky barely discernible through the twisted branches of the deciduous trees, Nicolas stopped, whirling on his startled father.

"It's my chest," Nicolas blurted in a strangled sob.

Alarmed by his son's burst of emotion Renee cried, "What's wrong with your chest? Are you having pains?"

"No!" Nicolas ripped open his winter shirt treating Renee's eyes to the sight of a baby-smooth, slightly sunken chest cavity dotted with two tiny nipples, shriveled up like pimples by the sudden rush of cold air. "Look at me!" Nicolas all but screamed. "I look just like a little girl. Just like Marie! All the other boys have chests that grow out. MINE is falling in. Everyone is teasing me about it. I'm ashamed to be seen without a shirt."

"Calm down, Nicky," Renee said unruffled. "Your old *Pere* knows something that will help you." Throwing off his winter robe and raising his right index finger, pointing skyward he said, "Observe."

Nicolas jumped back as Renee fell forward, Renee's strong arms preventing the near collision of his nose with the frozen ground. Then in that awkward position, balanced on stiffened arms, his legs straight out behind him, Renee began a series of neatly executed push-ups that had Nicolas's mouth hanging to his mid-pubescent sunken chest. With each push-up, Renee counted. When he reached fifty, he stopped abruptly and jumped to his feet, facing his aghast son.

"I learned to do that long ago. The movements strengthen the arms and the chest muscle. You give it a try."

Uncertainly, Nicolas shrugged off his robe, the heavy garment landing in a heap next to Renee's. Renee made encouraging noises as Nicolas carefully placed himself on the ground the way his father had done. After two fruitless attempts, Renee placed his foot on Nicolas's rump.

"Use your arms not your manhood to lift you. That part doesn't need more muscle. Keep your legs straight! Your arms and chest must do all the work."

After ten faulty tries, Nicolas collapsed. Renee looked down at his panting son, his thick arms folded across his chest as he shook his head in disgust. With one foot he scraped up snow and sprayed Nicolas's face with frost.

"Tomorrow you will do twenty. And the day after, thirty. In between times you will start lifting anything that looks too heavy for you. You can start by gathering wood for your mother."

Nicolas eased himself up slowly. Renee's foot on his spine pushed him down again—hard. "Get a lot of wood my little Nicky," Renee chuckled evilly in his throat. "It promises to be a cold night."

The one thing that Nicolas forgot but Renee remembered only too well was that it didn't do for a son to favor one mother over his other mothers. A natural mother, or First Mother, found no more favor than her sisters or aunts in this regard. By hauling in wood for Willow, Nicolas was then obliged to haul wood for ALL the other sixteen women of the Whistling Waters camped in the area, plus the wife of Buffalo Wallowing who had adopted him two months prior. All glowing mothers credited themselves for having raised such a considerate son and bragged about his generosity to the envious women outside their clan.

By the time Nicolas was finished being considerate and having his face kissed by each adoring mother, he fell into his own bed, exhausted.

Jacques and his fellow lodge mates were astonished by Nicolas's unseemly activity. On the first day they offered no comment. It wasn't *too* out of character for a son to oblige his mother and her sisters with a favor, but when the activity continued, day after day, Jacques became concerned. Sneaking over to Nicolas's bed in the dead of night, after making certain that the others were soundly asleep, Jacques shook Nicolas awake.

"Brother?" he hissed into Nicolas's blanching face. "Have you gone crazy? Everyone thinks you have. Why are you spending your days hauling wood when you could be doing other things?"

"*Pere*," Nicolas blearily replied. He turned his face away, trying to sink back into the deep sleep Jacques was determined to pull him out of. Nicolas's next words ruffled against the folds of the furred pillow. "*Pere* is making me do it." Nicolas grabbed the pillow with both arms and snuggled down into the warm maw of his blankets. In the midst of this movement Nicolas whined. "Leave me alone Jacques. Let me die with some dignity left to me."

Jacques sat bare-bottomed on the carpeted floor of the snug winter lodge. In the glow of the firelight that faintly lit the interior, he stared at the inert form of his brother. "Oh you must have done something bad," Jacques whispered mutely. "Something really, really bad."

Jacques kept a sharp eye on the situation for over a week. Every day proved the same. Nicolas was gone before Jacques and the others awoke, and stayed gone, only to be spotted later hauling wood and water for women, as if he were a captive slave. Nicolas was fast becoming a scandal among his peers. Unable to stand much more of his brother's odd behavior or their friends' teasing, Jacques slept lightly during the eighth night. Before dawn, when Nicolas slipped out, Jacques waited a moment then slipped out behind him, following Nicolas to their parents' lodge.

From a hiding place behind a tree, Jacques watched as Renee left the lodge. He followed after father and brother as they made their way through the small dense forest. Using stealth, he trailed them to a private clearing. When they stopped Jacques quickly dodged behind scrub evergreens and from this hiding place watched as Nicolas stripped down to skin and loincloth. Jacques received the shock of his life when Nicolas hit the ground, undulating as if he were in the throes of passionate lovemaking. Stunned out of all reason and forgetting stealth altogether, Jacques stepped out noisily from behind the scrub trees.

Both Nicolas and Renee heard him as Jacques staggered forward in his benumbed state. Nicolas froze mid push-up and Renee's head swiveled smartly on his thick neck. Relief sounding in his voice, Renee said, "It's only your brother. Keep going. You need twenty more."

Nicolas complied putting all of his strength into the renewed effort. As he worked and Renee counted, Jacques tottered forward, coming to stand alongside his father.

"What are you doing to him, *Pere?*"

Renee rushed his answer between counts. "Building your brother's chest."

"Is that why he hauls wood and water for all our women?"

"Yes," Renee snapped.

Jacques ignored the look of unbridled irritation on Renee's face as he persistently vied for his father's attention. "I think you'd better make him stop that, *Pere*. He's becoming a joke. Hauling wood and water for mothers might be nice for a time or two, but every day makes him look like he wants to be more with women than with men. If he continues he might be accused of being an 'unnatural.' "

"Hummmm," Renee hummed, twisting his lips to one side. "I hadn't consider that. I only wanted him to pick up heavy things and use his arms more. I'll have to rethink this."

Jacques continued to watch Nicolas while Renee, left arm folded across his chest balancing his raised right arm, index fingernail tapping his exposed lower teeth, thoughtfully considered the presented predicament.

"*Pere,*" Jacques quizzed, a near falsetto pitch to his voice. "Does this . . . this thing you're having Nicky do . . . does it really make a bigger chest?"

Renee rumbled a laugh. "Nicky," he barked, "stand up and come here."

Nicolas gratefully stopped the exercise and approached his father and brother, breathless from his exertions. Renee clapped Nicolas on the bare back pridefully.

"Look at him. He's looking more powerful isn't he? And this is after only a few days. Make a muscle, Nicky."

Nicolas raised his right arm and flexed.

"See that! That's what hauling heavy wood and large pots of water will do. No wonder men are afraid of women. They haul wood and water all the time. They're stronger than we are." Renee pushed Nicolas's arm down, running his hands over Nicolas's chest. "Do you see how muscle is developing across here?" Renee ran the flat of his hand down Nicolas's midsection. "Nicky is developing thick muscle all down through here. His belly is going to be as hard as a tree." Renee turned toward Jacques again. "When I was a young boy, I was skinny like Nicky. An old man taught me how to build myself up. Now I'm teaching Nicolas. So now what do you think about all this, my Jacques?"

Jacques's answer was to strip off his heavy coat and shirt. "I want you to show me too, *Pere*. I want muscles."

"You've already got muscles!" Nicolas shouted. "You have more than any of our friends."

"I don't care," Jacques replied flatly. "I want more."

"That's not fair of him, *Père*," Nicolas huffed. "I just wanted *some* muscles, but Jacques wants them all. Don't show him. I asked you first. Remember that."

"Shut up, Nicky," Renee said irritably. He rubbed a hand over his smoothly shaven chin as he stood between his two warring sons. "Jacques's coming along might be just the answer we needed."

"What answer?" Nicolas scoffed.

"Well," Renee drawled, "if your brother works with you, you can stop hauling for the women. Is that a good answer?"

Nicolas looked sharply from his father to his brother and then back to his father. "Really?"

"Really," Renee returned, a half smile tugging his lips. "As of today, your bondage to your mothers ends."

Nicolas grabbed Jacques's hand, yanking his brother over to him. "You have to get down like this, Jacques, and keep your back and legs perfectly straight."

CHAPTER FOUR

The next day, Renee found a short heavy log and had the boys haul it to their secret spot. After they performed a hundred pushups, he told his sons to lift the log up over their heads. Jacques and Nicolas struggled with the weight of the log, grunting with the effort, their arm muscles straining as they tried to keep it above their heads. Renee had them lower the log to one shoulder, raise it high overhead, then lower it to the other shoulder. They had to weight-lift the log until their muscles gave out.

After that morning, each day was the same—push-ups and log lifts until the two boys collapsed to the ground. But still, Renee would not allow them to quit. He made them run for twenty minutes, then walk for another half an hour. Each night, the boys fell asleep immediately when they stretched out on their hide beds.

Gradually, the early morning routines became easier as

the brothers learned to work as a team. This was another beneficial side effect. When Crow warriors went to battle, typically it was every man for himself and singularly competitive as warriors vied for war honors. Renee had another goal in mind for his sons. He wanted them to stay alive. Having each other to rely on was, in Renee's mind, already the greatest honor any man could ever own.

Along with the rigorous training, he had them practice various maneuvers such as pulling each other up into tree branches and running three-legged races, with one of each of their legs bound together by a leather thong. The purpose of this: the aid of a wounded brother should both boys be unhorsed. This was a skill Indians rarely prepared for, and until this training session, neither had Jacques nor Nicolas. But thanks to their Crow training, they were expert horsemen and highly skilled with all the weapons of the Crow including the rifle. Both Jacques and Nicolas could prime and load a rifle in under a minute.

Although Jacques and Nicolas were proud of the manly muscles they were developing, they became weary of the grueling schedule their father had mapped out for them. They began to pray for a colder, snowier winter.

But as the winter winds blew colder, Renee stepped up the pace of the training. He knew he was fighting time and soon the winter mornings would make exercising the boys impossible. Every night, when Renee went to bed, he worried about his sons. Their muscles had become strong, but they still lacked experience and wisdom, and these were things he could not teach them. After all, they were still boys; they had never been in an actual battle. They didn't know what they could expect from themselves or each other.

On the morning of their fifth week of training, Jacques and Nicolas awoke early and started outside to relieve themselves. As a groggy Jacques pulled the door flap aside, he came instantly awake letting go a loud whoop.

"What is it?" Nicolas asked, dashing to the lodge entrance.

"Look," Jacques said, as he went on outside.

"It's snowing," Nicolas cried when he saw the falling snow. His breath hung in the air like a miniature cloud.

He scrambled outside standing next to his brother. Both youths had their palms turned upwards, fat lazy flakes drifting into their hands as they smiled at the gray burdened sky. Beneath their feet the ground felt soft as if they were standing on a thick, deep quilt.

Nicolas's grin widened. The day was a complete whiteout. Snow had crept up the sides of all the lodges, covering wood stacks and supplies that had been left outside. Laughter and shrieks of joy rang out across the still valley as waking Crow children tumbled out of their family lodges frolicking like otters in the new-fallen snow.

"*Pere* won't make us work today," Jacques said as he looked up at the flat, dull sky. "On a day like this, not even the Cheyenne could budge *Pere* away from his warm fire."

"That means we can play," Nicolas said with a conspiratorial wriggle of his eyebrows.

"And I have an idea as to the game," Jacques grinned slyly. "But first we must go to see *Pere*. It wouldn't do for him to see us later."

"Why?"

Jacques leaned in close to his brother, wrapping an arm around Nicolas's shoulders. "It has to do with you and me, and all of those girls camped with their families on the other side of the river, our distant cousins, who don't know us or anything about us—yet."

Nicolas's head snapped back. "You can't be thinking what I think you're thinking."

"Then think again."

"Oh no," Nicolas groaned as Jacques walked him back toward the door of the lodge. "Not even WE can get away with THAT!"

"Yes we can. We just have to get *Pere* out of the way and then the day is ours." They edged back into their lodge, bundled up in their heavy robes, and set out to walk the quarter of a mile to the warmer lodge of their parents.

They were welcomed into the family lodge and gladly accepted the hot coffee and breakfast that their mother offered them. The boys gulped down food as their father watched them from the confines of his cozy bed.

"So what are you two lazy no-goods going to do with

the day, eh?" A scowl marked his face as he watched his sons slurp greedily from their gourd bowls.

"We thought we would go sledding," Jacques responded with his mouth full.

Nicolas, never one to speak while he savored his food, nodded in agreement.

"Sledding is a good idea," Renee replied lazily. "Take your sister with you."

"No!" both boys cried in unison.

Offended by her brothers' rejection, Marie began squalling loudly.

"*Mere,*" Nicolas pleaded. "We want to be with our friends. Marie has her own friends. Why can't she play with them?"

"Let them go on their own, Renee," Willow sighed. "It's natural for the boys to want to be with those of their own age."

Both boys sprang to their feet before their father could reply. "Thank you, *Mere,*" Jacques sang as they kissed her cheek and bolted for the door flap. Before they could duck through it, they heard their father's booming voice.

"At least get your mother more wood for the fire. I promise you'll only have to gather for her. It's payment for all the food you just swallowed at my expense."

Jacques and Nicolas scampered out and started gathering wood. When they returned later, carrying enough wood to keep the family warm for the rest of the day, Renee was asleep. After the boys stacked the wood for their mother, they tiptoed over to their father's bed and playfully shook off the snow that covered their winter robes.

Renee awoke with a roar. Willow and Marie laughed as the boys dashed out the flap to safety. Renee scowled and grumbled, then turned his back on them, settling in for the day like a hibernating bear.

"You're certain to be found out," Takes-The-Knife prophesied as he watched his two delinquent lodgemates. "And when you are, you are going to be in big trouble."

"We'll only be found out if you tell," Jacques warned. "So you better not."

"I won't, I won't," Takes-The-Knife promised. "But if any of our brothers see you, I would hate very much to be either one of you."

"We won't let them see us," Nicolas boasted. He had finished fashioning his own hair in the style of a warrior and now he helped Jacques with his hair. Their bangs stood straight up, high and stiff, as the water mixed with ash froze solid.

"How do I look?" Jacques asked anxiously.

"Older," Nicolas assured. "What about me?"

"You look good, too. Now let's get the sled." Jacques turned to Takes-The-Knife. "Do you want to come along?"

Takes-The-Knife rolled over on his side in his sleeping robes. "Oh, no," he said. "Thank you for the invitation, but I don't want to be anywhere near the two of you today."

"You're such a coward," Jacques tisked sadly.

"That's right," Takes-The-Knife cheerily agreed, waving a hand in farewell as he disappeared beneath his blankets.

Outside their lodge, the two errant boys kept the hoods of their robes over their heads, hiding their illegal hairstyle as they inspected the circular craft that would serve as their sled. It was constructed of bent willow branches with a stiff hide lashed tightly all around. It resembled a war shield for a giant warrior. Renee had made the sled for his sons two years ago, and it was getting old. After careful examination, the boys decided it still had a few downhill runs left in it.

Bundled beneath their winter robes, they sneaked out of the village of their close relatives, treading carefully on stones made slippery with black ice. The wintry, slow-moving river, heavy and ponderous, chugged threateningly around the bridging rocks. Safe on the other shore, the brothers made their way to the encampment of their distant cousins.

The DeGeer boys weren't the only young people taking advantage of the day. The best hill for sledding was already alive with happy youngsters gliding down the face of the hill, screaming with delight as they held on to the sides of their small sleds. Jacques and Nicolas stood and watched them for awhile.

Jacques's mouth twisted to one side in a thoughtful pucker. "The girls on this hill are too young. We haven't gone to all this trouble to impress babies. Let's go look for a better place."

Nicolas agreed and they moved off silently, dragging their sled between them. Their extra efforts were rewarded when they found another hill where some of the sledders were girls nearer their own age. None of the adolescent boys who were sledding there wore their bangs up. The DeGeer brothers smiled slyly at one another. This was the place.

Jacques and Nicolas threw back their hoods grandly revealing their supposed warrior status. Appearing to be young, yet seasoned campaigners, they were quickly surrounded by a swarm of admiring girls deserting their younger male companions in favor of the newly-arrived strangers. The abandoned boys weren't pleased.

"This is our hill," one courageous boy cried. "We were here first. Warriors should stay with their own kind."

"Out of the way, Rabbit," Nicolas growled, pushing past the protester.

"Warriors of many coups choose their own hill," Jacques said in his most menacing tone. Dragging their sled, they began ascending the rolling foothill.

At the top of the hill, the brothers stopped, their eyes suddenly focused on two pretty girls struggling with their sled. Nicolas and Jacques grinned and with a nod of mutual agreement, started walking in their direction.

The girls, after righting their bulky sled, popped inside then looked at each other rather stupidly. "Well, now that we're in, how do we push off?" asked one of the girls on the sled as she looked around for help.

"We'll help!" Nicolas called out as he and Jacques ran, as hurriedly as they were able through the deep snow, eager to offer assistance.

"Why, thank you," said the young lady who sat at the

front of the sled. Fluttering her eyelashes, she smiled demurely at Nicolas.

The boys crouched down, each one grabbing a side of the sleigh. They gave it a good push, then ran along with it, building up speed, until the sleigh took flight. The girls turned briefly to wave at the boys as the sled whooshed down the hill.

"Thank you!" the first girl laughed.

"Bye-bye!" yelled the second, waving a hand.

Realizing they had been had, Nicolas said in a panting, growling voice, "Let's get them."

The boys dashed back and grabbed their own sled. They raced with it until they had the speed they wanted, then easily jumped on to it and sailed away. Both of them jumping on at just the right time was a skill which had been hard-won. It had required two winters of painful spills before it was finally mastered. Jacques rode in the front and controlled the direction of the craft. Nicolas sat behind him. Both boys rocked the sled from side to side in order to gain even more speed as the sound of the girls' shrill shrieks and laughter floated back to them.

Jacques aimed the sled at the slower-moving one ahead of them. With proper maneuvering, he managed to pull his sled up alongside the girls'. As the two sleds bounced side-by-side down the slope, both girls glanced over, still smiling but thinly, and no longer laughing as the challenging sled bumped theirs and the speed toward the bottom of the hill increased.

With a quick jerk, Jacques again turned his sled into the side of the bigger sled. The two collided again, this time harder than he'd planned. The girls screamed in terror as they felt the hard jolt. Both sleds would have recovered had it not been for the submerged dead tree lying across their path, hidden from view. It tripped both sleds, sending the unsuspecting youths on an unscheduled flight. All four were thrown from their sleds. They flew into the air, ungainly as young eaglets, their arms and legs flapping, their hands clawing the frigid air before their bodies crashed back down into the soft snow.

Jacques landed on his back, inches away from the girl who had been in the rear of the bigger sled. Nicolas ended up almost on top of the other girl as both of them landed face down in the snow.

Nicolas sat up slowly, as if he expected some of his bones to be broken. The girl next to him moaned. Nicolas watched her in a state of terror as she rolled over onto her back and then went limp. Nicolas wiped the snow from his eyes and gasped when he looked down on the seemingly lifeless girl beside him. He leaned over and quickly brushed the snow from her face. Her eyes were closed and just by looking at her, he couldn't detect any movement that would indicate that she was breathing. He placed his hand on her neck, searching for her pulse. Just after he touched her, she opened her eyes and looked up at him, her stare vacant for a moment.

He brushed the last traces of snow from her face. When she smiled at him, he sighed with relief. He grabbed her hands and pulled her up to sit beside him. Both were breathing hard, and their breath made tiny clouds in front of their faces.

"Did you do that on purpose?" she demanded.

"No," Nicolas said. She looked disappointed at first, and then she stared at him, as if she were memorizing his face. He felt uncomfortable with her impudent scrutinizing of him.

"Are you hurt?" he asked.

She continued to stare, fascinated by his blue eyes, her heart fluttering as she stared into them. She had always wanted a man with blue eyes and she couldn't believe her luck. She thought he had a baby face, but she found that attractive for a young warrior. She decided that the past summer must have been his first season as a warrior because he seemed slightly unsure of himself. The brash swagger he affected rang false. She realized she was older than he both in years and experience, for he appeared about seventeen or eighteen and she was nineteen and already a widow.

She pushed away all concerns of his youth and inexperience. She was too caught up in his overriding beauty and radiating sensuality. Her late husband hadn't been young or pretty in the face. Worse, he had been a terrible and inconsiderate lover. Her father had given her over as a bride simply because her father and her late, unlamented husband had been good friends. She had honored her husband with her fidelity while he lived, for he had been a noteworthy warrior, and an excellent provider. Now that he was dead, she was free to choose her next husband. This strong young man sitting next to her seemed an excellent choice.

"I'm fine," she said, blinking her snow-covered lashes.

"Good," said Nicolas, smitten by the young lady. Her voice was sweet, like the distant trill of a meadowlark. It carried the tenderness of a lullaby, and wafted through Nicolas's fuzzed brain with such gentleness he wanted to sigh.

"I am Wolf Blanket," the girl said, with a coy smile. "What is your name?"

"Nicolas DeGeer," he said, hoping the husk in his voice wasn't obvious.

The reverie between them was suddenly broken by the noise of the other two sledders, who were obviously not quite as taken with one another. Nicolas and Wolf Blanket turned to watch them.

Jacques helped the girl to her feet and she clobbered his shoulder with her balled fist.

"You could have killed us!" she yelled. "That was the craziest thing I have ever seen. You deliberately ran us down!"

"I'm sorry," Jacques said with a grin.

The fuming girl saw through him like a pane of glass. "No you're not! We were having a fine ride until you ruined it. What if one of us had broken a bone, how sorry would you have been then?"

Jacques arched one brow. "Very, very sorry?"

The girl began sputtering in what was becoming a playful rage. "You brute!" she cried as she scooped up handfuls of snow and began pelting him.

Jacques laughed, defending himself by showering her with handfuls of powdery snow.

Nicolas helped Wolf Blanket to her feet and when they were standing side by side, Nicolas was all too aware of the girl's warm hand remaining in his.

66

"Let's leave them," she whispered, an impish look in her eyes. "Quick, while they aren't looking."

In a mad dash, Nicolas retrieved the sled that belonged to the girls. He helped Wolf Blanket inside and whisked off before Jacques saw them.

When Jacques noticed them sledding away, he let out a war whoop. He helped his young miss into the waiting sled and pushed off after his escaping brother. They met up again at the bottom of the hill, all four of them laughing and teasing one another.

"Let's go up again!" Jacques cried. His companion was in full agreement.

"I can't," said Wolf Blanket as she clung to Nicolas. "I have to go home. I'm all wet and I'm freezing cold. Perhaps we can do this again tomorrow."

Nicolas was disappointed but he gallantly offered to pull her sled and see her to her door. They walked away, leaving Jacques and his more adventurous darling to slog back up the hill for another ride down the slope. Jacques didn't display one ounce of pity or regret for Nicolas, who sulked as he walked away, disillusioned by the sour turn of events. How is it, Nicolas pondered, that Jacques always found the girls who were such good sports? Wolf Blanket was certainly pretty, but she was no sport. Was she afraid a little cold snow might kill her, he thought bitterly.

Wolf Blanket reached over and took his hand, then smiled at him. This was something at least, being allowed to hold a pretty girl's hand, Nicolas thought. It meant the day hadn't been a total loss. Perhaps she might even allow him to kiss her cheek. Hopefully, she was enough of a sport for that.

Nicolas saw her to her lodge door and chatted with her for a few minutes. Then, to his surprise and immense pleasure, she tiptoed and placed a gentle kiss, not on his cheek, but squarely on his mouth. When she stepped back, his pleased smile stretched from ear to ear. She held on to his hand, and led him inside the lodge. An old servant woman seated just inside the door fixed him with a hard look, but one word from the girl sent the old woman scuttling out, closing the door flap behind her.

"Please sit down," Wolf Blanket said sweetly as she indicated the place of honor.

Nervously, Nicolas seated himself where he was directed. Wolf Blanket settled across from him and hummed under her breath as she placed a small iron cook pot containing freshly brewed coffee on a stone near the fire.

Nicolas looked about the lodge and was impressed by the richness of it. Obviously this girl was not of humble birth and this revelation made him even more nervous. "Where are your parents?" he asked, his voice cracking. He was surprised when she placed a hand to her mouth and giggled into her palm.

"My parents?" she asked. "I don't live with my parents. I'm much too old for that. This is *my* home."

"All of this is yours?"

"Yes. All you see here came to me through my dead husband, even the servant woman."

"You mean you were married?"

"Yes, I am a widow."

"And all this is yours?" he asked.

"Yes."

Nicolas whistled as he surveyed the wealth all around him. Then he thought of something else that made him tremble. "If this is your lodge, then that means . . . we're all alone here," he said, his voice quavering.

"Of course we are, silly you." She smiled and fluttered her lashes. "Don't you want to be alone with me?" She moved closer to him, her hand going to his chest, rubbing her fingers in tight little circles against his winter shirt. "I mean, I know you are a handsome young warrior able to choose any woman you wish. A man such as you must have many, many sweethearts. Would it be difficult for a poor little person such as myself to find a place in your affection?"

Her puckering mouth was dangerously close to his and her ministrations were causing his heart to pound violently beneath the palm of her hand.

"Not . . . not so hard," he stammered. "I believe there is room for you in my regard."

She smiled confidently, realizing his inexperience and

pretense. "I like your name, Nicolas," she crooned, her full lips coming even nearer to his own.

"And, I like yours," he rasped.

"You do?" she purred. "My mother named me, saying I am soft like a wolf's blanket. Do you think I'm soft Nicolas?"

Sweat broke out of every pore in his body as he croaked, "Yes. Yes, I think you are very soft."

"Men always want to marry soft women, don't they, Nicolas?"

"Oh yes," he said, his voice trembling. He felt like his blood was on fire.

"Do you want to marry a soft woman?" she asked, breathing into his ear.

"I will only choose a soft woman," he declared.

"Me?" she murmured, kissing his earlobe.

Nicolas felt as if he were floating, all of his senses tingling, his thoughts tangled in sudden confusion. "Yes," he breathed. To his shock she placed her exploring hand inside his loincloth, directly on top of his hardening member. His eyelids flew open.

"I believe you," she giggled, her breath hot in his ear. "One of us seems ready for the honeymoon. Wait for me," she whispered in a sultry voice. "I'll get ready too."

She squirmed a few inches away from him and began slowly to undress. First she unwrapped her knee-length winter shoes, then the leggings. Finally, with Nicolas in a near swoon, she removed her dress. Nicolas was strangling on his tongue as he watched her full naked breasts sway free of the garment. Speechlessly, she began untying the leather cords of his boots and removed them from his feet.

Nicolas felt relieved that she wasn't trying to make further conversation. His throat was so dry and the lump in the center so swollen, he would not have been able to respond with anything other than gibberish.

Shortly after they were both down to skin, she began kissing his mouth in a way he had never been kissed before. Nicolas believed he was drowning. Her kisses were so expert. All Nicolas had to do was accept her offerings. And he did, gladly. He felt himself falling backwards with her weight full against him. When he was supine, she writhed on top of him, kissing him, touching him, moaning with pleasure from deep inside her throat. When she spoke, her voice sounded husky and far away.

"Do you want me to stay on top?" When he seemed confused, she smiled between her ardent kisses and said in a breathy voice, "It's all right. I don't mind." Her mouth locked on to his again as she blanketed him with her flesh, crushing her breasts against him, rubbing her loins against his.

Nicolas cried out as her hand grabbed his penis. She spread her legs and he felt himself entering the warmth of her body. He closed his eyes, his head rolling back as he entered her, his spine arching as he pushed himself farther into her. His arms locked around her and he was instantly lost to the new sensations of sex and the dizzying heat, his senses suspended in time and space, vividly aware, but only of the reality of just that blazing moment. Life during these frantic moments drifted into a blur as she moved on top of him. Nicolas gasped as he promptly climaxed in spasms of relief and pleasure.

They lay in her bed locked in a lovers' embrace, quietly watching the ebbing flames of the fire.

"That was wonderful, Nicolas," she whispered. "And I feel wonderful. How do you feel?"

Nicolas moved his head enough so that he could see her. He grinned bashfully. "I can't feel my legs."

"Nicolas!" she laughed, slapping his bare chest. "You are so adorable. We are always going to be this happy, aren't we?"

"Yes," he replied, ignorant of his present dilemma.

Wolf Blanket wriggled away from him onto her back where she stretched like a contented kitten. She was aware of Nicolas staring hungrily at her body. "Do you want to touch me?"

"May I?" he asked stupidly, still unable to believe all this was actually happening. For so long, he had yearned to touch a girl's naked body, explore the mysteries of female flesh. His young life had been a torment of fleshly desire. Now at last, here was a beautiful woman inviting his touch. A fire grew in his belly as his hand

70

anxiously stretched out for the soft, warm, fully rounded breast.

She giggled at his shy fumbling. "Nicolas," she sighed patiently, "if you want to love me some more, I don't mind, but this time, you will have to do all the work."

Nicolas edged closer. "I . . . I don't know . . . how," he confessed.

"What do you want to do?"

Nicolas chewed the inside of his cheek as he thought for a moment. "I'd like to kiss you. On . . . on your body."

"Then do it," she whispered. "I would like that."

Nicolas lost himself in the miracle of her. He loved her breasts and couldn't stop kissing them, especially when she shivered and moaned as her body undulated against him.

"Nicolas," she gasped. "Please. I need you inside me now."

Still uncertain he was doing everything right, he mounted her. She pulled him into her greedily, wrapping her legs around him as she held onto his backside with her hands. Bracing his weight on his arms, he stared down at her. After a moment she looked up at him.

"Nicolas," she bayed. "Move."

"Off?" he stammered.

"No!" she cried. "Move your hips, up and down."

Nicolas began, slowly at first. He uttered a short, sharp cry as his body began moving in the age-old rhythm.

Her head rolled from side to side. "More," she rasped. "I have to have more."

Nicolas did all he could to oblige, hoping his efforts pleased her. He shuddered and jerked as he felt her fingernails raking the flesh of his buttocks.

"Don't stop!" she panted. "Keep loving me. Keep loving me there. Oh yes. There."

His head was swimming as he lost all reason. He burned in a fever that would not break. He would have gladly given everything he owned, even his immortal soul, in exchange for this pleasure to never end. But it did end. Helpless against his own body, Nicolas went rigid as he emptied himself into her with an astonishing force. Spent, he lay on top of her, his lungs aching with every breath he stole.

"You're a strong lover, Nicolas," she whispered into his ear, "but you finish too quickly."

CHAPTER FIVE

Nicolas awoke to the muffled noises of the old servant woman crawling about inside the lodge. Still groggy with sleep, he wondered who she was as he watched her build up the fire. The lodge, too, seemed unfamiliar to him. Then, when he felt Wolf Blanket snuggle in closer to him, he remembered where he was. He smiled lazily.

"It's all right, young master," the old woman whispered, placing her thick index finger against her lips.

Nicolas, in a state of fatigue and sleepiness, missed the meaning in her words. He had no idea of the time as he lowered his heavy eyelids. He had no hint that the dawn had come and gone, taking with it the biggest part of the new morning. He was blissfully unaware that Renee had been on a rampage, searching for him during all of that time.

· · ·

Renee's temper didn't improve as the day lengthened. The answers he received from Jacques and his friends in regards to Nicolas's whereabouts were vague and non-committal. Their shrugging shoulders and avoidance of his eyes let Renee know without a modicum of doubt that his son was up to absolutely no good. Renee gave up trying to pry information out of Jacques and his tight-lipped lodge-mates. Early in the afternoon, Renee entered the camp of the River Crow, where he learned that a warrior closely resembling Nicolas's description had been seen in the company of a young widow known as Wolf Blanket.

"Sing your death song, Nicky. Here comes *Pere,*" he hissed as he stomped off in the direction of the young lady's lodge.

Nicolas bolted awake and sat up immediately when he heard the old servant woman squawking. Wolf Blanket woke up too, and sat up beside Nicolas as the two listened to the heated debate taking place outside the tepee. Wolf Blanket pulled the sleeping robe up to cover her breasts, then lightly touched Nicolas on the shoulder. Nicolas jumped at her touch, as if she'd struck him a hard blow.

"No!" the old woman shrieked. "You can't go in there."

Nicolas's heart stopped mid-beat as he heard his father's voice.

"Get out of my way, old woman!" Renee growled. He tore open the door flap and barged inside the lodge.

Nicolas made a dive for his clothes but before he could grab them, Renee had him by the back of his hair, jerking him to his feet. Nicolas winced in pain and wished he could find a way to hide his nakedness.

"What are you doing?" Wolf Blanket demanded. She jumped to her feet and flew to Nicolas's aid. She pounced on Renee's back and began beating on his shoulder with her balled fist. "You let go of my husband!"

Renee cast her aside as if she were no more than a bothersome butterfly. Wolf Blanket landed with a thud on the honeymoon bed. "Husband?" Renee roared. "Little girl, have you gone out of your mind? This boy is no one's husband. I am his father and I should know. Nicolas has a long way to walk before he is worthy of even holding the

74

horses of warriors. He pretends to be a warrior by dressing his hair, but he is not. He has played a mean trick on you, little person."

Wolf Blanket's mouth dropped open as she looked at Nicolas, then stared at Renee in disbelief. The old servant woman, who had followed Renee into the lodge, rushed over and wrapped a shawl about her mistress, covering the stunned girl's nakedness.

"You call him a boy?" Wolf Blanket said woodenly.

"Boy!" Renee affirmed. "My son is still a boy. He has never been on a raid. He has not counted a single coup. That is what you have taken into your bed, *Chere,* a long legged little boy who will now go home to his mother and be beaten for his deception. He will send you many fine presents to make his apologies."

The humiliation was too much for Wolf Blanket to bear. "Get out," she said with unnatural calm. "Get him out of here before I kill him."

Renee released his son and Nicolas hopped around the interior of the lodge, struggling to clothe himself. "Wolf Blanket," he pleaded.

She made a growling sound as she got up, then tried to get to Nicolas, her arms flailing, her composure destroyed by hysteria. Renee grabbed her about the waist and held her pinned against his side as Nicolas quickly finished dressing and made his escape through the door of the lodge. As Nicolas passed the old woman, she clubbed him viciously about the head and shoulders. Nicolas barely felt the blows. Abandoning his shoes and his winter blanket, he ran for all he was worth through the heart of the village, passing people who stood outside their homes wondering what all the yelling was about.

Renee held on to the girl, allowing her to work out the venom in her system. He wasn't fool enough to allow her feet to reach the floor of the lodge. Even a small toe-hold in her state of madness could prove fatal for him as he bore the brunt of her hatred for Nicolas. Wolf Blanket raged a good half hour before her anger finally dissolved into tears. Emotionally spent, she hung limply like a rag doll against Renee's side, her arms, head and hair hanging, her sobs small and pitiful.

"I am so ashamed," she said in a choking voice.

"No, little one," Renee crooned. He turned her around and hugged her to his chest in the same way he held his daughter Marie when she was troubled. "You thought you found a handsome husband," he said softly, stroking the back of her long smooth hair, turning her so she faced him. "There is no shame in that. You made a mistake, that is all. My Nicky does not look like a boy."

"He doesn't act like one either," she sniffed, running a hand under her dripping nose. Their eyes met and Renee's face split into a smile. Wolf Blanket fought against it, but she smiled, too. Her smile gave way to an embarrassed giggle. She blushed.

Gently, Renee set her down on her rumpled bed. Her old servant woman waddled to her side, tending her, clucking over her like a protective hen.

Renee watched quietly as he considered the girl's dilemma. Should Nicolas go about boasting of his illicit conquest, the young girl would be ruined. First, she would be teased until she wanted to kill herself, then she would be labeled a wanton, available to any man who desired her for as long as his mood lasted. Some women openly chose that sort of life and were not condemned for it because the Crow nature made allowances for women with amorous tendencies. This indulgent attitude, however, didn't allow the possibility of a wanton later reforming and having a respectable marriage. Only women above reproach were considered true wives. With this black and white mind set, bad women stayed bad, good women stayed good and woe be to the good woman who teetered on the edge. Once word spread that a woman had allowed a one night "marriage," her amoral destiny was sealed.

Renee knew that this girl had wanted a true marriage with Nicolas. Instead, she had received a broken heart. He grudgingly admitted to himself that Nicolas was a handsome little beast. So was Jacques, for that matter. Renee wiped a hand across his worried brow, knowing that he was going to have to use a firmer hand with his two sons, or there would be more little girls like this one to deal with. He would deal with the boys later. First, there was this girl to consider. He crouched down to look Wolf

Blanket squarely in the face, then took both of her hands in his.

"Listen to me, *Mon Cher*. Your reputation is safe. You have my word that no one will hear of this comedy. Your honor is secure. But you must never act as if you know my son. If there are rumors, I will deny them. You say nothing and play the innocent because the more you try to defend yourself, the more guilty you will appear. Do you understand?"

Wolf Blanket nodded meekly.

"You must keep still and allow me to put an end to whatever talk might arise. Can you do that?"

Again she nodded, her face puckering up to cry again. "I loved him," she whimpered.

He placed a fatherly hand on her shoulder. "I am sure you did. And I am more than certain that Nicolas felt love for you as well. But, *Cher,* he is still young. If you continued to have him as your lover, you would regret it. In the end, he would forsake you, for that is the way of foolish boys. I know many fine men who would be proud to take you for a wife. Your eyes should look to them."

"Are they old?" she asked softly, wiping her nose on the back of her hand. "I have had enough of old men. I want a husband who is young and pretty."

"I will find you one, little girl," he promised. "And he will be handsome, too." When Wolf Blanket looked at him and smiled, he knew his promise had been taken to heart. It was now up to Renee to make good his word. But first, he would go home and deal with Nicolas.

Nicolas screamed and frantically grabbed at the ground as Renee dragged him out of the bachelors' lodge by his heels. Willow made the scene worse, screaming as loudly as Nicolas while beating Renee's back with her balled fists. Inside the lodge, Jacques grabbed his brother's hands, trying to rescue Nicolas from the wrath of their father. Jacques and Nicolas locked hands and wrists, but their combined efforts were still no match for Renee. When Renee dragged Nicolas out, Jacques was hooked as well, the two like a pair of trout snaggled on one fishing line.

Nearly everyone in the camp came out on that blustery winter morning to witness the spectacle. Clan members usually spent cold mornings lounging by the warm fires of their lodges, but a scandal such as this was much too savory to miss. It wasn't every day a father administered corporal punishment to a son. A son's crime would have to be extremely serious to warrant such drastic punishment and the gathering crowd wanted to know the details.

"*Pere!*" Nicolas yelled. "It wasn't all my fault."

"You shut your lying mouth!" Renee bellowed. He slapped the side of Nicolas's head with his open palm, sending Nicolas reeling. Nicolas covered the injured side of his face with both hands. "I know what you did," Renee thundered. "That girl's old woman told me of your shame." He jerked both of his sons to their feet and stood glowering at them.

Ashamed, Nicolas and Jacques stood with their heads bowed in submission, staring down at their feet. Willow's face blanched as she stood behind her husband, tears streaking her cheeks, as Renee announced to the world the disgrace of her son.

"Did you think it was a joke to pester a girl of good reputation?" Renee roared as he glared at Nicolas. "A girl recently widowed? A girl who was once wife to one of the strongest warriors of our nation? You stupid puppy!" he spat. Again he slapped the side of Nicolas's head. "You have brought shame to our clan and I should kill you for what you tried to do. If you want to be with a woman, there are some who would welcome you, but Wolf Blanket is not that type of woman and for you to try to force yourself on her, is a crime no one should forgive you."

There was a general muttering of full agreement among the spectators. This boy had most certainly stepped beyond the boundaries of good conduct and they all agreed that Renee's actions fit Nicolas's crime perfectly. One of the clansmen suggested that Wolf Blanket herself should be present to administer the first blow to Nicolas. Renee quickly assured him that by her absence, and the fact that she was allowing the parents to censure their wayward child, spoke volumes as to her ladylike deportment.

"I am not going to beat you in front of everyone, though you deserve it," Renee announced, much to the disappointment of the crowd and the relief of Willow. "You two follow me and there will be none of your sneaky tricks or it will be worse for you." Renee turned on his heel, his back ramrod straight, and stalked away. His sons dragged after him amid the jeering hoots of the bystanders. This day would stand in Nicolas's memories as the most mortifying moment of his young life.

Renee led them through the deep snow into the sparse forest to their special place of training. As they followed him, the boys shivered, as much from fear as from the cold. When Renee finally halted and turned on them, he had a scowl on his face, but he was secretly pleased to see his sons standing together, awaiting mutual punishment. They were true brothers. If one was to be beaten, the other stood expecting the same treatment without excuse or complaint. Without a word, Renee reached over and grabbed his boys. He saw their startled looks as he hugged them tightly against him. He released them just as abruptly and walked a short distance away, rubbing his clean shaven chin. Without his beard, which Willow shaved off whenever she could, he looked a decade younger than his late thirties.

"I know what really happened, Nicky," Renee began. "I talked with the girl at some length." He stopped, turned, his eyes focused on Nicolas. "Because of your little prank, shall we say, she made a mistake. She thought you to be a man, so she took you for her husband. Maybe now you can appreciate how the truth upset her, and why I reacted the way I did. I felt it was better to embarrass you than to ruin her. You, after all, are a young boy and these things are halfway expected of you. On the other hand, she is a grown woman who would face disgrace for the rest of her life. What is folly for one is humiliation for the other."

"She has no need to be ashamed," Nicolas proclaimed, his chest expanding with pride. "I am her husband. I have taken her as my wife."

Jacques stood speechless, his eyes wide as he looked at his brother in a new light. "Really?" he croaked. "You mean, you . . . really?"

"*Mon Dieu!*" Renee implored the Lord High God above, his arms stretched heavenward. "Save me from the lunacy of my children. Do not allow them to make me crazy."

Caught up in the excitement of discovery, Jacques ignored his father's rantings. "But you didn't really get inside her," he said. "She didn't let you do that. Did she?"

Nicolas simply looked at Jacques without answering.

Jacques grabbed Nicolas by his thick winter shirt and held on. "When we're alone, you better tell me everything," he warned. "And I mean everything, Brother. If you leave out one little detail, I'll beat you myself."

Nicolas shook free of Jacques's grip and shouted to his father. "I accept the responsibility of being Wolf Blanket's husband."

Renee, who was dry-washing his face in his hands, spread his fingers and peeked at Nicolas. He took in a big gulp of air through his mouth and then expelled it, dropped his hands and walked slowly over to Nicolas. Suddenly, he raised his hand and slapped Nicolas on the skull several times. Nicolas tried ducking away and raised his arms in an attempt to defend himself from the blows.

"You are no one's husband!" Renee shouted as he whacked Nicolas. "You are a puppy with his brains hanging between his legs! I will kill you if you ever go near that girl again or if you ever repeat what you have just said to me. You are not to tell anyone else. Not even your mother!"

Nicolas's knees gave out and he slumped to the ground, his arms still shielding his head from further blows. "I'm sorry! I'm sorry!" he cried.

"You're sorry," Renee seethed, drawing back as he fought to control his temper. "I should say you're sorry. Now it is up to me to find that girl a proper husband to undo the wrong you've done her. And how am I to do that, I ask you? Young husbands eager to take a wife aren't hanging by their hair from the trees, crying 'Choose me. Choose me.' They are either already married or too interested in the war road to take a wife. But I promised to find her a man and so I will. But you," he bellowed, pointing an accusing hand toward Nicolas, "you will stay away from her. You will not talk to her, or try to see her, or send messages of love. If you do, then the only husband that will take her after such a proven disgrace will be a blind, deaf Shoshone, who has lived in a cave for most of his life and missed hearing the news. Do you understand now how serious this is? This is not a game, Nicky. You could easily destroy that young woman with just one word in the wrong ear."

"I . . . I wouldn't do that . . . " Nicolas stammered. "I love her."

"Then you must prove it," Renee replied, his anger abating. "You must love her enough to stay away from her and deny all knowledge of her and accept the ridicule of people who will say you tried to take advantage of her but failed. You must never tell anyone you were in her bed."

"Her bed?" Jacques cried as he helped Nicolas to his feet. "Really, Nicky? You were in her bed? Her own bed?"

"Jacques!" Renee shouted. "You didn't hear that."

"Yes I did," Jacques replied, confused.

"No you didn't!" Renee countered. "And if you ever act as if you did, I'll beat you half to death."

"I didn't hear anything, *Pere*," Jacques replied quickly.

"My Father," Nicolas ventured softly. "You are forgetting one thing. Maybe I put a baby in her."

Jacques's eyes rolled to the back of his head as he grabbed for his heart and sank to his knees. "In her bed," Jacques wheezed. "He was in her bed. Making . . . babies!"

"I have forgotten nothing," Renee retorted. He grabbed Jacques by the hair and pulled him to his feet. "I will just have to be quick in finding a suitable husband for her."

And that was the end of it, for the moment. Renee walked back toward home, the two boys following, sullen in his wake, heavy-hearted with the secret they both shared and could never reveal.

• • •

"Those two are out of control," Renee said to his wife after his return from the supposed beatings. "I should never have listened to you and allowed them to move out. It was too soon for them to be treated as young men." He allowed Willow to help him out of his soaked shirt and was glad she didn't comment. He was in no mood to hear that that decision had been his and his alone. "I've sent them to recover their things. They are coming back to live with us."

Willow looked away to set the shirt down, and again didn't respond to her husband's words.

"I know you do not like so many men to do for, Willow, but I have to keep my eye on those boys before they become as wild as the north wind. I am their father. They are still my responsibility." Willow dried Renee's body and his hair as he continued. "You are their true mother. It is your fault that they have so little respect for women. You should have taught them long ago that there are some women they can touch and some that they cannot touch. I can't raise them all by myself, can I?"

"No my love," she murmured, keeping a close guard on her tongue.

"I teach them to ride, hunt, fight and to think like men. It is up to you to teach them about . . . about . . . women. I do not have time for such things."

"Yes, my love."

"And you'd better teach them well, Woman, before our lodge is crowded with grandchildren!"

The verbal abuse Nicolas received from the members of his clan during the following weeks was hard to take, especially from those who thought it their duty to lecture him. His various mothers nearly wrenched his ears from his skull as they held on to him as if he were a naughty little boy while laying on lengthy sermons about correct deportment. Wolf Blanket was always considered the offended party. Eager to make amends for what one of their own had done, the entire clan of the Whistling Waters showered the girl with gifts and tokens of their esteem. Wolf Blanket played her part to the hilt and accepted the gifts as they were presented, as well as the earnest apologies of the givers.

While everyone concerned themselves with Nicolas, Jacques used the diversion to his advantage. Feeling that Nicolas had bested him, Jacques felt duty-bound to rid himself of his unwanted virginity so that he was once again on equal footing with his brother. Jacques began "night crawling," an expression the Crow used to describe the young bucks in a rutting fever who sneaked out from under the edges of their parents' tepee walls in the dead of night in search of willing females.

Renee and Willow, while they pretended sleep, knew precisely what their son was about. It irked Renee that Nicolas didn't sneak out as well. The boy moped constantly. Renee had no patience with first love, no matter how ardent and sincere. Jacques was simply in heat, and that Renee could close a blind eye to. Nicolas's depression over his lost love was beginning to grate.

Matters came to a head on the night of Wolf Blanket's honeymoon. After a lengthy search, Renee had found a willing husband for Wolf Blanket. The bridegroom was from the ridiculed Bad War Honors Clan, but he was young, strong and fairly handsome. These virtues outweighed the fact that he was also somewhat stupid. Wolf Blanket seemed pleased enough and the marriage took place. Nicolas reacted to the event by taking to his bed and refusing food.

That night when Jacques rolled out from underneath the tepee wall, he found himself sprawled across his father's feet. He looked up at Renee, eyes wide, terrified of what his father might do, in as much as Jacques had been caught, fairly and squarely, in the philandering act.

"Take your brother with you," Renee whispered.

Jacques collapsed with relief, then sneaked back into the lodge to wake his brother.

After a week of both boys rolling in and out at all hours of the night, Nicolas returned to his old self, his great love for Wolf Blanket set aside as merely a wonderful memory of his youth. Renee began treating his sons more like the men he knew they were fast becoming and as the winter weather retreated, their arduous physical training resumed.

Long before the warm spring months arrived, the winter camp slowly began breaking up. Family clans did not necessarily group together within encampments. Individual families set up housekeeping in whatever spot pleased them, turning their door flaps always in the same direction: the east. Indian people appreciated their privacy and their space. Consequently, tepees could be placed in such a way that there would be an acre or two between them. An Indian camp nestled in a valley and viewed from a high mountain gave the appearance of containing more Indians than there might actually be, especially when a few thousand horses roamed amid the settlement.

One day Renee arrived home with the news that an official Crow agency was being established and that an agent was needed to govern it. Certain that he was the right man for the new job, Renee packed up his family and headed toward Mission Creek.

There is wide, clear ground between a certainty and an absolute. It was a certainty that Renee DeGeer was more than qualified for the advertised position. It was an absolute that the powers governing Indian affairs would choose someone else less qualified. The requirement for the job, Renee learned, was that the agent must be an "Indian man," which meant, according to government officials, a white man who was married to an Indian woman and well-accustomed to Indian life and custom. There were many such men available, but none with the innate good sense and physical bearing of Renee. Renee's disqualification was that he wasn't an "American Indian man." He was a French-Canadian, who, over the years of riding with the Canadian Sioux, had wandered into Montana. To the American governmental mind, this made Renee a renegade foreigner, and less trustworthy than a Sioux or a Cheyenne. Had Renee known the mind-set of the people with whom he hoped to find employment, he wouldn't have bothered dragging his family the long miles across the area that would one day be the city of Livingston. Though if he hadn't, the DeGeers would have missed all the excitement about to transpire at the agency and for this, his family might not have forgiven him.

The "mission" wasn't really a mission at all. Missionaries hadn't founded it, nor at any time had they used it, although they were busy in other parts of the region. The mission was a ramshackle fort. A lone cannon entitled the cottonwood construction to be called a fort. What the loosely knit, rotted-out palisade walls were able to defend or protect, no one was quite certain.

On the very day the DeGeer family arrived and set about establishing a roosting spot, the fort caught fire. It soon became obvious that there was no way to quench the blaze. During the moments of pandemonium spreading through the fort faster than the actual fire, some unknown soul remembered the cannon was loaded. Hearing the even more startling alarm, a new panic quickly ensued, delirium soaring to a doubling height as people scrambled to salvage as much as they could before the fire took everything. The Crow were concerned with getting the horses and children to safety. White traders were concerned with rescuing their wares. Soldiers and officers ran about in a frenzy, not knowing what or whom they should rescue other than themselves.

As the blaze encircled the cannon, the weapon grew hotter and hotter. Frontiersmen, Indians, soldiers, and government officials scurried about in various directions screaming, scavenging, barking orders. Finally, they had sense enough to take cover behind boulders.

Two hours later, the cannon finally spewed its load. Although there was a loud explosion, the people had enough time to take cover and nobody was hurt, though some suffered rumpled dignities.

By the end of the day, the four-acre agency had been reduced to a charred pockmark on the ground with the ruined cannon sitting like a smoke-belching pig squarely in the center of the charred rubble.

Renee accompanied the two government officials who were temporarily in charge as they examined the devastation. Although the officials knew better, they continued allowing Renee's belief that he would indeed be the man to take over the agency after the organizing officials made their break back to Washington.

While Renee worried over his ruined post, his sons were having the time of their lives. Jacques and Nicolas decided that if their first day among the whites could be this exciting, the agency might not be such a bad place after all. Willow calmly took her little Marie by the hand and went back to her duties of housewife. It took more than a hell-blazing fire and one little cannon to ruffle Willow. Not after sixteen years with Renee.

The regular army officer who was temporarily assigned to the agency was Major Camp, formerly of Fort Ellis. He was a good man although somewhat stiff in his deportment, especially with Indians, and with the white men who aped the Indian lifestyle. He wasn't a mean-spirited man, nor was he dull-witted. He knew Renee not only by sight, but by reputation. He knew that if he was to maintain a semblance of control in this new, albeit burned-out agency, he would need Renee. So he hired Renee as the new building supervisor, even though Renee didn't know how to build anything.

Renee accepted Major Camp's offer, providing his sons were hired as well. Renee's plans were to keep the Crow agency business in the controlling hands of the Whistling Waters Clan, and having his sons on the governmental payroll was an absolute must for him.

Major Camp was slightly stunned when Renee introduced his boys. He hadn't really known what to expect when Renee broached the subject of his sons but the two gangly young men now before him, arrogant and belligerent to the core, had him mystified. He judged rightly from the way Renee continually whacked them on the backs of their heads, that the idea of working for a living left them both positively cold. The major had always been fascinated in the by-product of the mingling of white and Indian blood, so he couldn't help but stare at the taller of the two boys, the one who was introduced as Nicolas. If the sullen young man had been dressed differently, Camp would have sworn that he was full white. Yet as quickly as the idea came to him, the major dismissed it as an impossibility. The boy was obviously Renee's son. Renee had only one wife and she was full Crow. Still, the major thought, the lad's blue eyes were phenomenal, especially considering Renee had very dark brown eyes. He presumed that Renee had a blue-eyed ancestor somewhere back in his bloodlines.

As the three DeGeers left his tent, Major Camp shook his head, amazed by the wonders of heredity. He watched them walk away, the sons almost as tall as the father, and it never occurred to him that the fairer lad wasn't Renee's blood son. The boy named Nicolas walked exactly like his father. His hair was almost the same shade as Renee's, although Nicolas wore his hair loose while Renee chose to keep his in a ponytail. The bemused major would never know the long hours Nicolas had practiced Renee's walk until it had become as natural for him as it had come to Jacques who had inherited it by birthright.

Renee soon discovered that he was out of his element in dealing with the United States Government. He believed that Major Camp had hired him on the spot as agent, not simply as a man to help hold the agency together while applicants formally queued to interview for the position. Renee and his boys helped rebuild the agency from the ground up, using adobe instead of soft cottonwood for the buildings.

Meanwhile, a man named Pease bypassed the fort and went directly to Washington D.C., to apply in person for the job Renee thought was already his. Pease was no stranger to the Crow, though his Indian wife was of another tribe. He could read, write and conduct himself almost like a true gentleman in the white world and these noteworthy attributes landed him the job as supervisor of Crow affairs.

The day Pease arrived to take over, Renee pitched a blue-ball fit that threatened not only the budding agency, but the solid peace with the Crow, for they instantly and to a man, sided with Renee. Renee was one of their own, while Pease, who had bestowed upon himself the title of "Major," wasn't.

Major Pease, realizing that his entire career lay in the palm of this bellicose man, quickly adopted the manner of a diplomat. Aided by Major Camp, Pease called a powwow to discuss the issues at hand. This served to lengthen the fuse on the powder keg by three weeks, the time needed to assemble all the far-flung Crow chiefs. During the truced lull, Pease tried every ploy he could think of, desperate to sway Renee. In doing so, Pease overplayed his hand.

The meeting of chiefs took place in the newly constructed building. It was merely a large open room at that time, but they planned to partition off rooms to serve as offices. The chiefs, dressed in their best, entered solemnly, their demeanor displaying the gravity of the current negotiations. Pease watched them file in and as he went out of his way to extend a welcoming hand to each chief, he felt the first trickle of sweat run down his spine. If the chiefs all voted to throw him out, Washington, for once, might comply with their wishes, for the Crow were vital allies in the securing of the Western frontier.

Renee and his sons entered last and, bowing to the importance of their chiefs, took lesser seats. Renee had never been one to usurp his leaders and he wasn't fool enough to do so now.

The meeting began and, after four long hours, nothing had been accomplished. The reigning chiefs used the occasion for oratory that praised Renee. Major Pease and Major Camp were the only ones to grow impatient during the long meeting, as each chief droned on, outdoing the speaker before him, not only in length of speech but in flowery sentiment. Renee, smilingly interpreted each speech, not in the least embarrassed that the speeches were all in praise of him as a man, warrior and leader.

By midday the room was stifling when the chiefs rose to leave. In departing, most of the hot air exited with them. Renee and his boys remained seated, left alone with the two majors.

"What is it you want, Renee?" Pease asked in a somewhat defeated voice.

Feeling his victory, Renee rose and stretched to his full height. "You have heard what my brothers believe of me. You liked their words, no?"

"They expressed themselves admirably," Camp said, mopping his brow. "Now, may we get on to the real subject?"

"I'm sorry," Renee replied, spreading out his arms. "I thought I and my position with the Crow Nation to be the subject. Perhaps I should call back my brothers and explain to them our error."

"No!" Pease shouted. "That . . . that won't be necessary. I'm sure we're all perfectly aware of their stance on this issue. There is no need to have a rehash." With a jerk, Pease untied his starched necktie that had gone into a wilt in the heat of the long meeting. The chiefs were gone and he felt no more need for gentlemanly display. "It's been a long morning," he bristled. "Could we please just get on with the essentials?"

"Ah, *oui*," Renee agreed, taking his seat again. Flanked by his scowling sons who sat rigidly in their chairs, Renee began ticking off his demands. "One," he began in his heavy accent, "I and my sons will be the official interpreters for the agency."

Major Camp leaned far out of his chair and studied the boys, especially Nicolas. "Your boys speak English?" he asked, astonishment in his voice. He had only heard them speaking French with their father.

The inquiry put Renee on his guard. He didn't like the way the army major looked at Nicolas. It was common knowledge the Crow didn't take white captives, however, there could always be that one exception. If the major suspected Nicolas to be an American, the army might take it into its head to liberate the boy, whether Nicolas wanted to be liberated or not. It wasn't as if he were a grown man free to choose his own destiny.

Casting a warning glance toward Nicolas, Renee lied smoothly. "Ah, no. My boys do not speak American, as yet. But I teach them. They will learn quick. They both smart, like they Papa."

"I find this request reasonable and perfectly in order," Pease said.

Camp sat back in his chair, still uncertain. Something wasn't right here. He couldn't put his finger on it, but something was definitely amiss.

"An' I want land for a permanent place for my family," Renee said. "In fact, I think it would be a good idea to map out the reserve and assign each family in the tribe their own land. This, I believe, would avoid confusion later on and give everyone their rightful due. The Crow will one day stop their roaming and will need a place to go. You cannot expect to huddle them all around the agency like children waiting to be fed. They would never stand for this treatment."

The two majors stuck their heads together and whispered back and forth. Finally Pease spoke for them both. "That is an excellent idea, Renee. And very responsible of you to protect the future of your kinsmen."

"*Oui,*" Renee nodded and smiled slyly. "I am a responsible man. An' while we discuss the future of my brothers, I have this to add. There are too many whites at this agency. I know we need the soldiers and the families of the men who assist with the agency, but the others we don't need. Get rid of them. This is Crow land. Get rid of the extra whites before they settle and plow up the land that is not theirs."

"That could be trouble," Pease worried aloud to Camp.

"There will be more trouble if you don't do it and do it quick," Renee promised.

The two men huddled again, for a longer spell of time.

Jacques and Nicolas glanced sideways at each other, smiling slightly.

"We will have to begin the evacuation tomorrow," Camp said. "But I agree with you. Sending the settlers away before they have a chance to take root is the only fair thing for all concerned."

"My feelings exactly," Pease agreed.

"I am happy we all agree with each other so easily," Renee chimed. "It will make further discussion possible."

"What do you mean, further discussion?" Pease snapped. "You couldn't possibly have more demands!"

"Ah, but I do," Renee returned boldly. "Make yourselves comfortable, *mes amis*. This will take a little bit."

After an hour of arguing back and forth, the group disbanded in order to have a meal and clear their tempers. Two hours later they were back at it, Pease having the presence of mind to bring with him paper and pen to make a permanent record of all the requests they agreed upon. When they were through, he read them aloud.

1) The Crow Reserve belonged absolutely to the Crow and their descendants. Any white attached to the Reserve for whatever reason was required to learn the Crow language.

2) Any whites residing on the reserve must mingle with their Indian hosts without hesitation. The Crow were not to be treated as second-class citizens in their own country.

3) A school must be provided and white children living on the reserve would attend this school with the Indian children.

4) The trading store being built would not sell the Indians items or food goods sent by the government. These items were entitlements, not trade fare.

5) A doctor would be in residence at the agency. A man of high morals and worthy skill. Any doctor proving himself unworthy on either standard would be promptly dismissed.

6) On the matter of missionaries. A church was permitted but Crow attendance was not mandatory. Any missionary caught calling his red brother a heathen was to be expelled immediately.

7) Building materials would be freely provided to all families who wished to build permanent structures on their allotted portion of land. That, and a few head of cattle, the number of cattle depending upon the size of the family.

8) Crow scouts. The Crow were not to be forced into actual fighting when such fighting ensued between the army and enemy tribes. The Crow duties ended when the designated enemy was located. All dispatch riders, couriers, and agency workers, save that of government officials, were to be of Crow origin. (This last demand, Renee hoped, would stem the tide of whites drifting in and being hired on at any little job that might be available.)

9) No policies were to be made regarding Crow welfare without a council with the chiefs. Any policy made

without this council would be considered nonexistent by the Crow.

10) The Crow would continue to choose their own chiefs. When a death or vacancy occurred in the chiefly ranks, the replacement would be made in the time-honored fashion. Governmental appointees were unacceptable.

"Gentlemen," Pease said, running a handkerchief over the back of his neck as he looked away from the list, "I think we have an agreement. Provided Mr. DeGeer will keep his bargain and not cause any further dissension at the agency."

"You have my word," Renee nodded. "As long as my chiefs agree to this list and have nothing further to add."

Pease froze, a stricken look on his face.

Renee threw back his head and laughed loudly. "So soon you have forgotten number nine, eh, *mon ami?*"

Renee and his immediate family stood quietly as they surveyed the four hundred and fifty acres they were considering as their allotted parcel of land. It seemed to be a good place. The land curved and dipped gently and there was an abundance of trees. There were three streams, one meandering through the center of the section, the other two cutting through the upper corners. Fresh water would never be a problem for family and animal use. The section was situated in the very heart of the Crow reserve. Renee thought that to be the most desirable of all the section's qualities. His children and his children's children would always be a well-established part of this land he loved so fiercely.

Since Jacques and Nicolas were fixed employees of the agency, they, too, had the right to choose their own sections. Renee glanced sideways at Nicolas. Legally, Nicolas had no claim to any piece of the reserve. The government didn't know that, and the Crow, having adopted Nicolas into their number, weren't inclined to divulge this piece of information, but Renee had to make certain Nicolas's future was as firmly settled as Jacques's. The only real way Renee could seal Nicolas's Crow destiny was to find him a wife. A full-blood Crow wife. Nicolas was still too young to be married, but that didn't prevent him being betrothed. Renee's ferrety mind set to the task of selecting a likely candidate.

Two weeks later, he had one.

CHAPTER SIX

The Crow didn't ordinarily betroth their daughters. When girls became of marriageable age, a suitable husband was duly selected. The case of Nicolas was an extraordinary circumstance and Renee's old-time friend, Rides-The-Buffalo-Down of the Streaked Lodge Clan, happily, was quick to see Renee's point.

"They might kick him out if they knew," Rides-The-Buffalo-Down nodded as he counseled with Renee. "The whites can be funny like that."

A week later, Nicolas found himself sitting in the lodge of Rides-The-Buffalo-Down, dressed in his finest shirt, positioned between his father and his brother. He looked straight ahead as he listened stonily to himself being discussed as if he weren't there, while a ten-year-old girl blatantly inspected him.

Her name was Eyes-That-Shine and the name suited

her. She was as bright as a new copper penny and was as tenacious as gummy pine tar. Nicolas was appalled that this little bothersome child was the bride Renee had chosen for him. Nicolas had imagined something a bit more promising when Renee informed him of a match he was considering. Nicolas had naturally assumed that his unknown bride would be a girl old enough to visit on the quiet while they awaited the blessing of their wedding day. This infant would take years to mature and Nicolas's needs were more immediate.

"He has too many sweethearts," Rides-The-Buffalo-Down said as he puffed on the pipe. He passed the pipe toward Renee and waited further comment as Renee made the sacrificial offering of smoke to the four corners of the earth, to the sky and then to the earth itself, before answering the charge leveled against his son.

"He has known many," Renee admitted. "But that is because he is a beautiful person. Your daughter is lucky to consider a man many women seek to call their own. Such a husband is a pride for a wife."

Renee passed the pipe to Rides-The-Buffalo-Down. The prospective in-law smoked as he nodded in agreement. In a nation where male vanity was everything, a man with many sweethearts added to a wife's luster, not her shame. Custom aside, Rides-The-Buffalo-Down was still a father.

"If I am to agree to this future marriage," he stated firmly, "your son must curb his attentions toward other females. He must openly court my daughter and express his desire for her. He must do this until the marriage day as a sign to others that Nicolas is no longer available to the women who would seek to be his wife."

A groan almost escaped Nicolas's throat when he heard his own father say, "We agree to your terms."

Satisfied, Rides-The-Buffalo-Down rose. "Now we will leave the young ones alone for a moment to become better acquainted."

Panic reached out a cold hand and gripped Nicolas's heart as all the men left the tepee, leaving him alone with the little girl and her watchful mother. Pretty Stone, Eyes-That-Shine's mother, was now a woman Nicolas could no longer speak to, for it was forbidden for a man to say even one word to his mother-in-law. The actual marriage, while far off in the future, was all but concluded. All marriage customs, with the exception of the one held dearest to Nicolas's heart and loins, were now enacted.

Eyes-That-Shine scooted on her knees and sat in front of Nicolas, resting her bottom on the backs of her legs, her knees lightly touching his. She inclined her head from side to side as she openly studied this boy husband of hers.

"You're skinny," she said after a long scrutiny.

"You're short," he snarled in retort.

The girl's face puckered at the insult. "I don't think I'm going to like you."

"I'm glad," he fumed. "I don't like you either. Especially when you stare and pick your nose."

She waggled her hips and stuck our her pink tongue. "Too bad for you," she sneered. "You still have to court me and bring me pretty gifts. Father said so."

"Father said so." He mimicked her infantile tone. His imitation promptly caused her to squall at the top of her lungs. Nicolas didn't try to stop her or to apologize. He merely plugged both of his ears with his fingers.

Pretty Stone bent her head and concentrated on her fine needle work, biting her lower lip to suppress the laughter she would share later with her husband.

While the handshake between the fathers in front of witnessing clansmen was still warm on Renee's palm, he presented himself at the agency to secure Nicolas's portion of land, claiming it for Nicolas and his legal Crow wife, Eyes-That-Shine.

Nicolas and Jacques waited for him on the covered front porch, just outside the agent's office door. Because it was a hot day, the door had been left open to permit a breeze and the DeGeer brothers were able to listen to the business being transacted inside. They heard Renee proudly explain Nicolas's recent change in marital status.

Major Pease, seated behind his large oak desk, leaned to the side so he could see the recent bridegroom. He shook his head in distaste. Of Renee's two sons, he much preferred Jacques, who looked like an Indian and had a somewhat pleasant personality. Nicolas, on the other hand, had too much white in him and seemed surly in disposition. Pease considered him a born troublemaker.

"Not one word from you," Nicolas cautioned Jacques as the two brothers saw the look on Pease's face. Jacques grinned, but said nothing.

When Renee walked out with the tract map in hand a few minutes later, he slapped it down over the top of Nicolas's head.

"It's done," he said proudly. "You now have your little place on this earth, my Nicky."

Nicolas expelled a long stream of air through his flaring nostrils. "I don't want to be married to her *Pere*! She's a spoiled brat. Her father has ruined her."

Renee shrugged as if this were the common complaint of all married men. "Her father has overfavored her, but you have to remember she is his only child. It's natural for a father to shower a lone child with too much attention. It's up to the husband to teach her better manners."

Renee pushed his sons aside and headed for their tethered horses. With one swing of his leg Renee was mounted, then he waited for his sons to mount up.

On horseback, Nicolas was just as tall as his father, and he looked him directly in the eyes. "She's only a baby," he said as firmly as he dared, trying to make his father see reason.

"Babies grow," Renee countered.

"But she's no older than Marie," Nicolas yelled. "And you want me to court a girl that age? I'll feel like I'm courting my own sister." He shuddered at the incestuous thought. "*Pere,* you also agreed that I had to stay away from other women. What am I supposed to do while I wait for that baby to grow up?"

Renee chortled as he rapped Nicolas's chest with his curled knuckles. "You use the time to become a warrior, my little man. It is time you thought of other things besides pleasure."

Several family groups of the Whistling Waters Clan moved onto Renee's acreage, set up their lodges and made themselves at home. Renee enlisted the aid of a few of the young men to go out with him and his sons to the upper region of Mission Creek to cut trees. Willow had definite ideas about her permanent home. She wanted it built of logs.

"I want a big home, Renee," she informed her husband. "The white women have nice houses but they look so small."

"Want to outshine them, eh?" he grinned.

"No," she replied with a casual shake of her head. The thought of status hadn't occurred to her. "They have small families," she explained. "I have a big family. I need more room than they do."

"But I don't want to cut down all of our trees just to make a big house," Renee barked.

Willow merely turned and walked away from him, avoiding an argument. "Then get the trees you need from someplace else," she said in a final tone.

Renee stood there, hands on his hips, fuming mad, speechless in that moment. He knew his limits with Willow. And he knew that as blustering as a man might be in the Crow world, it was the women of that world who quietly ruled the households. In well-learned wisdom the women seemingly gave their men their heads, never arguing when their men left them for months on end. They saw it as their duty to keep the family home together while their husbands were gone. However, when the men came home and the wives made requests of their husbands, they expected said requests to receive proper attention.

"Willow," Renee bellowed after a minute.

Willow paused in the entry door of their lodge and looked back at him patiently.

"I'll have to drag all those logs down from the hills," he complained. "This is going to be a very hot season and that kind of hard work in this heat might kill me."

"Then please remember to sing your death song," she said flatly. "It would not do for your spirit to get lost looking for the Sky Road." She ducked inside the lodge, ignoring his thunderous expression.

· · ·

Still holding Pease firmly by the testes, Renee and his group of loggers made for the supply building at the agency. From the beleaguered agent they commandeered two wagons, ten mules, coffee, sugar, bacon, beans, saws and axes.

"You'll let me know if you need anything else," Pease said sarcastically.

"*Oui*," Renee grunted, flicking the reins of the lead mules, aiming the wagons away from the bustle of the growing agency.

Jacques, who rode his horse close to the side of the wagon, passed the open-mouthed Pease. He leaned over and smiled impishly at the stricken agent. "*Au revoir, Monsieur Agent,*" he said.

Nicolas laughed out loud, much to Major Pease's discomfiture. The other Crow in the logging party were quick to pick up on the agent's plight. They, too, laughed as they rode past him, kicking up dust into his face like salt spray off a rolling ocean wave. Indignant, Pease stood in place and listened to the mocking laughter as the taunters rode out of the compound.

The group of fifteen men worked hard the first week, felling trees and stripping the logs of branches. The first few days were exciting, but after a week of hard work, everyone, including Renee, became bored with the project and voted to vacation the following week.

Medicine Crow was one of those in the work party and the two fledgling DeGeer warriors followed after him as his devoted disciples. Renee knew his boys held Medicine Crow in their highest esteem and encouraged the hero worship. He was not jealous in the least that Medicine Crow usurped him in the eyes of his sons. At times Medicine Crow could grow too melancholy for Renee's tastes, turning any conversation toward the morbid thoughts that forever plagued him, but he was a seasoned warrior with a sound logic about him, and in Renee's mind, his sons had made a wise choice.

"My death is close. I hear the old ones who came before

us whispering in my ear when I sleep. I know this means I am to join them soon."

While such statements ordinarily might not make for lively repartee, they deepened Renee's respect for his younger brother. In Renee's experience, any young man overly concerned with his premature demise, real or imaginary, tended to last longer on the war road. As a rule, warriors in their prime were out for glory and oblivious to dangers, especially when they believed their "medicine" made them invincible. Medicine Crow was extremely cautious and he was a planner. Renee admired both attributes so much he trusted his sons to the younger chief.

Renee's opinion would stand the test of time. Medicine Crow, a veteran of many bloody confrontations with the Lakota, Cheyenne and Blackfeet where hundreds of strong Crow warriors fell by his side, lived to see the early 1920s. Both before and after his death, he was hailed as one of the greatest chiefs known to the Crow Nation. He would go to Washington D.C., be presented with medals, have his portrait made in various poses and be written of in glowing terms in newspapers up and down the eastern coast. Though a fierce war chief, Medicine Crow was also terminally shy, and fearful of the attentions favoring him above all the other chiefs present. Primarily because of his youth and extreme good looks, he would be photographed, his newspaper-printed image setting white female hearts fluttering. In the year 1880, Medicine Crow would be a media success. He was a powerfully built man possessing gracious manners which invited trust and admiration from every corner of the white capital. After his departure from the capital, fiction novels involving white lovelies being captured and held as love slaves by handsome Indian males became the most popular of all the Penny-Dreadfuls. Rumor has it that Medicine Crow also cut trail for the swarthy silent film star, Rudolph Valentino. This may or may not have been true but the overriding theme of the celluloid sheik certainly smacked familiar to those who knew Medicine Crow.

•   •   •

THE GLORY DAYS OF BUFFALO EGBERT

The week off from grueling toil was a week of boyhood revisited for all of the warriors. They hunted, swam and lazed in the warm sun, happy to be away from wives and sweethearts nipping at their heels, goading them into one useful activity or another. Life free of women held a rosy glow until they ran short of food. There were still plenty of beans, a little bacon, game meat and wild onions, but the Crow had grown accustomed to other luxuries such as coffee, sugar and cigars. When these items ran out, the grumbling began. Before it escalated, Renee took matters in hand. He sent his two sons back to the agency.

"Tell the majors we need soldiers, too."

"Why, *Pere*?" both asked.

"Just do what I tell you," Renee replied. "Tell the majors that there are a lot of bad Indians in these woods."

The boys shrugged it off as some wild whim of Renee's, and rode out to do as they were told.

Renee's message threw the majors Pease and Camp into a dither. "Hostiles!" they cried. "Hostiles rampaging inside the Crow Reserve." The two majors discussed the possibility and decided that if DeGeer couldn't hold the aggressors back, the invaders might break through and destroy the agency itself. They quickly agreed to Renee's request and outfitted a column of cavalry, and sent them out under the leadership of Sergeant Dankins.

After the DeGeer boys secured all the coffee, sugar and tobacco they could legally draw against their entitlements, they helped themselves to more, quietly pilfering the sutler's store. Although they were still novice warriors, they were practiced thieves. While the agency people were busy with their new fears, Jacques and Nicolas easily purloined all they could carry. The souls of innocence, and with supply packs bulging, the brothers calmly rode a half mile ahead of the enlisted soldiers, leading the cavalry toward their father.

"Men, keep your eyes on them two bucks," Sergeant Dankins ordered, nodding toward the two brothers who rode ahead of them. "If they get picked off, don't wait for my orders. Just duck for cover."

An hour after sunset, the soldiers arrived at Renee's camp. Three bonfires burned, illuminating the base camp, staving off the crowding darkness. Nicolas and Jacques dismounted, ignoring the soldiers. The tired cavalry, still on their horses, looked around for telltale signs of warfare. None of the Indians in the camp looked wounded; in fact, they seemed quite comfortable. The only tension seemed to arise from the squabbling among the warriors over fist-fuls of cigars that the DeGeer brothers weren't keen on sharing.

Renee wandered toward the confused horsemen and greeted Sergeant Dankins. "I'm pleased to see my sons led you safely through."

"Through what?" the sergeant barked. "We didn't see any hostiles."

"Oh they ain't so much back that way," Renee replied with a wave of his hand. "They more up there,"he said, pointing to the north. He wasn't lying. He knew that north was where the Lakota would be. He just didn't see any reason to mention *how far* north they were. "Come down from your horses. You welcome at our fires. Come," he said with a broad smile. "Soon we have the *cafe*, eh? You men, you hungry, *oui*?"

The group of uniformed men looked to the sergeant before making a move. Sergeant Dankins exhaled loudly and then gave the hand signal to dismount. "There ain't no way we can ride back tonight anyhow," he reasoned aloud.

Eight days later, Major Camp sat as quiet as a stone while his "Toppy," Top Sergeant Dankins, made his oral report. Camp was paralyzed by what he heard.

"There was lots of hostile activity, sir," Dankins recounted. "And the woods were too heavy for a column attack. Since DeGeer and his Crow were used to the area, it was agreed he would fight the Sioux back while me and my men finished up the detail."

Camp's entire body tightened, his face a stolid mask, his voice incredulous as he asked, "You're saying you cut trees?"

"Yessir!" Dankins replied with pride. "Me an' the men, we cut 'em as fast as we could. DeGeer wouldn't pull out

of there until the detail was done. He said he'd rather face
the whole Sioux tribe with only one bullet than to go
home to his woman without the logs he'd promised her.
He must be mighty scared of her, sir, 'cause him and his
Crow took some heavy losses. When he come back one
day, he was miss'n three men. Three! We cut a lot faster
after that, believe me."

"Oh I believe you, Toppy," Major Camp said calmly,
even though he was seething inside. "You're dismissed.
On your way out, kindly send in Mr. DeGeer."

"The gunfire was all around us, sir."

"That's enough, Sergeant!" Camp shouted, refusing to
hear another word. The sergeant saluted smartly. Camp's
returning salute was a limp wiggle after which he used the
hand to cover his eyes.

Renee didn't stand on formality. In fact, he didn't stand at
all. He sat back comfortably in the ladder-backed chair,
one leg crossed over the other as he tipped the chair back,
rocking it slightly, savoring his cigar. He studied the major
through a haze of smoke.

The arrogant son-of-a-bitch, Camp thought in disgust.

Renee was wearing a new set of buckskins Willow had
crafted for him while he was out cutting trees for her. A
man who worked hard to provide for the woman he loved
deserved a new suit of fine clothing. As an added display
of wifely love and gratitude, Willow had heavily fringed
both sides of the leggings. The fringes were so long, they
fell to the floor like cascading water whenever he stood up.
Despite his anger, Major Camp had to admit that Renee
cut a natty figure.

"I know what you did, Renee," Camp began slowly,
measuring each word. "I can't prove a thing of course, but
we both know what really went on out there."

"It was horrible," Renee said as he lazed in the chair.
"The Lakota were thick like the fleas."

"God's eyes, Renee!" Camp thundered. "The only
thing thick out there was your pack of lies. You used my
men like a gang of darky field hands!"

103

"*Monsieur* Major," Renee replied, feigning astonishment. "You wound me to the quick."

Seething, Major Camp stood. Renee remained seated, which further kindled the major's ire. "We'll just see," Camp said. "We'll just see how wounded you are after you spend the rest of the summer doing every scum job I can find for you and your plundering sons!"

"You calling my sons thieves?" Renee demanded in a low, menacing tone, one eyebrow raised.

"Yes I am!" Camp roared, his face red with anger. "And I have the sutler's accounts to prove their theft. Jacques and Nicolas are no longer allowed in that store. Am I making that clear enough for you?"

Renee had the major by the uniform lapels before another second passed. His movements were so swift the officer hadn't even seen him coming. Until that moment, Camp hadn't realized just how dangerous Renee could be when aroused. In his better moments, Renee was like a fearsome panther with only the sheerest veneer of restraint, and now wasn't one of those better moments. Camp realized this as he dangled in Renee's grasp, their faces only inches apart. Renee's mouth was set in a threatening snarl.

"Them boys are the grandsons of a big chief," he growled as he showed more of his strong, even teeth. "A bigger chief than you ever meet, you poor little man. It ain't for you to say where they go an' where they don't go. You understand?" He shook the dangling Camp roughly. "This their country. Their land. Your damn store sit on their ground. So if they tell you get your store off it, you get it off. They go where they wanna go and don't nobody better tell 'em they can't. I kill the one who says it. You tell your storekeeper that, *mon* major, an' you tell him quick. Is this clear enough for *you*?" Renee let the major go with a push.

He left the office without another word.

CHAPTER SEVEN

The DeGeer house went up quickly. The men of the Whistling Waters hauled and set the logs while the women mixed the mud mortar, filling in the gapped spaces between the placed walls. Within two weeks the house, with its flat board tar papered roof, was ready to live in. All the workers brought in their sleeping mats to share in the warmth and security of the walled house.

With almost seven thousand square feet of living space, the DeGeer house was enormous. It had four fireplaces made of natural rock which Jacques and Nicolas had hauled in with wagons and mules. They had worked night and day. As yet, the house had no windows. Renee ordered glass panes, but they weren't due to arrive from Bozeman for another month, so they had left the walls intact. They saw no reason to cut holes that could not be filled.

The house was one large open room with a dirt floor. With no windows, it was dark inside and they burned wood in all the fireplaces to light up the dank interior. Willow had been right in saying she needed a large house. Even as big as it was, with all of her relatives crowded inside, there was barely enough breathing room. And there certainly wasn't any privacy. The wall-to-wall family slept in typical Indian fashion—wherever they could find a clear space. Those couples in the mood for love had to slip out quietly, taking refuge either in the woods or a vacant lodge. Slipping out wasn't a problem. Slipping back in again was. Too many family members were on hand to greet the amorous married couples with grins, quietly implying, "We know what you were doing."

Willow and her sisters tried cooking on the stone hearths once, but with no ventilation, the nearly fifty people who lived there were quickly overcome with smoke. They all rushed outside, coughing and choking as smoke billowed out the open doors. It was then that the people of the Whistling Waters learned that dripping buffalo grease and enclosed walls weren't a good mix.

Renee and his brothers built an outside barbecue pit by digging a deep fire hole and setting stones around it. With an iron grate placed across the stones, they were able to cook steaks and keep coffee simmering throughout the days and nights. They dug another fire hole and used a heavy tripod to hold a cast-iron pot, which had been designed for use as a wash pot, but instead was used for stews. With the cooking problems solved and in the presence of such bounty, none of the relatives was in any hurry to leave. After a few weeks of family unity, it came as somewhat of a relief to Renee when a Crow courier rode in with the news that Major Camp had a job for the three DeGeers. Renee knew it would be a scum job, as Camp had promised, but anxious to get away from his cloying relatives, he decided to take the job and allow Major Camp to save face at the agency.

According to the courier, Renee, Jacques and Nicolas had been assigned to help escort a white family out of the reserve. The man, a blacksmith, had been employed at the agency and was living rent-free on Crow lands. Because of the policy Renee helped set down, the man had been discharged from his job and, after he'd trained several Crow in his smithy craft, he had been evicted from the house he'd built. Major Camp found it only fitting that the man primarily responsible for the blacksmith's eviction should also be the man to assist the family in packing up and moving on. Renee and his sons were also to see the Russell family safely on to the township of Absaroke, due to reports of hostiles having been seen in the area. When Renee heard the last part of the major's message, he threw his head back and laughed until tears rolled.

"I'm glad to know the major isn't a fool who loses his head in anger, yet is tricky enough to find a good way to get even," he told the courier. "Good. It is done. Tell the major I will do this thing for him and then we will be even. After this, maybe we can be friends again. Maybe."

The courier remounted and rode off to relay the message from Renee.

Since the Russells had been evicted, the ownership of their house was to be decided by lottery. Mrs. Russell, already upset because she had to move, was besieged by Indian women coming and going, blatantly inspecting her house. She was not in a good mood when the DeGeers arrived to help her pack her belongings.

"This is inhuman," Mrs. Russell cried, as Nicolas and Jacques chased around the yard, trying to catch her squawking chickens.

Nicolas vaguely understood the English being spoken as he stuffed the flapping birds into the holding cages. After four years of speaking only French and Crow, English sounded abrasive to his ears. He wanted to tell the woman to shut up but if he did, Mrs. Russell would know that he not only spoke English, but that he understood it as well. That was something Renee had warned him about. Renee had said that something bad might happen if Major Camp ever found out Nicolas had once been an American, and Nicolas wasn't anxious to find out what that something might be. He remembered only too well the dreariness of American life and he wasn't eager to go back to it.

Crow life fulfilled his every want and desire. Tall, tanned, half-naked in his breechcloth and ankle-high

moccasins, long dark hair fanning out behind him like a
bird's wing in flight as he walked proudly, he looked
exactly the part he played of Crow half-caste. Only his
blue eyes vexed him. Overly conscious of them, he kept
his lids lowered, which gave him a sullenly lazy, and
intensely insolent, expression. Whites working at the
agency gave him a wide berth, thinking him one of the
troublemakers peppering the tribe who were bent on
threatening the peace.

"Will you two stop playing with those birds and come
over here?" Renee stormed in French. He was helping Mr.
Russell haul the furniture out and load it into the transport wagon.

Mrs. Russell stood helplessly to one side as the foreign-
speaking Indians manhandled her worldly possessions.
They jabbered away in what she knew to be French
mingled generously with the guttural grunts and growls
she recognized as Crow. She couldn't comprehend any of
it and was secretly amazed that her three evictors could. It
was almost as if they were making up a language as they
went along, just to devil her further.

The Russells had one child, an eleven-year-old named
Charlotte. Mrs. Russell had called her daughter Lottie
since birth but the child was a hopeless tomboy who
answered only to Charlie. The girl always wore overalls,
boots and a hand-me-down faded plaid shirt. When she
had acquired an old hat from somewhere, Mrs. Russell
had tried to keep her from wearing it, telling her daughter
that the hat might have vermin.

On that occasion, Charlie had thrown one of her
famous temper fits, promptly taking the sewing shears to
her hair. She snipped off one golden plait, then the other,
leaving donut-shaped gouges with erratic sprigs of hair
sticking out, an act which put an end to all her girlish
charm. The shock of her daughter's mauled appearance
had caused Mrs. Russell to faint dead away. To hide
her daughter's disfigurement, Mrs. Russell parboiled the
old hat and gave it back to Charlie. After that incident,
Mrs. Russell lived in constant mortification of her only
offspring.

Ironically, on this black day of official eviction, it was

the fact that her daughter looked like a pug-nosed boy that gave Mrs. Russell some consolation. She shuddered to think what the two near-naked Crow youth might do if they knew her Lottie was actually a girl. Everyone with a brain knew that breed Indians inherited only the worst traits from their mixed parentage. It was unnatural to mix the two bloods. Whites weren't meant to produce issue from the biblically-cursed darker races. Nothing good could ever come from it. This was an opinion which Mrs. Russell held close to her heart and for this reason, for the first time in her life, she was glad that her only daughter looked and acted like a pugnacious boy.

She would have been even more relieved to know that Nicolas and Jacques didn't give a hoot one way or the other about her child. The boys were a long chalk from being rapists and certainly children held no interest for them, be they male or female. However, they couldn't help but notice this child because Charlie seemed bent on giving them as much pain in the posterior as humanly possible.

The day of the move was uncomfortably hot. The sun burned with a fiery intensity in the noonday sky and the child buzzed them like a pesky fly as sweat poured in rivers down their bodies.

"You two smell," the child sneered as she held onto her button nose with one hand. "Pew-yooo! Stinky Indians!"

The working boys ignored her and her insults as much as they could. Jacques couldn't understand her words. Nicolas understood everything. The child reminded Nicolas of all the nasty little children he had ever known in the white world and the memory grew too close for comfort. Before he could stop himself, his foot flew out and struck the child's hind end.

Charlie screamed, and Mrs. Russell flapped around, looking like one of her chickens.

"Oh!" she cried as she held her arms out for her crying daughter. "Charlie . . . oh my darling Charlie. Come to Mama."

"Your son accosted my baby," she railed at Renee.

"Madame," Renee replied evenly as he leaned against a chifforobe. "Your baby's bottom attack my son's foot. See it does not happen again or I will not be responsible for your child's injuries."

"Oh!" she squawked again, as she grabbed her child's hand and hustled her away. Charlie paused to make a face at the two young men.

"She is going to ruin that boy of hers," Renee said to his sons.

"She has already ruined him," Jacques snorted.

"Never mind them," Renee said. "It is white people's business. It has nothing to do with us. Let's just get this thing into the wagon so we can be quit with them."

The three of them grunted as they lifted the plainly crafted oak and cedar chifforobe. The drawers of the combination wardrobe and chest-of-drawers slid out when Jacques tipped it forward, his hands vainly searching for a grip. With a great deal of clatter but very little damage, the drawers landed at their feet, sending up a spray of dust. Hating the woman and her silly cabinet, Jacques frowned, his mouth twisting wryly. "I hate white people," he shouted. "I just hate them. It's too much work to be around them. Why can't they be normal and have normal possessions?"

"I don't know, Jacques," Renee said. "But we're never going to be rid of them if all you do is stand there and complain. Nicolas, pick up those pieces before she comes out of the house and starts another fuss."

The wagon was finally loaded by three o'clock that afternoon. Normally, travelers set off in the early morning hours, but Renee wanted these people off his hands quickly so he insisted they depart immediately.

The Russell family rode together in the wagon and as it pulled away, Mrs. Russell turned for one last look at her former home. It was a depressing sight as she saw an Indian family already taking possession. The lucky winners of the lottery were swarming in, obviously unconcerned about pushing the former owners out, as they arrived with their horses and all their earthly goods loaded on a travois. The horses and children quickly trampled the flowers that Mrs. Russell had planted in the front yard and nursed into bloom. She forced herself to turn away and then sat rigidly in the wagon beside her husband, hugging her child against her.

"That house never suited me anyway," she murmured through the tight slit of her mouth. "Living in a proper town is what my Lottie needs. Whoever heard of raising a young lady stuck off on Indian land with nothing but Indian children to mix with. Small wonder she's as wild as a March hare." She looked over at her husband, angered further by his passiveness. "I was four shades of a fool to let you talk me into it in the first place. The Indians need us, do they, Elmer? Well you just take a good look at how grateful they are for what you taught 'em at the smithy. They took all we had to give an' showed us the gate! After we get to that town, we're sticking to our own needs and no more playing the missionaries."

While Mrs. Russell lambasted her husband and watered her sour grapes, Renee rode well in front of the wagon. Jacques and Nicolas brought up the rear, herding the Russells' two cows. It was nearing midnight when Mrs. Russell put a halt to the caravan.

"I will not be bumped about in the dark one more mile, Mr. DeGeer," she said after they had stopped. "Do I make myself plain?"

"All too well, madame," Renee said, bowing at the waist from the saddle. He called his sons and they rode up from behind. The boys drew up hard on the reins when they reached the wagon, the dust flying as the hooves of their horses dug into the dirt. Mrs. Russell fanned the dust from her face in exaggerated strokes.

"We stop here," Renee told the boys.

"What for?" Nicolas asked, annoyed.

"The woman is tired."

"But we're almost there," Jacques complained.

"Don't make me crazy," Renee shouted. "She wants to stop so we stop. Where are her rotten cows?"

"Somewhere back there," Nicolas responded.

"Well, bring them in," Renee snapped. "We will have to tie them to the wagon. I don't want to waste tomorrow morning looking for the stupid beasts because they wandered off in the night."

Jacques turned his horse and Nicolas was set to follow.

"Not you, Nicky," Renee said. "You must gather wood. It will be too cold to sleep without a fire." An impish smile played on Renee's lips, and in the light of the bright full moon, Nicolas didn't miss it. "Nicky, does this misadventure bring back any old memories?"

"No," Nicolas lied, although it wasn't a total lie. The journey with Renee so many years ago on this very route seemed more like a dream now than an actual event.

Renee's smile broadened. "Get a lot of wood, my good son."

Everyone in the camp slept with a heaviness brought on by trauma, physical labor and boring travel. Everyone except Charlie. She couldn't get comfortable in the crowded wagon and huddled alone, she was cold to boot. Quietly she clambered down, dragging her child's quilt with her. The first group of bodies she came across were Jacques and Nicolas sleeping a foot apart. They looked comfortable and warm in their sleeping robes, their backs to the low burning fire. Without hesitation she plunked herself between them, stirring Jacques.

He opened his eyes slightly and saw the child. Her hair stuck out in all directions, an untidy halo in the glowing light. She wrapped her quilt around her shoulders and shivered as she mouthed the word, "Cold," trying to make him understand. Still half asleep, Jacques sighed and raised his warm buffalo robe with one arm. Charlie scampered into it and snuggled her small back up against him, grateful for the precious warmth he provided. Content at last, Charlie drifted off into sleep.

"Ahhhhhhh!" Mrs. Russell screamed. "Ahhhh!" she screamed again as if she were being scalped alive.

Renee awoke with a start and sprang to his feet. He saw the woman standing over his sons, and his first thoughts were that they had been killed in their beds. He ran toward them, jumping the fire pit that smoked in the cool morning air.

THE GLORY DAYS OF BUFFALO EGBERT

As Mrs. Russell started to scream again, both boys sat up in their blankets.

Relieved to see his sons alive, Renee stopped just behind Mrs. Russell and immediately saw the cause of the woman's hysterics. It was impossible to miss the small blonde head half submerged under Jacques's blanket.

"He's got my baby!" Mrs. Russell cried like a woman demented. "He's got my baby!"

She was set to let go another air-sundering wail when Renee whacked her soundly on the back. She swallowed her scream as it rose halfway out of her throat and began choking on it after Renee's blow sent it back to the pits from which it stirred.

"What's all the fuss?" Mr. Russell said as he ambled over to join the gathering.

Renee waved the matter aside with a casual hand. "Nothing. All is well. Our children simply sleep together. You wife take it too seriously."

"Our children did what?" Mr. Russell quavered, his face going ashen.

Renee looked at the man with surprise. Renee knew the Russells to be prejudiced people but this display went a bit too far.

"Our children," he repeated more slowly, "share blankets. It is an Indian custom to share warmth. The night was too cold for the little one to sleep alone, ah *oui*?"

"Hi, Daddy!" Charlie twittered, the buffalo robe draping her head as she peered out.

When Mr. Russell realized that his daughter had slept the entire night nestled in the arms of the Crow youth, he was appalled. He grabbed her small hand and hauled her bodily out of the blankets. He heaved a sigh of relief when he discovered that she was entirely clothed except for her boots.

Jacques made a face at all of them, and threw his blanket up over his head, shutting out the early morning intruders. Nicolas followed suit, glad to let his father handle the bizarre attitudes of the child's parents.

"Just what do you think you were doing?" Mrs. Russell asked her daughter.

"I was cold," Charlie replied.

"Then you should have come to me," hissed Mrs. Russell.

Renee had had enough of this woman and her over-protectiveness. "It was correct for the child to seek my sons," he declared. "It is only proper for a child this age to be with warriors. To wait for them to be older, wastes them. They mature faster when you allow them to bed with men."

Renee was nonplussed by the parents' reaction to his simple statements of Indian fact. He would have sung a different tune had he an inkling the child was female. Still in the dark about Charlie's sex, Renee was startled when both her parents caterwauled about the indignities foisted upon their innocent child as they dragged her away, Charlie kicking and screaming, "I wanna stay with them! I'm still sleepy!"

Absaroke was in plain view by dusk of that long wearisome day. There, the DeGeers gladly bade a fond farewell to their charges.

While Renee said goodbye to Mr. Russell, the boys waited for him at the rear of the wagon. They used this final opportunity to make faces at Charlie who had begun the display when she stretched her lips with her fingers, crossed her eyes and stuck out her tongue at them. Jacques crossed his dark eyes and slid his mouth sideways as he waggled his head. Nicolas stuck his thumbs in his ears and waved his fingers. Charlie matched them goofy look for goofy look.

"I'm glad this is over," Jacques said. "One more day and I would happily kill this brat." He had no idea that he would see her three years later. She would be mature and quite lovely. But, alas, still a brat.

The wagon lumbered off, the two cows in tow. Renee and his sons crested the hill, then watched as the Russells ambled their way toward the town. His foster fatherhood beginning to weigh on him, Renee turned to Nicolas.

"Do you ever think of your life of long ago, Nicky?"

"No," Nicolas replied curtly. Renee and Nicolas locked

eyes for a somber moment. "My mother is Tall Willow. It was she who gave me birth into the Whistling Waters. The life of the whites you speak of, I don't know it. I don't accept it."

Renee's heart took flight, soared like the hawk. He turned his horse eastward and called to his sons. "*Bon.* We go home! *Allons, mes fils!*"

CHAPTER EIGHT

Renee's allotted land was teeming with visitors when they arrived home. Tepees dotted the landscape. Cook fires flecked the living areas along with meat-drying racks heavy with curing flanks of buffalo meat. It was clear that even more guests had arrived during Renee's absence and were prepared for a long stay, the new company having settled in amongst the Whistling Water relatives.

"*Mon Dieu,*" Renee breathed with an air of helpless resignation. "Our land has become the Crow capital." There was nothing left to do but ride into the center of activity and endure the cries of welcome and hearty handshakes.

A high-ranking chief of the Lumpwood Warrior Society dragged Renee from his saddle, hugging Renee hard as he shouted in Renee's ear. "Welcome home, Brother! We thought you had gotten yourself killed."

The other men laughed heartily at the joke. No self-respecting warrior died without a proper witness to his valor.

"Come join our council, Brother," the chief bade, his arm tightening around Renee's shoulders. "We have brought food and many fine gifts for your wife and yourself."

Renee's heart, leaden with dread, beat in slow motion. He knew now the reason of the visit from his warrior brothers, though it took them two full days before coming to the point. The chiefs had come for his sons. But before the actual claim was made, there were other things to be concerned with. Feasting, dancing until the long hours of night, speeches made in regard to Renee and Willow having raised such fine strong sons and, best of all, light hearted pranks to be played on unsuspecting victims.

Finally, at the close of the second day, with Renee's patience strained beyond the limits of endurance, the Lumpwoods, dressed in their finest regalia, stood at Renee's front door. The fraternal order was ready to plead its case.

The Crow tribe has always been a matriarchal tribe. Clan membership came to the sons through their mother, and her alone. However, sons were likely candidates for their fathers' warrior society. During the 1870s, four such bands dominated the Crow culture.

The Lumpwoods. The Foxes. The Big Dogs. The Muddy Hands. Each club had its own leaders, forms of dress, songs and dances. They were brothers who fought together and socialized with one another freely.

After two years as a Crow, Renee joined the Lumpwoods. One of his first friends within the Crow had been a member and so Renee chose his friend's group. Serious and open competition existed among the war clubs, each always striving to outdo the other. One favorite shenanigan was to encourage their younger men to kidnap wives of rival clubs. The natural targets were wives having had more than one husband. Ladies known for enjoying the company of many men. Now and again a "purchased" wife was caught up into the snare. When this happened, of course, the wife of honor lost her good reputation.

However, high honors were bestowed on the male who had lured the woman to her downfall in stature.

Her "disgrace" might be as slight as to ride on the wooing warrior's horse, or as serious as full-blown adultery. The outcome always proved the same. Instant divorce. Such were the pitfalls of women following their hearts and not their heads when listening to a rival club member espouse his love and admiration.

The principal chief of the Lumpwoods was a man called Flat-Land-Rider. Known for his splendid oratory, he was selected to speak on behalf of the society. He stood out from the gathering, proudly displaying his bent staff covered with otter skin, the sign of his high office.

"My brother," he began, addressing Renee loud enough so that all could hear. "You are the proud father of two young men who have gained our attention. We have discussed them many times and we have decided that they have now reached a good age to die."

These last words, though they might have chilled the marrow of any father outside the Crow world, were the highest praise a Crow could give. Old age for a man among the Crows was viewed as a curse fraught with evil. It was preferable for a warrior to die while still young and handsome. An early demise was certain to provide the surviving widow and her family with many wailing mourners. If a man died while old it was highly likely his longevity had stripped him of friends who would grieve his passing. Then too, there was the uncertainty of admittance into Crow heaven, a place crowded with brave young men who might ridicule and chase away an old spirit.

"You honor my sons," Renee replied gravely. He had long dreaded this moment. During the last two years Renee believed he was prepared for it. Now that it had arrived, he knew he wasn't, just as he knew too, that he was powerless to fight against it. He mentally chided himself for not feeling the expected pride. All of his work and worry had been for this day, the day his sons would shake his hand and go off with warriors to make their own lives. It was time for them to earn their scars and their coup feathers, to cut their ties with their parents and fend for themselves.

THE GLORY DAYS OF BUFFALO EGBERT

Willow stood by Renee's side, stoic in her resolve. Renee wondered if she were dying inside as much as he. Floundering for words, and choking on his torturous emotions, Renee tried to speak. "They . . . they are only naughty little boys," he mistakenly blubbered.

That remark caused a great deal of disconcerted discussion. "Naughty little boys" was a title for novices of the Foxes' tri-level club structure. To a single man, the Lumpwoods turned on Renee.

"Are you telling us you have allowed your sons to join up with the Foxes?"

"No!" Renee cried, putting the lid down on the ugly mood rising like proving yeast. "I only meant to tell you that these two louts aren't worthy of the trust you are placing in them. They still act like children needing to be milk-fed by their mother. They are going to be a lot of work for you and for that I apologize."

This explanation smoothed out the ruffled feathers of the gathered tribesmen as the Lumpwoods accepted Renee's explanation. Smiling broadly as Flat-Land-Rider turned first to his club members then back to Renee, the chief spoke confidently. "We will make men of them, my brother. It is time for them to come out from the cover of your lodge and build a home for themselves. You were generous parents. It is past the time these two puppies learned to be hunting wolves. In their trials, they will realize just how generous you were and will bless your names for the happy childhood you provided them."

It was finished. Renee was outnumbered. He had no choice but to sit mutely and watch as his sons were initiated into the warrior society. Their feet were set on the war road now and there was no way Renee could call them back. His hand went to his chest. The wrenching pain he felt was terrible, made worse by his sons' excitement over their new life. Arms about each other's shoulders, they were brothers by clan, society and spirit.

"Stay alive," Renee whispered to their broad backs.

Four days later Renee's sons left, riding out with the experienced members of their new society. They were allowed to take only the possessions they could carry in their arms or on their backs. They would have to earn

119

their own way. However rich or poor they became in life was solely their own responsibility. The days of accepting meals from kindhearted mothers were over.

Willow waited until her sons couldn't see her face before she allowed herself the privilege of tears. When they came, they came in a deluge, bathing her beautiful face. She leaned heavily in Renee's strong arms, her eyes glued to the image of her boys as they grew smaller on the horizon.

"Our time with them passed too quickly," she said in a low voice. "Where did it all go?"

Renee couldn't speak, the constricting knot in his throat silencing his vain efforts to comfort his wife.

They were even denied the sympathies of their relatives as the Whistling Waters, taking a cue from the departing Lumpwoods, packed up and moved out on the same day. By mid-afternoon, the land that had once seemed so crowded, was empty, save for the three remaining DeGeers who were left to clean up the camp remains.

"Now this place feels too big," Willow said as she surveyed her desolate homestead.

CHAPTER NINE

Whatever Nicolas and Jacques expected in their new status, it certainly wasn't what they received. All their young lives they had seen only the glory of being men on their own, missing entirely the lousy side of the adventure. Suddenly on equal status with orphans, they were miserably poor. They had no lodge for shelter, no food but what they could hunt up on their own. When the summer storms came crashing in, the brothers hunched up together under their sleeping robes. They didn't dare ask to be sheltered by their clansmen for they knew they would be ridiculed. As tempting as the thought incessantly became, they knew also that they couldn't go back to their parents' warm house. They had to prove themselves as men, capable of providing for themselves and the wives they would one day take. The pressure to succeed was greater for Nicolas than Jacques because Nicolas already had an in-name-only wife, plus a father-in-law who kept sharp eyes on him, quietly demanding Nicolas to hurry and make good as a provider.

Working to put an end to such a humble existence, they joined every buffalo hunt that was organized. On the first such hunt, even though between the pair of them they shot down five large bulls, they were shoved out by eager skinners who not only got the hides but the tongues, leaving the two lesser warriors the scraps.

On the second hunt, they were ready to assume more aggressive roles. Jacques, riding in the middle of the thunderous stampede of terrorized buffalo, took out a huge old bull. As it skidded to its knees, rolling to the ground in its death throes, Nicolas jumped from his horse, wielding his knife. Leaving his brother to protect and butcher his first kill, Jacques went after a young cow. An expert marksman, Jacques put a bullet in its heart and as the creature charged on, vaguely aware it was dying, Jacques leaped onto its back, skinning knife clenched in his teeth. The brothers hunted in this way almost every day for the next sweltering weeks.

The tongues of their kills were presented with pomp to the wife of Rides-Down-The-Buffalo. Eyes-That-Shine clapped her hands and went about bragging to all of her playmates about her brave husband. Nicolas soon doused her smug attitude with a cold splash of reality.

The two DeGeers had collected twenty green hides, the number needed for a lodge of their own. "Who better qualifies to clean these hides and stitch them together than my little loud-mouthed girl-wife?" Nicolas grinned wickedly to Jacques. When the request was made of Rides-The-Buffalo-Down, Eyes-That-Shine's temper soared.

As a daughter of a rich man, Eyes-That-Shine wasn't accustomed to menial labor. Her family had a Piegan captive woman as a servant. Cuts-Off-Her-Hair, so called because she was forever mourning her fate as a slave, said nothing as she served the food to her master and his two invited dinner guests. Cuts-Off-Her-Hair paid no attention when the young girl lost her temper.

"Let the old woman do it," Eyes-That-Shine told Nicolas. "I'm not going to."

"You tell everyone quickly enough you are my wife," Nicolas shouted. "Here is your opportunity to prove yourself the same way I have to prove myself."

No one in the lodge became concerned over the argument between the espoused couple. Nicolas and Eyes-That-Shine fought all the time. It was their way. They disagreed on every issue. Their courtship was heated, though not in the normal manner. Nicolas paid his perfunctory calls and Eyes-That-Shine was always ready for him in her prettiest dress. They were always pleasant to one another for a brief second and then the shouting began. During the first weeks, all the yelling disconcerted the bride's father. Then, Rides-The-Buffalo-Down became so accustomed to their booming debates that had the quarrelsome pair suddenly changed attitudes, he would have hauled one or both off to a healer, convinced of some terrible illness.

But as he listened to this particular argument, he became uneasy. What sort of daughter have I raised, he thought. What kind of wife has this young man agreed to accept? In disgust he threw his charred piece of half-raw steak down onto the wooden slab platter resting between his crossed legs.

"My daughter," he began, his softly spoken words shutting up the warring couple with a start.

Eyes-That-Shine sent Nicolas a "you're in trouble now" sly smile. Then she looked at her father and waited.

"This man of yours makes a reasonable request," her father said.

Her eyes flared wide, the whites a swimming pool for the dark orbs which stared disbelievingly at her father.

"You are more than ready to share in his victories," Rides-The-Buffalo-Down stated. "I know you are happy with the gifts he works to bring you. I have heard your boasts of his courage and his beauty. How is it, then, you are so quick to shun him when he comes to you with a natural demand? He is right when he says this is his proving time, and more than right when he says it is yours as well."

"But, Father!" she cried.

The elder man raised one hand to silence her. "It is time

you took seriously your duties toward him. When you go to live with him in only two seasons, you will have no servant. Young couples never do. Your mother had no servant when she first married me. She had to know all the things a wife is expected to know. Things you have yet to learn. This is the way of life, Daughter." Then he began his lengthy oratory, instructing all three young people present within his lodge walls.

"In the beginning, the earth was covered with water. Old-Man-Coyote was alone and his shadow wandered the landless earth. He was very sad this world was so empty. He found four ducks swimming, all male like himself. He encouraged the ducks to dive beneath the waters. Three found nothing. But the fourth duck brought up a soft root which he gave the Old Man.

"The Old-Man-Coyote became very excited and told the ducks to go back under the waters. They did, bringing up mud which Old-Man-Coyote dried into dust. He blew some of the dust all around and made the dry lands. With the root, he made all the grass and trees and plants. With a pinch of the dust, he made many animals—the elk, antelope, beaver, buffalo and the bear. He also made the prairie chicken and gave this bird a wonderful dance, and told the bird to dance for him every morning and every evening as a celebration of life.

"But soon, the Old Man became bored with these creatures and taking more of the dust, he made men. There were no females of any kind and soon all the creatures of the earth, including the men, requested females so that they could reproduce after their own kind.

"The men said, 'You have taught us, Old Man, how to make weapons, how to hunt to feed ourselves, to use sticks to make fire. But what use are our weapons with no one to defend, and hunting skills when we have no one but ourselves to feed? And there is no warmth at our fires without someone to share them.' So the Old Man said, 'All right. I hear you.' And taking the very last of the dust, he made females for all the creatures.

"The human females were glad about the life given to them but after awhile became jealous of the gifts the Old Man had given only the men. They felt useless and so they asked him for special powers of their own. Again he said, 'All right,' and he gave the women the knowledge to make warm homes, to prepare the food the men brought them, to sew clothing for protection against the winter winds and best of all, the gift to make children inside their bodies and nourish the young ones with milk from their breasts. These are all things men cannot do. These gifts are blessings from the Creator, making women necessary and special.

"Both the men and the women were happy with their gifts. The men were so pleased they copied the dance of the prairie chicken to celebrate the fine life they were given." Casting a stern eye toward his pouting daughter, Rides-Down-The-Buffalo finished his story. "This was in the beginning of time. It has never changed. The powers given to the first women have been passed on to their daughters since that day. The special partnership between men and women remains the way Old-Man-Coyote planned it. It is the way it will continue into forever."

Eyes-That-Shine kept her mouth clamped firmly shut for the rest of the evening.

Eyes-That-Shine hated manual labor. Her carefree days had always been spent playing in her toy tepee with her friends. But she was too old for such games now, so lately, she tagged after the older girls. She was accepted into their company because she was becoming of marriageable age, and already had a promised husband. Nicolas was a husband many of her new friends envied her for. The others had their eyes on Jacques, so it was to their benefit to be a friend to this offensive little person. They suffered her spoiled disposition while they laid plans to attract the attention of one or both brothers. They listened as she went on about how Nicolas adored her. All of them knew that for a lie. Anyone with one functioning eardrum knew how Nicolas really felt about his intended. She was kept in the dark by her new friends in respect to Nicolas's willingness to be waylaid after leaving her father's lodge, the ever-eager Jacques always at his side. The nights of stolen romance were secrets giggled about behind Eyes-That-Shine's back.

Scraping away the spoiling flesh from the staked-out hide in the drumming heat of the afternoon sun was cruel work, so cruel that Eyes-That-Shine forgot Nicolas's handsome face and strong body. All she saw was Nicolas's smirk after her father delivered his damning lesson of Crow genesis. Toiling away in the oppressive heat, she almost hated Nicolas. Hated him as the cause of ending her lighthearted days of childhood and burdening her with a slave's work.

The scraping tool felt too big in her little hands. Her back ached and the top of her head burned unprotected under the relentless sun. Yet she was expected to work until the hide was cleaned and ready to smear with the concoction of brains, gall, blood and urine to soften and waterproof the prepared hide. Since the hide was intended as a lodge covering, it didn't have to be perfectly smooth and for that, the struggling girl was grateful.

She toiled all that day, determined not to quit. Determined because even though she loved Nicolas, she knew he didn't return her affection. If she were to quit her task, she might provide him his golden opportunity to reject her publicly. Not only would she lose him, but she would shame her parents and she would also lower her prospects for another husband. Eyes-That-Shine worked on stubbornly, even when her mother twice tried calling her away for a rest.

"I have to keep working," she said to herself over and over. "I can't lose him. I can't let him go to another woman. I am his wife. I am his wife."

At sunset, she finished. She sat on the ground next to the completed hide, her legs crossed in an unladylike fashion, the empty bowl that had contained the slops used in the tanning process cradled in her lap. She was as coated as the hide pegged into the ground. She was so exhausted she was oblivious to the flies that swarmed her and stung her thin arms. Her exhaustion turned to satisfaction when Nicolas walked toward her, leading his horse.

"You finished," he grunted. He sounded extremely disappointed and that made her feel even more proud.

"Yes I did," she said, struggling to her feet. "I will do one a day until all the hides are completed and then you will have your house. Are you pleased?"

Nicolas twisted his mouth to one side and raised his eyebrows. "I suppose so. Jacques and I need a place out of the rain. It would be nice if you could work a little faster."

Eyes-That-Shine puckered her soiled face, her eyes a close squint. "You mean thing!" she screamed, raising her fist at him.

Nicolas ducked as she flung herself at him, her arms a buzz saw. He laughed as he held her off. "Look out," he cried. "You're a filthy mess. I don't want you on me."

"I'll show you," she cried.

Before he could stop her, she grabbed his hair and pulled his face down, whereupon she planted a wet, smelly kiss on his surprised opened mouth.

"Ukkk," Nicolas blubbered, wiping his mouth on the back of his hand as he pushed her away. "Stop that! That's disgusting."

"What's the matter, Nicky?" she teased, going after him as she made kissing noises. "Don't you like the taste of a little buffalo blood and urine?"

Repelled, Nicolas began spitting the ground. "Is that what that stuff is?" he gagged. She smiled and nodded, as he retched loudly.

Eyes-That-Shine's parents stood watching the young couple quietly from the side of their lodge where they were partially concealed. "That's the way a young couple should play," her father said with a wide smile. Her mother snickered in her hands as she watched them.

"Stay away from me, 'Shiny'," Nicolas shouted.

Eyes-That-Shine chased him, her arms thrown wide for hugging.

"Shiny!" Nicolas threatened. "I mean it!" He quickly leaped onto his horse, steering the shying animal away from the girl.

Eyes-That-Shine's shrill laughter rang the air as Nicolas took flight.

•   •   •

Jacques and Nicolas left the main camp the next morning, taking two young men of their class with them. They headed up the Yellowstone and there they all cut lodge poles for the lodge under construction by Eyes-That-Shine. When the work was done, they took the next two days to loaf. They stripped naked and cannonballed off ledges of a cliff embankment into the clear running river below.

After a full day of swimming, as they lay on the banks basking in the sun, the subject of women arose. Suddenly, to Nicolas's discomfiture, Eyes-That-Shine's name entered the conversation. They all teased Nicolas unmercifully about being henpecked. They joked about him having to resort to 'night crawling' again. Nicolas passed the teasing off as he lay on his back enjoying the feel of the sun on his body. The youths, realizing they were getting nowhere with their ribald jests, grew quiet.

Takes-The-Knife, who was lying on his stomach chewing a blade of grass, somberly stated, "My oldest brother married last season."

"Again?" Jacques hooted.

Takes-The-Knife threw a handful of grass in Jacques's direction. "This time it's official. My brother, Elk Hunter, took a young girl. A virgin girl. He paid eight horses for her."

All the young males whistled over the high price of the bride.

"He's had nothing but trouble ever since," Takes-The-Knife stated glumly.

Nicolas, his interest titillated, rolled his head toward Takes-The-Knife. He squinted against the sun, one eye closed. "What kind of trouble?" he asked.

"The worst kind," Takes-The-Knife confided. "Sex."

No one spoke. All eyes were on him. Takes-The-Knife knew he held his audience spellbound. "Have any of you had a virgin?" They all shook their heads. "Well, don't try it. My brother is an old man. He thought everything would be fine, but it hasn't turned out well for him at all."

Jacques crawled in closer to Takes-The-Knife. "What happened?"

Takes-The-Knife raised up on his arms and spoke as if he and Jacques were the only two sharing the confidence.

"He took her off to a special honeymoon place. You know, so they could be all alone. He worked for over a week making everything nice for her. When he finally had her alone and tried to take her, that's when things went badly for him."

Jacques, a stickler for detail, asked, "Are you going to tell what happened or am I going to have to hurt you?"

"All right, all right." Takes-The-Knife grinned devilishly. "According to Elk Hunter, it's hard to get inside a virgin. You have to push hard and sometimes virgins fight a lot. It turned out his new wife was a fighter. And," he added dramatically, "a screamer." All the youths sat up and perked their ears as Takes-The-Knife went on dramatically. "Elk Hunter stuffed blankets in her mouth to quiet her so he could concentrate. He said his doing that made her crazy and she screamed louder and fought like a demon. Her fighting him made him take longer and finally, after he was finished, she tried to stab him with a knife."

Nicolas's face turned ashen.

"It's true," Takes-The-Knife nodded. "And she still goes after him whenever she gets her hands on a weapon. He thought she would calm down after awhile and get over it, but she hasn't. Now he's afraid to go to sleep. He's afraid he'll wake up one morning and find his manhood missing."

"I don't believe any of this," Jacques scoffed.

"You'd better," All-The-Animals-Running replied. "My uncle, Ties-Up-His-Horse's-Tail, has the very same problem. He traded for a Nez Perce girl last winter. You've seen her, Jacques."

Jacques agreed that he had.

"Beautiful, isn't she?" All-The-Animals-Running said.

Again Jacques agreed.

"Well, she's mean. And she hates my uncle. She tortures him."

"How?" Jacques asked.

All-The-Animals-Running moved into the group as if afraid of being overheard as he lowered his voice to a mere whisper. "It all started on their wedding night. My uncle, who's *really* old, almost forty winters, thought he knew exactly what to do. He tied a stick in her mouth to hold down any screaming. But then while he was taking her, she bit right through the stick. It stabbed her in the tongue and there was blood everywhere. So, not only couldn't she walk for awhile, she couldn't eat either because her tongue was all swollen and black. I guess that's when she started hating him and turned so mean. She gives him the worst kind of torture. She has a beautiful body and she undresses in front of him all the time."

"That's torture?" Nicolas chortled.

"It is when you're not allowed to touch the body," All-The-Animals-Running replied solemnly.

They were all stunned into morbid silence trying to comprehend such a horrible state.

"But can't he force her?" Jacques cried.

"No," came the answer. "She made him promise he would never force her again. He made the promise because he was so sorry about her tongue. He's been even sorrier since. He's tried begging, but that only seems to make her more pleased with herself."

"Why doesn't he just throw her away?" Takes-The-Knife quizzed.

"Would you if you had a woman that looked like her?" All-The-Animals-Running scoffed. "Besides, only a few know that they aren't happily married. I'm not even supposed to know. I heard him talking about it to my father. If any of you tell, they'll know I was listening, so on your honor, you don't repeat any of this."

"We swear," Nicolas and Jacques vowed.

"Did you see their faces?" All-The-Animals-Running cackled to Takes-The-Knife. "Nicolas looked green."

Takes-The-Knife laughed. "I thought Jacques was going to empty his stomach when you threw in the part about the stick stabbing the girl's tongue." He fell back, wallowing in muffled laughter. Then a thought occurred to him and he sat up smartly. "Jacques and Nicolas are going to kill us when they find out she's carrying a baby inside her."

"They won't find out for a long, long time," All-The-Animals-Running said dryly. "My uncle has taken her to be with her parents for the birth of their child. In the meantime, we can make the bridegroom Nicolas as crazy as we like."

The boys slapped each other with glee, trying to muffle the laughter that bubbled from their mouths.

CHAPTER TEN

Nicolas became remote and withdrawn. The joy of being amid the magnificence of the Yellowstone vanished. He finished gathering the lodge poles by himself. When his brother offered his assistance, Nicolas responded gruffly, "It's my responsibility."

Having gathered twenty-five sound poles, he signaled to the others it was time to leave. Each youth secured the long poles on either side of their mounts and trailed after Nicolas as he plodded homeward.

Eyes-That-Shine stood close to her mother as the young warrior procession journeyed their way through the large encampment dragging the poles. Cuts-Off-Her-Hair stood well behind her mistress, Pretty Stone. Nicolas stopped the procession and dismounted. Although he stood before his mother-in-law, he spoke only to Cuts-Off-Her-Hair. He had no words for Eyes-That-Shine either.

"Here are the lodge poles my wife needs to make a home for me and my brother. Try to see that she doesn't break them."

Cuts-Off-Her-Hair pulled in her upper lip and bit down hard to squelch the smile that threatened when the young girl sucked in a sharp gasp of air. The old slave woman decided she liked this young warrior, even if he was Crow. She also decided to take over the task of finishing the lodge, ensuring that the project would be done correctly. It was the first time since her capture that she willingly took on a task. That in itself would have been a high compliment to Nicolas had he known. He left the women, Eyes-That-Shine sputtering with rage, seeking out the one brother he knew might offer him solace. Medicine Crow.

Medicine Crow lazed in his lodge, smoking a short clay pipe as he listened to Nicolas's tale of woe in regard to the enforced marriage. When he was certain Nicolas had finished, Medicine Crow offered the only solution he knew. "You need to take yourself to a high place. You need to deprive yourself of food and water. You must set up an altar and on it, offer a piece of your flesh. When you've done all this, and if the One Above hears you, He will tell you what to do."

"About marrying Eyes-That-Shine?" Nicolas asked hopefully.

"No," Medicine Crow replied, dashing the hope. "That has been decided. Unless she does something shameful, you can't throw her away. You have to take her. Our clan is too close to the Streaked Lodge Clan for you to tear up the marriage. It would mean a feud between the Whistling Waters and the Streaked Lodges. Then everyone in the Whistling Waters would be mad at you for causing the trouble. You would be lucky if anyone in our family spoke to you again. You might even have to quit being a Crow and go back to your first people."

Medicine Crow leaned against the woven willow branch back support that crowned his bed as he smoked and considered the terrible consequences. He was a man who liked to be absolutely certain of the advice he gave. "Everything I've said is true," he said, kicking away any hope Nicolas might have.

Nicolas washed his face in his hands. His tired blue eyes rose like summer moons to meet those of Medicine Crow. "Then why must I offer up the sacrifice of myself?"

"I won't take you out with me until you do," Medicine Crow shrugged.

When Nicolas told Jacques of his plans, Jacques asked permission of Medicine Crow to go as well. This offering-up of his flesh became more popularly known as the Vision Quest. It was an essential ritual for a young man before he was permitted to journey the war road. An untried warrior needed to know where he stood in the Eternal before he gambled his life. These things were told him by other elders as Nicolas made preparations to go on his Vision Quest.

Visions were profoundly important to warriors. They were keenly sought in all important matters. Conversely, they were sometimes a handy excuse. He learned that a warrior who had received a vision might say he hadn't had a good one if he wanted to change his mind and back out of going on a raid. That was certainly an honorable excuse, though used about as frequently as a buffalo wandering into a village and offering itself up as a sacrificial meal. Many young warriors, after enduring this horrific torture, claimed to have had a vision when all they actually had was unendurable agony.

The heaviest burden of the quest remained ahead, in that if a man maintained he had experienced a vision, it needed proving. This need of proof did away with the possibility of outlandish claims. Warriors who hadn't had a real vision but wanted to have people believe that they had, tended to keep their retelling of their vision on the drab side, while those who had actually had one could get quite carried away.

One such warrior went into a trance. In that state he saw a Cheyenne village. In the heart of this village he also saw a buckskin horse with large brown spots on its flanks. The horse turned to the visionary and said, "I am waiting for you." After the vision faded, the warrior lay in his bed for ten days recovering his strength.

THE GLORY DAYS OF BUFFALO EGBERT

Taking eighteen men with him, he set out on foot, walking the many miles to the place he had seen in his dream. Upon finding the Cheyenne village, he tarried until nightfall. After instructing his men to stay low and keep quiet, he went right to the place he knew the horse would be, cut the tether and rode out with it, proving to everyone his trance had been the unvarnished truth.

"Many such tales are told among the Crow," Medicine Crow told Nicolas and Jacques. "Too many to be disregarded."

The scheduled day came when the DeGeer brothers were to follow Medicine Crow. Other boys had already gone away from the camp on similar quests.

Medicine Crow, mounted on a sturdy horse, rode behind Jacques and Nicolas, who were on foot.

"You must stay ahead of my horse, but always know where I am without looking back over your shoulder," he told them.

At first the feat seemed quite workable. Medicine Crow set an ambling trot which felt easy enough. The boys were confident runners. Along toward the middle of the day, the steady pace, the methodical tattoo of the horse's hooves, combined with the broiling heat, proved to be killing. The boys were half dead, foam flicking their faces and chests. They ran on, aware only of the subtle movements of the horse behind them. When it changed direction, they numbly changed as well. The run continued until about four in the afternoon, ending when Medicine Crow reined up and dismounted.

Quietly he walked toward the two brothers, who, by sheer determination, remained on their swollen, aching feet. Each leaned against the other, lending strength. Their arms dangled past their knees, their backs stooped, their heads hung down. They labored to breathe, each breath causing them enormous pain.

"I will give you some water," Medicine Crow said. "Then you will rest until the others arrive."

The brothers treasured every drop of water, sucking on the tube of the leather parfleche like babes at a nursing mother's nipple. Medicine Crow allowed them only a small amount, then grabbed the water bag, snatched it away. When he said, "Enough," he was more than pleased that they stopped drinking immediately. Renee had trained these two well. Medicine Crow began to feel privileged at being the spiritual father of such enduring and readily obedient young men. If they remained so, he determined, he would keep them close to him.

"You may rest now," Medicine Crow said.

Grateful, Jacques and Nicolas crumpled before him, not bothering to look for a likely spot of shade. Their legs simply buckled beneath them and they lay close together in a heap.

Medicine Crow laughed silently as he tied off the drinking end of the water case. He quietly walked away to tend to his horse as he waited for the other vision seekers to join them.

"They rode here!" Jacques hissed to Nicolas when they saw the other four vision seekers arriving at the foot of the craggy mountain on horseback. They carried bed robes and food supplies.

Jacques and Nicolas were stunned. Medicine Crow had allowed them nothing, not even a change of clothing, and the moccasins on their bruised and wounded feet were worn through. Their bodies ached from the long, punishing run in the sun. They were hungry, tired and thirsty, and Medicine Crow seemed to hoard the water case as if its contents were the last drops to be had on earth.

The brothers knew better than to complain about their treatment, and Medicine Crow knew full well what was in their minds. Later, when they all sat around the fire waiting for the first light of morning, Medicine Crow took the opportunity to speak privately to Jacques and Nicolas. "I made a promise to your father a long time ago about the two of you. That is why you receive my special attention."

The boys looked at each other and, as always, knew what the other was thinking. "What did he promise? To kill us?"

All the young men in the small camp stayed awake the whole of the night talking, waiting for the coming dawn.

THE GLORY DAYS OF BUFFALO EGBERT

The other young men ate a small meal. The brothers DeGeer neither asked for, nor were offered, any of the food. Their lack of complaint pleased Medicine Crow but what pleased him even more was the way they ignored the boys who were gulping their food. He knew Jacques and Nicolas were starved. They hadn't eaten all day and the energy spent during the twenty-five mile run had left their bodies depleted. Still, they acted as if they'd just finished a big meal and were too full to pay attention to the food being consumed in front of them. Their brave front truly impressed Medicine Crow. They were indeed Renee's sons.

Before the morning sun emerged from the center of the earth, Medicine Crow took the boys aside and allowed them a small ration of water. "I want you both to cleanse your systems," he said. "Before we climb the mountain, move your bowels."

He didn't offer this advice to the others. They hadn't asked for his expert help, nor had he promised their fathers anything. His only concerns were Jacques and Nicolas. The others had come along because they had heard the brothers were to seek visions and they had decided that they, too, were ready. Medicine Crow didn't believe they were, but he did nothing to prevent their joining them. It wasn't the Crow way to chastise or rebuke children. Bad treatment crippled a child's spirits. It was better for children to learn from their mistakes than to prevent them from making them. Lessons learned the hard way were lessons learned for life.

The climb up the face of the mountain was as arduous for Jacques and Nicolas as the long run had been. Somehow, from deep within, they found the strength they needed to accomplish the task. Medicine Crow led the way, the two brothers never letting him out of their sight, each hearing Renee's voice drumming in their minds: "Never let go of Medicine Crow's hand. Never let go of his hand."

The top of this particular mountain was a very special place for Medicine Crow, and because these two young men were his special charges, he wanted to share with them the place where he had received his first vision.

When the others had signaled their intentions to remain behind on the lower ridges, Medicine Crow hand signaled back that they could. He was quietly glad the others wouldn't be at the top with them. He wanted to guide the DeGeer brothers through their quest in private and the other boys might prove to be a distraction.

Lying on his stomach, Medicine Crow leaned over the sharp boulder atop the embankment and called out instructions to the boys on the lower level.

"Make a small altar. Cut yourselves. Offer small pieces of your bodies to the Old Man. Eat nothing. Drink not even a sip of water. Do not sleep. Lie down to conserve your blood. Keep your eyes to the sky above and pray without ceasing."

When he returned to Jacques and Nicolas, they had already finished building their altar and stood before it, their shoulders touching. Medicine Crow nodded his approval as he withdrew his metal knife from its sheath.

He turned his back on the pair as he cradled the large knife in both hands and offered it up to heaven. "Old Man," he intoned. "I have brought you two young men I find without flaw. They are honest. They do not lie. Their hearts are brave and strong. They are the precious treasure of the Crow. Our young men and women are our wealth, but these two young men are especially worthy of your notice. Hear their prayers. Take pleasure in the sacrifice of themselves to you. Bless them with your images from beyond. Help them to understand the meaning. And remember always their courage on this day."

The amen to this prayer was quick and stinging. Medicine Crow took each boy by the left arm and sliced twice across the upper biceps, taking up the thin wedge of flesh from between the two incisions. He handed the boys the strips of their own flesh and pointed toward the altar. Blood poured down their arms and dripped from their fingertips as they placed the skin offering on the stones. Medicine Crow waved his arms wide, and the brothers parted, each seeking his own place to lie down and stare up into the heavens.

THE GLORY DAYS OF BUFFALO EGBERT

· · ·

"You must be careful with these," Eyes-That-Shine's mother instructed. The young girl sat enthralled as she watched Pretty Stone carefully removing the sharp quills from the skinned hide of a porcupine. The women of the tribes used the quills for several purposes. Some they cut and dyed and then used them for embroidery work by sewing them onto treated hides. Other quills were left long and used for brushes by adhering them onto rawhide-covered wood.

Today, Eyes-That-Shine was learning to make a roach, an ornamental headpiece worn by men. In her education as a young wife, it was necessary for Eyes-That-Shine to make a roach for Nicolas. It would be her gift to him upon his return. Her parents also prepared gifts for him. Rides-The-Buffalo-Down was making Nicolas a war shield and a tripod so that the shield would not touch the ground when not in use. The tripod would sit outside Nicolas's new lodge, the one which Cuts-Off-Her-Hair labored long hours to complete, having relieved Eyes-That-Shine of the cumbersome task.

Pretty Stone, as her gift to her son-in-law, had gone to the tribal craftsman and commissioned an even dozen of projectile points, commonly referred to as arrowheads.

All tribes boasted of such craftsmen. The Crow considered No Talker the best of their nation. He was an old man who valued his solitude and preferred to camp away from the bustle of village life. With many customers, No Talker was a wealthy man, even by white standards. He was also a miser. He had no wife, mainly because he was too beggarly to buy one. In his long-past youth, he had had women who came to live with him, but when they were kidnapped by younger men, No Talker didn't seem to mind. He wasn't the sort who ached for company, male or female. His one true love was the perfection of his craft, a craft that left his hands calloused and horny.

His hands had become so disfigured as his age increased, that when the honored wife of Rides-The-Buffalo-Down came to him to commission his skill, her eyes sought relief by looking up into the cerulean sky and watching the scudding clouds as she spoke to the artist. His fingers were permanently curled into his palms after so many years of holding the promising stone securely while striking out the edges with his cutting tool.

Pretty Stone was a woman who judged another woman's worth by the strength and capability of her hands. This man's hands, however capable, were a sight she did not cherish. Misshapen, bony, lined with thick veins and forever chalky from stone, his hands—though ugly—were also his best form of advertisement. No one outside his own tribe would ever wonder how he made his living. Being a master craftsman, he was able to live on the fringes of the village without fear. A man of his caliber evoked such natural respect that even warring tribes passed his homesite, leaving him in peace.

There was no mistaking his housekeeping as that of the ordinary hermit. He had three tepees. Two contained his tools and earthly treasure, the third was used to house him. The litter of his craft lay strewn everywhere. Like all artists, he was a die-hard sloven.

No Talker held up a finely-crafted arrow point and examined it for flaws. True to his name, he seldom spoke to anyone who patronized his establishment. Today, however, he was unnaturally chatty.

"You are blessed to have such a fine new son," he gruffed behind sore gums and gapping teeth. "If the Creator had blessed me with a daughter, I would seek one of Renee's sons for her. Tall Willow is an exceptional woman. She raised fine sons. You are lucky to get one of them, and you were smart to come to me for your wedding present for your son-in-law. Too many young men prefer the rifle to the weapons which made our people great. A Crow without a strong bow and quiver of straight arrows is no Crow. He is only a watery reflection of the white man."

Swiftly he grabbed her hand, pressing five completed arrowheads into her palm. Nearsighted, he didn't see the look of revulsion that passed over her face as he clung to her hand.

"You take these now," he commanded. "You take them to a strong man of medicine to have them blessed. I will finish the others as quickly as I can. As my wedding present to your son-in-law, I will make twelve more arrowheads for his brother. Jacques should quit the rifle, too. It won't save him. Only the old way will save him. Tell both young men I said this when you give them my gift. Don't forget."

He let her go as quickly as he had grabbed her. He picked up a fresh stone and studied it, then placed it on the leather protective strip draping his thigh, and began the meticulous chipping away of the outer edges, forgetting her presence entirely.

Clutching the projectile points in her hand close to her chest, Pretty Stone backed away, then made a run back to the main camp. She resolved to send her husband to fetch the remaining points. She had had enough of the strange No Talker.

Throughout the years the Lakota (Sioux) enjoyed a certain reputation as being the "Scourge of the Plains." They might well have been a "scourge" to the white man, but to the Crow, they were more of an annoyance. The Lakota were Johnny Come Latelys to the plains and were obstinate in their claim to the Yellowstone, the traditional homeland of the Crow.

In 1833, Prince Maximilian of Germany traveled with his entourage to Fort Clarke on the Upper Missouri, now known as North Dakota. There he met the Mandan, the Hidatsa, and the Crow. The Crow, an offshoot of the Hidatsa, shared with the Hidatsa a common language, as well as customs. Maximilian was thoroughly impressed with the tall Crow and their picturesque long hair. He thought the Crow were the most handsome men and women of all the Native Americans and it was obvious to him that they believed this of themselves as well, judging from the way they behaved, both in manner and ornate dress.

His impressions of the Lakota were somewhat less glowing. His journals stung the Lakota, described as being overbearing, bellicose, eager to shed blood and overtly hostile with anyone having anything to do with

the Crow, especially white men. Maximilian described
the Lakota (whom he recorded as being "Sioux" misspelling the Chippewa name for the Lakota, "Nadowe-
is-iw," which roughly translated means "enemy") as
being tall, though not as lanky as the Crow. The Sioux,
he wrote, tended more to be bowlegged and barrel-
chested and generally an "unlovely people," an opinion
probably well enhanced while fleeing the Lakota homeland in flight for his life.

Throughout the long history of animosity between the
Lakota and the Crow, there have been many chiefs
on both sides who have caused one or both nations
grief. One Lakota chief, legendary for bedeviling the
Crow, was a bandy-legged, full-chested man well in his
fifties, of Hunkpapa origin, known as Bear Ribs. Bear
Ribs's personality could only be described as dramatic.
He was a man to whom calamity, large or small, was no
stranger.

His smaller trials could be laid at his own door for, in
many ways, he was as big an enemy to himself as he was
to the Crow he was determined to root out. Sitting Bull
couldn't abide Bear Ribs, though he was wise enough to
keep his distaste to himself. Bear Ribs was a powerful
chief and Sitting Bull was as yet only a medicine man,
though he would later become a chief. Bear Ribs, during
the early 1870s, wielded the war club of the Hunkpapa
and he wielded it often. He held the treaty which deeded
the Yellowstone to the Crow with nothing short of contempt. With this attitude, he encouraged his warriors to
harass the Crow agency which they did with aplomb
until 1876.

Bear Ribs had one enemy he considered mortal. Renee
DeGeer. This feeling was worsened in that, at one time,
Bear Ribs had loved Renee as a precious brother. Renee
had only betrayed Bear Ribs slightly when Renee married
the Crow woman. This had been a transgression easy to
forgive when compared to Renee's sin of coming to the aid
of a white man and in the process, killing three good
Lakota warriors. There had been two young boys along
with the three experienced warriors who were in charge
of the horses while the late, lamented trio rushed the

wounded enemy to finish him off. From nowhere, the two youths testified, Renee and his accursed Crow had appeared and backshot the Lakota warriors. Renee then, according to eyewitness testimony, carried off the white man. Having at one time been with the Lakota, Renee declined to scalp the fallen warriors but that courtesy failed to soothe the enraged Bear Ribs. Bear Ribs promptly passed the death sentence on Renee for his crimes against the Hunkpapa.

It scarcely mattered that the vengeance wasn't exactly swift in the offing. Indians have never been ones to pace their lives according to the ticking of a clock or the passing of seasons. Vengeance was theirs—when they got around to it.

Now, after almost six years of being otherwise engaged, Bear Ribs turned his mind once again toward thoughts of Renee.

Renee and Tall Willow were asleep in their bed when the attack began at three in the morning. Renee opened his eyes at the first crack of rifle and instinctively cringed as the bullet whizzed through the newly-installed glass window pane, streaking inches above his nose before impacting with the wall that separated his and Willow's bedroom from their daughter Marie's.

Willow rolled off her side of the large bed and hit the earthen floor with a muted thud. A second shot rang out and Renee followed suit, landing on top of his wife, shielding her with his body. More rifle shots broke the still night air. Renee had an even bigger fight on his hands trying to contain Willow once she heard Marie screaming.

When Renee heard the window in Marie's room crash, a cold fear crept through his veins. Willow tried to charge out from under him to go to their daughter, clawing like a wild animal bent on protecting its young. As a last resort for a man who adored his wife, Renee hit Willow with his fist, delivering an undercut blow to her jawbone. Willow fell back to the floor, unconscious. Renee shoved her underneath the bed, then grabbed up his rifle from the bedpost and made a dash for Marie's room.

Renee was horrified when he saw two Lakota dragging

his thirteen-year-old daughter out through the shattered window. He took careful aim and fired at one of them. His bullet hit the brave squarely in the face.

The other warrior, a large hulk of a man, held on to the squirming Marie and dragged her on through the smashed window. He paused for a second to look Renee in the eye.

Then he was gone, with Marie still trying to fight him off. Renee cursed the rifle he had to reload. Cover fire for the retreating Lakota and his captive pelted the house. Renee didn't bother to duck. Only a cannon ball could penetrate the log walls and the distant marksmen were missing the open window.

Reloaded, Renee took aim out of the window at the shadow he knew to be his target. He didn't waste his load on the flashes of gunpowder coming from the surrounding sides. His aim was only for the fleeing specter. Breathing hard, his face bathed in sweat, Renee fired. And missed. His target danced away and became lost in the darkness.

Renee's heart stopped beating. In that small moment of death, he stared out the window in disbelief. It had been such an easy shot, one he should not have missed. Yet he had. He went cold all over when he heard his daughter's distant voice as she cried out for him. He leaned heavily against the window frame, his eyes vainly searching the darkness, his useless rifle dropping from his hands.

"Hello, Renee!" a disembodied voice called out from the distant blackness. For a moment, everything grew quiet, then the crickets resumed their chirping. "My name is Wolf's Tracks. I am nephew to Bear Ribs. I have your daughter. She is mine from this night on. If you look for her . . . and I know you will, Renee . . . you will find her in my lodge heavy with my child. Sleep well in your white man's lodge, Renee, knowing your little girl is in mine."

Renee shook involuntarily as he heard the mocking laughter as it mingled with his daughter's frantic cries.

Wolf's Tracks called out again. "She will be working under me in her duty, to replace the three good men her father murdered like a coward."

"Pere!" Marie screamed before her voice was muffled.

Renee's legs buckled under him and he crashed to his knees, his body curling as he slumped to the floor. Tears flooded his eyes as he heard the sound of horses' hooves fading away into the night.

CHAPTER ELEVEN

Tall Willow was inconsolable. For three days she cried and wailed as only a grieving Indian mother can. Then she went into shock and retreated from the world altogether.

Renee wrapped her up, gently placed her on a travois and headed for the agency. There, he left his wife in the care of Mrs. Pease.

The tragedy which had visited the DeGeers moved Major Pease to pity and sympathy, something he wouldn't have extended to Renee under ordinary circumstances. He watched quietly without complaint as Renee helped himself to more than his share of entitlements. Pease even offered Renee a hand as Renee balanced the load on his pack horse and bound it securely.

"You'll never get her back, you know," Pease said solemnly. "You'll have to ride straight into the heart of the Lakota lands and they will be waiting for you, Renee. It's what they want you to do. You'll be dead before you ever get to her."

"I'm dead now," Renee answered brusquely.

"No, you're not," Pease shouted. He grabbed Renee by the shoulders, spun him around and shook him. "You are alive. Willow is alive. Hell, Marie is alive. They won't kill her. She's more valuable to them whole and healthy. And like it or not, she's a wife now. She's . . . Lakota."

Renee pushed the agent from him as if Pease were an infectious carrier of the Black Plague. "She is my little girl!" he raged. "*Ma bebe.* She wants her PaPa. I will bring her home where she will be safe and her MaMa will be well again. *Adieu, mon ami.*"

Renee mounted, accepted the reins of his pack animal from Pease and kicked his horse into a canter.

As was her habit, Marie had retired that fateful night wearing her soft, doeskin sleeping skirt. The shirt had once belonged to Jacques, and after he had outgrown it, it had passed to his baby sister. Along with her nightshirt she wore a feminine version of the breechcloth. Safe in her bedroom, she had slept snugly until the shots sounded, breaking glass showered down on her and two pairs of rough hands pulled her from her warm bed. Then there had been the frightening, jostling dash across the yard, clutched in strange arms, a stranger's labored breath on her cheek as gunfire broke all around them. She cried out for her father but was slapped and then gagged by a leather thong that stretched her mouth and indented her cheeks. After that she had no memory, for she fainted from the trauma of being helpless in the hands of the fearsome Lakota.

When Marie came to, her arms were tied behind her back. Her legs were immobile, tied at the ankles, the leather rope lashed under the horse's belly so that she wouldn't fall off. The painful gag was still in position as she slumped on the back of the horse. She bowed her head, tears streaming down her face as she rode, a prisoner, into the dawning light.

Becoming a captive of the Lakota was a young Crow

girl's worst nightmare. All of her life she had heard stories of Crow girls kidnapped by the Lakota and now, she remembered the women who had told their stories. She shut her eyes tight and could see those women as they sat, their heads bent over their needlework. She could hear their voices as they whispered fearfully.

"The Lakota always take Crow maidens whenever they can," one woman said.

"They want us for our fair skin and pretty bodies," whispered another.

"It is like a sickness with them," a third voice added.

"Guard Marie close," said the first woman to Willow. "She would be their greatest prize."

"The Lakota would kill themselves in a big fight, each warrior eager to claim her."

Wolf's Tracks noticed when his prisoner rallied. He fell back so that his horse was in step with hers, then tugged the strap at the base of her crown to let the gag fall away. He watched Marie as she worked her lower jaw, encouraging blood circulation, her head deliberately turned away from him. Cautiously, he placed a hand on her shoulder.

Marie gasped involuntarily and swung her head in his direction. Her dark hair, long enough to reach her waist, flew in a thick mass as she swirled her head around. Her eyes, luminous with fright, were big, bright and golden brown. Her high cheeks had a natural flush of color and her lips were full and perfectly sculptured. As the morning sun grew brighter, her face seemed to light up and glow with the new day.

"Thank you, my Uncle, for sending me after this girl," Wolf's Tracks said, verbalizing his wonder of her. "You are wise beyond your knowing."

Marie inclined her head as he spoke, trying to make out what he was saying. He seemed to be speaking more to himself than to her. She only knew a few words of Lakota, so she couldn't be certain. She trembled as he leaned his weight against her horse and pushed his face into hers. He mouthed each word carefully, trying to make her understand.

"We will stop now. We will rest."

She nodded and he gave her a smile. He kicked his horse and rode to the front of the scattered warrior column. The group of over twenty braves stopped and talked for five minutes, each casting a vote either to go on or stop for breakfast. The hungry ones won out. Marie watched as the warrior who had just spoken to her took charge, leading them all into a gully sprinkled with tall cottonwoods. Where cottonwood grew, there would always be water.

Marie's legs tightened against her mount's sides as her horse descended the foothill. The warriors surrounding her mount didn't seem particularly concerned about her riding ability. Tied to the horse, there wasn't much danger of her falling off. Her escorts merely saw to it that she kept pace. When they reached the bottom of the hill, her body-guards left her as they went to water their horses and themselves. The only one to come to her aid was the warrior who had released her mouth gag. Now he came to untie her arms and legs so that she, too, could dismount.

"Thank you," she sighed, as she slid from the horse, her feet touching the ground. The warrior, tall like a Crow, but thicker in the chest and arms, dismounted and stood by her side. Marie stood a solid five feet four inches and was still growing, but she felt like a dwarf next to this man.

"Do you have thirst?" he asked. Marie shrugged her shoulders indicating she didn't understand. So he used sign, and smiled broadly as she nodded. He took her by the hand and led her toward the stream, where they both knelt down. Wolf's Tracks used his large hand as a cup as he offered her water. A thrill he had never experienced before overpowered him as she placed her lips in the center of his palm and drank the cool water. While she drank, he lightly touched the hair on the back of her head. The instant he touched her, Marie stopped drinking, begging with her eyes for reassurance that he wouldn't hurt her or misuse her.

He looked old to her. Older than her brothers, about the same age as her cousin-brother, Medicine Crow. This man, being Lakota, wore his hair in braids, not long and

149

free and beautiful like the Crow. His facial features were heavy, his nose broad. By Crow standards, Wolf's Tracks was not a handsome young man. While the young men of her maiden's fancy had been lithe, this man who presented himself as her benefactor was burly.

"Do you have hunger?" he asked.

Marie nodded again. She knew that Lakota word, *locin*. Her father spoke Lakota and sometimes mixed it with Crow.

"Come," he beckoned. He signed for her to walk behind him, tucking her hand inside the belt that covered his breech string. She followed him in this manner to the place where the others lolled and ate. He began a conversation with his fellows that, judging from the volume, turned rough.

Marie very nearly jumped out of her skin when he bellowed at the resting men. She realized that not only was he a man of stature, but of importance as well, for when he spoke, the others moved quickly. Marie watched in alarm as the other warriors quit the makeshift camp, mounted their horses and rode off, leaving her alone with the stranger.

Satisfied to see the backs of his comrades, Wolf's Tracks led his prize toward the abandoned blanket, instructing her to sit. He stood as he rummaged through the food bag and produced two large strips of jerked meat. He joined her on the blanket and handed her a strip. Marie didn't put it to her mouth until he began to chew on his piece. While she gnawed at the toughened dehydrated meat, she saw that he was watching her, his eyes absorbing every part of her.

Her trim legs were exposed. Her sleeping shirt came only midway to her thighs when she stood, but when she sat, it was much shorter.

"What is your name?" he asked.

She looked blankly at him.

He thudded his chest with a curled meaty fist. "Wolf's Tracks," he said. Then he touched her chest lightly.

"Marie." She repeated her name several times before he attempted it.

"Ma-Rie." He smiled and grunted his approval. He touched her again. "*Mitawicu*. Ma-Rie. *Mitawicu*."

Marie couldn't swallow the piece of dried meat in her mouth. She understood only too well the Lakota word for wife, *tawicu*. Her heart pounded in a wild panic. She now knew why he had sent the others away. He was going to rape her. Although, to him, it wouldn't be rape. She was his *tawicu* and this was supposed to be their honeymoon. Marie scrambled to her feet and tried to make a dash for freedom.

His size was a poor witness to his agility. Marie had barely moved when he had her in his arms, holding her tight against his chest. She began to cry, tears streaking her face. Gently, he touched her hair, then traced the outline of her face with his fingertips as he made shushing sounds and spoke to her with tenderness, words she didn't understand.

"Don't," he said. "Don't run from me. It hurts my heart that you are so afraid. I know you are a maiden. I will be gentle with you. I would hurt my own body before I hurt you. Be still, my little bird." He continued to caress her and, slowly, Marie gave up her struggles. "I am not going to take you here. This is not a place for loving. This is only a place to become acquainted."

He released her then, on guard if she should tried to run again. A wide smile stretched across his face as she stood stock-still, her chest expanding and contracting as she breathed quickly. She looked like a captured fawn wanting to trust her captor, yet unable to.

"I will go very slow with you," he said. "I want your heart. Your loyalty to me. I do not want to always worry that you will try to run back to your father."

As if she were a baptism candidate, he took her in his massive arms again and lowered her down to the blanket. Marie stiffened, prepared for the fate that doomed all women. He lay down next to her and held her tightly in his arms.

"Isn't this nice?" he whispered against her hair. "This is the way you will sleep from this day on. Safe in my arms. I will protect you from all harm. I will feed you and give you the biggest lodge any woman ever owned. And servants. I will give you servants. And you, Ma-Rie, you will give me your love and fine sons. You will be happy with me. My happy day will come when you tell me how much you care for me."

Marie was appalled when he brushed her lips lightly with his own, and yet, the Lakota's kiss was gentle. The only man who had ever kissed her mouth before was her father, a man who stood accused by his family as being a maniacal kisser. Renee was well-known to plant big wet kisses on anyone who would hold still for it, especially Willow. Marie and her brothers were always dodging Renee's puckered lips.

The thought of her family caused her lower chin to tremble and she began to cry. Wolf's Tracks' large hands wiped away the tears as he shushed her, cradling her against him. An hour passed before she finished weeping, and during every moment of it, the Lakota held on to her, patiently allowing her to cry it all out. When her tears were spent, she lay exhausted, snuggled against his bare chest, in a deep sleep.

To him, her even breathing against his skin felt like the silken flutter of a butterfly's wings. "I have waited for you all of my life, Ma-Rie," he whispered as he lightly kissed her forehead. Wolf's Tracks, for the first time in his life, felt the misery, the aching, bittersweet agony of falling in love.

By noon it was unbearably hot. Marie awoke in the Lakota's arms, feeling wet and sticky with the perspiration beading her skin. She looked up into his eyes and he said, "I'm hot too. The stream is cool. Let's go into the water."

He led her by the hand, hers lost inside the paw of his palm. As they stood on the gravel shore of the stream, he signed for her to remove her shirt and breechcloth.

Marie shook her head emphatically.

Wolf's Tracks laughed. With a slight tug, he pulled her shirt off her, then pivoted and tossed the shirt onto the grassy bank. When he turned again, he saw that Marie was doing her best to cover her breasts with her folded arms. The attempt was futile. Marie was too well-endowed to be hidden by her thin arms. Having begun her menses at the tender age of eleven, at thirteen-and-a-half, she possessed a body grown women envied. The discovery of such desirable bounty had its effect on Wolf's Tracks. For just a moment he forgot his vow of patience and gentleness. He forced her arms away, holding them down by her sides as he ogled his child bride.

His breathing became thready as he feasted on the sight of her. He was so preoccupied, he failed to notice her humiliation or feel her body go rigid in his hands. Her hair was the perfect backdrop for her lovely naked form. His right hand sought the breech string and with a rough pull, it fell away, leaving Marie without a shred of privacy or dignity. Wolf's Tracks came out of his euphoric dream-state when she lowered her head and began crying again.

"Oh no," he moaned. He lifted her under her arms and held her against him, throwing her limp arms over his shoulders, trying to pretend that she was hugging him the way he hugged her.

"I'm sorry," he said softly. "I know I embarrassed you. Forgive me, but you are just so beautiful, I couldn't help but stare. Ma-Rie," he crooned in her ear, "please don't cry anymore." He knew the joys which lay ahead for them if only he could get her past this rough introduction. Wooing a maiden was easier when the maiden was of one's own tribe, but Marie was an alien . . . a war trophy. He knew that captive brides were always more skittish than most, especially because of the language barrier. And winning a fair maiden's heart by using sign was not made easier. Sign language might be the common language of the plains, useful when talking to friends and enemies of different tribes, but it was a poor alternative in pitching one's woo.

Wolf's Tracks set her on her feet and gently nudged her toward the water. As she entered the small river, he tried to keep his greedy eyes off her little rump while he kicked off his moccasins. He toyed with the idea of keeping his breechcloth on, because taking it off would reveal only too well how she affected his senses. However, he knew that if he didn't take it off, the wet leather would have him chaffed raw by the end of the day. He took it off and dove quickly into the creek.

As they swam, he stayed chest-deep in the water. It was

doubtful she had ever seen a man fully naked before and the sight of one built like a horse and fully erect might set her on the run again. His hope was that the cold water might kill or wound his passions before he lost his head completely. Swimming hard to use up his excess energies, Wolf's Tracks left his captive alone. After lapping the river ten times, he stopped to rest, sitting in the shoals. His body shivered as the cold stream swirled around him, but when he looked down, he realized all of his efforts had failed, as the male third eye peered back at him through the clear tide passing overhead. It wanted that girl and no amount of exercise or water was going to work as a substitute.

Marie wasn't going out of her way to curb its appetite. Wolf's Tracks sat on the bottom of the creekbed, water up to his neck, as Marie floated like a dead person on her back, her breasts pointed skyward, her legs parting and coming back together as she languished in the cooling water. Wolf's Tracks blew air from his mouth, puffing his cheeks as he did so.

"I can't stand it anymore," he groaned. He pushed off the bottom and swam toward her.

Marie screamed when he grabbed her at the waist. He held her with one arm and treaded water with the other. He swam with her until they reached the shallows and then he sat down, forcing her to sit on his lap, her legs straddling him.

Marie's eyes bulged with fright when she felt the hard obstacle between them. Timidly she looked down and then quickly back to him.

"It's only me," he smiled. "You cause that."

Marie moaned as she tried to twist away but he held on tightly to her arms.

"Do not worry," he assured her. "I am not going to make love with you now. I only wanted you to know what you do to me. And, I want you to know how much it hurts me to want you so much," he said, his voice raspy.

He pulled her closer, his lips touching hers, lightly at first, then full and demanding as he kissed her in the fashion she had once seen her father kiss her mother. She felt his lips part, his teeth pressing against her lips and his tongue as it invaded her mouth and began to explore. His breathing became deep and he moaned inside his throat, his arms tightening to crush her against him. Suddenly, he pushed her back, panting as he looked into her frightened eyes.

"I . . . can't. Not here. It isn't right. We should be in our home, in our bed. And you will need women to care for you . . . after." He tried to swallow, his Adam's apple moving slowly in his sand-dry throat. "We have to go home now, Ma-Rie."

There were a number of captive Crow women who were married to Lakota husbands at the encampment, but the arrival of this particular Crow girl set off a flurry of excitement. This captive was the daughter of an old and feared enemy. Wolf's Tracks' successful capture of Renee's daughter was hailed as a tribal victory.

Marie rode behind her self-proclaimed husband on his horse, her horse trailing on a lead rope. Her arms tightened around his waist as they entered the large village of the Hunkpapa. Women poured out to greet him, surrounding the horse he and Marie rode. Wolf's Tracks had trouble guiding his mount through the press of female flesh.

Bear Ribs stood proudly in front of the assembled chiefs, his arms folded across his chest. He smiled smugly as he watched his favorite nephew arrive with his prize. Wolf's Tracks looked around and when he couldn't locate his mother in the crowd, he called out for her. Only-Cooks-With-An-Iron-Kettle pressed her way forward, waving her arms to gain her son's attention. When she stood beside his horse, Wolf's Tracks dismounted and turned the horse's rein over to her.

"Take her safely to my lodge, my Mother," he said to the old woman. "Let no harm come to her or I will be very angry."

Only-Cooks-With-An-Iron-Kettle, feeling her importance, accepted the responsibility of her daughter-in-law, pushing back spectators, as she led the horse away from the Council of Chiefs.

Marie looked back over her shoulder and watched as

Bear Ribs embraced Wolf's Tracks. Then Wolf's Tracks and his proud uncle ducked low, entering the council lodge to smoke with the gathered men.

Only-Cooks-With-An-Iron-Kettle hurried Marie inside the giant lodge, which was twice as big as any lodge Marie had ever seen. Marie's arrival had been anticipated and Only-Cooks had worked for two days providing the lodge with every luxury known in the Indian world. The girl who stood before her looked very young and thoroughly frightened. As this was to be the female who would present her with grandchildren, Only-Cooks treated Marie with the respect accorded to young brides.

"I have a dress for you," the old woman said, scuttling about the spacious tepee. "I made your bride's dress myself the day my son left to claim you. It may be too big. I was expecting someone . . . someone older." She looked at the bleached doeskin dress and shook it out. "It will have to do, too large or not. When a child grows inside your belly, it will be just right."

Only-Cooks-With-An-Iron-Kettle was dressing her new daughter when two women entered. Marie's heart leapt as she recognized them. They were Crow women. They embraced her and shouted shrill cries of joy. The oldest was called Little Knife. The other, Makes Peace. The pair, longtime captives, wept and stroked Marie's hair as they talked excitedly.

"We were told you were coming," Makes Peace blubbered, "though we refused to believe it."

"But I knew that if anyone could steal away Renee's daughter, it would be Wolf's Tracks," Little Knife said. Then she leaned her forehead against Marie's. "Watch out for him," she warned. "He is an important war chief to the Hunkpapa. He has a bad temper. Everyone gives him a clear ground when he is in a bad mood."

"At least now I know his name," Marie sniffled.

Only-Cooks-With-An-Iron Kettle didn't understand the Crow language but she knew by her mother's instincts that these two women were talking badly about her son to his new wife. Infuriated, she shoved them away from Marie, screaming for them to get out and go to their own homes. When they obeyed, Only-Cooks pressed Marie's head

156

to her shoulder, in an attempt to mother the child. "There, there," she crooned. "Do not believe a word they say. They are jealous because my son did not choose either of them. Do not let their spite turn you against such a fine husband."

Marie was several hours in the care of her mother-in-law. The old woman fed her boiled meat, a Lakotan favorite, rubbed her with a sweet-smelling oil and brushed out her tangled hair. They were in the middle of a heated argument about Marie's hairstyle when Wolf's Tracks entered the lodge. Both ceased their fussing and looked to him as he stood inside the door flap.

"She won't let me braid her hair," Only-Cooks complained.

"I am glad," Wolf's Tracks replied. "I like her hair the way it is."

His mother's cheeks swelled as she fumed. "Loose hair will get in the way of her work. How will she be a proper wife if she has to tend her hair all the time?"

Wolf's Tracks was on the verge of telling his mother that he had no intention of allowing his wife to spoil her looks, or her body, with drudgery, but held his tongue. His mother had worked hard for his father all of her life. She wouldn't understand his wanting to pamper this girl.

"We will consider the problem of her hair in a few days," he said, trying to please his mother. "But while we begin our married life, I prefer her hair untied." He knew he had hit on just the right response when his mother lowered her head in modesty and giggled like a girl. He walked toward his mother, knelt down and took one of her workworn hands in his. "Now . . . if you want to be a grandmother . . . I think you should leave us."

Only-Cooks-With-An-Iron-Kettle quickly kissed her son's cheek and scurried from the lodge. She didn't enter again for several hours, when at last she was beckoned by her son. In the interim, she kept watch, shooing away anyone who might approach and threaten the lovers' privacy.

.   .   .

157

Marie's knees quivered as she stood watching Wolf's Tracks. He untied his own hair and perfumed his chest with the oil his mother had left. He stood in profile, Marie examining his male form. The more she looked at him, the more he seemed to grow in bulk. When he bent his arms, his biceps trebled. His chest was larger than her father's. His long legs were thickly corded with muscle. She closed her eyes, shuddering at the thought that he could kill her without half-trying. When she opened her eyes, he stood before her, his questioning eyes probing hers.

"Do not become more afraid of me now, little one," he smiled. "Not now that I am about to make you truly mine."

Marie felt herself being led to the far left of the lodge in front of the bed of furs. Her mind went blank. The moment she feared most had finally arrived. Her only defense was to detach her spirit from her body. Dully, she saw the dress pass her opened eyes as he lifted it over her head. She was only dimly aware of his hands touching her hips and breasts. She barely felt him lifting her up in his arms and placing her on the bed.

He kissed her mouth and held her against him. Marie blocked out all his attempts at foreplay. She closed her eyes, telling herself that everything was all right as he moved on top of her, his shadow engulfing her.

Marie came crashing back into her physical being when the pain proved too intense to will away. All she saw was chest but she could feel every inch of his masculinity pushing itself deeper inside her. She heard her own voice crying, and his voice answering in strangled groans. Marie arched her back and screamed one long torturous shriek. Wolf's Tracks stopped trying to enter her, pausing a moment to wipe her face which was bathed in sweat.

"I'm sorry. I know this hurts. It will be over in just a little bit and then my mother will tend you." He pushed again as Marie begged him to stop. "Oh my love," he crooned. "My little love. Try not to fight. Welcome me and it will be easier for you."

Marie's eyes were wild. He held her pinioned wrists over her head with one hand while he caressed her with the other, and all the while he continued hurting her in her most private place.

"Ma-Rie," he gasped as he finally broke through her hymen. The warmth of her vagina closed around him as he slid slowly inside. He kissed her deeply, his eyes heavy and closing. "I have to finish, or the fire inside me will kill us both." He ignored her pleas and her sobbing as he lost himself in the pleasure of her.

As he undulated on top of her, Marie gradually realized the pain was subsiding. It didn't go away completely, but it didn't tear her apart as it had moments ago. She was then able to enjoy the former bliss of detachment. This uncomplicated state allowed her to witness the male response to sex.

His face held the expression of a man being flayed alive, though the sounds he made seemed to express intense pleasure. He let go of her wrists and balanced the weight of his torso on his stretched, taut arms. He was heavy but surprisingly, not as heavy as he appeared. Realizing he wasn't going to crush her after all, she relaxed, waiting patiently for him to stop thrusting inside her. He stopped for an instant but only long enough to adjust her legs into a bent position.

Marie gasped in surprise, not pain, as she felt him go deeper into her. When she gasped, he seemed to go out of his mind. His speed increased and he ground his teeth. With one last great thrust, he went rigid, his head rocking back to his shoulders, his mouth opened as he convulsed. She felt something warm and liquid spilling inside her as his rocking lessened and he slowly crashed, his weight smothering her.

Only-Cooks-With-An-Iron-Kettle and her group of three medicine women inspected Marie's abused and broken genitalia. Marie was mortified, but the old women seemed to know what they were about. They forced her into a sitting position and instructed her to hold on to her ankles while they went about their business and talked among themselves. They cleansed her with warm water and cloths, then her most personal wound was salved with a cream that took the stinging pain away. As they tended to Marie, the women could hear the heavy, thudding footfalls of Wolf's Tracks' moccasins as he paced outside the lodge.

"Mother," he called through the lodge hide walls. "Is she all right?"

"She will live," the old woman answered. "You broke her cleanly."

"I want to see her."

"You shouldn't come in yet," his mother yelled at her son's shadow on the lodge wall.

Impatient, Wolf's Tracks didn't wait to be invited back into the lodge. He burst in, his concern for his wife too great to keep him in proper check. His mother tried to order him away, but he wouldn't hear her. He went directly to Marie's side, sitting next to her on their bed. Only-Cooks-With-An-Iron-Kettle covered Marie with the robe while the departing medicine women took away the washing bowls of bloodied water.

Only-Cooks-With-An-Iron-Kettle was overcome by dismay watching her son's display of tenderness as he kissed Marie's closed eyes. When his lips left Marie's little face, Only-Cooks-With-An-Iron-Kettle tapped her son's shoulder and offered him her motherly advice.

"Try to stay off of her for the rest of the night. When you mount her again, use this." She handed him a clay jar filled with bear grease. "It will help you enter her and it will soothe her at the same time. She is very small. It will take a while before she is used to you. But then that is the way of virgins. They must be stretched before they know pleasure."

"Thank you Mother."

Wolf's Tracks folded Marie gently into his arms and held her cradled against him for the rest of the night.

CHAPTER TWELVE

Wolf's Tracks tried to concentrate as he sat in the council lodge while his bravado and virtues were being extolled. As the guest of honor, he wasn't required to speak, only smoke when the pipe was passed his way. This left him room to daydream, which he did, the voices in the lodge becoming a droning background for his thoughts. He had been married now for nine weeks and although he'd thought that he would have grown tired of being a husband by now, he hadn't. It worried him slightly that Marie held him in such a grip of desire. The more he had her, the more he wanted her. I feel like a dog, he thought. I go into heat the moment I see her or hear her voice.

She no longer fought him or cried when he took her. He was glad about that, but it worried him that she still seemed to endure him rather than desire him as he was certain she should. She should like it by now, he thought glumly. I must be doing something wrong. He was half-tempted to ask the advice of the assembled men but quickly squelched the impulse. It wasn't right to discuss such personal matters. Especially when his manhood was being so loudly proclaimed. He wondered what they would think if they knew that, by her remote behavior in his bed, the little Crow girl counted the most injurious of coups on their praised war chief.

He sat frowning as Bear Ribs recapped for the hundredth time, the valor of Wolf's Tracks' abduction of Marie. Suddenly, Wolf's Tracks couldn't stand being holed up in the lodge another second. During Bear Ribs' most glowing oratory, Wolf's Tracks arose and walked toward the opened door flap.

"Where are you going?" Bear Ribs chided.

"Home," Wolf's Tracks replied, ducking through the door.

The chiefs watched as Wolf's Tracks walked away with quickening strides through the village.

"It would seem your nephew hasn't as yet finished his honeymoon," Sitting Bull chuckled. He sat back enjoying both his turn at the pipe and Bear Ribs' chagrin. "Perhaps in a few weeks he will be ready to sit and waste the day with old men."

Bear Ribs threw the medicine man a scathing look. He was developing a festering hatred for the daughter of Renee. He blamed her for his favorite nephew's unprecedented bad manners. He chewed his lower lip as he floundered, searching for a way to dissolve the marriage that had been his vengeful scheme in the first place. His revenge on Renee was turning sour in his mouth. But, perhaps, he thought, when Renee attempted to rescue his child, Bear Ribs could see to her death as well.

Wolf's Tracks found Marie sitting outside their lodge sunning herself in the company of his mother who, while she sewed, gave Marie lessons in the Lakota language. Marie, a quick student, was now able to form complete sentences.

Only-Cooks-With-An-Iron-Kettle was surprised, and not pleasantly so, to see her son approaching. His early return caused her to fear that things had gone wrong in the

162

council. That worried her. Her brother, Bear Ribs, could be so contrary. It wouldn't do if her son fell out of his favor. As a dependent widow, she was a woman who lived in worry of her younger brother's abusive temper. She tried to question her son, but Wolf's Tracks brushed her off. He wasn't interested in conversation with anyone other than Marie.

He grabbed Marie's hand, quickly leading her over to the tree that kept his favorite horse sheltered from the sun. He jumped on the gray and white horse and as Marie offered up her arms, Wolf's Tracks pulled her up and placed her behind him. He kicked the animal in the sides and rode out, Marie's back a miniature against his.

The village wasn't far from the river. The Lakota, like the Crow, always preferred to camp near a good water source. He set Marie down before dismounting, then picketed the horse. He took Marie's hand and walked with her toward the craggy shoreline.

"We must talk," he said as he sat down on a boulder.

Wordlessly, Marie joined him and waited for him to speak. She could tell her husband was troubled.

He tried to look her in the face several times and finally gave up. When he looked at her, he wanted her, and at this juncture, an open dialogue was more important to him than making love.

"Ma-Rie," he began clumsily. "I am troubled in my soul." He took a long breath and expelled it. "I care for you so much it makes me crazy. You are always in my head . . . and my heart."

She said nothing and her silence was deafening. Bashfully, he glanced up at her, hoping that if she had understood at least some of what he was saying she wasn't crowing her final victory. To his relief, she wore an expression of concern as she listened intently. Encouraged, he groped for the right words to continue.

"I have to know . . . do you care for me? Even a little bit? I have tried to be patient . . . and gentle. I have provided you every comfort. But still, you don't respond. When I take you in my arms sometimes, you feel like a

163

piece of carved wood." Cautiously he took her face in his hands and spoke more softly. "I need to feel your love. I need to feel you wanting me." He swallowed hard. "I love you so much."

"I know that," she quipped matter-of-factly. "That's why I have a baby inside me."

Wolf's Tracks looked dazed. "W-what?" he stammered.

Marie tilted her head inside his hands with the innocence of a child, resting her cheek against his palm. "My mother told me long ago that babies come from men who love you. I have a baby, so you love me."

Wolf's Tracks' brain tried to register the statements made in an almost monotone delivery. "Y-y-you have a b-b-baby inside you?"

Marie wondered at his faltering speech. She took his hands away from her face and held on to them as she nodded her head. "I thought you knew." She smiled shyly.

"How would I know?" he gulped.

She sighed as if she were dealing with a moron. "Because you are the one who put it in me."

Wolf's Tracks shook his head as if trying to clear his brains. Can she be that ignorant, he thought. Has no one ever told her anything about men and women? He looked back at her and saw that she was watching him closely. Clearly, he concluded, she wasn't making fun of him or putting on a cruel act. She was truly ignorant.

"It's wonderful about the baby," he said. He edged in close to her and carefully placed his arms around her. "Very wonderful." He looked down into her upturned face. "Tell me, my little darling, everything you've ever been told about the ways of men and women."

What Wolf's Tracks heard he found incredible. By the simplistic nature of her answers, it was woefully apparent that Marie had been raised in the most sheltered life imaginable. Protected by her parents and zealously guarded by her older brothers, Marie had been shielded from all knowledge of the pleasures of sex. What she did know about life she proudly proclaimed as if she were an ancient sage.

As she explained it to him, her menses was a sign of womanhood from the Creator. Babies came from men who loved and respected their wives. It was a wife's duty to grow children in her body. When there was a long absence of menses, it meant that a woman had a baby inside of her. That was all.

"But did you ever think about what it would be like to be with a man?" he asked, his voice unnaturally high.

"*Ma mere* said that sleeping with men is a lot of trouble because they snore. It is true." She nodded, trying to look like a woman of great experience.

Thoroughly amused, and fighting to hide the smile that played on his lips, Wolf's Tracks quizzed her further. "But didn't you ever once think about the pleasure it might give you?"

"Is it supposed to?"

"Yes," he boomed as he laughed.

"Then why didn't you tell me?" Marie shouted at him. "*Ma mere* said my husband would teach me what I should know."

In the face of such logic, Wolf's Tracks was dumbstruck. "I didn't know I had to tell you. I thought you knew. I thought after a time you would begin to ask me to make love to you. I have waited for one sign, one word. I feel like the biggest fool who ever lived."

Wolf's Tracks didn't notice Marie lowering her head and blushing. When she spoke, he turned and looked at her.

"Then it's all right for me to like it?" she said in a soft voice.

"Yes," he breathed fervently.

"Well," she drawled. "I like it more than I thought I would at first. It gets nicer all the time. I like the way you kiss me and hold me." She looked up at him, a pleading look in her eyes. "Can we *really* make love whenever *I* want to? I thought I was supposed to wait for you to want me."

That night, in the privacy of their darkened lodge, they lay naked in one another's arms. Breathing hard, their bodies damp with sweat and spent passion, they were perfectly content together. "I love you, Ma-Rie," Wolf's Tracks husked. "*Wastekicilakapi.*"

"I love you, too," Marie cooed. "*Wawowastelaka.*"

During the next weeks, as Marie's body began to swell, Wolf's Tracks was even more of a stranger to the company of men than he had been. Now that Marie loved him, he was absolutely besotted with her. If all Marie had had to offer was mere physical attraction, Wolf's Tracks' interest would have slackened. But Marie was so much more than just a beautiful face and body. He could talk to her, confide in her. Besides being a lover, Marie became his best friend.

"I would lose my own life before I would lose you," he said. The statement was not made hastily in the heat of the moment. It was made on a fine clear morning as they stood knees deep in a creek, dunking the water skins, filling them for the day's ration. He wrapped an arm around her and kissed the top of her head. Birds twittered in the trees, insects droned, fish now and again slapped the surface of the stream as she stroked his nippled breast. Standing with his wife as they performed a perfectly normal daily function was, for Wolf's Tracks, one of their most glittering moments. She loved him and he trusted her love. It was a fact as simple as collecting water, and more wonderful than the perfect day they shared.

The only people of the Hunkpapa who saw him with any regularity were the women who served them. He was tender with his wife, yet brutal to the women who served her needs. His mother was appalled. Only-Cooks-With-An-Iron-Kettle became openly dissatisfied with her daughter-in-law, pregnant or not, and took her complaints to her brother.

Bear Ribs listened carefully to every word his sister reported, though he offered no suggestions. He needed Only-Cooks-With-An-Iron-Kettle's hostility. Her condemnation would make disposing of the girl easier after Marie had served her purpose. He even went so far as to plant the seed that perhaps the girl was an evil witch-child. How else could she enslave such a powerful man as Wolf's Tracks? This malicious nudge was something for Only-Cooks-With-An-Iron-Kettle to ponder, which she did, night and day.

The couple in the center of the furor was unaware of the plots threatening their happiness. As far as they were concerned, nothing could ever touch them. They were young, strong and wildly in love with one another.

THE GLORY DAYS OF BUFFALO EGBERT

The Crow women who had warned Marie of Wolf's Tracks' temper were proved right time and time again. Marie witnessed it each time their sacred privacy was unnecessarily intruded upon. Their absorption with each other and their solitary attitudes further enabled them to win the prize as the most unpopular couple in Lakota history.

"Try not to breathe so much," Wolf's Tracks whispered. He pressed his ear against Marie's swelling belly, his hearing strained as he listened to the child inside her.

Marie couldn't hold her breath a second longer, expelling the air in her lungs in a long stream of relief. "Ahhhh," she sighed as she hungrily sought more air.

"Just one more time, Sweetheart," Wolf's Tracks pleaded. "I think I heard something."

"No." She used her arms to push herself up into an awkward sitting position. "What you heard was me dying. I don't want to play this game anymore."

Wolf's Tracks hurried to put the wolf's-fur-covered backrest behind her so that she could sit comfortably. That done, he lightly kissed her mouth. "What present would you like after our child is born?"

"To visit my parents," Marie said without hesitation. "I want them to meet my husband and see our child. I don't want them to worry about me anymore. I want them to know how happy I am."

Wolf's Tracks recoiled slightly. This was the one gift he wasn't prepared to give. For the past six years he had been fed a steady diet of hatred for Renee. After falling in love with Renee's daughter, it became easy for him to forgive Renee for marrying a Crow woman and deserting the Lakota. If Tall Willow were even half her daughter, Wolf's Tracks found no fault in Renee's action, though he would have approved more had Renee brought Tall Willow to live among their own as he had done with Marie.

"I will think on this," he said softly.

But Marie was too happy to hear what her husband was really saying.

CHAPTER THIRTEEN

Wolf's Tracks had clear memories of Renee. As a small boy, Wolf's Tracks had respected and admired the French-Canadian. Renee had been with the Canadian Lakota for most of his life so in Wolf's Tracks' mind, Renee wasn't a real white man. Renee had always been much too Indian for that pronouncement. Wolf's Tracks remembered Renee as being friendly and very popular. So popular that it had stunned the Hunkpapa the day Bear Ribs reported, "Renee now rides with the Crow. He is still our brother, but has become a brother we can kill without guilt if we are forced to do so."

It was left at that. The break between Renee and his Lakota brethren had been clean and civilized. Until Renee ruined the standoff by killing the three Lakota warriors. Wolf's Tracks had been nineteen at that time and rising fast as a noted warrior. Though Wolf's Tracks claimed no blood relation to the fallen three, he did vow his own vengeance, boasting that he would be the one to collect the bounty placed on the traitor Renee's scalp. And for Wolf's Tracks it had been irksome that Renee had avoided punishment for so long a time. This further inflamed Wolf's Tracks' already seething hatred of the deserter.

Wolf's Tracks' love for Marie gradually lessened his loathing of Renee, though Wolf's Tracks sincerely doubted he and his new father-in-law would ever extend one another the hand of friendship. Out of fear of losing Marie's hard-won love and trust, Wolf's Tracks realized that fighting against Renee or Jacques and Nicolas was now totally out of the question.

During their moments of quietude, Marie verbally painted Wolf's Tracks a different portrait of Renee. Listening intently, Wolf's Tracks could almost hear Renee's booming laughter and he enjoyed the stories of Renee's helpless defeats against Tall Willow. From Marie's detailed descriptions, Wolf's Tracks conjured Jacques and Nicolas in his mind. He had them set so well in his mind, he believed he could easily identify them, even if they stood amid a mob of young Crow men. Absorbed and thoroughly amused by the tales of Jacques and Nicolas and their youthful exploits, Wolf's Tracks began fostering the strong desire to call them brothers. But sadly, he pushed such notions away. Having Jacques and Nicolas as brothers was a thing that could never be. Jacques and Nicolas were Crow. Wolf's Tracks was Lakota. A pragmatist, Wolf's Tracks concentrated instead on filling Marie's life completely, hoping that with time she would begin to forget her Crow family as she became more and more Lakota.

"Will you give me that present?"

Marie's voice brought him abruptly back to the present. With heavy heart, he turned his face away so he wouldn't have to look her in the eye.

"After the child is born, and after the two of you are strong, past the dangers of sickness, we will talk of this again." He kissed her forehead as she lay her head against his shoulder, his feeble half-promise satisfying her.

• • •

169

Though Wolf's Tracks' sentiments were softening toward his in-laws, the DeGeers steadily heated up their wrath against him. Jacques had taken the news of Marie badly. Nicolas retreated into himself, becoming remote and stony. Of the two brothers, Renee worried more for Nicolas. Jacques's screaming tantrums and grief-stricken histrionics were natural. It was healthy for the inner spirit's system to vent such powerful emotions. But Nicolas wouldn't.

"I'm going to kill him," Nicolas said in a hoarse, determined whisper. His eyes went blank and he didn't seem to see Jacques as Jacques went into a fresh fit of rage. Nicolas sat like a chunk of wood inside the council tepee as Jacques drew his knife and had to be wrestled to the ground by Renee and Medicine Crow and physically held down by Renee. Jacques's grief was so powerful, Renee knew that Jacques meant to cut off his little finger as an outward sign of his inner torment. Renee sat on Jacques's chest, his knees pinning Jacques's arms to the ground.

"You will need every part of yourself if you are to rescue your sister," Renee yelled at Jacques. "Your finger lying dead on the ground will not save her."

Jacques's face contorted, a mask of fury and loathing. "He has raped her," he spat. "He has thrown away her purity. He has defiled her body!"

Renee was nonplussed. He knew every word Jacques screamed to be the truth, though as Marie's father, he wasn't especially eager to hear it. Nicolas and Jacques, the brunts of a practical joke played on them by their boyhood friends, remembered all the made-up horror stories now long forgotten by the original tellers. That such a brutal fate had befallen their baby sister twisted their minds.

As Jacques seemed to grow more rational, Renee slowly released him. He watched carefully as Jacques retrieved the knife from the dust. Standing straight, his handsome young face set hard with a look of anger, Jacques showed the gleaming blade to his father. "Don't worry. I won't use this on myself. I will use it on the one who has abused my sister. When I am finished with him, he will have to squat behind his heels to pass his water like a woman."

THE GLORY DAYS OF BUFFALO EGBERT

It would seem that the fates had joined hands in an effort to doom the happy life of Marie and Wolf's Tracks. The pair hadn't a friend in the world. While Renee, his sons and their volunteering brothers of the Lumpwood war society scoured the countryside for months, tracking the nomadic Hunkpapa, Bear Ribs baited Renee's hook while at the same time secretly plotting against the unsuspecting couple.

There was but one cloud of relief on their horizon—Sitting Bull. Sitting Bull didn't really care about the couple one way or the other. He was simply sick of Bear Ribs. Four raiding parties had gone out of the camp during the months of Wolf's Tracks' marriage and Wolf's Tracks had turned down recruitment from all of them, preferring to stay home in the comfort of his wife's arms. Wolf's Tracks' reputation as a fierce warrior and defender of his people seriously suffered. Sitting Bull saw Wolf's Tracks' actions as a waste of talent, but he was inclined to be a little more tolerant of the love-struck young man than his fellow tribesmen. Sitting Bull, having been in love himself several times, thought he understood the younger man far better than those who had taken up the sport of bashing Wolf's Tracks' reputation on a regular basis. Sitting Bull came to the conclusion that until Marie gave birth and the tempers among the Hunkpapa cooled, the two lovers would be safer elsewhere. Since neither of the pair in question seemed predisposed to come to him for his sage advice, Sitting Bull called on them.

Sitting Bull was welcomed into their lodge and was fed and treated like an honored guest. As he watched the young couple, he was astounded by the magnitude of their affection for one another. As he witnessed their unbridled devotion he remembered several of his favorite long past loves, though he admitted, none of his romances ever went to this extreme. Sitting Bull sighed heavily as his hosts reinforced his original conclusion that the lovebirds would have to fly the nest while he was still able to offer them his failing protection. If the pair were to survive intact, they would have to live someplace else until their unnatural passions for each other simmered down and they were able to conduct themselves normally.

Sitting Bull took Wolf's Tracks outside and when they were well out of Marie's hearing, laid out the simple truths, pointing out to Wolf's Tracks what he should have seen for himself. After listing the long inventory of village grievances, Sitting Bull was sorely tempted to find a stout stick and beat the doltish young man over the head with it, for not only did Wolf's Tracks act surprised by what he heard, he also literally reeled as if scandalized.

How can he be so stupid, Sitting Bull thought. Has his love making for month after month turned his brains to dust? Didn't he notice that no one was being friendly with him, not even his own mother?

"What do you suggest?" Wolf's Tracks asked after long sulky deliberation.

"Leave," Sitting Bull replied tersely.

Wolf's Tracks sighed. "All right, we will pack and leave tomorrow or the day after."

Sitting Bull's patience finally snapped. Using his fist, he struck Wolf's Tracks a hard blow to the chest. "I have to tell you everything," he hissed as Wolf's Tracks staggered from the unexpected blow. "Now you walk with me, and if you value your life as a married man, you pay attention to every word I speak."

Like a pet dog trotting behind Sitting Bull's heels, Wolf's Tracks followed the older man into the shadows of the night where they would neither be seen nor overheard.

Marie was asleep, though she awakened rapidly in alarm when her husband placed the palm of his hand against her mouth. The fire in the center of the lodge burned low, the soft light highlighting Wolf's Tracks' strong profile.

"Listen to me, my darling," he whispered.

They left in the dead of night, leaving their tepee standing in hopes that they would not be missed for several days. Bear Ribs might despise their presence, but he certainly didn't want them out from under his thumb. As Sitting Bull had so aptly pointed out, Bear Ribs needed Marie, and while he needed her, Wolf's Tracks and Marie were

172

essentially Bear Ribs' prisoners. With Marie heavily pregnant, Wolf's Tracks needed all the time he could gather in putting distance between his plotting uncle and his little family.

Wolf's Tracks and Marie rode separate horses, Wolf's Tracks leading two pack horses. They left behind the luxurious comforts of their home, fully prepared to live rough while they journeyed toward Wolf's Tracks' distant relatives, the Minneconjou.

Nicolas rode as west scout. On a distant hill he made out the small vague form of a horse and rider he knew to be Jacques, who was scouting to the east. Over the months, they had been in and out of the Crow main camp a total of three times. The long search was beginning to wear down the volunteers who had begun voting daily on quitting the futile effort. Only Renee's determination kept them all together and moving farther north.

It had been raining a solid drizzle during the last five days and Nicolas felt despondent under the oppressive darkness of the sky. As he crested a knoll and cleared a stand of trees, he spotted movement off to his left. He reined in and sat perfectly still on his horse.

Off in a distant gully, two people were riding with their heads covered over by robes for protection against the relentless weather. Heavily burdened pack horses followed the riders. Nicolas frowned as he wondered who would be so witless as to venture the prairies virtually alone. He turned his horse before the travelers spotted him and backtracked his trail.

A mile's distance lay between himself and Jacques. After silently attracting his brother's attention, Nicolas held his rifle in both hands and pressed it up and down over his head several times. Jacques understood and they both rode in the direction of their trailing father.

"Only two?" Renee quizzed. "And they are Lakota?"

"Yes, *Pere*," Nicolas panted.

"Well," Renee replied. "Let's pay them a little visit and see if these two travelers can be persuaded into talking with us."

. . .

The Crow, bellies down in the tall grass, waited in ambush as their victims neared.

Wolf's Tracks halted abruptly as gunshots sounded all around them, but his warrior's abilities were hampered by Marie. Terrified, she wouldn't get off her horse to take cover. She fought him again, as she had in the first days of their marriage, as he tried desperately to drag her down from her mount. In the midst of her struggles, her blanket fell away.

It was then that Renee saw his daughter for the first time in over seven months.

"Marie . . ." he breathed. Nicolas and Jacques, by his side, shared their father's astonishment.

Jacques was the first to recover. Watching the big Lakota manhandle his sister proved more than he could endure. He scrambled to his feet, rifle in hand, and charged into the battle on foot, screaming as he ran down the incline into the small valley. Nicolas, caught up in the fury of the moment, slipped his father's grasp and ran after his brother. The Crow quickly halted their gunfire so as not to accidentally murder the foolhardy brothers.

Renee lay his face in the soddened earth and groaned. "Help me, God. I've raised . . . idiots."

In all his warring experiences, Wolf's Tracks had never seen the likes of the two kiyiing Crow running toward him. After shoving Marie behind him, he raised his rifle and took aim.

Suddenly, to Wolf's Tracks' surprise, Marie grabbed his rifle so he couldn't shoot.

"Jacques! Nicolas!" she screamed.

Her brothers took that as further sign of her distress and increased their speed. Before Wolf's Tracks knew it, they were on him. Jacques swung his rifle like a club. Nicolas brandished a knife.

Wolf's Tracks did not want to fight them, especially in front of Marie. He was bigger and stronger than either of them and he used all his strength and agility in ducking and dodging, fending them off without doing either of them anywhere near the damage they were determined to inflict on him. Again his undoing was Marie.

"Stop it! Stop it!" she cried shrilly as her brothers stepped up their hand-to-hand combat. She took hold of Jacques by one arm and he swung her this way and that, so maddened he didn't feel his sister's hands clinging to him. When Wolf's Tracks saw Marie's little feet leave the ground, his heart leaped with fear that she would be critically injured. He dodged Nicolas's flashing knife and grabbed his wife as Jacques spun her around for the third time. When Wolf's Tracks grabbed Marie, Jacques slammed the back of Wolf's Tracks' head with the sawed-off rifle stock. Wolf's Tracks was knocked cold. Marie was safe, though hysterical, when her father and the rest of the Crow reached her.

It wasn't a friendly group Wolf's Tracks met upon returning to the living. Someone had tied a rope around his neck and tied his wrists behind his back. Marie stood weeping pitifully while all of the capturing Crow argued loudly with her. Groggy, Wolf's Tracks knew only that he had to get to her and so made an effort to stand.

His movements attracted Jacques's attention. Jacques swirled and cocked his rifle, aiming it at Wolf's Tracks' heart. The expression on Jacques's face made him appear more like a cruel caricature of himself. His mask of un-adulterated hatred stole away his handsome features. Nicolas snarled as he advanced on Wolf's Tracks and with a swing of his arm, back-handed the downed Lakota's face. Wolf's Tracks knew he would receive no mercy from these two if the vocal Crow were voting his fate. Marie tried to rush to her husband's side, but Renee caught her and held her back.

Wolf's Tracks hadn't seen Renee in years except for the long look they had exchanged through Marie's bedroom window. The night had been dark and he had only seen Renee's silhouette, the shadows of his eyes. Now, as Wolf's Tracks looked at Renee, he was aghast. That beard. That legendary beard. There was not one thread of gray in it. Renee hadn't changed a day in Wolf's Tracks' remem-brances of him. Didn't Renee age like normal men? Renee

had to claim the same total of years Bear Ribs owned, yet
Bear Ribs was almost an old man now. Yet here stood
Renee as fit and trim as ever, so fit in fact Renee could
easily claim to be the older brother to his two sons and
strangers would believe him.

Wolf's Tracks shook away his concerns of Renee,
returning them to his wife. He watched as Marie tugged on
her father's shirt, pleading with him in the Crow language.

"Ma-Rie!" he called to her.

For having dared to utter her name, Jacques pushed his
rifle into Wolf's Tracks' chest. After slurring the history of
Wolf's Tracks' parentage, Jacques sideswiped Wolf's
Tracks' lower jaw with the rifle's stock, the impact of
wood and bone cracking the air like a tree limb splitting
away from the main trunk. Wolf's Tracks fell to his knees
and Marie screamed as she tore herself from her father's
grasping hands.

Wolf's Tracks' mouth filled with blood as he slumped
on his knees, his head bowed as his dazed brains wafted
for anchor inside his skull. His watering eyes faintly recognized Marie's little feet in front of her brother's larger
ones. He heard distinct slapping sounds and thought
Jacques was abusing Marie for her efforts in trying to protect her husband. He tried hard not to black out again.

"Do not hurt my wife!" he cried. "Do not hurt our
child! Please!"

The only two people to understand him were Marie and
Renee. Marie rushed to him, taking his poor wounded face
in her hands.

Renee pushed himself between his two sons, standing
between them and the captured Lakota.

"Let me have him," Jacques seethed, looking over his
father's shoulder as Marie tended her husband. "You
promised I could have him." He pushed his weight against
Renee's chest, trying to go through his father to get at the
accursed Lakota who stood on his knees cringing like a
beaten dog.

"You stop it!" Renee shouted. He pushed Jacques back.

Nicolas made a move to the left. Renee, with a panther's speed, grabbed them both by the fronts of their
shirts and hauled them close to his face, sending spittle

into their blinking eyes as he spoke through gritted teeth. "He said, 'Please.' Do you know what that is to the Lakota? That is one thing they never, ever say. Not for themselves. But he said it. . . ." Renee's eyes flooded with a look of pain and his voice took on a rasping edge as he finished, ". . . for his . . . wife. He does not beg for himself. He begs for her . . . and their child."

"I don't believe you," Jacques seethed behind barred teeth.

"You don't believe me?" Renee bellowed. He pulled his sons around and forced them to view the truth they refused to accept. Marie, pregnant, down on her knees, using her dress to wipe the face of the big Lakota. Marie, crying over him, kissing his face, murmuring words of endearment in the Lakotan language. "You don't believe me!" Renee repeated. "Would the Creator above you both find women to love you like that?" He pushed them roughly forward, his palms against their spines. "Go help him to his feet."

"Why does he have to be tied *Pere*?" Marie sobbed. "Why are you treating my husband so cruelly?"

Renee turned away from his imploring daughter, his face set southward as they rode through the drizzle. He couldn't concern himself with his son-in-law just at this moment. He had to get Marie home. That was all that mattered. He couldn't leave the Lakota behind, alive to go for help. And Renee couldn't kill Marie's captor considering the way Marie loved him. Though why she did, Renee couldn't fathom. Her Lakota husband looked like a churlish brute, built like a grizzly bear and twice as mean. Then too, Renee didn't particularly want to untie him. He knew that when this Lakota had stolen Marie, he had most certainly tied her, and he wanted his prisoner to have a taste of his own medicine. It would do him good. This small act of vengeance was certainly doing Jacques and Nicolas some good.

Jacques held on to the rope tied around Wolf's Tracks' neck. Wolf's Tracks' hands being bound behind his back saved the arrogant Jacques from being pulled off his horse and the brothers-in-law having another go at one another, this time Wolf's Tracks feeling less and less protective of Marie's tender feelings.

Another point in Wolf's Tracks' favor, thereby causing Renee to allow the Lakota to live, was that by the Lakota's very size, he could have easily smashed Jacques and Nicolas during his first opportunity. Realizing his attackers were his wife's brothers, Wolf's Tracks, instead, had only taken the stance of self-defense. That impressed Renee, though it also left him with a bigger problem of what to do with their captive. It wasn't as if Renee could throw his arms around the strange young man and say, "Welcome to the family." He knew a Lakota wouldn't voluntarily seek to become part of a Crow family. He also knew that Marie's husband hadn't been taking her home to the Crow when they were discovered. They had been traveling northwest, not southeast.

Marie told her father the story of Sitting Bull coming to Wolf's Tracks with his words of warning and advice. Learning that Bear Ribs had become embittered against his own nephew, Renee encouraged further haste in leaving enemy country. He knew the tenacious Bear Ribs well enough to know he would have the Hunkpapa searching for his fleeing nephew. If Bear Ribs found Wolf's Tracks in the company of Crow, he wouldn't bother with the pesky fact that his nephew was a prisoner. Not until after he had wiped everyone out, including Wolf's Tracks. Then he would loudly mourn his nephew while privately worrying that everyone of his tribe considered him an evil person.

Only when they were on the fringes of Crow country did they finally stop for a night's rest. The rain was slashing down like silver lancets. Winter seasons on the plains were typically plagued with storms until the cold winds turned the rains into snow. The retreating Crow party took refuge in one of the many hillside caves that pocked the countryside. The cave was large enough to house the horses as well.

Marie was in a high pout against her father and brothers and ignored them at every opportunity. They watched her as she unpacked one horse, found a dry robe and took it over to her husband, who sat soaked and dyspeptic, glaring at all of them. Jacques still held on to the rope around Wolf's Tracks' neck.

Finally, Marie had had enough of Jacques's haughtiness and she was angry. She pulled defiantly on the lead rope until Jacques let go. Then she loosened the noose and slipped it over Wolf's Tracks' head. She stood up and faced Jacques.

"I want your knife," she demanded.

"No," Jacques spat.

Renee found a space by the fire the Crow shared and settled in. He watched his sons and daughter arguing as if they hadn't been separated for more than a few hours. Knowing they were all safe and hearing them yelling at one another again as if no time had separated them, was sheer bliss for Renee. His family was complete again.

"Nicky," Marie railed. "Jacques won't loan me his knife. I want you to give me yours."

Nicolas stood shoulder-to-shoulder with Jacques. "I won't give it if you're going to use it to cut that Lakota loose."

"I hate you both!" she smoldered. "I'm going to tell Mother how mean you both are."

Renee's face split in a smile as his eyes danced, adoring his feisty little daughter. His eyes flickered to Wolf's Tracks and he saw that the Lakota was also watching the feuding trio. And like Renee, he smiled slightly, finding a certain pleasure in the verbal combat.

"You just tell Mother," Nicolas countered. "You always tell her everything anyway."

Jacques pointed an accusatory index finger at Marie. "You know you haven't changed at all," he shouted. "We have been beating every bush and tree looking for you. We thought the Lakota were torturing you, when what they were really doing was spoiling you even more rotten than you were before."

"I'll bet you didn't escape at all," Nicolas piped. "I've never heard of anyone escaping from the enemy with two pack horses and a guide. The Lakota probably begged you to leave."

Wolf's Tracks watched Renee. Renee had been hand-signing the sibling barbs for Wolf's Tracks' benefit. Nicolas's last comment caused Wolf's Tracks to lower his head and laugh soundlessly. When Marie began to bawl, he looked first to her, then to Renee, watching Renee's hands translate the words he couldn't understand.

"You two are so mean," she wailed. "I'm cold, I'm wet, I'm hungry and I'm going to have a baby and the uncles of my child don't even care."

Alarmed, the brothers rushed to their squawling sister and quickly wrapped her up in a blanket. While they tried to console her and apologized repeatedly for being such unfeeling louts, she cried even louder, fueling higher the flames of their guilt. While his children were otherwise amused, Renee left his place by the fire. He walked over to Wolf's Tracks and cut his son-in-law free.

Wolf's Tracks rubbed his wrists. "Are they always like this?" he whispered to Renee.

"Yes," Renee whispered back. "And hearing them all yelling again, gives me such joy."

CHAPTER FOURTEEN

They traveled hard for over a week. Wolf's Tracks made no effort to escape or steal guns from his Crow guardians. After awhile, the Crow party relaxed, though they kept watchful eyes. Renee assured his brethren that Wolf's Tracks wouldn't do anything foolish which might endanger Marie.

Renee's words proved true. Wolf's Tracks tended his wife, and she him, the pair keeping to themselves a good deal of the time. Marie refused to speak to her brothers whenever they were rude or openly hostile toward her husband. "I'm telling Mother," she warned time and again.

There were always Indians in the agency now. More and more of the Crow enjoyed the easy life of unrestricted Reservation Indians. Permanent homes, along with tepees, freckled the sprawling landscape. The agency boasted a school with two teachers. There was a church as well, but it had remained empty of congregation, except for the worshipping white families living in and working at the agency, until a Bible-banging, hellfire-preaching missionary, a young Indian zealot of an unknown tribe, (he had been raised by a white family of missionaries from infancy and had no idea of his origins) walked in and took over the pulpit. Unlike the missionary before him, the new preaching man didn't mind that the Crow refused to dress up like white people to attend his church services. The sight of half-naked males in his congregation didn't gall him one whit.

Plains Indians enjoyed the benefit of several articles of clothing, both sexes wearing the breechcloth. The men also had shirts and leggings. The women wore either one-piece dresses, or blouses and skirts. But the main mode of dress, for men at least, was simply the breechcloth and moccasins. During the summer seasons these were all the men wore. They didn't bother with any other clothing until the winter cold became too great to overcome with just a robe wrapped around the head and shoulders.

The previous missionary had run himself ragged trying to fully clothe Crow men while at the same time wooing them into his church. With the summer temperatures topping one hundred degrees outside and one hundred and ten inside, the Crow weren't very enthusiastic about going to church. And they made it clear that if they weren't welcomed in the 'Medicine House' wearing their casual native dress, then the 'Medicine House' wasn't welcome on their land. Poor church attendance among the indigenous people yanked the floor boards right out from under the browbeating preacher's feet. Before the next month was out, he was out as well.

Although the supplanting preacher had been raised as white, he had natural instincts in dealing with Indians. He ordered a pump organ for the church and the music it wheezed out attracted the Crow in droves. He stood on the small dais waving his arms as he led his congregation in song, not caring one jot that the Crow make up their own words to such hymns as "Bringing in the Sheaves." He smiled broadly when everyone joined the chorus, suddenly breaking into English as if right on cue.

THE GLORY DAYS OF BUFFALO EGBERT

"Bringing in the sheaves, bringing in the sheaves ...
basakapupe'cdec akapupapa'patdetk, bringing in the
sheaves."

Translation: "My people who went to the Nez Perce are
not wearing Nez Perce belts."

Under the new parson's tutelage, babies were christened
(the preaching-man was a Methodist person) and weddings were performed. The Crow men hated the unnatural
ceremony, but the women dragged in their unwilling husbands by their ears because each woman married by the
preaching-man received a heavy brass wedding band that
clasped the lower joint of the left ring finger. Then, too,
there was the added thrill of hearing the reluctant husbands promising to keep their wives until they were dead.
This strange newfangled custom added a new prestige for
married women. And so popular were the wedding bands
that women took extra pains to flaunt their left hands into
the faces of women as yet uninitiated.

One of these women happened to be Tall Willow. Now
she had two pressing reasons to watch anxiously for
Renee. One, because she was sure that when Renee finally
returned, he would have their daughter with him. Renee
had promised to find Marie and he was a man of his word.
The second need was the wedding band. Willow lusted
after that piece of brass with an unquenchable desire. Her
sisters of the Whistling Waters were driving her crazy with
theirs. Tall Willow might have a bigger house, but they
had the wedding bands and it irked her to the marrow to
look out her flour sack-curtained window and see her sisters coming for a visit, knowing they would bang their
ring fingers against their coffee cups, treating her ears to
the sound of brass clinking against thick chinaware.
Willow vowed quietly that when she got her ring she
would march to their homes and bang her ring finger until
she chipped the patterns right off their china.

Until that day however, Willow filled her long lonely
days setting the social pace at the agency. Mr. Pease had
recently built a house in Bozeman and he and his wife now
lived there, but before they moved, Mrs. Pease and Willow
had developed a friendship of sorts. Mrs. Pease, a dark,
sharp-faced woman who spoke in precise language, never

183

allowed anyone to call her anything other than Mrs. Pease, not even her own husband. She was proud of her ample bosom, accentuating it with perfect posture, walking regally behind them, like the prow of a ship. Mrs. Pease took it upon herself to give Willow lessons in being white, calling Willow "my dear Mrs. DeGeer."

Mrs. Pease spoke fluent Crow as well as English. But she was desperate to learn French, which Willow knew as a second language, so a symbiotic relationship formed between them. Willow taught the woman French and Mrs. Pease taught Willow how to pour tea and make curtains.

The Pease home in Bozeman was quite elegant. Mrs. Pease, a full-blood Indian herself, was never inclined to divulge information as to her former tribal affiliation. She dressed like white women, right down to the tight buttoned shoes and whalebone corset. She belonged to women's leagues and boasted many white women friends, who whispered behind her back.

"You know, Ethel, sometimes I have to pinch myself to remember she's Indian. An' sometimes when I'm with her I forget to look at her skin."

To which Ethel always replied, "I have the same trouble myself, Gert. But it just shows what those people can do if they just half try."

Gert and Ethel would have been positively teary-eyed had they known how hard Willow tried. But they didn't because Willow never graced the house in Bozeman. On lesson days, every Tuesday, Mrs. Pease went to Willow's house to spend the day until Mr. Pease fetched her in the surrey and took her home. This snub, of which Willow was unaware, turned out to be to Willow's advantage. Or so both women thought. Having access to the DeGeer mansion, Mrs. Pease now knew exactly what Willow required in order to make her transition into the white world complete. Mrs. Pease poured over the mailing catalogs and placed orders right and left. She never bothered to look at the prices of any of the items. She was spending government money and the United States, as far as Mrs. Pease was concerned, was a bottomless well.

A wonderful cast-iron cook stove arrived from Cincinnati, along with a kitchen sink and water pump. Willow stood by wringing her hands as Mrs. Pease saw to the installations, bossing around the Crow men as if they were her personal slaves. Before the kitchen could be over-hauled, proper wood flooring had to be placed throughout the house. The agency had started a fledgling sawmill, so planks were not a problem. Though keeping the Indian men working often was.

"Why do I need to walk on dead trees?" Willow asked shyly.

"If you don't have good floors, your rugs will ruin," Mrs. Pease told her. She also saw to it that the house was subdivided into several room groupings instead of the simple two bedrooms.

When the work was completed, there were five bed-rooms in the house and Willow was told emphatically by Mrs. Pease that under no circumstances would anyone be allowed to sleep in the "sitting room" any longer. That once-spacious place was soon crowded with rocking chairs and settees. And of course . . . rugs. The dining area was a Victorian showroom with a lovely beeswaxed mahogany triangular table, ten chairs, two of them captain's chairs placed at opposite ends, and a sideboard. A china hutch stood against one wall and was filled, oddly enough, with Blue Willow pottery plates, cups and saucers which had been shipped in all the way from Staffordshire, England. Tin plates and cups remained in the kitchen hutch which stood close to the trestle table and benches that Renee had built, suffering under the delusion that these few pieces would be the only furniture his wife would ever need. Willow would not allow Mrs. Pease to throw Renee's handiwork out, so the crude table and hutch were shoved out of sight into the kitchen for informal meals.

Mrs. Pease also taught Willow not to throw away her flour rations. The flour was sacked in bags of splendid calico. The Crow women were enthusiastic in drawing this particular ration, though not for the white powdery product. The Crow women either poured the flour out on the ground or gave it away to white women, for the Crow ladies wanted only the colorful cloth bag the fifty pounds of ration was sacked in. They used the material to fashion cool cotton blouses for themselves or dresses for their little girls.

Mrs. Pease taught Willow to store the flour in a barrel as protection from weevils and fashion window curtains from the vivid cloth. Using the flour, Willow learned to bake biscuits and yeast bread and to fry flapjacks. Willow didn't particularly care for these foods, but Mrs. Pease always enjoyed biscuits, which she called 'scones,' heavily smeared with butter, with her tea, so the ever-patient Willow complied. Willow's family would find many surprises when they returned home. The only one who would appreciate even part of it would be Marie.

Eyes-That-Shine was growing like a weed, all arms and legs. Immature breasts budded and her knees were losing their knobby look. She began spending more and more of her time with Willow, her future mother-in-law. She was thrilled with the redecoration of the house. She sat for hours with Willow in the warm kitchen, the two of them at the trestle table, a kerosene lamp in the center, its soft light pushing away the winter darkness, as they pored over the wonders of the mail-order book. Eyes-That-Shine attended the agency school and always brought her precious lead pencil with her when she visited Willow so that she could circle items in the catalog she wanted Nicolas to buy for her someday after they had their own house. It never occurred to either of them as they passed the time dreaming over the items that the men in question might rebel. Eyes-That-Shine circled the advertisement for the George and Martha Washington knobby white decorative bedspreads, telling Willow this type of blanket would be perfect for the newly installed wrought-iron beds.

The little girl stayed the night with Willow as the thunderstorm grew more dangerous. Eyes-That-Shine was afraid of lightning. On this night as the lightning lit up the darkness, revealing the yard outside like a flash of noon sun, she trotted off to sleep in what had been designated as Nicolas's room. She tossed in the bed, unable to sleep because of the long rolling thunder that sounded like hundreds of cannons in the sky. She cowered under her quilts, wishing fervently that she was back in her parents' small three-room house and snuggled in the wood-framed bed between her mother and father for security. Every time she moved, Nicolas's iron bed creaked and squeaked.

Eyes-That-Shine was in the middle of a good creaking toss when she heard a noise outside. She lay perfectly still and listened. When she heard the sounds of horses and voices in the outer yard, she sprang from the bed and rushed across the wide room to the window. As she pulled back the curtains, she saw five riders just as the lightning streaked again. She recognized Nicolas immediately, then Renee and Jacques. The other two she didn't know. Wearing the cotton nightdress Willow had made for her, Eyes-That-Shine raced out into the hallway and collided with Willow.

"They're home!" the young girl cried.

They dashed into the sitting room and when Willow saw her daughter, she wept with joy. She hugged her, pressing Marie's head to her bosom.

Renee, Jacques, Nicky and Wolf's Tracks stood wide-eyed in the front sitting room, the three DeGeers thinking they were in the wrong house. Wolf's Tracks was in awe having never been in a white person's house before. The four of them were speechless during the flurry of finding dry clothes for all of them and the making of hot coffee to warm their cold insides.

"You have been very busy," Renee observed as he stood next to Willow at the new kitchen stove.

"It kept my mind clear," she said with a shy smile as she poured coffee into the waiting tin cups. She looked back at Wolf's Tracks, who sat nervously on the trestle bench next to Marie, wearing some of Renee's borrowed clothing. Wolf's Tracks looked uncomfortable, for as large as Renee was, his clothing proved much too tight a fit for Wolf's Tracks.

"Is he going to stay, do you think?" Willow queried.

"I did, when I came to the Crow," Renee said flatly.

"That was different," Willow said biting the side of her mouth as she set the coffeepot back on the stove. "You were a white man before you became Crow."

"No," Renee corrected. "I was a Lakota before I became a Crow. Just like him."

"But we trusted you," she whispered.

"I see," Renee frowned. "Does this mean you don't trust Mitch?"

The simple question rocked Willow back on her heels. She didn't think often of Mitch Boyer, but now that Renee called him to mind, his face swam before her eyes. Mitch Boyer was French/Lakota. He had been with the Crow for fifteen years and now scouted for the soldiers. He was married to a good Crow woman and they had two children. Everyone, including the soldiers at the fort trusted Mitch.

Willow stole another glance at her son-in-law. Guardedly Wolf's Tracks' eyes met hers.

"I think maybe he will stay," Willow decided aloud.

The fifth bedroom was the only room without a bed. Willow used it as her sewing room. With Eyes-That-Shine using his bed, Nicolas quickly volunteered to sleep on the living room floor. Willow grabbed him by the nape of the neck and the belt of his breech string and frog-marched her ill-mannered son into the kitchen for a quiet word.

"Do you want to hurt Eyes-That-Shine's feelings?" she hissed. "How would it look to her or her family if you refused to share a blanket with her? Rides-The-Buffalo-Down will be insulted as would I be if she were my daughter. The two of you will be officially married this time next winter. It won't hurt for you to be considerate and sleep nice with her once or twice before she gets her ring."

"What ring?" he asked, his upper lip curled at one corner.

Willow forgot her recent education hadn't as yet had time to extend itself to her family. She tried to explain patiently. "She will get a ring from the preaching-man on the day Rides-The-Buffalo-Down accepts your presents and gives Eyes-That-Shine over to you as a wife."

"Why does she need a ring, Mother? You don't have a ring."

Willow blasted a short stream of air through her nostrils. Angrily, she went nose-to-nose with her accuser.

"I am going to have a ring! As soon as your father is

rested, he will go with me to the church and the preaching-man will give me my ring. Marie will go, too. She needs one herself. All married women wear shiny rings. But you have taken me off the subject. I want you to go right back in there and ask Eyes-That-Shine in front of everyone if she will share your blanket with you. She is so embarrassed you preferred the floor to her company she's about to cry. Everyone feels sorry for her, even that huge Lakota, and they never feel sorry for anyone."

"That Lakota isn't feeling sorry for her, Mother!" Nicolas sneered sarcastically. "He's afraid to sit on your new chairs. So is *Pere,* Jacques, and even Marie!" Nicolas's astute observation earned him a clip on his shoulder from his mother's open palm.

"Oww!" he yelped. "All right, all right. I'll do it," he grumbled.

Nicolas was positively gallant when he entered the sitting room, all but bowing from the waist before Eyes-That-Shine who huddled alone on one of the settees, her head hanging down. When Nicolas asked her to share his blanket, she instantly reasserted her position in the DeGeer family. She became smug and full of her own self-importance.

"Yes, I will sleep with you," she said softly. "But you are going to have to remember that I am not your full wife yet so you will have to keep your hands to yourself." She left the settee and minced off proudly toward the hallway and Nicolas's bedroom door.

Nicolas followed Eyes-That-Shine, but paused long enough to glare at his mother. "See what you are forcing me to sleep with," he whispered harshly, an exasperated expression on his face.

After Nicolas's bedroom door closed, the rest of the family in the living room sputtered and snorted giggles behind their hands. Confused by it all, Wolf's Tracks looked to Marie for a translation. Marie pulled Wolf's Tracks down onto the sofa next to her and translated the scene in whispers. He started to laugh out loud but Marie smothered his face with one of the settee throw pillows.

Renee stood with his back to the hearth, rocking on the balls of his bare feet, enjoying the warmth, peace and normal mania of being home again. "My poor Nicky," he chuckled.

No one enjoyed their bedrooms. Renee hated the new influx of furniture. "Why do we have to have these stupid closets and dressers? I'll break my toes on them in the darkness when I go outside to pass my water."

Willow, lying on her stomach, stretched over the side of the bed and pulled a brightly painted chamber pot out from underneath the bed and smiled up at him. "You don't have to go out anymore. Mrs. Pease says we are supposed to use this."

Naked, Renee stood with one leg bent, his hands firmly on his slender hips as he stared hatefully at his wife. "I don't care what that white-red woman says! I refuse to sleep over my own urine! The idea is filthy. Only a white person could think of such a thing."

Before Willow could stop him, Renee grabbed the piece of pottery, ran to the window, opened it and chucked the offensive bowl outside, where it splintered against a rock. He swirled on Willow. "And don't you ever let me find another one in here! I'll smash it as well!"

In another room, Wolf's Tracks stared at the bed. "Let's make a place on the floor," he begged. "This bed is too short for me. And it makes noises that sound like ghosts." Squatting beside the offensive bed, he raised the covers and made a quick search underneath, making certain there were no ghosts. "Why does it stand so far off the ground?"

Too exhausted to put up a fight, Marie kicked the covers off with her legs. "All right. We'll sleep on the floor."

Wolf's Tracks didn't object to the mattress. He pulled it from its lodging place of wire mesh and threw it down. He and Marie adjusted the cotton sheets and lay down, smoothing the blankets over themselves. Marie assumed her rightful position in his arms and they were soon asleep, oblivious to the battle taking place in Nicolas's room.

"I have to sleep on the right side," Eyes-That-Shine complained. "I get headaches sleeping on the left."

"I don't care where you sleep," Nicolas fizzed, "as long as you sleep!" A second later, he let out an "Ooomph," as she scooted across him, her knees digging into his chest.

She wriggled in against him. "You're taking up all the room," she complained. "Move over."

"If I move over, I'll fall off," he grumbled. "You're too little to need more room." He tossed onto his side and cradled his head in the pillow. He closed his eyes and was trying to drift off when she tapped his bare shoulder with her index finger. "What now?" he groaned.

"I want to ask you a question." She sat up and then curled herself half over him, trying to look into his face.

"Ask."

"Everybody says sleeping with a man is fun. This doesn't feel like fun. When does it get to be fun?"

He opened his eyes and looked at her. "It will be fun when you are built like a woman and I'm so desperate I've forgotten who you are. But until that time . . . shut up and go to sleep!"

"No," she snipped.

That tore it. Nicolas was so exhausted he was dotty. He shot up into a sitting position, grabbed her by her arms and shook her until her teeth clattered. "You are going to go to sleep or I am going to break your neck!"

Eyes-That-Shine began caterwauling.

Before she could rouse the house, Nicolas pulled her into him muffling her mouth against his bare chest. "Stop that," he ordered in a sharp hiss. "You will wake everyone up. Do you want them to think bad thoughts about us? Now stop it."

"You scared me, and you hurt my feelings," she blubbered. "I don't think I want to marry you anymore. And I missed you so much when you were gone, too."

"I'm sorry," he said. "I didn't mean to scare you or hurt your feelings. It's just that sometimes you make me so mad I forget you're only a little girl."

"But I'm not a little girl anymore," she wailed. "I have my woman's time now and mother says next year you will give me a baby. Marie isn't much older than me and she's going to have a baby. But you won't give me a baby because you are mean and hateful." She blubbered more

191

loudly. "You probably won't even build me a little house," she accused, tears streaming down her face.

"All right, all right, all right," Nicolas yelled in a hoarse whisper. "I'll give you a baby. I'll build you a house. But not tonight."

Her tears dried up as quickly as they had come. "Really?" she asked pertly. "Do you promise?"

"Will you go to sleep?"

"Will you hold me in your arms?" she countered.

Nicolas steamed, his lips a compressed gash across his face. "Yes," he finally said through clenched teeth.

"Then I'll go to sleep," she said brightly. She scooted back down into the bed, and immediately snuggled up against his chest.

Nicolas felt her yawn and her steamy breath felt pleasantly warm against his skin.

"I guess you could call this fun," she said in a dreamy tone.

Jacques paced in the large, square shaped room pronounced as his. He looked through the chiffonier and found articles of his clothing, and on the shelf, his personal grooming equipment. His brush and comb were there, and the copper tweezers he used for erratic facial hairs. Sometimes Jacques envied his brother. Nicolas had to shave his face like their father. Nicolas even shaved his arms and legs because too much body hair might give away the fact that he was white. Nicolas always despaired the shaving, but Jacques was fascinated by the ritual.

Jacques dropped his tweezers back onto the shelf and wandered the room again, trying to come to terms with it. He had a chair, a nightstand by the bed with an oil lamp, and a dry sink complete with water pitcher, washbowl and a supply of towels.

He sighed heavily. My place, he thought. This is my place. And I am alone in it. I am the only one in the house who is alone. No one shares my bed. I am so alone I don't even see my shadow.

He felt confusion about his sister. Why hadn't she allowed them to kill that Lakota? Why was she so protective and loving toward him? The Lakota was an evil person who had stolen her away, raped her, and ruined her life. Any one of those acts merited his death, yet she seemed so happy. And *Pere* allowed him in the house and Mother fed him! It was incredible. They were all so nice to him and the Lakota was the ugliest, meanest looking villain Jacques had ever seen. In Jacques's eyes, Wolf's Tracks was big, clumsy and stupid. He owned not one physical attribute or well-mannered grace to recommend him. Nothing that could ever turn a well brought-up Crow maiden's head.

And yet, the Lakota had turned Marie's.

It was a puzzle to Jacques, and worried him so, it was a long time before he could sleep.

CHAPTER FIFTEEN

The Russell family didn't find easy times in the township of Absaroke. There were three smiths in the town and Mr. Russell was only able to find employment as a lowly helper, doing all the heavy work his employers preferred not to do themselves. Mrs. Russell, to supplement the family income, took in laundry. The only house they could afford was a small rental. The owner of the house was Mrs. Cooksey, lately known as Mrs. Andershot. The late Mr. Cooksey, like Jeffery Higgins, never returned from the northern gold fields. Five months after receiving the news of her husband's death, the Widow Cooksey married Elton Andershot, the new owner of the War Shield Saloon. Mother Irene, feeling "too puny to whore no more" (actually dying, wasting away from a mysterious ailment), hadn't been too under the weather to make a profit. She died, however, a few weeks after the deal was set, leaving a considerable fortune to her "daughters." They squandered her money the way they had squandered their lives, both ending up broke, homeless, and alone just a few years later and in different areas of the country.

The new owner, Elton Andershot, was not a bordello keeper or a card-playing sharpie. He was an opportunist. A tall gaunt man who seemed more to stagger forward, rather than walk. Plagued by congested nasal sinuses, Elton habitually breathed through his opened mouth. With his lower jaw hanging, he clumped the main street of the prospering town looking more like the village idiot than one of its richest members. He had one saving grace which had drawn the former Mrs. Cooksey to him like a magnet. He knew how to turn a profit with every venture he tried. Herself being one of a rare breed—an unmarried, white Christian woman, and not too unattractive—Mr. Andershot jumped at the chance to marry her. The former Mrs. Cooksey wasn't terribly shy about jumping herself, accepting the proposal immediately after it fell from his loosely hanging jaw. She'd had enough of dreamer husbands. What she wanted now was filthy lucre, barrels and barrels of it. And having money was the one and only charm Elton Andershot could lay claim to.

The former Mrs. Cooksey now dressed in the finest clothes and lived in a large house attended by two live-in maids and a cook. She was thrilled down to her toes with her new and more comfortable life. She also ruled the town's social scene with an iron and merciless hand. One well-intentioned mention of the tyrannical queen's early midwifery days saw that poor remembering lady banished forever from the strata of the ruling social set.

Now that she finally had the gold her first husband had promised her, the once earthy Mrs. Cooksey was not a kind person. Her children lived in terror of her and family pets habitually died or ran away. She had devolved into one of those humans who should not be allowed to freely associate with any other living thing. Inanimate objects, however, were more than safe in her hands because expensive whatnots were her pride and passion. Her children became walking whatnots, always dressed in the best of fashion and displaying perfect manners. The poor children were mentally abused beyond all hope of salvation, but were always seen to be well-dressed, cleaned and pressed, thanks *in toto* to the slave-wage labors of Mrs. Russell.

Miss Charlotte Russell, still preferring to be called Charlie, was supposed to be in school. Her parents, much too busy eking out a living to see to her properly, truly didn't know that instead of attending class, she ran the streets of the bawdy town dressed like a boy, earning beer money by running errands for some of the more unsavory of the town's denizens.

Little Charlie had gone from tomboy to worse. Working as a street courier in her boyish garb, she learned to play a mean hand of poker, swear like a trooper, and roll cigarettes with one hand. Laws concerning minors hanging around or drinking in saloons weren't as yet in force. The War Shield became Charlie's daily haunt. Mr. Andershot failed to recognize her as the child of one of his tenants, for his wife collected the rents, a hobby the overbearing woman thoroughly enjoyed. Then again, Mr. Andershot rarely noticed children, his own stepchildren included.

Charlie was well on her way to becoming Montana's newest Calamity Jane until two calamities of her own nipped her chosen career in the bud.

Breasts.

These being the only two natural disasters ever known to have bypassed history's erstwhile Jane completely. Charlie fought back by binding her breasts down, though it soon became apparent to everyone that this was a ruse she had so easily fobbed off in the past. Charlie became welcomed into the War Shield for more than simply sweeping the floors and sitting in on poker games. But to save herself from the groping hands which were becoming an ugly habit among her former chums, Charlie was forced to quit the pub altogether.

The middle years of Absaroke's history were far from years of pride. Almost every establishment began displaying signs announcing, "Whites Only" or "No Indians Allowed." The Crow were unaffected, for they no longer went to Absaroke. The town was overcrowded with gold seekers, opportunists, and ex-war-veteran vagabonds. Few residents remained who actually remembered the old days when the Crow camped in the heart of the town, sharing an easy relationship with the townspeople. The peace-loving community was now rife with street brawling, race hatred, and bloody, drunken reenactments of the Civil War by ex-Confederate and ex-Union veterans. With so many trading posts available and the agency stores well-stocked, the Crow had no need or desire to wade through the muddy quagmire of blood and beer currently serving as the asphalt of Absaroke's main street.

There were a few Indians in the town, mostly Shoshone, a scattering of Bannocks and even one or two expelled Piegans. From these wastrels of their tribes Charlie formed a poor mental opinion of the Indian peoples. She couldn't really remember the Crow. She had only a hazy recollection of three who had taken her family away from their former home. The memory of the eviction was reinforced by her parents who cursed the Crow with almost every breath they drew. No one could ever accuse Charlie of being an "Indian lover."

On the day of Charlie's fourteenth birthday, the Russells finally admitted to themselves that something had to be done about Charlotte. They decided their only option was to marry her off. For Charlie's birthday present, she was forced in a dress which revealed to the world that she was indeed quite a lovely girl, and taken off to Sunday church. The Russells repeated this ritual for several months of Sundays with nary a nibble at their feminine bait.

Had they actually known the reason for the indifference displayed toward their coquette, the Russells would have been horrified. Several likely suitors had, after the first church service, presented themselves to Charlie as her parents met and shook hands with the rest of the flock who were eager to greet the Russells and welcome them into the fold. Charlie promptly cussed the lads a blue streak, reeling the young Christian-minded swains into speechlessness. Every Sunday after that she sat with her ignorant, disheartened parents on the church pew, all pink and innocent, her cold eyes warning off any young man she caught shooting glances her way. The elders of the church, hearing the reports of the flabbergasted parents of the young men, were either too kind or too rattled to brace the Russells on the subject of their daughter's unseemly behavior.

Charlie, for all her faults, and they were legion, was a lovely looking girl. She was petite, though she had a left hook that could knock a mule to its knees. She had a well-endowed figure and the loveliest golden hair, with enough natural curl to spare her mother the ordeal of grappling with Charlie, the heated curling tongs a weapon between them. All of this natural beauty was enhanced by soft cornflower-blue eyes. Anyone not having had the pleasure of an introduction would have considered Charlie a prize catch. Unfortunately, too many young men knew her, and Mr. and Mrs. Russell despaired that their Charlie was on the threshold of becoming an old maid.

All good things come to an end and one dreary morning Charlie's luck ebbed like the tide.

Hector Yates was a lummox. Those of his acquaintance would be the first to admit that however disparaging the term, in the case of Hector Yates the term was the highest praise possible. After alighting from the stagecoach, he stood and surveyed his surroundings, his heart thumping with joy. Hector had heeded the call to go West, answering without a shred of an idea as to what he would do with himself after his arrival "way out yonder." He hadn't a real trade nor an education. Built like an ape, he also enjoyed a personality which would cause the aforementioned primate to wince. He had a crop of rusty red hair and vivid pink skin. He always appeared to be sunscorched, especially his brick red face. He sported a handlebar mustache which drooped, despite heavy waxing. Thinking himself quite dapper and more than a match for the backwoods one-horse town, he looked pathetically like a bloated pink walrus in a buttoned down wool suit.

Mr. and Mrs. Russell met him on the day he arrived in town and decided Hector Yates was just the man for their Charlotte.

Hector found work first with the Webbs, but when making correct change for customers proved too much for his limited mental capabilities, he promptly moved on to a job at the post office. He was able to read so he was given the job of sorting mail into the proper slots.

THE GLORY DAYS OF BUFFALO EGBERT

Before Charlie's reputation could precede her, the Russells invited Hector to supper. Under her parents' watchful eyes, Charlie was forced to be somewhat pleasant, and the oafish, addlepated Hector fell madly in love with her. Having little experience with women, he misread her stilted manner of conversing as maidenly shyness. The Russells were careful not to allow their daughter to be alone with him because they didn't want him to change his mind. At the end of one month, Charlie was dressed in white and forcibly dragged to the altar.

The ceremony, sparsely attended, was kept as short as possible. The minister, upon the Russells' urgings, left out the phrase "If anyone present has objections to this union, let him speak now. . . ."

The holy vow, "Do you take . . ." was only asked of Hector. The minister was tempted to add, "And are you very, very sure?"

The Russells cried tears of sweet relief as Charlie was pronounced as wife, to be had and held somewhere other than under their own roof. Their means were singularly limited, but what little they had managed to save, the Russells paid over to Hector as a dowry.

Being a dolt of the first magnitude, Hector sagely invested the paltry sum into a run-down soddy on the lone prairie with the aim of trying his hand at farming, something he knew even less about than counting out the change of a dollar. After the short shrift wedding, the Russells fondly waved good-bye to their grim-faced daughter squatting like a gargoyle in bridal dress on the wagon seat next to her jubilant husband, going off finally, to make her way in the respectable world. So happy were the Russells to see her go that they never once entertained the thought that they might not ever see her again. In all truth, it would have grieved them sorely had they known.

The honeymoon campout was not the stuff of Hector's manly dreams. His blushing bride had refused to speak one word to him all during the long day's travel. As dusk fell, they stopped and wordlessly made a crude camp. Later that evening, feeling romantic, Hector made a grab for his bride as she lay on her separate sleeping mat.

"Well, Honey," he said, "I know you're as curious as

me about all this, so we outta get naked an' get this thing done."

To his astonishment, the barrel of a six-shot revolver stabbed his abdomen as he fumbled with the buttons of his fly.

"You lay one hand on me, you peckerwood, an' I'll blow a hole through you an' wear your guts for garters," she snarled.

"B-But Charlotte," he gasped, unable to take his eyes off the deadly weapon pointed at his midsection. "W-We're husband an' wife."

"Get off me, you butt-hole, or I'll aim lower and we'll be sisters."

When she cocked back the firing lever of the revolver, Hector backed off, scurrying on his hands and knees over to his own blankets. "I'll forgive you, Charlotte, cause I know you're nervous. You'll be more relaxed when we're in our own house."

"And the sun rises in the north, Ass-brain."

Hector Yates was a sound sleeper. Charlie could have awakened the dead as she went through her belongings, found her old coveralls, bound down her breasts, slipped into the faded work shirt and finally drew up the denims. She pinned up her hair, and stuffed it under the battered hat. As she sat on the ground lacing up her boots, she watched Hector, prepared to send her newly-wedded husband into the world beyond should he make the mistake of waking. Dressed, she packed up food, ammunition, and an extra rifle. She mounted the best horse and then nonchalantly rode away.

As dawn rose, so did Hector, only to find himself abandoned. Four weeks passed before he got around to reporting his wife missing.

During the two and a half years it took the Russells to marry Charlie off, the DeGeer family enjoyed a certain amount of peace and harmony. Marie gave birth to a hefty son. Nicolas went through with the marriage to Eyes-

That-Shine. Nicolas had made as happy a groom as Charlie had a bride, for there was nothing about Eyes-That-Shine which attracted him to her. And too, they continued to fight like a pair of Tasmanian devils trapped in the same sack. Eyes-That-Shine held close the secret of her love for him while Nicolas felt free to voice his disdain of her. Instead of settling down and giving her the baby and house he had promised, Nicolas escaped for the war road.

During the first weeks after his arrival in the household, the problem of what to do with Wolf's Tracks had posed an interesting dilemma, one which was eventually solved by Mitch Boyer. This happy solution arrived at the DeGeers' door long before Marie gave birth and Nicolas entered holy Methodist wedlock. A week after Wolf's Tracks' arrival, all the Crow knew about him. The DeGeers suffered a slight shunning while the tribe watched to see which way the Lakota would fly. When it became clear that the enemy among them wasn't going to murder his host family in their beds, the Crow gradually came to accept this alien in their midst.

When Mitch first appeared he had with him his shadow, Tom LeForge, another "Indian-man" married to a Crow girl. Despite his French name, LeForge was an American. Renee didn't care for LeForge all that much but tolerated him when he was in the company of Mitch, which was more often than not. In years yet to come, LeForge would be hailed as being a "white Crow." LeForge was a friendly person, but Renee's distaste stemmed from LeForge's lack of direction. In Renee's mind, LeForge was one of those people life was forced to carry on its weary shoulders. LeForge, though a good-hearted soul, was simply too wind-tossed to develop a strong relationship with Renee. Renee might appear to be happy-go-lucky, but in truth, he planned all of his moves with care, whereas LeForge ambled from day to day, content if nothing really serious happened to upset his lifestyle. A man heard often to say, "I'm easily satisfied," had only two anchors in life, his wife Cherry and his friend Mitch. After their separate deaths, LeForge disappeared only to reappear decades later at the Crow agency an old and destitute man. The Crow obligingly took him back in, making his last years comfortable while he penned his memoirs.

Renee's absence from these published recountings angered the DeGeer descendants. Renee's extraordinary life had been summed up simply: ". . . there were many white men married to Crow women of my acquaintance."

Wolf's Tracks took to the French-Lakotan Mitch immediately. Mitch convinced both Renee and Wolf's Tracks that Wolf's Tracks should apply for work as a scout with the army. But in order to do this, Wolf's Tracks would have to learn to speak passable English.

Renee agreed to act as Wolf's Tracks' tutor. Time being of the essence, total immersion became the hard and fast rule. Jacques and Nicolas, too, were caught up in the scheme, Nicolas suddenly being made to remember a language all but dead to him. For days, all three young men sat outside the house on benches looking to Renee as their teacher. Soon after they began, they all spoke haltingly and with the same heavy accent Renee employed. Though Jacques was the only one of the trio to claim French blood, all of the DeGeer men ended up sounding as if they had just arrived from Montreal.

Though everyone else in the family seemed willing to accept Wolf's Tracks into their bosom, Jacques continued nursing his hatred for his Lakota brother-in-law, working in subtle ways to make Wolf's Tracks' life unbearable, hoping against hope that each new day would find the Lakota gone and out of Marie's life forever. Nicolas and Jacques both knew how to make sex, but not love. Neither of them had a notion of how stubborn the emotion was, nor how a man afflicted with it found the courage to stay where he wasn't welcomed, simply to be near the object of his devotion. The building storm between Jacques and Wolf's Tracks broke the same day Marie began heavy labor.

Renee knew Jacques's blood was up on the crisp March morning. Mitch and LeForge had stopped in, as they were frequently wont to do. The more Marie ailed, the more jittery and sullen Jacques acted toward Wolf's Tracks. On this morning, Wolf's Tracks, worried about Marie, was overly edgy himself. Renee realized that if he didn't intervene, the situation would erupt into violence between Jacques and Wolf's Tracks as the pair became more openly menacing toward one another. The house, large by any standards, had become small and stifling with the feuding pair stalking one another underneath its roof.

Marie moaned in her bed and clung to Willow's hands. Renee ushered all the men outside to have their cups of morning coffee. They were all out in the backyard, Nicolas, Jacques, Wolf's Tracks, Mitch, Renee and LeForge. They sat on benches and had just barely poured their coffee when verbal sparks flew between Jacques and Wolf's Tracks. Hard words were passed and as Jacques threw his filled cup to the ground, the pair jumped up, Jacques pushing himself against Wolf's Tracks, the taller of the two. Wolf's Tracks didn't back down, not even when Nicolas jumped up to side with his brother. Renee quickly stood and pulled Nicolas away and stood between Jacques and Wolf's Tracks.

"It is time you two settled this," Renee said. "The words of peace have not helped. You only want to fight each other. Fine. You will fight here, where your secret will be safe with us. It is a shameful thing for brothers to hate one another."

"He's not my brother!" Jacques spat. "He's only the violator of my sister."

"I didn't do that," Wolf's Tracks bellowed. "I didn't rape Marie."

"Yes you did," Jacques seethed behind barred teeth. "And I swore to turn you into a woman for your crime."

"Then your time has come to try, Little Baby Man."

It really wasn't much of a fight by Queensberry pugilistic standards. Indians weren't adept at fighting with their fists, and the tussle between Jacques and Wolf's Tracks was more like a wrestling match. They tripped and threw each other around, or rather more accurately, Wolf's Tracks threw, Jacques landed. Jacques weighed one hundred and fifty pounds while Wolf's Tracks was a beefy two hundred and fifteen pounds. There was a lot of sweating, grunting, tripping and charging, but as Renee sat calmly drinking his coffee, he knew no real physical damage was being done to either one of them. Being a great admirer of tenacity, he gave his battling sons credit. Neither of them was going to stop until one or both dropped from exhaustion. He also admired fair play, which was why he was mortified when Jacques drew a knife.

Renee stood, his eyes popping, as Jacques held a shining knife against Wolf's Tracks' ribs. Nicolas, Mitch and LeForge stood as well, each man afraid to move, for the look on Jacques's face warned them off. Despite appearances, Wolf's Tracks was still in command of the situation. His right paw grabbed Jacques's hand. Amazingly, instead of forcing the knife away from his body, Wolf's Tracks strained the knife inward, the sharp point penetrating his chest. Paralyzed, Jacques watched as his brother-in-law's skin seemed to open up and suck in the knife blade past the curved point stopping a fraction above where the blade widened. Blood poured forth, both sickening and mesmerizing Jacques.

"You've never drawn blood before . . . have you, little brother?" Wolf's Tracks rasped between great heaving breaths. "Terrible the first time, isn't it? I remember the first man I killed. I see his face all the time. Dreams can be horrible. In dreams the dead come back and punish the living. But you've always slept well, haven't you, little brother? Maybe not tonight after you've killed me, eh?" Wolf's Tracks grimaced as he gripped Jacques'ss hands more tightly. "Don't be afraid. All you have to do is push it through. I will help you."

"No!" Jacques cried out frantically, trying to free himself from Wolf's Tracks' hold.

"Where is your vengeance oath now?" Wolf's Tracks gasped, his voice thick with the agony his face failed to register. "You should never swear to things you don't mean. You wanted my blood. You have it. Here it is."

Horrified, Jacques's eyes bulged as Wolf's Tracks pushed the knife a half inch farther into himself. Jacques heard a grating sound as metal touched bone. He watched in terror as blood gushed over the knife, staining their locked hands.

"Stop it! Stop it!" Jacques shrieked. With all his

strength he pulled himself and his knife free. Wolf's Tracks, holding his hands over his wound, fell to the ground in a curling slump.

Renee rushed to his son-in-law, ignoring Nicolas, who jumped to his feet in a state of shock. Jacques was equally stunned, and Renee shoved him aside. Mitch helped Renee set Wolf's Tracks on his feet as they dragged him up the two short steps leading into the kitchen.

When Willow heard the commotion in the back part of the house, she left her daughter and ran to the kitchen. She gasped when she saw Wolf's Tracks slumped over the trestle table and blood dripping all over. She looked at her husband and glanced around at the others. Then, without waiting for them to explain, she dashed back to her sewing room and gathered up her medical supplies.

"What happened?" she asked Wolf's Tracks a few minutes later as she tightened the bandage around his chest in an effort to stop the bleeding.

"I cut myself," Wolf's Tracks rasped.

Jacques stood shamefaced in the corner of the room watching as his mother ministered to Wolf's Tracks. He was surprised that Wolf's Tracks hadn't told her that her cheating son had used a knife against him in a fair fight.

He became even more distraught when Marie came wandering in, unsteady on her feet, her face pale and sweaty. Jacques wanted to go to her, but Marie didn't even notice him. She went straight to her wounded husband. With a cry Jacques would never forget, Marie threw herself at her husband's feet.

"Oh my darling," she wept. "What has happened to you? You are bleeding."

"I'm all right," Wolf's Tracks assured her. He stroked the back of her head and kissed her damp forehead. "I'm fine, Sweetheart. I just had a little accident. I want to know how you are. Our little one . . . is his wanting to come out hurting you?"

"I'm fine. Our child is fine," Marie sobbed as she held on to her wounded husband. She turned to Willow. "Mother, he's still bleeding. Can't you do something?"

Willow pulled Marie away and went back to tending Wolf's Tracks' wound. Jacques couldn't stand it anymore and stepped forward to confess his sin. But a scathing look from Renee sent him back to his corner. Jacques crumpled under the fresh sting of shame and covered his eyes with his blood-soaked hands.

Marie suddenly noticed Jacques's hands. "Mother, Jacques is bleeding, too," she cried.

Renee tried to step between his wife and their errant son. With a duck to the left, Willow evaded Renee's grasp and before Renee could recover his footing, Willow held her son's hands in hers. She turned both of Jacques's hands several times. Finding no wound, she looked at him with a hard questioning expression in her eyes. When Jacques turned away from her, unable to look her in the eyes, Willow instantly knew the truth and shared her son's disgrace.

"Your brother is all right," Willow reported to Marie. "He can wait. I will tend to him later."

At the end of the day Marie gave birth to her son. Jacques offered Wolf's Tracks his hand, not only in congratulations, but in friendship. Renee closed his eyes in relief when Wolf's Tracks accepted both. The feud was over, although it would be another year before either young man admitted to actually liking the other. The truce set, Jacques stopped meddling in Marie's marriage and looking for the day Wolf's Tracks would go back to the Sioux. Wolf's Tracks' willingness to shed his blood had more than earned him the right to stay. Jacques, although he couldn't understand it, finally forced himself to admit his sister's love for her ugly Lakota husband.

Eyes-That-Shine made a pretty bride. Nicolas was a handsome groom. Once again, the male Crow preened and strutted. Willow had toiled for a year preparing her son's highly decorative shirt and heavily fringed leggings. Every day for a week prior to the church wedding, Willow had brushed and oiled Nicolas's waist-length hair. On his wedding day Nicolas's hair hung straight and smooth, his somber face framed by myriads of frothy feathers of varied hues. When she wove the feathers into his hair, she had attached small shells which clinked as he walked nervously to the altar.

Eyes-That-Shine wore a pretty, white doeskin wedding dress that bore designs of wild roses made with hundreds of tiny red glass beads. The sparkling beads had become very popular among Indian women, and replaced the dyed porcupine quills that had always been used for embroidering. Eyes-That-Shine wore a wreath of black-eyed Susans on her head and carried a small matching bouquet in her hands.

The couple stood before the preaching-man on a warm spring morning in 1873. Eyes-That-Shine was not quite thirteen, Nicolas was nineteen. According to Crow custom the bride was well past marrying age, while the groom was considered still far too young. Girls married before or during their first menses and men typically married in their late or mid-twenties. This long bachelor period provided the valuable time young men needed in order to develop, unencumbered, into notable warriors. This wedding was the first known breach of tribal custom, but in the quiet conspiracy surrounding Renee's adopted son, this exception was but one of many the compliant Crow allowed. In the case of Nicolas, protecting him as a full Crow was deemed more important than following normal custom.

Many of the men who were there to witness the marriage ceremony recalled fondly the good old days when a man and a woman merely chose each other, exchanged gifts and then moved into the groom's lodge. With the old custom, a man could have as many as five different wives in his lifetime. The Christian wedding custom brought with it the added formality of dressing up, standing before throngs of onlookers while making promises the men had some difficulty tolerating, though the women savored each spoken vow with a fervent passion.

The church was filled to overflowing and those who were unable to find room inside, stood on the outside leaning in through the opened windows. The Crow men weren't as moved by the proceedings as their womenfolk, generally agreeing amongst themselves that the marriage was a waste of precious bachelorhood days for Nicolas. The women of the Whistling Waters and Streaked Lodge clans wept joyously as the bride took her place beside the groom to stand before the minister. They were enjoying a glorious day.

Jacques and Renee stood beside Nicolas for moral support. Eyes-That-Shine was flanked by two of her giggling best friends acting as her attendants. Willow sat on the groom's side of the aisle on the front pew beside her daughter, her grandson in Marie's arms. Wolf's Tracks sat next to Marie, his long legs stretched out, a smile on his face. Having gone through this ceremony himself on the same day his son had been christened, he was thoroughly enjoying Nicolas's comical plight.

Wolf's Tracks listened as Nicolas mumbled the promises to love, protect and stay with his wife until death did them part. The promises, so difficult for Nicolas, had come easily for Wolf's Tracks. The church vows were the very same promises he had made to Marie in the privacy of their marriage bed eighteen months before. Saying the words again in front of his wife's family hadn't discomfited Wolf's Tracks in the slightest. But Wolf's Tracks knew Nicolas's heart. He knew his younger brother-in-law didn't love Eyes-That-Shine.

Wolf's Tracks, an army scout and a working member of the DeGeer family, had taken time off from army duties to lend his male in-laws a hand in setting up the honeymoon lodge on the side of a peaceful stream. The spot chosen for the lodge was some distance from the DeGeer holdings, skirting the edge of land held in claim by Nicolas and Eyes-That-Shine. Wolf's Tracks was struck by the beauty of the wooded land and the verdant grass, and commented about the site being a perfect place to begin a marriage.

Jacques shuddered at the comment and expressed his sympathies for Nicolas loud enough for his father and Wolf's Tracks to hear. Jacques was heavily involved with an older woman, a River Crow named Makes War, and he extolled the joys of being with an older, more experienced woman. Makes War was the on-again, off-again wife of a white trapper who had headed for the hills shortly after the birth of his second child, a little girl, and hadn't been heard from in over a year. Until news of her husband's death or his return, Makes War was more than happy to dally with Jacques before seriously seeking a second husband.

Wolf's Tracks worked side by side with Renee as they set the lodge poles firmly into the ground. While they worked, both men listened as Jacques told the sour-spirited Nicolas what to expect during the honeymoon. He told tales of screaming, bloodletting, histrionics and revenge, and Renee and Wolf's Tracks had a hard time believing Jacques was describing a honeymoon. His graphic tales were more in keeping with an all-out warring assault.

"Where does he get such notions?" Wolf's Tracks whispered.

"He doesn't believe half of what he's saying," Renee grunted as he slammed the pole into the hole. "He's just making his brother crazy. My boys have always done that. It's been a game between them since they were young."

"Strange game," Wolf's Tracks mused.

Nicolas didn't kiss the bride, although the minister's final words gave him permission. Instead, Nicolas shook hands with Eyes-That-Shine and muttered, "I'll try not to make you nervous." The remark puzzled some of those who were within hearing range and each drew their own conclusions. Jacques, who radically feared a virginal bride more than his own slow torturous death at enemy hands, believed the comment meant Nicolas would try not to hurt her any more than was absolutely necessary.

Renee concluded, given the couple's long history of heated battles, that Nicolas was promising to make a better attempt for the future.

Willow believed Nicolas was promising not to expect too much of the young girl as a wife right away, and she was proud of her son for being so considerate.

Rides-The-Buffalo-Down, the father of the bride, sat on the other side of the aisle and was both wide-eyed and baffled.

Eyes-That-Shine understood only too well what Nicolas meant. She and Nicolas, both the proud possessors of flaring tempers, fought in private far more than anyone realized. The heated discussions were caused by Eyes-That-Shine's intense jealousy of Nicolas. The older she grew, the more she realized just how handsome her chosen husband was and his looks attracted flirting females in droves. Nicolas's happy response to their attentions caused Eyes-That-Shine to react violently. She became even angrier when Nicolas gleefully reminded her that until their official wedding day, he was perfectly free to do exactly as he pleased. She knew that Nicolas loved women and that he had never been much in the way of celibacy.

Three days before the wedding was scheduled to take place, Eyes-That-Shine followed her wayward fiancé. She saw him enter a lodge and after waiting a few moments, she dashed in unannounced and caught Nicolas with his breechcloth down and in the arms of a hated rival. She screamed hysterically and tore into Nicolas with her fists. The frightened girl with Nicolas scampered out of the lodge and streaked to a friend's home where she could find safety and clothing to cover her naked body.

With the other woman gone, Nicolas and Eyes-That-Shine vented their mutual fury. Nicolas had his hands full trying to hold Eyes-That-Shine at bay. In her hysterical rage she pelted him with her fists and kicked him with her feet. Nicolas dodged most of her blows and grabbed her, covering her mouth with his hand. He held her tight as she continued to kick her legs and swing her fists.

"You can't tell me what to do," Nicolas yelled. "We're not married yet. And when I want a woman, I'll take a woman. It's your own fault your feelings are hurt. You shouldn't have followed me. If you want to spare your nervous nature, never follow me again."

Nicolas's roving eyes made him blind to the growing beauty of Eyes-That-Shine. He didn't see her pretty face or her maturing figure. He only knew that he didn't like her bad temper and her screech-owl demands. The iron door of his mind slammed shut against her and remained firmly bolted against any changing image.

After the ceremony, the bride and groom descended the steps of the church into the churchyard where they stood hand in married hand accepting the congratulations of the well-wishers. Eyes-That-Shine was radiant, laughing as she flaunted the shiny brass ring on her third finger, left hand. After an eternity of waiting, Nicolas DeGeer officially belonged to her. The days of sharing him with secret sweethearts were over. In front of everyone he had promised the Creator he would be faithful and love only her, and Eyes-That-Shine fully intended that Nicolas would be a man of his word. Her wedding day put all the females on notice who shamelessly panted after him.

Nicolas stood beside her, his expression blank as he mentally kissed each one of the lovelies who had serviced him so ardently, *adieu*. Married only five minutes, Nicolas missed his carefree bachelorhood as only an entrapped groom can. He knew people were hugging him and shaking his hand but he was too numb to feel the press of their bodies or the grip of their hands.

Jacques was the only one to reach through Nicolas's mental fog. He hugged Nicolas hard, as if he were sending his brother off to die. "I shall pray for you all this night," he whispered.

When it was Wolf's Tracks' turn to congratulate the new groom, he read Nicolas's expression correctly and felt a genuine concern for him. "It won't be that bad. I promise you," he said quietly. "Don't let Jacques's teasing upset you." But Wolf's Tracks' words went unheard.

CHAPTER SIXTEEN

The Whistling Waters and the Streaked Lodge Clans gave
Eyes-That-Shine and Nicolas a lavish wedding reception in
the churchyard. Trestle tables groaned under the weight of
the food the women had prepared. An enormous firepit
played host to two roasting hindquarters of buffalo. As
more and more Christian weddings were performed, the
Crow women went to further extremes to make the happy
events last as long as they could. The bride and groom's
presence wasn't generally required during the entire time
of the joyful celebrations because the parties sometimes
lasted for two days. In the case of Nicolas and Eyes-That-
Shine, their wedding fete lasted exactly forty-six hours
longer than the honeymoon.

After receiving gifts and well wishes, Nicolas and his
wife mounted their separate horses, waved good-bye and
left the revelers to their festivities. As they slowly rode

away, Nicolas looked back over his shoulder in resignation. He knew his private party wouldn't be half as high-spirited as the one in the churchyard, but he steeled himself to make the best of it. He was duty-bound now.

It wasn't every day a Crow was saved by Blackfeet. And, if the raiding Piegans hadn't been shooting at him with intent to kill, Nicolas would have gladly rushed out from his cover and kissed each and every enemy warrior smack on the mouth. Nicolas and Eyes-That-Shine had been in their honeymoon camp a short hour when the first rifle shot sounded. Like the distant rumblings of thunder on a sweltering afternoon, Nicolas received the first sounds of the attack like the promise of sweet relief. He and his bride had been sitting in the lodge staring vacantly at one another. Eyes-That-Shine finally took the initiative and removed her clothing, then lay down on the bed robes. Nicolas sat fully clothed beside her, impotent and mouth cotton-dry. He was about to suggest that they postpone the inevitable when the first shot zinged the air. He quickly threw her dress to her, grabbed his rifle and began firing out of the door opening.

"Seven!" he shouted to his wife, who hurried to dress. "I count seven, seven that I can see."

Just then a bullet ripped through the lodge-skin walls, missing Eyes-That-Shine's head by inches. She screamed and dropped to the ground.

"We have to get out of here," Nicolas shouted. He grabbed her hand and ran out of the lodge, carrying both rifles and his hunting bow and quiver of arrows. Eyes-That-Shine crouched as she followed him. She carried the water skin and the extra ammunition pouch Nicolas had thrown to her. He stood in such a way to attract the enemy fire away from her as Eyes-That-Shine slid on her backside down into a dry gully, taking cover behind protruding boulders. An instant later, Nicolas slid down next to her.

The newlyweds worked together, and made an impressive team. As Nicolas fired one rifle, Eyes-That-Shine reloaded the other, ready to hand him the freshly armed weapon when he needed it. They were pinned down in the ambush the entire first night of their marriage. By early morning, Eyes-That-Shine was as mad as hell at the entire Blackfoot Nation.

When it came to dancing, Jacques rarely knew an equal. He knew he was beautiful *au naturel*, but dressed up in his feathered bustle and porcupine quill roach, he felt truly splendid. While his brother fought off the Piegan band of Blackfeet warriors, Jacques danced on the outer edge of the circle of male dancers, giving the female spectators a taste of *joie de vivre*. Jacques was a young man who possessed it all: good looks, a good build, virility and best of all, bachelorhood. As Jacques danced, first arching his back, then crouching as he turned small circles, his feet thumping to the rhythm of the drum and the voices of the singers, he made a pact with himself never to marry. Life was much too good exactly the way it was.

A Piegan rushed the hiding couple from their left. As he darted between rocks and trees, Nicolas drew a bead on the charging man, and fired. The Blackfoot spun on his feet and heeled forward, shedding his mortal coil. Two more Piegans peeked up and Nicolas's bullet grazed one on the side of the head. He handed the empty gun back to his wife to reload, but Eyes-That-Shine wasn't there.

Panic-stricken, Nicolas abandoned caution and stood up to look for her. He spotted her as Eyes-That-Shine crawled toward the body of the dead Blackfoot. Too late to reload either one of the emptied rifles, Nicolas grabbed up his bow and arrows. No Talker, the artisan who had crafted the projectile points, must have been a visionary. He had warned Nicolas's mother-in-law, Pretty Stone, that the rifle wouldn't save Nicolas. Pretty Stone hadn't bothered passing on the message, thinking the wily No Talker to be merely drumming up more trade for himself.

Eyes-That-Shine was in mortal danger, as two Piegans were also rushing toward the body of their fallen comrade and hadn't noticed her. From his vantage point, Nicolas was horrified because he knew Eyes-That-Shine didn't see them coming.

Sweat poured into his eyes as Nicolas drew back the ninety-pound pull bowstring. He focused on the two approaching Blackfeet and fired, first one arrow, then rapidly a second. Each arrow flew silent, swift and true, hitting their marks in proper succession. The first arrow went through the neck of the farthest Piegan, the second, straight into its victim's heart. Each man fell soundlessly, and Eyes-That-Shine remained blissfully unaware of her recent danger.

Afterwards, Nicolas sat behind the boulders, holding his bow with both hands, the bottom point of the weapon stuck deep in the soft grit of the earth. His entire body was shaking when Eyes-That-Shine slid in beside him. Beaming, she presented her husband the fallen enemy's rifle.

"I counted coup on that dead Piegan," she said proudly.

"You were almost killed, you little fool," he flared. "Don't you ever leave this safe place again."

"But I just wanted . . ."

"Shut up!" he ranted. "I don't care what you wanted. Don't you understand? I hate it that I'm trapped here with you. With any luck at all, I'll die today. So please, don't torture my last day alive with the sound of your voice." He recoiled from her outstretched hand. "Everyone wanted us to be married. All right, we're married. If nothing else our marriage means I no longer have to play your stupid courting games just to keep you happy. Married people don't have to be happy if they don't want to be . . . and I don't want to be."

With death so imminent, Nicolas could no longer pretend that he could actually make a go of his marriage. The preaching-man had said, "Until death do you part." With that fatal parting so close, Nicolas felt he had nothing more to lose in speaking the words he had long kept choked off.

Eyes-That-Shine listened to him and understood what he was telling her. She now realized what her childish tantrums and carping had cost her. She might wear

Nicolas's ring on her finger but she didn't have his love. No one, not even her powerful father or father-in-law could force Nicolas to love her. That responsibility had been left to her and in this awful moment she realized just how miserably she had failed.

The Piegan branch of the Blackfeet preferred making war on foot, stealth being their primary weapon. Masters of camouflage, they could appear and disappear at will. This ability demoralized the enemy into making disastrous mistakes, firing at shadows while the Piegans moved in for the kill. But the Piegans on this raid were learning how difficult it is to kill a man who didn't actually care if he lived or died. They soon learned that fear had no effect on such a man because he didn't panic. He just coldly went about his business of making certain his enemy died along with him.

Nicolas renewed his love for his bow, taking each aimed shot carefully and calmly. He shot with deadly accuracy. The Piegans, who had begun twenty strong at the onset of the attack, limped quietly away, seven alive, four wounded, the nine that had fallen, abandoned. Nicolas's honeymoon, though not a marital success, earned him the distinction of being a full Crow warrior of many coups.

Medicine Crow himself came to witness the body count. Nicolas had reported that he had killed three, perhaps four. That in itself was a major claim, but the Crow searching party kept finding bodies, and all but two of the recovered Blackfeet had been felled by arrows with Nicolas's markings. Nicolas was as stunned by the results of the count as everyone else was because he honestly couldn't remember hitting any but the two who had threatened Eyes-That-Shine. After that, he had simply shot and ducked, not waiting to see if his arrows had struck.

Nicolas hadn't loitered in the battle area to take scalps or assess the damage. During the last night of their two-day siege, when he realized the Piegans had lessened their attack, Nicolas immediately set his mind to getting Eyes-That-Shine to safety. He retrieved their horses picketed some distance from their camp, fetched her and then galloped nonstop to the DeGeer stronghold. He deposited his wife into his mother's keeping and left with the summoned

Crow men. Heartbroken, Eyes-That-Shine waved him good-bye. She wasn't to see him again for a year.

The news of his bravado spread quickly throughout the Crow Nation. Nicolas, in high demand by various war chiefs, accepted the pipes offered him and sojourned off on raid after raid.

Jacques went with him on the raids. "You know," he said, "it doesn't feel like you're married, Nicolas. It still feels like the old days, only better because now we are men."

"Marriage isn't important enough to come between us, Brother," Nicolas replied. "And I don't see it as any reason to stay in the camp. I like being out, so I go."

"But what does Eyes-That-Shine say?"

Nicolas worried his lower lip before replying. "She has what she wants." He then closed off the conversation which he found too embarrassing even for close brothers to discuss. He knew that Eyes-That-Shine wasn't about to admit to anyone that she was still virgin, and Nicolas couldn't bring himself to shame her, not even to Jacques, whom Nicolas trusted with his life.

Eight months to the day of Nicolas's marriage, Charlie stood at the altar and listened to Hector pledge his troth. Charlie wasn't asked anything, had promised nothing and didn't for one second consider herself married and most assuredly, under no conjugal obligation whatsoever. She lit out for high country the same day Nicolas and Jacques prowled the countryside with a beleaguered raiding party under the leadership of Shakes-A-Rattle.

The omens at the beginning of the raid against the Shoshone had boded ill. Shakes-A-Rattle, a veteran in his mid-thirties, a man of rock-hard physique with a face to match and small restless eyes, chose to ignore the warnings for two reasons. One, he had had a powerful medicine dream. But seeing how badly things were going, the dream more probably was the side effect of gastritis caused by poorly treated meat. Two, he had Nicolas, a young warrior the fates seemed destined ever to favor. Shakes-A-Rattle threw out the warning omens and proceeded with his plans. Plans which misfired disastrously.

Not only had the raiding Crow lost the herd of horses

stolen from the Shoshone, they lost their own few mounts as well. The fifteen Crow wandered footsore some two hundred miles deep inside enemy territory, without food or shelter and the encroaching winter weather turning as cold as a witch's heart. Everyone had rifles except for Nicolas. After his stirring battle with the Piegans, Nicolas preferred to use only his bow, with No Talker happily supplying all the arrow points his satisfied customer ordered. Nicolas's having the bow was a real piece of luck for Shakes-A-Rattle's beleaguered campaign.

Desperately hungry, the Crow were afraid to hunt game with their rifles because the Shoshone tracking them were bound to hear the shots. After the fourth day of starvation, Shakes-A-Rattle finally gave his permission for Nicolas and Jacques to hunt with the bow. If the DeGeer brothers came back with fresh meat, he planned to chance a fire long enough for his men to cook the food and eat. Four hours later, Jacques and Nicolas returned. They had found a small herd of buffalo, shot a calf, took the tongue, liver and hind leg and hurried back to their starving companions.

The men were so hungry they fell on the fresh meat, barely waiting for it to be warmed over the fire. They stuffed themselves until they could hold no more, went to sleep and awoke a few hours later, all of them vomiting violently as their shriveled innards proved unable to cope with the sudden feasting after so long a fast. They retained enough of the meat so that when they tried eating again, this time more slowly, their bodies managed to process the food normally. Recognizing that they were all physically ruined, Nicolas and Jacques decided that they had had enough of Shakes-A-Rattle's foiled raiding party.

"He's going to get us all killed," Jacques muttered. "I vote we break away from him and go home."

"I vote with you," Nicolas agreed, though the other three Crow standing with them were still undecided and remained mute.

The brothers didn't wait for them to make up their minds, but left in the middle of the night, walking southward, finished for the time being with the war road. All they wanted was to be home in their warm beds and enjoying their mother's cooking. Shakes-A-Rattle, after his return to the Crow village, would have to do a lot of explaining to the elder chiefs in an attempt to justify the abuse his misadventure had inflicted on fifteen good men. The DeGeer brothers weren't anxious to stand as witnesses against him. Public chastisement of a war chief is a hard thing to play party to even though the humiliating censure might be warranted.

A two-day walk away from the ill-fated raiding party, the brothers had an sudden change of luck for the better. They found a horse. The poor beast was wandering, searching for browse, having a rough go because the cold had killed off surface vegetation. This was a horse accustomed to being grain-fed and ignorant in the ways of pawing the ground for undergrowth. The horse, catching the scent of man, galloped toward them, knowing that where humans were, there would be food. By the animal's action, and by the bridle the animal wore, the brothers knew the horse belonged to white people. Indian horses, equipped for life in the wild, shied away from anyone other than their rightful owners.

Stroking its head, Jacques muttered into the horse's ear to calm it. "We have no food for you, you poor thing. We are hungry, too. I know you are weak, but you must try to take us home." The horse tossed its head and grumbled a throaty whinny.

"Ah-hey," Jacques smiled, cheering the beast's show of courage.

The stray horse belonged to Charlie. It ran off from her on the same day that Hector Yates strolled into Fort Ellis and reported Charlie missing. Also on the same day, Hector sold his parcel of land to a mustering-out soldier for twenty-five cents an acre less than what he had paid for it and left Montana, never to be heard from or seen again.

The horse had bolted because Charlie had met up with a few hostiles. Charlie wasn't certain what tribe the attackers belonged to as she was too busy returning their fire to note their tribal markings. The Indians had taken her by such surprise she hadn't had a spare second to secure her horse's reins. The few precious moments she had, she used as time to cut the saddle cinch. She had done so because her extra rifle and ammunition were in her saddlebags. Cutting the cinch was a waste of a good saddle, but it was faster than unpacking.

Charlie shot at anything that moved. She didn't mortally wound anyone but she tried, nicking one warrior's ear, giving the advancing hostiles pause. As her aim improved, her attackers backed off, going for reinforcements. When the Indians returned a day later, Charlie was nowhere to be found, her tracks having been washed away in the rains.

The warriors were a small scouting group still vainly searching for Wolf's Tracks and his Crow wife. Wolf's Tracks and Marie were thought to have been with the Minneconjou, so Bear Ribs sent a delegation asking the couple to come home. The Minneconjou had no idea what their cousins were carrying on about. Wolf's Tracks was certainly not among them nor had he ever been. Bear Ribs quickly searched among the other bands of Lakota with the results just as negative. In a fit of pique, he decided Wolf's Tracks must be in hiding on the prairie. Not once did he entertain the notion his nephew might be with the Crow. So ludicrous was the idea it failed to niggle a single brain cell. Going forward with what he believed to be true, he continually sent out searching teams. In order for Bear Ribs to regain his pride, Wolf's Tracks had to be brought back for public punishment.

Finding Charlie, the small hunting party thought they had at last succeeded in their seemingly endless search. On this hazy drizzling day, Charlie kept them at bay. They were incapable of getting a clear look at their opponent. All they knew was that they had found a lone rider who was a fair shot. They grew excited. This person could indeed be Wolf's Tracks. They began a highly vocal voting to decide who would ride back to the main camp and report the news and who would stay to keep an eye on their quarry. During that moment of polling, Charlie's well-aimed round pierced the ear of a warrior in a spot he wouldn't have chosen on his own to wear an earring and the voting polls closed, all of them preferring to ride back for additional men.

The following day, the Hunkpapa returned with sizable

reinforcements. Charlie had made the mistake of leaving the safety of her cave to search for her horse. The long absence of the hostile Indians lulled Charlie into a false sense of security. As blind luck would have it, she saw the large party of Hunkpapa just minutes before they picked up her spoor. Some of the warriors were on horseback. The main scouts were on foot, walking ahead of their mounted brothers as they searched the ground for some sign they may have missed because of the rains.

Charlie ducked behind a cluster of boulders, holding her breath, her eyes squeezed tightly shut as she heard them talking back and forth and moving all around her. She gulped down a choking lump in her throat as one of the walking scouts found a trace of a booted footprint.

"Ho!" he shouted. The others sped toward him and gave vent to a heated debate over the find.

"It's a child," one declared after inspecting the footprint. "A white child."

"What kind of child holds off the Hunkpapa?" another bickered. "I think it's a very small man."

"Or a woman," a sage offered. The warriors looked from one to the other and slowly began to snigger.

"If this turns out to be a woman," the bandaged-ear warrior chuckled, tenderly brushing his wound with his fingers, "then I have a better way of making her pay for the damage she has done me. I'm telling you all . . . if these are a woman's tracks, then I claim her. I will teach her what it means to shoot a Hunkpapa."

"But," responded their leader soberly and loud enough to be heard over his warrior's ribald joking, "should this turn out to be a child, I vote we take it back with us. A child of such courage deserves to be made a Lakota."

They stood for a moment quietly, considering the motion placed before them. One by one they began to voice the opinion that their leader was right. Any child able to protect itself so well, earned the honor of adoption. Now all that was left for them to do was catch it. The wounded warrior continued to hope that the track belonged to a woman. It was an inexpensive way to acquire a wife, and a wife so wily and courageous would

be most exciting to bed. Then too, it was a widely held
belief that women of spirit bred notable sons.

"We must all try to capture this little person," the
nicked eared warrior said. "Without using our weapons
too much. We don't want to wound it."

They all agreed, picketing their horses and fanning out
to cover a greater range.

Charlie scurried to a different hiding place, leaving
behind her a blizzard of telltale tracks. They were found a
half hour later and the Lakota formed a crescent arch
around the well entrenched Charlie. Their intentions were
now tempered with a self-serving mercy, but Charlie, not
understanding their conversations, hadn't a notion of their
plans for her. Her plans toward them hadn't changed one
iota. She was still determined to take out as many Indians
as she could before they could get their hands on her.

One tracker, excited about the easy trail left for him,
ventured too close. Charlie let fly a rifle shot that struck
him in the arm, knocking him to the ground. Two of his
fellows sprang to his aid, dragging him back to safety as
Charlie's expensive repeating rifle sounded again and
again, whizzing bullets over their ducking heads.

"I claim that gun," the wounded warrior exclaimed as
he held on to his profusely bleeding arm.

"We'll get it for you, Brother," a comrade promised.
"You deserve your reward."

Nicolas and Jacques stopped the horse abruptly when they
heard the gunfire. Riding in front, Jacques twisted to the
side to confer over his shoulder with his brother. "Someone's
in a fight. Do you think it's Shakes-A-Rattle?"

"It can't be," Nicolas reasoned. "He couldn't have
gotten this far on foot."

They remained quiet, listening to the distant gunfire.

"That's close," Jacques said thoughtfully. "Close enough
for us to go take a look."

"No," Nicolas shouted. "We should let whoever is in
the fight go ahead and fight. It makes our escape that
much easier."

Nicolas spoke good sense, but Jacques simply could not

resist temptation. "But what if one half of the people fighting are friends of ours? Can we abandon them? And if we help them, they will give us food and another horse. We need another horse, Nicky. This one will not take us far. If we are to make it home before the first snow, we need the help of friends."

"We're close to the Flatheads' winter camp," Nicolas snapped angrily. "This horse will take us that far. The Flatheads are our traditional friends. They will give us food and horses. There is no need for us to risk our lives."

Jacques smiled a mischievous grin. "Ahhh . . . but what if the fighters over there are Flatheads defending themselves? You know Flatheads are poor warriors who depend on the strength of the Crow. If we turn our backs on them then we will be in big trouble with our own people. And we're in enough trouble now, Nicky, just for leaving Shakes-A-Rattle."

Nicolas took a deep breath. "All right," he growled. "We will go over there, but only to look. Maybe we can steal some horses if the fighters are too busy to notice they're being robbed."

"That's a good plan, Nicky," Jacques hooted.

"Oh shut up," Nicolas frowned. "If we get killed, I'm coming back in a spirit dream and telling Mother it was all your fault."

High atop the battle area, lying flat against the ground, Jacques and Nicolas viewed the scene below with wonder. They watched as the Hunkpapa, strangely oblique in their method of making war, snaked around on their bellies, inching toward the little white boy they were in the process of surrounding.

"They're trying to take him prisoner," Jacques whispered.

A second later Charlie stood in a half-crouch and fired her rifle. The bullet skimmed the ground, missing one warrior's head by a millimeter.

"Good luck to them," Nicolas chuckled. "That little man-child won't be so easy to take."

"I want to help him," Jacques said, his muscles tensing.

"You're crazy," Nicolas hissed.

"No I'm not. You go find their horses. Take three and scatter the rest. I'll go down and help him with this fight. When you have the horses, ride for us. We'll jump on and leave the miserable Lakota to walk home in disgrace. It will be a fine coup for us, Nicky, and we'll have that boy to stand as witness of our courage. Go on," Jacques urged. "They're getting closer to him. I'm losing my chance to get down there."

"I still think you're crazy," Nicolas replied, slithering off to do as he was bid.

Charlie began firing rapidly. The Indians were very close on her now and she rattled, becoming more frenzied in her self-defense. She was about to fire at a subtle movement ahead of her when she heard a noise behind her. She whirled around.

Jacques grabbed her before she could squeeze off a fatal round, tackling her to the ground. As he sat on top of her and tried to hold her down, Charlie bucked beneath his weight like a green-broken mule.

"Crow," Jacques hissed, then continued speaking in his thickly accented English. "I . . . Crow. My brother and I help you against the Lakota, eh?"

"You friendly?" Charlie panted. "Friendly Injun?"

Jacques nodded enthusiastically.

Charlie pitched and wriggled, renewing her efforts to free herself. "You got a hell of a way of showing it, Pard. You wanna get your ass off me before we're both shot to pieces?"

Slightly dazed by this unchildlike mode of speech, Jacques moved off, his hands raised parallel with the sides of his head, his eyes glued to her. "You not shoot. I friend."

Charlie rolled out from under him and retrieved her gun. Her hat fell off and her hair pulled loose of the hairpins which had given up trying to restrain it. "I heard ya the first time, Peckerwood," she growled.

Jacques was dazzled by the discovery he made. "You . . ." he breathed. "You . . . a . . . womans."

Charlie whacked her old hat against her thigh. "Course I'm a woman, Ass-eyes. What the hell did ya think?"

Before Jacques could respond, a shot rang out and in unison they splashed the ground. Charlie turned her back on him and began firing. Pausing mid-round she looked back over her shoulder to her bemused rescuer. "You gonna help out or did you just come down here to stare?"

Jacques scrambled to her side and fired off a shot, mortally wounding one of the invading Hunkpapa. When he began the arduous work of reloading, Charlie grabbed his gun and shoved her repeater into his hands. "The best shot should have the best gun, don't cha think?"

"*Merci, ma petite,*" Jacques breathed, in awe of the weapon he held.

"Well, don't make love to it," Charlie bawled. "Shoot it!"

Jacques put the rifle against his shoulder and began firing as Charlie reloaded the single-shot rifle.

"What a dick," she said under her breath as she worked quickly.

Nicolas found the picketed horses without any trouble. The Lakota, anxious to capture the child, had been careless. They had left only one guard for their horses, and the guard was distracted, intently watching his brothers crowd in around their prey. Now that more shots were being fired, the young guard's attentions were completely diverted. Nicolas aimed his deadly arrow and with the combination of his strong bow-arm and the artisan skill of No Talker, he didn't miss. The unwary guard fell forward, a victim of his own negligence.

Nicolas ran in a crouch toward the horses. Quickly he cut all the tie ropes, mounted one and led two extras, one for his brother and one for the child Jacques was defending. He raced through the small herd, scattering them in all directions. Holding onto the lead ropes of the two trailing horses, Nicolas galloped down the rocky arroyo, his voice resounding his high pitched war cry to alert Jacques.

"My brother," Jacques shouted to Charlie. "*Allons.* We leave."

Charlie wasn't adept at leaping onto a horse galloping straight at her. She missed the horse intended for her by a wide country mile. Nicolas kept a firm hold of the lead rope of the animal as shots from the enraged Lakota fired the air by his head. Frightened, the horse ran with its head held high and seeing the clumsy human jumping at it, the beast's eye went wide as its body turned sideways to avoid the would-be rider. Charlie's feet left the earth and as the horse bolted past, she landed squarely on her rump with a thud, the wind partially knocked out of her. Benumbed, she sat still on the ground and groaned in shock.

"I sure as hell hope I didn't break nothin' important," she wheezed.

Jacques reined in and turned as if he had been lassoed. He saw Charlie sitting like a wad of rumpled clothing with her legs spread out in front of her. He made a dash back for Charlie, leaning half off the side of his mount as he rode straight for her. Not trusting her to grab hold of him, Jacques snatched the back of her coat and breeches and pulled her on board. Charlie hung bent double, draped across the horse's thick neck like a killed doe. She screamed bloody murder at the indignity but Jacques was not in any mood to help her into a sitting position. The Lakota were now running toward them, firing both bullets and arrows at his retreating backside. His own safety had by far a greater precedent over the girl's graceless retreat.

"I wanna go back," she shouted at the brothers after ten miles had been placed between them and the Lakota. The brothers dismounted with their ward and gave the horses a much needed rest.

"You want to what?" Nicolas flared.

"Go back," she said adamantly. "What are ya? Deaf?"

The brothers looked at each other in puzzlement, then looked back to her. Charlie, her long blonde hair blowing away from her grimed face, took a deep breath and tried in a more patient voice to explain.

"Listen," she began more slowly. "Everything I own in this world is cached in a little cave back there. I gotta go an' fetch it."

"No," Jacques replied with a shake of his handsome head. "We go forward . . . not back."

"Then you just explain to me how I'm gonna get myself to Oregon without my supplies," Charlie screamed.

The brothers held a small council while Charlie fumed and watched them, ignorant of their conversation as they spoke to one another in French. Finally Jacques addressed her and what he said really gave her temper a toss. "You don't go Oregon. You come with us, eh?"

"When pigs sprout wings and circle the moon," she bellowed at the top of her lungs. "I ain't going no place with you two."

The brothers looked at one another and shrugged their shoulders.

"There's extra rope on my pony," Nicolas said in French. "We're going to have to use it on her."

Jacques looked at the girl and smiled knowingly.

And suddenly Charlie realized she wouldn't be going to Oregon right away.

CHAPTER SEVENTEEN

Charlie's entrance into the Flathead village was not that of a regal queen, nor did she possess a serene composure. Her ankles were tied, the rope securely lashed under her mount's belly. Her hands were tied behind her back and her mouth was gagged. Unfortunately, the gag hadn't prevented Charlie from screaming, even though her throat became rough and swollen. Jacques held on to her horse's lead rope and she trailed after the brothers as their unwilling, noisy guest.

Charlie continued to make as much noise as she could while the brothers dismounted and warmly embraced the head chief of the Flatheads.

The chief was an old man with long, silver-white hair. He was known to all as Shot-His-Horse's-Foot, having thus been renamed during his middle age after a rather unfortunate incident occurring in years long passed. The

Flatheads, never ones to get too close to whites if they could possibly avoid it, gave Charlie their undivided attention as she was just one little white person and seemed tied up nice and tight. They were drawn to her because of the wonder of her hair. Everyone crowded around her horse, wanting to touch her tresses or perhaps snatch a little for luck. Enraged by so many hands grabbing her, Charlie continued her screams behind the gag. She was relieved when Jacques turned and noticed her plight.

Jacques excused himself from Shot-His-Horse's-Foot and dashed to Charlie's aid. He cut the belly rope and hauled her down from the horse. He put a protective arm around her, pushed through the crowd and ushered her toward the chief. The cut rope, still bound to both of Charlie's ankles, trailed behind her like long, untied bootlaces as she scuffled along beside Jacques.

The old man raised his eyebrows as the pair stood before him.

"I didn't think the Crow were allowed to steal white women anymore," he said, his voice grating. "It does my heart good to see that the whites don't run the Crow and that the Crow still do as they please about women. I approve of your prize, my son. You honor me by coming to us for safety while you enjoy her. We will make room for you so that you can have a nice long stay." He smiled and winked. "It's going to snow tonight. My bones began aching this morning and my bones are never wrong about snow." He turned to Nicolas with a broad smile. "Your brother has brought his own woman, but we will send you one of ours. It isn't comfortable for a man in the winter season to sleep alone. What kind of woman do you want? A big hot one or a small quick one?"

Nicolas threw back his head and laughed heartily. Being a DeGeer, he wasn't one to look a gift woman in the mouth. "I would like a small pretty one that smells nice," he answered. "I don't care if she isn't quick."

The old chief laughed and clapped Nicolas on the back. "That is a good answer," he cried. "I must remember it."

The brothers were provided with separate, hastily constructed lodges so that they might enjoy privacy with their women. Nicolas was more than pleased with the woman

229

provided for him. Her name was Rainbow and aside from having a skull shaped flat and broad, a style forced on children during infancy, earning the Flatheads their name, she was small, young and in the Flathead way, pretty. She was also quite eager to please Nicolas, and after a year of celibacy, Nicolas was more than ready to be pleased.

Jacques, on the other hand, was in a quandary. He circled the long-striding Nicolas like a pesky fly. "What am I supposed to do with her?" he asked.

Nicolas, hot on the trail of Rainbow, stooped to enter the lodge door. He turned in the narrow opening and faced his brother.

"I don't care what you do with her," he said. "You're the one who saved her. If you had just left her to the Lakota, you would be enjoying the hospitality of our friends and one of their women. But you had to have the glory of saving her, so she's your problem, Brother. Not mine."

"But you just can't leave me alone with her," Jacques yelped.

"Yes, I can," Nicolas retorted as he shut the door flap in Jacques's face.

Jacques stood outside the lodge, feeling lost and abandoned. Finally he called his brother's name.

"I'm busy," Nicolas yelled from inside the lodge. "Go away before I kill you."

Dejected, Jacques ambled off in the direction of the lodge that had been prepared for him and his captive.

Ordinarily, as Hector Yates could firmly attest, a cornered Charlie is a thing to reckon with. While Jacques had purposefully stayed away from his assigned lodge, the Flathead women had gone to work on Charlie. She was tired and there were simply too many of them for her to fight off. The women bathed her, dressed and redressed her, and argued as they each demanded a turn at brushing out her washed hair. The women planned to save the strands of golden hair that came away entangled in the quill brushes from Charlie's skull. Little did Charlie realize that her hair would later be used in good luck amulets, glued on dolls' heads for little girls, or boiled with love medicines to be slipped into drinks and given to unsuspecting males. Providing Charlie with a nice dress and warm shoes seemed to the Flathead women a fair exchange for bits of her strange colored hair.

The women were long gone by the time Jacques steeled himself to enter the lodge. Charlie was asleep on the bed in a sitting position, resting against the chair-like backrest. Thunderstruck, Jacques stood mesmerized as he gazed at her. Gone was the grime from her face. Gone were the sexless overalls and clodhopper boots. Her hair, which had been a stringy mass, was now golden smooth and shining in the firelight.

"*Mon Dieu,*" Jacques breathed, awed by the transformation of the girl. "If Nicky could see you now, he would fight me to trade places." Not wanting his brother to discover what he'd thrown away, Jacques tied the lodge entrance securely. With the flap tied down on the inside, no one could enter without his permission. And Jacques had no intention of inviting anyone in.

He crossed the lodge toward her, standing a small distance away as he removed his heavy winter clothing, then stripped down to skin. He kneeled in front of her and when he touched her face softly, Charlie's eyes fluttered, but she was too tired to open them completely.

"Shoo, little one," he whispered. "Is all right."

"I'm so tired," she whined nasally.

"I know, *ma petite.* You sleep. You safe." He took the backrest away and carefully eased her down into a comfortable position. He inched himself into the bed of furs alongside her and covered them both with the heavy blanket as he cradled her in his arms. Charlie wriggled in closer against him, her face resting against his bare chest. "This nice, eh?" he asked. He nuzzled the top of her head with his cheek.

Charlie nodded mutely and the movement of her cheek against his naked skin sent a rush of heat through Jacques's body. He prayed that the old Flathead chief's bones could be relied on. He prayed for snow. Snow, thick and deep, to seal him in with this lovely girl, making travel impossible, hopefully for several weeks.

Charlie's last conscious thoughts as she sank into sleep were more of a wonderment as to why this sheltering warmth felt so familiar.

During the night, Shot-His-Horse's-Foot's bones proved accurate. The snow began as a slushy drizzle during the night, then turned into a light snow. By dawn, the snow was falling heavily, the large flakes sticking to the icy glaze covering the earth. As the flakes piled up, the snow began crawling up the lodge walls of the sleeping village. The morning sky was so gray and oppressive, the Flathead village people slept in, not realizing it was morning until it was well past noon.

When the fire grew cold in the center pit, Nicolas kicked Rainbow out of their bed to fetch more wood while he wallowed inside the covers, pulling them over his head to keep in the warmth. He ignored Rainbow's quietly spoken complaints about having to go outside. Nicolas was more Indian than a lot of Indians. He knew a woman's work was never done and therefore reasoned she should always be in a hurry to at least keep up with it. If there was one thing Nicolas couldn't abide, it was a malingering woman.

"There is so much snow," Rainbow sighed, bundling herself up against the elements.

Her remark caused Nicolas to throw back the covers and watch her exit. After she had gone, he crawled on his hands and knees to the doorway and looked out. The high country of the Yellowstone gleamed under the virginal blanket of first snow, glistening more like a diamond instead of the natural yellow rock it had been named for. This immense land of steep gray stone mountains, thick forests of tall, straight pine, juniper and aspen, lush wide meadows with meandering creeks, pristine clear blue lakes, rushing whitewater rivers and thundering waterfalls which dropped hundreds of feet straight down the faces of mountains, inspired only one comment from its adopted son trapped snowbound within the bosom of its wonder.

"Merde."

•   •   •

Jacques was more merciful to Charlie than his brother was toward Rainbow. Jacques left the lodge early and retrieved their firewood himself, carrying it back in the leather tote women used for hauling. Charlie slept so soundly she didn't hear him leave, nor did she hear him come back in. Jacques dumped the wood next to the entrance, and fastened the flap shut against the wind and intruders. He was a happy man. He had gotten his wish about the snow. As he built up the fire, the low flames snapped and crackled with the addition of wood. Smoke curled up to the hole in the middle of the lodge. Jacques shivered as he removed his soaked shirt and leggings. He hung them to dry on the pegs set into the lodge poles. Half-frozen, he wormed his way back into the bed. When his cold skin touched Charlie, she woke up with a start.

"Tarnation!" she cried as her eyes flew open. "It's freezing cold in here."

"Is not the air, *ma petite*," Jacques said though clattering teeth. "Is me. You make warm, eh?"

"Do what?" Charlie squawked, bolting upright.

Jacques sat up beside her, grabbed her by the shoulders and forced her back down beside him. "Make warm. I cold."

"Well, I'll get 'cha a blanket," she replied, trying to squirm out of his tight grasp.

"Have blanket," he said, hanging on to her with all of his might. "Want you in blanket with me."

"Maybe after we've both died and learned how to ice-skate in hell," she cried. She finally broke free of him and made a dive for the end of the bed.

Jacques caught her by the waist and pulled her roughly back. "Stop that," he shouted in her face. He gripped her shoulders and shook her like a naughty child. "You don't run way from me. Is not nice. Have you no manners? I save you life, *mais non*? I bring you here. Give you comfort. You be good woman. You be wife, eh?"

"Wife?" Charlie hooted. "Mister, I ain't nobody's wife. I ain't wife to that loony I got shut of and I sure as hell ain't no wife to no red stick."

233

Jacques, normally a mild-tempered sort, could only remember losing his temper a few times in his life. And there was no time he felt as angry as he felt at this moment. In all the years of his loving and leaving women, he had not once said the word "wife" to any of the girls who had longed to hear it said. He was appalled that he had said it to this small, ill-tempered, mocking stranger, but for her to throw the proposal into his face as if it had been some horrible insult to her, angered him more. His brows knitted as he stared at her, his dark eyes flickering with fury.

"You don't say who you wife to," Jacques thundered. "I say!" He thumped his chest with his closed fist. "You wife. That is *finis.*"

"Look, Bub," Charlie snorted, "I don't care if your name is 'Finney,' I still ain't your damn wife."

"You are," Jacques roared.

Charlie, her mouth puckered for a fight, fired a flat-handed slap across his face. Jacques didn't flinch, but drew back his opened palm and treated her to the same abuse, except his slap sent her flying backwards. Charlie sprawled on her back, her eyes crossing, her ears ringing as he took hold of her limp arms and dragged her back into the sitting position.

"You not hit!" he seethed. "You hit, I hit. I don't like for to hit you."

Charlie, somewhat addled, responded weakly. "Can't say I'm all that crazy about it neither."

Eyes-That-Shine told no one of her ruined honeymoon. It was a bitter secret she kept close to her heart. After six long months of neglect, she finally sought the counsel of the one woman whom she knew she could trust. Yet even with Pretty Stone, her mother, she remained too ashamed to admit the whole truth.

Pretty Stone listened to her daughter's hedged questions on marriage and came the closest in guessing what ailed her child. Her voice took on a conspiratorial edge as she began giving her daughter the benefit of her hard-won wisdom regarding marriage.

THE GLORY DAYS OF BUFFALO EGBERT

"Marriage, my daughter, is not a natural state for men. I have never known one man to care for it for any long period of time. If a woman is to have a good marriage, then it is up to her to have it. Men won't try. It goes against their nature. Men must be led as husbands, never followed. But lead gently or they will rebel. While they admire women of spirit, too much spirit can work against a woman. A husband will always want to know his wife can take care of herself and their children while he is away, but when he is home, he is her protector and provider. Men can be very strange creatures. It took me a long time to learn what I am saying to you, so listen well."

Eyes-That-Shine moved in closer to her mother, resting her head against the warm and familiar shoulder. She watched Pretty Stone's deft hands as they worked to create beauty on a piece of soft leather which would become new dancing shoes for her father.

"You have a man of temper in Nicolas," Pretty Stone continued. "He is like his father who raised him. Renee has always been more difficult than most men. I think that comes from his being with the Lakota for so long. The Lakota all have very bad tempers and they make the worst husbands. Too much passion in their blood. Nicolas is no better than Jacques or Renee. It takes very strong women to hold on to those three. And do you see how easily Marie's husband fits into that family? He feels at home with those men and wouldn't with anyone else. Now ask yourself. How does Marie live with such a man?"

There was a long period of silence while Eyes-That-Shine recalled domestic scenes in the DeGeer home. She chewed the corner of her mouth as she vividly recalled Marie's public moments with Wolf's Tracks. The big Lakota was fearsome in appearance and one look from him cowed the normally mouthy Eyes-That-Shine. Yet Marie seemed impervious to his warning glares. He could kill his little wife with one sweep of his arm, but Marie didn't seem to understand the danger. She fussed over him as if he were a child unable to care for himself. Then Marie would settle contentedly under the protection of the very same thick arm that could so easily hurt her, smiling in pride and satisfaction. Wolf's Tracks' response to this tender treatment was beyond belief. He did very little in life before discussing it with Marie and always accepted Marie's decisions. On one certain occasion their spousal unity had thrown Renee into a rampaging fit.

"You don't need your own house, *ma chere,*" Renee shouted at the breakfast table one morning. His face was red, his neck veins extended. "I built this big house for all of us. You are too young, the baby is too young for you to move out. I demand you stay. That is all I have to say. The subject is closed."

Marie hadn't cried nor argued. Her own house was almost completed and was close enough that it could be seen from the kitchen windows. In the mornings after her father and Wolf's Tracks left, she stood at the kitchen window and watched them as they worked like a pair of teamed mules to finish her house. When the men came in for their noon meals, Eyes-That-Shine clearly remembered, she heard Marie gush as she served her laborers.

"It was such a fine idea for you to put the house so close to Mother's," Marie had said sweetly. "I would not have been able to live far away from you, *Pere.* Now I won't have to." She hugged Renee's neck and sighed. "Oh, *Pere,* I would have missed you so. I'm so happy we will always be close."

Satisfied that he was still lord and master, Renee replied gruffly, "I said you were too young to be away from your parents and I always mean what I say. My little Cody will play on his *Pa-Pere's* land. The boy needs to know who he is. He can't know that growing up without all of his family." Renee fondly chucked the six-month-old under the chin as Wolf's Tracks jostled the baby on his knee. The naked baby smiled and drooled, basking in the attentions of his father and grandfather. Two months after his birth, the baby had been named The-Lakota-Wolf's-Son. Renee called the baby Cody and the rest of the DeGeers took to the name.

"You must learn from the women in that clan." The thin trickling voice of Pretty Stone recalled Eyes-That-Shine back from her day-dreaming. "The women of our clan can't help you. Those DeGeer men are just too different. My advice to you, my daughter, is to watch Willow closely. She trained Marie. She is the only one who can train you. A mother knows her son. Seek her counsel, but remember mine as well. Your father wasn't easy either, but he was tame compared to Renee." She let go a long sympathetic sigh. "I don't know how Willow has managed over the long seasons with such a hothead. But, she has and she has always appeared happy. So watch her closely."

Eyes-That-Shine changed after that, not only in temperament but physically. She gained an inch in height and her figure filled out. The little-girl face softened as she bloomed into mid-adolescence. Using Willow as a role model, she learned how to cajole her father-in-law and slowly lost her fear of Wolf's Tracks. She put away her need to compete with Marie, becoming Marie's friend and ardent admirer. Accomplishing all of this was hard, especially during the first months of effort. Eyes-That-Shine had always been prone to pout whenever Marie was given a gift or special treatment. It was a trial learning to curb her jealousy but after the first few weeks of all out effort, it became easier and her efforts in unselfishness were duly rewarded.

Renee came home after two weeks away. He had led a scouting party of soldiers into the Blackfoot lands. Wolf's Tracks was still out with his assigned troop of soldiers. With Nicolas and Jacques away as well, it had been only the women to tend the home fires and to work on Marie's nearly completed house.

At first, it had been very peaceful without the men. After a week, the peace turned to boredom. The night Renee finally arrived home, blustery and demanding, it felt as if the house of women had received a much needed transfusion. They swarmed Renee with attention, Eyes-That-Shine right in the thick of it. After the initial excitement wore down, she sat with baby Cody on her lap as Renee handed out gifts. Willow proudly displayed her crocheted shawl with long fringes. Eyes-That-Shine extolled the beauty of the wonderful gift, genuinely happy for her mother-in-law.

"I'm glad you like it," Renee said with a sly smile. He dipped into his travel bag and brought out two matching shawls. "I got one for each of my daughters, as well," he said proudly.

Eyes-That-Shine tenderly wrapped her shawl around her. She didn't know which pleased her more, the actual present, or the fact that Renee thought of her as his daughter.

"We all look alike," Marie laughed.

"Ah *oui*," Renee smiled. "You are all DeGeers."

An hour after their argument, Charlie's head was still splitting from the whack Jacques had given her. And she was beginning to realize something that, until this time, had always been alien to her.

Fear.

As long as she didn't resist and acted halfway docile, her captor seemed content enough. But all the cuddling he insisted on made her nervous and she had nowhere to run or any way to get there. Charlie was a person accustomed to having people dance to her tune. Even being dragged to the altar had neatly fit into her plans. If nothing else, Old Yates, as she thought of him, had been good for a respectable ride out of town. A way to get out on her own without breaking her parents' hearts by simply running away in the night.

This present situation, however, was proving to be a horse of another color. As much as Charlie put her pain-riddled mind to it, she kept coming back to the same conclusion. She was trapped. She was terrified that if this Crow even suspected she was planning an escape, he just might tie and gag her again. Ever practical, Charlie certainly wasn't silly enough to count on being saved by the cavalry.

She scotched that notion, thinking, what cavalry is likely to show up in an Indian village in the middle of winter to save one scrawny white girl?

The Fort Ellis cavalry rarely showed up in time to save anyone so they would hardly consider her a special case even if they knew where she was. There were long running jokes around Absaroke in regard to the soldiers of Fort Ellis. Charlie's favorite was:

THE GLORY DAYS OF BUFFALO EGBERT

Question: How do you get a soldier out of a tree?
Answer: Wave to him.

It didn't help their reputation any that most of the soldiers had never been on a horse in their lives and had to be taught to ride after reporting for duty. New recruits were more popular than the Comic Opera Players Troupe which toured Absaroke once a year. The town's citizenry showed up on training days, taking up the best vantage points to watch the nervous new riders work out in the center ring. The recruits were invariably thrown or trampled, but Charlie's favorite moments were when the horses chased the unseated riders around in the training ring, adding to the soldiers' humiliation.

No, she thought to herself wistfully, don't be looking for any help out of Fort Ellis.

The side of Charlie's face was bruised and her eye was forming a temporary squint due to swelling. Jacques fussed over her, placing a poultice of raw meat on the side of her head while he held her tucked up under one arm.

"Oh, Little One," he crooned, "I am so sorry for this. I do not mean to hit hard, eh? You feel better?"

"It stings," she grimaced.

"Ah *oui*," he exclaimed. "Is good the stinging. Make you well, eh?"

"It's real jolly of ya to be so concerned," she sneered. "But now I got a question for ya."

"*Oui*," Jacques nodded.

She pushed his hand and the steak aside and looked him in the eye. "Are you ever gonna let me go to Oregon?" she asked.

Jacques thought about it for a long moment, then shook his head and grunted. "No."

"What?" she cried. "Not even if I was real, real nice to ya?"

"Ah *oui*," Jacques smiled broadly. "You make nice," he said, dropping his voice to a hush. "But not for to leave."

"Why?"

Jacques began stroking her long hair, his heart brimming with a new-found love which he couldn't express as he spoke slowly in his thickly accented English. He wanted desperately for her to understand. "You pretty, eh? And

239

soft, like . . . fawn. But so brave. Ah, *tres* brave. Have fine strong heart. Be generous with you heart, Shar-lee." In a pleading voice he finished his statement. "*Voulez,* give love to me, eh? *Voulez, voulez?*"

"Hey," Charlie barked, pushing him away. "Wait a minute. Maybe I'm gett'n this all wrong but it sounds a whole lot like your askin' my permission about this love'n stuff."

"*Oui,*" Jacques nodded, watching her suspiciously.

"Is this a joke?" she piped incredulously. "What are ya? A polite rapist or something?"

"Eh?" Jacques puzzled with a slight shake of his head. "What is 'jooke'?"

"I'm askin'," Charlie said two decibels louder, as if he were hard of hearing, "are ya try'n to fool me?"

Jacques gasped. "*Mais non, ma chere.* I would not fool you."

Charlie grinned mischievously as she felt the relief of being back in control. "Well now . . . ain't you a pip?"

Wolf's Tracks didn't go directly home after his three week detail of scouting duty ended. Instead, he went with Mitch to Mitch's home in the heart of the main Crow village. The clan villages were growing smaller each year as more and more of the Crow abandoned their hide lodges in preference for log homes. The reserve had become dominated with log homes as families of the Crow claimed their parcels of land, abandoning their nomadic days.

Mitch, the half-caste Lakota turned Crow, wasn't in any particular hurry to build a stationary home, no matter how much his wife cried or pouted for one. Neither he nor Wolf's Tracks could find any attraction in living in one permanent place. It went against their nature. When the earth became tired of humanity living in one locale, it was the human's responsibility to move on and allow that place to recover from the toll their temporary habitation had imposed. That was the natural order of things. As warm and dry as Renee's home was, and aside from the fact that he was building one almost exactly like it to please Marie, Wolf's Tracks preferred a tepee over an unmovable house.

THE GLORY DAYS OF BUFFALO EGBERT

A roaming hunter by heritage, Wolf's Tracks often felt trapped inside four walls. The only thing that kept him in was his love for Marie. He would happily tear the walls down with his bare hands if it were not for Marie's loving persuasion. In deference to Marie, he bore the confinement with stoicism. But still, she hadn't managed to talk him into sleeping in the creaking bed. Cody slept in the bed while his parents slept on the floor. This was a concession to her husband Marie made without complaint. Wordlessly, Willow supplied them with thick quilts to make their floor sleeping more comfortable.

Sitting inside a tepee and with a fellow Lakota after so long in the arid white world wilderness, Wolf's Tracks' spirit breathed a huge sigh of relief. Mitch's wife served them an excellent meal of boiled tender buffalo flavored with wild onions, just the way Lakota appreciated it. Then she left, taking the children with her while the men ate, smoked and talked. The peace and the Indianness of it all seeped into Wolf's Tracks' bones. He felt so at peace he almost dreaded having to leave his friend's lodge.

The peace ended much too quickly when Mitch's wife stuck her head into the lodge entrance and said in a quivering voice, "There's trouble."

Shakes-A-Rattle adhered to the Crow etiquette pertaining to raiding parties which had gone awry. When a returning party came home bearing bad tidings, they weren't allowed to ride directly into the village. It didn't matter that the returning men might be starving. They were, by tradition, forced to make camp well away from the village and suffer their starvation a little longer, sending in just one of their number to inform the chiefs of their whereabouts. In the meantime, the worst was always assumed and the entire village went into a wailing and keening mourning even before hearing officially who of the stricken party was lost or dead.

Food was packed and the chiefs rode out to Shakes-A-Rattle's meager campsite. The village was in a flurry when Mitch's wife hustled back to her lodge to inform her husband. Mitch and Wolf's Tracks stood side-by-side watching the chiefs riding out. The trilling wails of the women were deafening and Wolf's Tracks had to shout over the din. "Who led this party?"

"Shakes-A-Rattle," Mitch's wife shouted back.

Wolf's Tracks went as pale as a full Hunkpapa is able. He turned and gave Mitch an uneasy look. "My brothers," he said.

Mitch grabbed Wolf's Tracks' shoulder to stabilize him. "I'll get our horses."

Though the food was spread out before them and warm blankets were provided, the hungry and cold warriors were not allowed to eat a single morsel or accept the warmth of the blankets until Shakes-A-Rattle finished his report. His report was given to his superior chiefs with a heavy helping of malice after learning the DeGeers were nowhere near the village and hadn't been heard from.

"They are deserters," he shouted. "They left in the thick of battle. We were surrounded by Shoshone and they stole away like cowards. I don't know where they are and I don't care. I couldn't risk the lives of my brave ones to look for them. It is not my fault they are lost."

He would have continued his denunciation had it not been for the arrival of Mitch and Wolf's Tracks. Their skidding dismount momentarily took the wind out of his bellows. It was one thing to discredit the DeGeers to his chiefs, quite another to carry on in front of their brother-in-law.

Medicine Crow stood quickly as Wolf's Tracks approached the council. He placed himself between the Lakota and Shakes-A-Rattle, stopping Wolf's Tracks' advance by placing his hands on Wolf's Tracks' shoulders.

"It's Jacques and Nicolas," Medicine Crow said to Wolf's Tracks in a somber voice.

"Dead?" Wolf's Tracks cried.

"We don't know that," Medicine Crow said quietly. He indicated with his chin toward Shakes-A-Rattle, who stood with his arms folded across his chest. "That one says they ran away from a fight."

"I don't believe that," Wolf's Tracks spat.

"It is true," Shakes-A-Rattle charged. "Here are all my witnesses. Question them. They will tell you I speak the truth."

Wolf's Tracks looked from shamed face to shamed face of the seated warriors. All of them tried to avoid his eyes, especially one of them. And it was that very one Wolf's Tracks called on.

"You!" he shouted while pointing a hand at the youth of his choice. "I know you. You are Winter Beaver. I know you to be a friend to my brothers. If you tell me this thing said about them is true, then I will believe it. But you must stand and say this to my face."

Winter Beaver felt trapped. Returning home, he had thought that if he simply said nothing to anyone he would be safe from the feuding that was certain to split the village in half. He had planned to allow Shakes-A-Rattle to make his report then go to the safety of his father's lodge admitting to nothing. But now everyone looked to him, demanding him to speak. He forced himself to his feet and stood with his head hanging like a condemned man. He was a tall youth, fair-skinned and almost as pretty as a girl. He had never been a good liar, so lying was something he avoided, and he knew that now was not the time to try something he did badly, no matter how hard Shakes-A-Rattle scowled in his direction. Tired, hungry, his body numb from cold and the long ride home, he began his report, knowing his words would anger everyone who heard them.

"My name is A-Winter-Beaver-Trapped-Outside-His-Lodge, and this is what I have to say." He went on to affirm the fact that the DeGeers had left of their own accord, but stated that they did not run from any battle. He explained that two days after their departure, Shakes-A-Rattle's party met up with the Shoshone who had been tracking them relentlessly. They quickly laid a trap for the Shoshone, killing three and stealing their horses. Then Shakes-A-Rattle turned his men toward home, riding, as Winter Beaver so graphically phrased it, "until we wore our buttocks out."

Shakes-A-Rattle's eyes suffused with blood. He looked as if he were going to have a fit.

"I knew it," Wolf's Tracks said, standing taller in the sudden light of his brothers' vindication.

Winter Beaver sat down after relieving himself as group confessor. He knew he had made a bad enemy of Shakes-A-Rattle, but Renee and Wolf's Tracks would be even worse enemies. The boy felt he had had no choice in the matter and felt, too, all the shame of having been the one to expose Shakes-A-Rattle as an incompetent Pipe Holder.

"They didn't leave during a fight. My brothers are not cowards." Wolf's Tracks pointed an accusatory hand at Shakes-A-Rattle. "The shame is yours. They left because they lost faith in you and for no other reason. And you, you great woman of a man, you worried more for your own reputation than the lives of my brothers. You didn't even look for them after you gained horses. You hurried back here instead to spread your lies against them."

"That is not true," Shakes-A-Rattle bellowed. "Winter Beaver didn't tell it right." He turned to the other members of the group. "You. Mule Eye. You stand and speak. You tell them how it really was."

The young warrior known as Mule Eye lowered his head and refused to stand. His refusal was eloquent. Shakes-A-Rattle was condemned. As the war chief, the Pipe Holder of a warring party, his had been the sacred trust of leadership and the heavy responsibility of bringing home the young warriors placed in his command. The DeGeer brothers' desertion, while a grievous sin, paled beside Shakes-A-Rattle's failure to search for them once horses had been gained.

Wolf's Tracks sent Shakes-A-Rattle a new tremble of fear when he spoke quietly. "This will go hard for you when I tell Renee."

Medicine Crow mounted his horse to ride with Wolf's Tracks and Mitch. Shakes-A-Rattle, blustering to the end, shouted after them. "You tell Renee that he has little girls for sons. And you tell him that I, Shakes-A-Rattle, said it."

"I will," Wolf's Tracks promised. He then spat on the ground, showing the war chief his utter contempt. The three turned their horses and galloped out of the council.

•　　•　　•

"My sons!" Willow shrieked. Renee held her in his arms as Willow lost the power to stand on her own.

Marie whimpered meekly against Wolf's Tracks' chest as he embraced her.

When they heard the noise from the next room, they turned and saw Eyes-That-Shine shaking as if she were having convulsions. Medicine Crow rushed to her, catching her just before she fainted. "Nicky . . . " she breathed softly before passing out.

"Take her to her room," Renee barked. "Marie," he shouted, bringing his daughter abruptly to her senses. "Show your brother the way. Then stay with your sister."

Marie pushed away from her husband and scurried out of the kitchen. She led Medicine Crow down the hallway as he carried Eyes-That-Shine in his arms.

After the three were clear of the kitchen, Renee turned his attentions to his wife. "They are not dead, Willow," he shouted. He shook her roughly. "Do you hear me, woman? They are alive! If our sons were dead I would know it. There would be no life left in me if even one of them were dead. But I feel alive so I know they are alive."

"Really?" Willow said meekly, still trembling. "Do you promise me this is true?"

"Yes, I do," he said, holding her in a tight embrace. He kissed her tenderly on her neck. "Our sons are alive."

Willow's arms tightened around him as she wept with relief.

"But I will kill them when I get my hands on them," Renee promised in a husky voice.

The threat infused new life in Willow. She pushed Renee back and glared at him like a mother wolf protecting her litter of pups. "You better not hurt them," she growled. "My sons are lost, cold and hungry. All they want is to come home. As their father, it is your duty to find them and bring them to me. And if you abuse them, they will tell me. I will leave you forever if you beat them. I mean it, Renee."

"All right," Renee stormed. "I won't beat them. I'll just push them around a little bit."

"Oh, no you won't," Willow railed.

Neither of the elder DeGeers heard Wolf's Tracks pull

up a bench to enjoy a ringside seat at the fight. Actually watching Willow pull Renee's horns in was far better than any story Marie had ever told.

"I know how you push, Renee," Willow accused. "You broke a white man's arm five seasons ago giving him a little push. And when he lay there screaming in pain, you played the innocent. 'He just fell down'," she said, mimicking him. "Neither Jacques nor Nicolas had better fall down. I will not allow you to do that to my boys."

They glared at each other, so far divided on the issue at hand that neither could see the other's point of view.

"Woman," Renee steamed through flaring nostrils, "you make it hard for me to be a good father."

"I really don't care," she said, tapping an impatient foot as she folded her arms under her breasts. "You just go find my sons."

Jacques needed air and exercise. In the three days he had been holed up with Charlie, he had not seen much in the way of sexual gratification. Charlie appeared thoroughly disinterested while he was constantly on his knees, begging her. She always said no and he couldn't believe her willpower.

How can she sleep night after night with a naked man and not want to make love, he wondered as he slogged through the knee-deep snow. Isn't she human?

The horrible rub was that the more she rejected him, the more he wanted her. Jacques felt he was going insane wanting a woman the way he wanted Charlie.

"I am going crazy," he determined aloud as he dragged his legs through the deep snow. He walked through the heart of the village with his head down, lost in his anguish. When he heard his brother's voice calling him, Jacques turned. He was glad to see Nicolas running toward him, waving his arms over his head as his winter robe flapped like a cape behind him. Jacques ran toward Nicolas and the brothers embraced for a long moment, clapping each other on the back, thumping their snow covered robes.

"Where are you going?" Nicolas asked, his breath fogging the crisp air.

246

"I don't know," Jacques said dejectedly. "I'm just walking."

Nicolas studied Jacques's downcast face. "Brother, you look upset."

"I am," Jacques replied flatly.

Nicolas hugged his brother again. "Let's go hunting," he suggested.

Here at last was Charlie's chance to get away. Her captor had finally left her alone and unguarded. She could simply walk out and with any luck, steal a horse and head for the hills. It was easier than anything she had counted on. So why couldn't she get up and go? As she sat staring into the fire, she honestly didn't know the answer to that question. For three days she had only wanted to escape, looking for any opportunity.

"An' what am I doin' now that I got my chance?" she squawked. "I'm sittin' here on my butt wondering where he is and when he's come'n back, that's what I'm doin'.."

Charlie picked up a twig and jabbed the fire with it, producing a small puff of smoke along with its tangy sharp odor, which stung her eyes and nose. She pulled away from the firepit and slumped inside the robe, draping her shoulders. With a surrendering sigh she admitted aloud to her lonesome self, "I think that red-stick's grown on me."

She knew the way he said her name certainly had. With his rich accent and deep voice, he had taken a name so flat and unappealing as Charlie and had turned it into music, pronouncing it, "Shar-lee." The empty tepee felt suddenly cold without his presence and she pulled the blanket tighter around her, pretending it was his strong arms blocking out the cold. But try as she might, her imagination wasn't that sound. To her deep chagrin, Charlie realized she needed the real Jacques to keep her warm. And in that instant she admitted to herself the real reason she hadn't run away.

She no longer wanted to.

"Tarnation," she swore. "Of all the men in the world, I hafta go and get squashy over a red-stick." She was about to chide herself further when she thought of Jacques's handsome face. "Might as well get use to it, Charlie-Girl. Looks like this is home sweet home."

She heard the sounds of footsteps crunching loudly over the snow. She held her breath, her heart beating excitedly, her stomach in a wild flutter. And then a deep despair came over her when the footsteps grew distant, the person, whomever it had been was moving away. She was disappointed that it hadn't been Jacques, whom she called Jock. She snuggled deeper into the blanket, lowering her head as she huddled inside it, and silently begged Jacques to come back.

"Have you tried kissing her?" Nicolas asked as they tramped the woods on their supposed hunt.

"What?" Jacques replied, his grieving mind in a muddle.

Nicolas put out a hand to stop their progress, puckered his lips and made exaggerated kissing noises.

Jacques threw Nicolas's hand off and walked on. "No," he grumbled.

"No!" Nicolas bellowed, causing Jacques to halt.

Jacques stood with his back to his brother, his eyes closed, his shoulders stooped. "I asked her once if I could kiss her and she laughed at me, so I haven't asked again," he admitted.

"You're not suppose to ask," Nicolas laughed. "You're just suppose to do it."

"B-But," Jacques stammered, "that would be rude."

Nicolas grinned as he sloshed through the snow to catch up with his brother. "Not to a white woman. In the white world it's rude to ask. If a man asks a white woman for a kiss, she's been trained to say no. I don't know why that is, I just remember it as a custom among the whites."

Jacques looked at Nicolas dumbfounded. "What about asking to make love? Is it rude to ask for that as well?"

Nicolas scratched his head through the robe's hood. "I can't remember. I don't think I was old enough to find out when I lived with those people. But did you ask her?"

"Yes," Jacques confessed. "She said no to that, too."

Nicolas thought for a moment. "Well, as I see it, there's only one thing left for you to do."

"Yes?" Jacques breathed hopefully.

"You're going to have to rape her."

"What?" Jacques cried, rocking back on his feet.

"Now listen, Brother," Nicolas said as he grabbed Jacques's shoulder. "Consider this. If she has any feelings for you but is too shy to express them, it will only be rape for a few minutes. But, if it turns out that she really hates you after all, then you are going to have to give her a nice present. Even if that present is to take her all the way to Oregon."

"But I don't want to go to Oregon!" Jacques thundered.

"Do you want to make love to that woman?" Nicolas smirked.

Jacques stood his ground and thought about it. With a heavy sigh that filled the cold air with a new cloud, he began clumping silently back toward the village.

"How many days would it take to get to Oregon, do you think?" he asked feebly as they neared the snowbound village.

Charlie was half out of her mind with worry when Jacques finally returned. Night was already setting in and it was dark behind him as he stood in the doorway. She jumped to her feet and greeted him like a nagging wife of many years.

"Where the hell have you been, Jock?" she ranted. "You had me worried plum to death. I thought you had gone off an' left me to rot. I was give'n you just one more hour before I took off myself."

He stood in the doorway and stared across the lodge at her. He slowly raised his right hand, then flexed his index finger several times. "Shar-lee, come here," he said firmly.

Charlie's mouth snapped shut as she eyed him, wondering at his intent. "What for?"

"You do what I say, Shar-lee," Jacques commanded. "You come here."

Hesitantly, she walked across the lodge until they stood toe-to-toe. Jacques grabbed her by the waist and lifted her

249

up, her feet dangling above the ground. He covered her pink lips with his mouth.

As he kissed her, Charlie's heart crashed around inside her chest. Her arms went up and wrapped around his neck as Jacques kissed her more deeply, his tongue penetrating and exploring her mouth. He held the back of her head with his hand, afraid that she would pull away from him. Their heads twisted and turned as they devoured each other.

Then, with her legs still dangling against him, Jacques carried her across the lodge. As he walked, wet snow fell from his hair and dripped onto her face. The sudden chill on her cheeks startled Charlie and she opened her eyes.

"Damn it, Jock. You're freez'n half to death," she said as she brushed the offending snow from him.

"You make me warm, Shar-lee?" he asked, his voice husky.

She stopped brushing and looked at him, fear beginning to shine out of her eyes.

"Shar-lee," Jacques said in a half-whisper. "I ask you for the last time. Make love with me."

Charlie couldn't speak as a flooding passion welled up in her. Instead, she nodded weakly.

Jacques threw his head back and laughed from sheer gratitude. "*Mon Dieu,* Shar-lee. I love you so much."

CHAPTER EIGHTEEN

Jacques stripped down to his breechcloth and knelt down on his bed, his arms draped across his bent knees. He stared at Charlie, who stood in front of him, stark naked. She was so beautiful, much more so than he had dared imagine, and his imagination during the days and nights spent with her had been wild. As he gazed at her naked body, his mouth became so dry, his tongue stuck to the roof of his mouth.

Charlie was short but she certainly was not stunted. Everything she owned was exquisite and in perfect proportion. Her breasts were full and high, her waist small and her belly flat. Her pelvic bones protruded slightly. He loved her legs the best. They were well-muscled and perfect in contour. She was the color of fresh cream, except for her face, which now held a full blush, extending to her neck as the embarrassment of his scrutiny became intense.

Jacques felt himself hardening and the heat of his body rose in waves from his skin. He rose on his knees and extended a hand to her.

Shyly, Charlie placed her hand in his, her knees buckling as she knelt down in front of him.

Jacques's heart beat like a wild bird against the prison of his rib cage when he touched her. Her breasts quivered in response, her nipples growing erect and hard. He lowered his head, his mouth finding hers.

"Oh Shar-lee," he whispered against her lips, "you are giving me the most wonderful gift."

Jacques heard her cry out in pain and he wanted to stop. He ordered himself to stop, but his demanding body possessed a will of its own. He kept pushing, his hips undulating as he forced himself inside her, hating himself while loving her for not fighting or screaming. He felt her knees bend and touch the sides of his waist. Then he charged through her hymen, felt the blood, heard her soft plaint as he pushed deeper inside, his mind spinning, his body out of his control.

I'm no better than a dog, he thought. I'm hurting her. Forgive me, my Shar-lee . . . I can't stop. I would if I could . . . but I can't. He would have kissed her, but Charlie was so tiny her face was buried in the center of his chest and Jacques couldn't reach her mouth. When she grabbed hold of his buttocks and pulled him farther into her, some of his guilt faded away.

He propped himself higher on his arms and watched her face. A new heat exploded in him as he realized that she was beginning to enjoy the coupling. Her hips began to move, clumsily at first, completely out of step with his. He slowed, waiting patiently for her to find the correct rhythm and when she did, he cried out with the intense pleasure her movements produced. Thinking she was doing something wrong, she froze for a second.

"Don't stop, Shar-lee," Jacques begged. "Please . . . don't stop. You feel so good."

Their love dance continued as they both grew too hot for their bodies. Jacques was ready to explode.

"Shar-lee," he growled in an animal voice, his eyes glazed, looking far away, his expression the tight mask of a man in agony. "I can't wait. I have to . . ." He couldn't complete his sentence. His loins erupted, hot, volcanic, as his hips pushed hard against hers. He gasped as he emptied himself inside her, the volume and length of his orgasm sending him into a world of darkness illuminated by blasts from a million stars. There, he floated through waves of an inexpressible ecstasy.

"Don't move, Sweetheart," he ordered.

Charlie relaxed on the backs of her arms, watching him as he dressed quickly and then ran barefoot out of the lodge door. She flopped back on to the bed, shaking her head. Everything he did was such a mystery to her. She glanced up through the smoke hole and watched the snow slowly drifting down, white specks against a blackened sky. She winced in discomfort when she shifted her hips. Everything below her waist felt uncomfortable and sticky. Still, sex hadn't been quite as awful as she had expected. She had always dismissed what little she knew of the act as a supreme joke played against humanity. Her response to the motherly confession delivered by the chagrined Mrs. Russell on the occasion of Charlie's first menses to the ways of men and women had been a laughing, "You're kidding, right?"

But as painful as it had seemed at the time, it had also proven, for the naturally audacious Charlie, to be wildly exciting. Even now, she became a trifle warm thinking of Jacques on top of her, pushing himself between her legs. She hadn't realized men were built that large and wondered how Jacques could walk or ride a horse with all that between his legs.

"I guess being a man is a whole lot rougher than it looks," she said aloud. "I mean, a few wrong moves and a fella could really put a hurt on himself."

Her thoughts were interrupted when an old woman entered the lodge. Jacques stood behind her. "Shar-lee, this woman will care for you," he said. "When she finished, I come back, eh?" He turned to go, pausing briefly in the doorway, his eyes large and fearful. "Shar-lee . . . you not hate me, no? For the hurting of you?"

"Jock," she sighed. She wanted to laugh but he looked so helpless, like a little boy who thought he was in trouble. Her heart went out to him. "Come back quick," she said softly. "I miss you too much when you're gone."

His handsome face split into a wide smile of relief. "I be here, Shar-lee. I don't for to leave you."

"Jock?"

Jacques paused as he crouched in the doorway and looked back to her. "*Oui,* my darling love. What is it?"

"Don't 'cha think you ought'a put on some shoes? It's snowin' outside."

The only payment Jacques had been able to offer the medicine woman for her services was the promise to hunt for her the entire time he stayed among the Flatheads. She seemed more than satisfied, and fetched her healing herbs and balms, trotting along behind him. Knows Everything had earned her name late in life because she was the type of woman who had to be in the know regarding all aspects of village life, no matter how trivial the gossip. Jacques hadn't really needed to offer her any present. She would have paid him to poke into his business. But being invited in was much better. Now, when she discussed the couple's affairs with the other women, it would be like a mother worrying over her own children. Outside the tepee, unmindful of the biting cold, Jacques mirrored his brother-in-law Wolf's Tracks, as he paced back and forth, while the woman he loved lay inside being tended by Knows Everything.

Tepees were constructed with inner walls that were formed by draping blankets all around the lodge, extending halfway up the inside lodge poles. In the summer, thin blankets were used. In the winter, thick fur robes were preferred for insulation. In both seasons, the blankets insured privacy. Hide tepee walls alone were transparent enough to allow silhouettes of the occupants to be seen from the outside.

Jacques could see the crown of the old woman's head as

she bobbed about inside, although her silence as she tended Charlie unnerved him. He paced vigorously in the cold night air, his ears alert to the slightest sound from within the lodge. Finally, he saw the old woman stand and make for the door. He raced around the width of the lodge, meeting her as she stepped out.

"You have a fine wife," the old woman grunted. "Small, but strong."

"And she is all right?"

"Of course," Knows Everything chuckled. "Why wouldn't she be?"

"I injured her," Jacques blurted.

The older woman wheezed a laugh. "You Crow are so strange. You worry too much about your women. First time loving is natural and right." She placed a motherly hand on Jacques's shoulder to reassure him. "You didn't hurt her. No more than you had to penetrate her." She patted Jacques again and began to totter off in the direction of her own lodge.

"Wait," Jacques cried, hurrying after her. She paused as he covered the small distance between them. "I need your advice," he said. "It's about making babies. I need to know how to make one quick. It's very important that I do that."

"Why?" she asked. She stood back, studying him through narrowed eyes. "You are both very young. You should enjoy your youth together before you make babies."

"I know, I know," Jacques interrupted, "but we have a special problem. I have to put a baby in her quick."

"Oh," the old woman breathed, believing she realized their special problem. "You are afraid that since she is white, she will try to run off and leave you."

"Something like that," Jacques stammered. "Can you help me?"

She gave him another fond pat as she again wobbled off in the direction of her lodge, Jacques walking along with her, listening to every word she spoke. "Making babies is easy but you must do it right if you are to make a strong one. Listen to me carefully and do exactly as I tell you." Jacques's intense expression led her to believe that he would follow all of her instructions. Satisfied, the old woman began what she loved best, lecturing and advising the younger generation.

"First, whenever you take her, her hips should be high. You must place thick blankets under her hips to hold her in that position. It might be uncomfortable for you both but it's necessary, for you must plant the baby deeply. If babies are placed wrong, they fall out before they are ready to be born."

"Really?" Jacques said.

"Yes," Knows Everything said, feeling most important. "Next, and this is the hardest part for young men, you must not love her every day. Every other day is best. A day's rest will make the seed in you stronger. If you love her too much, your seed will be weak. Weak seed causes many babies to die before their first year because men refuse to listen to this good sense. I know. I have to help bury those poor babies and comfort the broken-hearted mothers. And it's always the man's fault! If you want a strong child who will survive its infancy, then you must remember everything I am telling you. Every other day, and no more."

"I will remember," he promised.

During the next few days, Charlie couldn't help feeling that Jacques was acting bizarre, even for Jacques. One day he couldn't keep his hands off of her, and the next day he would be as frigid as the snow covering the earth. He would even push her away when she tried to initiate sexual foreplay. She put up with this erratic behavior for five days. On the sixth day, after a night of torrid love-making which had left her spent, breathless and tingling from head to toe, she discovered that he was gone in the morning. He stayed away the whole day and half the night, staggering in half-dead from exhaustion, falling asleep the instant his head touched their shared pillow. He lay heavy in the arms of Morpheus snoring like a bear, oblivious as she removed his heavy clothing.

She awoke the following morning tight in his arms,

Jacques raining kisses on her face. "Wake up, my lovely Shar-lee," he cooed. "I have some loving for you."

Charlie's temper exploded.

"You better get off me, Jock, or I'll punch your eyes black."

"What is the matter, Shar-lee?" he asked, startled by her threat. He allowed her to push him back as she pulled herself up into a sitting position, her lovely breasts swaying seductively as she moved.

"I'll tell you what's the matter," she fired. "I'm fed up to death with your hot-cold attitude, that's what. One day you're all lovey, the next day you act like you can't even stand for me to touch you. You go off to God knows where, leaving me all day an' all night, lettin' me worry myself half blind. If this is being an Indian, Jock, I don't like it. I don't mind the tepee, the funny food, or a bunch of people who I can't talk to always pulling at my hair, but I do mind your half-assed attitude. Now if you've decided that you really don't love me after all, then just give me a horse and point me toward Oregon and I'll get out of your life. But if you want me to stay around, you better start acting like it."

"Oh, Shar-lee," he breathed, his hand lightly touching the side of her puckered face. "I am so sorry. I don't know I hurt you. I don't want for you to leave me. Is why I work for the *bebe*. Is for *bebe* I act as I do. But I tell you this, Shar-lee, eh?"

"Yeah," she agreed. "You're always going on about the 'Bob-bee,' she snorted. "All the time it's 'bob-bee, bob-bee, bob-bee,' just like you're all the time sayin' 'eh.' Eh, eh, eh, bob-bee, bob-bee, bobee. Big yippee. But what's that got to do with you treatin' me like a sack of mule cookies? That's what I'd like to know."

"For *bebe*," Jacques shouted. *"Bebe."* He ran a hand through his hair in frustration as she continued to look as blank as a board. As a last resort he folded his arms into a cradle and began rocking, as if he were rocking a . . .

"Baby?" Charlie cried. "Are you trying to say baby?"

"Ah *oui, ma chere,*" he said. *"Les enfants."*

Charlie fell back onto the bed, her blue eyes bulging, her mind in a stupor. Jacques lay down beside her, his fingers touching her hair as he placed tender kisses on her temple.

"Jock," she said, her voice trembling, "I don't know if I'm ready for Bob-bees." She turned her head to look at him, her blue eyes misting. "That stuff scares me, Jock. Having babies I mean. I don't know how to take care of a baby." Tears spilled down her cheeks. "What if I kill it? They're kind of fragile, Jock. If you don't know what you're doing around 'em, you can hurt 'em real bad."

"You no hurt *bebe*," Jacques chuckled. "When *bebe* come, *ma mere* help Shar-lee. *Ma mere* know about *bebe*. She teach Shar-lee, eh?"

"Does *ma mere* mean your mother?"

"Ah *oui*," he chimed. "*Mere*. Mother."

Charlie's mind wheeled as she listened to Jacques relate in his slow, heavy accent, the instructions given to him by the old medicine woman. She didn't know whether she was relieved or even more frightened as she listened, at last understanding his past behavior.

"But I still don't understand what the rush is in us havin' a baby," she said.

Jacques was lost for an answer. He had hoped he could quietly impregnate her without having to explain. Charlie was so young and there were so many things she didn't understand. The foremost being his niggling fear of his parents' disapproval of her as his wife. A cold hand gripped his heart as he mentally heard his father demand that he throw her away while Renee chose a suitable Crow girl for him, the way he had chosen for Nicolas. He couldn't bear the thought of losing Charlie and yet, he couldn't come to terms with the possibility of losing his home and family in order to keep her. But if she were carrying his child, he reasoned, even Renee would think twice before interfering with the marriage. There was nothing more precious in the Crow culture than a woman heavy with child.

"You must have *bebe*, Shar-lee," he said in a determined tone. "Our marriage not ..." he floundered, searching for the right word, "good ... until *mon bebe* inside you. You understand, eh?"

"Do you mean we're not really married until I'm ...

pregnant?" Her eyes went slightly glassy as she marveled over this supposed custom of his people.

"*Oui,* Shar-lee," he nodded rapidly.

Charlie whistled between her teeth. "Boy hi-dee," she said in an awed wonder. "You people sure got a hell of a way of tying the knot. But I guess it sorta makes sense," she said, studying his face. "I mean, it keeps you from being stuck with a woman who can't have kids, right?"

"Ah *oui,* my Shar-lee," he laughed in relief. "You understand now, eh? You help me make *bebe?*"

Charlie twisted her mouth to one side as she considered the request. "Oh, all right, Jock," she said, throwing up her hands in surrender. "But you've gotta tell me what to do."

Jacques leaned over and kissed her mouth quickly. "Not for to worry, Shar-lee," he said as he lifted her hips and wadded bed robes under her elevated pelvis. "I do all the work. I put *bebe* deep inside you."

While Jacques was busy impregnating Charlie, and Nicolas was lying in Rainbow's arms, safe and content, Renee went to each clan member one by one, enlisting aid in the search for his sons. He had a major problem with recruitment—the weather. Indians hated to be away from their home fires in the winter. In the end, there were a stalwart five in his party, ready to brave the cold season in order to find Jacques and Nicolas. The volunteers were Mitch Boyer, Wolf's Tracks, Medicine Crow, Little Eagle and He-Won-Against-The-Cheyenne.

By the time Renee and the Crow party set out in the final week in December, Jacques and Nicolas had been living happily among the Flatheads for eleven weeks. The Crow literally slogged through the hard terrain, hampered by bitter winds and deep snow. Renee wouldn't have gone out on this fool's errand if it had not been for Willow pushing him out the door. He had enough faith in his sons to know they would seek shelter somewhere and that they were skilled hunters. It wasn't as if they were helpless children. But Willow shut her ears against reason. She wanted her sons home and as far as she was concerned, it was

Renee's duty to find them. And Eyes-That-Shine couldn't stop crying for Nicolas. Renee was a little undone by his daughter-in-law's tearful devotion to his son.

So began Renee's four-week odyssey with his faithful band. They endured cold, poor rations and pitifully slow travel for days on end. By the end of the third week, all of the horses were too weak to travel further. Walking and leading their exhausted animals by the reins, Renee turned his group in the direction of the stationary winter encampment of the Flatheads. Renee's plan was to trade for fresh horses before pushing further into enemy territory.

Weeks prior to Renee's odyssey, Nicolas sat beside Jacques, the pair of them spellbound as they watched Knows Everything chanting over Charlie, who sat next to her. The old woman held a slim string in her hand, with a single bead attached to the bottom end. She spun it over Charlie's exposed abdomen. Her chanting grew more intense as the bead began to rotate in a circular motion, beginning small, but like a ripple in a still pond, growing wider and wider with each rotation. The bead stopped suddenly, vibrating violently over Charlie's navel. It held that way for a long moment and the startled woman stopped singing. The circling motion began again with such a frenzy that the old woman gasped sharply.

"What is wrong?" Jacques cried as he jumped to his feet.

"Nothing," the old woman cackled in a high, excited voice. "You have a strong son in there. His spirit has touched mine. This is the best sign I have ever known for a new mother." Her old, weather-worn face creased in a wide smile as she looked to Jacques. "You did a fine job, young warrior. This child is strong and very healthy."

Nicolas stood and the brothers excitedly hugged one another.

"I am to be a PaPa!" Jacques roared with joy.

Nicolas, ever the stickler for detail, held on to Jacques as he questioned the medicine woman. "When will the child be born?"

The woman ticked off the months of waiting on her calloused fingers. "Before the hot season ends," she announced. "Long before the weather is cold. That is important for new babies. Cold isn't good for them." She turned back to Charlie and covered the expectant girl. She had grown quite fond of the white girl and after she had tended to her, she offered Jacques more advice. "You must see to it that she gets plenty of fresh meat with a lot of blood in it. Also, I will leave herbs you must boil in water. She must drink this tea every day. Has she wasted her food?"

"Twice," Jacques blurted anxiously. "One time in the morning, two days ago. Again yesterday, only late in the afternoon. That's when I knew I should send for you. Does this mean the baby doesn't like the food I give him?"

The old woman smiled, her face softening as she enjoyed the ignorance of the young but doting father. "No," she said gently. "This is the time when the baby takes over the mother's body. It causes a fight between them. The fighting makes her throw away her food. The herbs will help her keep her food down until this fight is over."

The old woman pushed her heavy weight upwards as she stood to leave. As she patted Jacques's shoulder, her smile faded and her expression grew somber. "This is also a dangerous time for her, so listen well, young warrior, if you wish this child to be born."

Jacques nodded, his gesture fearful.

"You must stay off of her while she and the child come to terms with one another," Knows Everything cautioned. "If you don't, she might begin to bleed and if she does, the child will lose his grip and come out. If you need a woman, you must take another until I tell you this danger has passed. Too many stubborn men ignore this and kill their own children. I hope you will not be one of those. If she needs me for anything, you must come at once. Do not wait for her discomfort to pass. You might come for me too late. Will you guard my words?"

"Yes, Mother," he said reverently, bowing to her. "I will do everything just as you say."

Jacques and Nicolas walked the old woman outside and watched as she toddled off through the village and waved down a group of her friends, anxious to tell them all the news.

"I have to hunt," Jacques said. He stared down at the leather case that held the herbs. "We haven't any fresh meat."

"Don't worry, brother," Nicolas said. "I will hunt for you. And Rainbow will do the cooking. Stay with Shar-lee and make her the tea."

"You are good to me, Nicky," Jacques said gratefully.

Nicolas threw his arms around Jacques and hugged him hard. "You are my brother and you are making me an uncle," he said with a big grin. "I am so happy, Jacques. I can't wait for him to be born. I hope he looks just like you, tall and strong."

"You forgot beautiful," Jacques laughed against the side of Nicolas's head.

"On purpose," Nicolas snickered.

Charlie sipped at the freshly brewed tea suspiciously. After the first small taste, her eyes crinkled in pleasant surprise. "Hey, this ain't half bad. Kinda sweet and nutty flavored." Eagerly she sipped some more.

"You may have all you wish, little Shar-lee," Jacques beamed. "Is good for *bebe*."

"An' his mama likes it, too," she said between loud slurps. "Guess we're really married now, huh?"

"*Oui,*" he agreed, the relief evident in his voice. "Now you mine forever. You happy, Shar-lee?"

"Yep," she beamed. "You're one good looking fella, Jock. Your hair's a lot longer than mine, but I don't hold that against ya. I like your face too much to care about your hair."

"*Merci,* Shar-lee," he said, trying to hide his smile.

"You're welcome," she returned, polishing off the herb tea and handing the bowl back to him. "Hey, Jock," she said, catching his arm as he turned from her. "Let's make love to celebrate." She didn't care for the look that passed over his face. It was filled with sadness and his mouth turned downward in a frown.

"No, Shar-lee," he whispered. "We cannot."

"Why?"

Jacques moved in beside her. He wrapped his arm around her and snuggled her against his side. "For *Bebe*," he began. "Old woman says is dangerous time for you and little one. She says my loving you might harm *Bebe* and make you bleed. For both of you, I must ... not, until danger has passed."

"What?" Charlie cried. "Is there something wrong about the baby that you're not telling me?"

"Non, ma petite." He took her little face in both of his hands. "No, no, no. *Bebe* good. You good. But you must stay good, Shar-lee. Is so important for you and *Bebe* to be well. Is only for a little time until the wise woman says *Bebe* has firm hold inside you. He is so small I could make him fall out of you and die. Shar-lee want *Bebe* too, eh?" A single tear slipped down her face as she nodded. "You are my Shar-lee," he crooned, cupping her face in his hands. "I love you. I love *Bebe*. I protect you both, even if it is myself who is danger to you. We be patient, Shar-lee. Is only for a little time."

"But I was just getting the hang of lovin' ya, Jock," she squawled.

"I know, my love," he soothed, kissing her tears away. "And I have enjoyed your learning." As his soft full lips met hers, his tongue gently caressed the inside of her mouth. Charlie's blatant passion sprang to life. She kissed him back ardently, her tongue meeting his, then exploring his mouth as she pressed her body against his. He felt himself growing hot and quickly pushed her away.

"You kiss too nice, Shar-lee," he said, wiping sweat from his forehead.

"Tarnation!" she yelled. "I got me a long-legged beautiful husband and now I can't even kiss him."

Jacques looked back at her, wanting her so much he was shaking all over. "Shar-lee ... just remember how I love you, eh?" He rose, dressed only in his breechcloth and moccasins, stooping as he went through the door hole of the small lodge. He left the village, found the privacy he needed and threw himself to the ground, rolling in the snow. Finally he came to a stop, face down, arms and legs spreadeagle, welcoming the cold that seeped through him and cooled his blood.

"Creator of all things," he mentally prayed. "Give me strength and courage. You have sent me this beautiful woman. Help me protect her and the child. Cool in me this fever I cannot control."

As if in answer to his prayer, snow drifted downward from the gray sky. The large flakes landed on his back, melting instantly as they struck his warm skin.

"Thank You," he said aloud to his Lord.

CHAPTER NINETEEN

Jacques sat in Nicolas's lodge, unable to follow the small talk Nicolas and Rainbow offered. He absently chewed on his thumbnail until it was a bloody pulp. Knows Everything was with Charlie for a private examination. Four weeks had passed and Jacques was delirious from the enforced sexual abstinence. During the third week, half-maddened, he went off secretly with a willing Flathead girl. It had been all for nothing. The stolen tryst proved a dismal failure. Jacques hadn't been able to raise his temperature or his penis. He slumped off home slightly guilt-ridden at having tried to replace Charlie but highly concerned for his flaccid masculinity. His worries over his manly vigor ended after entering his tepee. At the first sound of Charlie's voice his penis rose and knocked demandingly at his abdomen wall, very much alive and in a zealous frenzy.

As he waited now in Nicolas's lodge, he knew if the medicine woman came in and reported that he would have to be patient even for another day, Jacques would put a gun to his head. The trouble with old people, he reasoned, was that they had forgotten what it was to have hot blood in their veins. And Nicky. Jacques was beginning to hate Nicky, especially now, as Nicolas sat teasing the giggling Rainbow. Nicolas seemed oblivious to the torment Jacques was feeling. But why should Nicky be concerned, he thought. Nicky didn't want a baby. Making a baby was something Nicolas guarded against, because when they left the Flathead camp in the spring thaw, Rainbow wouldn't be coming with them. Though Nicolas had led Rainbow to believe otherwise. He had laughed to Jacques saying that if Rainbow knew she wouldn't be going with him, he ran the great risk of ruining his bed-warmed winter.

Jacques very nearly jumped out of his scalding skin when the old woman appeared and squatted in the opened doorway. Her face gave nothing away.

"How is my wife?" he asked.

"Perfect," the old woman said. "The baby has a firm hold in her. It kicked like a dozen little butterflies against my hand."

Jacques, in his rush to go to Charlie, knocked the old woman aside and she landed on her well-rounded rump. Nicolas, Rainbow, and the news-bearing Knows Everything watched him as Jacques flew with winged feet in a desperate run for his lodge. Men, women and children cheered the footrace he held against himself as he passed them. Dogs barked and chased along. Jacques was oblivious to it all, for his one consuming thought was Charlie. Charlie, now capable of loving and waiting for him.

Jacques and Charlie were still joined, though he lay off to the side, his face buried in the rumpled pillow. He breathed in great gulps of air, his lungs ballooning to their fullest capacity. "Shar-lee," he murmured, "that was wonderful. So wonderful. Are you all right? Am I too heavy?"

"Shut up, Jock," Charlie panted, her hands holding his hips prisoner against her, afraid he would leave her completely even though she could feel him shrinking inside her. "I ain't talkin' while this feelin' lasts."

Jacques escorted Charlie on her early morning constitutional during the second week of February. She liked to have her daily exercise before the rest of the people in the village plunged too fully into their daily activities. Charlie hated it when the Flathead people stopped what they were doing to stare at her as she walked by. It wasn't just Charlie they stared at. The Indians were as fascinated with Charlie and Jacques as a couple as they had been in the beginning with her hair. The newlyweds were as opposite as two people could possibly be. Jacques towered over his bride, and many of the adults in the village secretly wondered how such a pair could possibly make love with any degree of comfort, never mind find pleasure.

Their coloring was another fascination. Jacques, though he was half French, leaned heavily toward his mother's complexion. He was a lustrous copper, lighter than the average Flathead, though not exceptionally lighter than his fellow Crow. And, his wife was so fair, her white skin was nearly luminous. Her golden hair, worn in braids, framed her small face. Her red rosy cheeks and large blue eyes were a splash of color to her pale face. What really caused the villagers to teeter were the times when the couple paused in their stroll long enough for Jacques to exchange pleasantries with one of his hosts. Jacques had formed the habit of resting one bent arm on the top of his wife's head as if he were using her as a cane. She didn't seem to mind being his support and neither of them realized just how comical they looked.

It was during one of those times when Jacques was chatting with two men and Charlie, like a cane, stood patiently beside him when the camp scouts rode in. With their horses' hooves spraying snow and mud as they charged through the center of the village, it was obvious that the scouts were in a hurry to cry out the alarm. Visitors were coming. More Crow! The early morning drowsy village instantly sprang to life as women scurried to prepare for their arriving guests.

267

"What's happening, Jock?" Charlie twisted her head out from under his arm. He didn't seem to hear her. His eyes were intent in the direction from which the village guards had come. "Jock," Charlie cried, seizing his arm and shaking it.

"Is all right, *ma cheri*," he said in a remote voice. This was something he hadn't expected. He hadn't counted on his brothers sending out a search team in the heart of winter. He experienced a rush of apprehension that slowly turned to dread. He knew of only one person with the ability to pry the Crow from their warm fires and agree to suffer the cold of long travel. *Pere*.

Jacques grabbed Charlie by both shoulders and pushed her in the direction of their lodge. It was hard enough for Charlie to understand his English under normal circumstances, but in his agitated state, it was almost impossible. "Shar-lee, go home," he ordered. "Stay there and do not come out for even to peek, *oui*? You stay inside, Shar-lee. You don't come out for nobody but Jacques." He gave her fanny a mild swat. "*Allez!*"

Charlie ran in one direction while Jacques long legged it in the other. "Holy moley," Charlie huffed as she scampered along. "We must be havin' a war."

Jacques's legs stretched out like a thoroughbred's as he ran frantically toward the outer recesses of the village. Horses' hooves sounded behind him. Nicolas drew up smartly, tossing Jacques the reins of a spare horse.

"It's *Pere*!" Jacques yelled as he climbed aboard the horse.

"I know," Nicolas breathed. Both mounted, they looked panic-stricken at one another, saying in unison the only French expletive they knew, "*Sacre merde*," which translated to "Holy shit."

The brothers kicked the sides of their mounts and rode like thunder through the dense stand of pine and aspen. Nicolas took the lead, half-standing in the saddle as he charged forward.

"I knew it. I knew it!" Renee shouted at the top of his lungs as he hugged and shook both of his sons and lifted them off their feet as they were held prisoner in his tight bear's grip. "I knew you were both alive and well." With his arms tightly around their shoulders, he beamed proudly. "I tried to tell your mother that you were all right. They are warriors, I told her. They know how to take care of themselves. But would that woman listen? No. I should take a stick to her." In a hushed, laughing tone, he added a comment for their ears only. "But I don't because she hits back, eh?" He whirled them around and presented them to the exhausted, mounted men of his party. "You see what I tell you? My sons know how to take care of themselves. I trained them myself. They are not little boys lost in the cold."

The others looked at each other with weary expressions, thoroughly aware that it would have saved them all a long ride if Renee had been able to convince Willow of that fact.

"Pere," Nicolas ventured. "You didn't have to come for us. We were only staying here until the warm season."

"I know that," Renee laughed, bussing the side of Nicolas's head. "But I am here now. And, when the weather warms a little more, we can all leave together, eh?" A dark look passed between his sons, a look Renee found disconcerting. "What's the matter with you two? Why aren't you happy your PaPa found you?"

"We're happy you're here, *Pere,*" Jacques blurted. "We're just embarrassed you came looking for us like we were lost children."

Renee's happy mood faded. He released them and stood with his legs wide apart and his fists on his hips. "I told you that was your mother's fault," he barked. "I am glad you are men enough to find this embarrassing, but we are all your family. You do not have to turn shamed faces toward us." He looked from one boy to the other and got no response. Infuriated, he clipped the back of Jacques's head. "Stop that at once!"

"Stop what, *Pere?*" Jacques cried, touching the back of his head.

"This funny looking you're doing with each other. I don't like it. It reminds me of when you were small boys in big trouble. Didn't I tell you you were not in trouble with me?"

"Yes, *Pere*," they nodded rapidly.

"*Tres bien*," Renee gruffed as he stomped away from them toward his horse. "Now we go to the village of our friends," he said as he mounted.

Renee rode past his sons, fuming that they weren't as joyful with his presence as he believed they should have been. He had come a long way for such a lackluster welcome and was genuinely hurt by their attitude.

Medicine Crow and Wolf's Tracks kicked their horses into a walk paralleling the standing brothers. "What have you two done now?" Medicine Crow hissed as he rode by. When neither boy answered, Medicine Crow looked at Wolf's Tracks. They both knew that their younger brothers had done something all right. Something even worse than deserting Shakes-A-Rattle.

Shot-His-Horse's-Foot was very proud to have what he called the "Big Guns of the Crow" in his lodge. Jacques and Nicolas were nice boys, but they were just "Little Guns" compared to the men honoring him with this visit. The old chief made room for all of his dinner guests, the Little Guns included, treating them to the best feast his village could provide.

"Thank you for having my sons," Renee said, as he gnawed on the charred meat with gusto. With his grown-out beard he looked like a wolf greedily tearing at its prey.

"They are no problem, no problem," the chief assured. "We have enjoyed them. They have been most useful to us and very entertaining. I wish we could have them forever."

Renee's eyes squinted meaningfully in the direction of his sons. Was this the reason they weren't happy to see him? Had they decided to ride with the Flatheads and abandon their true people?

"We think the little captive wife is quite sweet, too," the old chief added.

Jacques spewed pieces of meat as he hacked loudly. Nicolas and Mitch began pounding his back as Jacques gagged, his eyes watering.

Renee stopped eating. He eyed Jacques coldly. "What wife?" he asked the startled chief.

"His," the old man replied as he pointed at Jacques.

Renee threw his portion of meat down on the platter that rested between his crisscrossed legs. He wiped his greasy hands on his leggings, then bellowed at his sons. "Outside!"

Jacques and Nicolas stood stiffly at attention while their father paced back and forth in front of them. "Now," Renee said as if reasoning to himself, "that old man said 'captive wife' so that means she's not a Flathead bride." He paused, his hands clasped behind his back. He raised up and down on the balls of his feet as his sons watched his every movement. They knew that to be one of their father's most dangerous movements. It meant Renee was struggling with his temper.

"My son was told he wasn't old enough to take a Crow bride, so, what does he do? He steals one from someplace else. And why? Because his brother has a wife, and what one of my sons has, the other wants as well, *oui*?"

No response. The faces of both young men were dewy with sweat.

Renee took two steps and stood nose-to-nose with Jacques. "Tell me about your wife, Jacques," he growled.

"I . . . I found her," Jacques stammered.

"Ah, you found her." Renee smiled and nodded, as if he fully understood. "So that means, of course, that you had to keep her, eh?"

"Yes, *Pere*," Jacques bungled.

Renee jammed his face farther into Jacques's. "No, it does not! Just because you find something nice doesn't mean it belongs to you. Now where did this woman come from?" His nerves frazzled as he saw his sons pass a look between them again. Without giving Jacques a chance to speak, Renee jumped in with his own hastily construed conclusion. "Piegan!" he raged. "You found a Piegan and you took her to your bed?"

"No, *Pere*," both sons said at once.

Renee staggered with relief, running a hand over his face.

"I would never take a Piegan woman," Jacques said, almost laughing that his father could think such a thing.

"Thank you, my Jacques," Renee muttered. "For a moment, my heart almost stopped beating." He thought for a moment. "But what does that leave? Lakota? Shoshone?"

Both young men shook their heads as if they were controlled by an invisible puppeteer.

Renee's hands flew to his chest as he careened around in front of them. "No!" he bellowed. "No . . . not . . . Cheyenne! Your mother would never survive it."

Jacques and Nicolas were surprised at their father's thick-wittedness. Neither of them could remember a time when their father beat at a bush so many times and still came up empty-handed.

Renee grabbed the back of Jacques's neck and pulled him forward until their foreheads were touching. "My Jacques," he murmured. "My beautiful, beautiful, Jacques. I loved you before you were ever born. I will continue to love you long after I have passed into the other world. There is nothing . . . nothing," he said, stressing the word by knocking heads with Jacques, "you can ever do anything to stop my love for you. And for the sake of that love I'm telling you, you must throw this woman away."

"*Pere,*" Jacques offered in a near whisper. "She carries your grandson inside her."

Renee released Jacques with a rough fling, throwing his arms skyward. "*Mon Dieu!*" he shouted. "Show mercy on this poor fool of a man who has fathered such a son. Spare his mother the disgrace of a Cheyenne daughter-in-law. Show us how. . . ."

"*Pere?*" Jacques timidly interrupted.

"Show me. . . ."

"*Pere,*" Jacques said louder.

"What is it?" Renee snarled, his arms still aloft. "You're interrupting my prayers."

"She isn't Cheyenne."

"What?"

"I said," Jacques repeated, "she isn't Cheyenne."

Color returned to Renee's face as he slowly lowered his arms, his eyes set on Jacques. "Not Cheyenne?"

"No, *Pere.*"

Jacques was treated to a rib cracking hug. "Oh," Renee

exclaimed as he held Jacques tightly. "You gave me such a fright. Your mother's father was killed by the Cheyenne. She would kill me if I brought one into the house. And Jacques," he added, dropping his voice a decibel, "you don't want to know what she would have done to you for having had sex with one." Suddenly feeling quite jolly, he threw a spare arm around Nicolas and heaved a sigh, filling the air with his frosty breath. "I feel better now," he said. "Much better." He bumped his head against Jacques's temple. "Of course I am still angry you married when you knew I said you couldn't. Still, the girl is pregnant, eh? You know this without a doubt?"

"Yes, *Pere*," Jacques said quickly. "The child is already kicking and the medicine woman said it's a boy child."

"Ha!" Renee boomed. "Of course it is a boy. Any fool would know that. When they kick early, it's always a boy. Now where is she? I want to see my daughter and place my hands on her belly and feel my grandson."

The brothers passed that look again. Renee was tired of this cat and mouse game they seemed determined to play. "Listen to me," he said, giving their necks a squeeze, "I have given you my forgiveness. You have said the girl is not one of our worst enemies so no matter what tribe she is with, I will be nice to her. I promise. It's a pity she isn't Crow but what is done, is done. My grandson will be Crow. And all of his brothers, too, eh?" He laughed, playfully increasing the pressure squeeze on their trapped necks.

"*Pere*," Nicolas wheezed as he clawed at the strangling pressure against his esophagus. "It would be better for you to meet her in private. She's a very shy person."

"Shy!" Renee shouted. "DeGeers are not shy."

"She hasn't been a DeGeer that long, *Pere*," Jacques managed in a rasping voice, his hands frantically pulling at his father's suffocating forearm. His face was turning a dangerous blue from his father's affectionate strangulation.

"That's true," Renee mused, ignoring them both as they writhed and kicked and tugged at his arms.

"*Bien*," Renee said resoundingly. "I will meet her in private. Jacques, I will go at once to your lodge."

"No!" both sons gasped, finally wrenching themselves free of his chokehold.

The sudden rush of cold air on his all but crushed Adam's apple proved too much for Jacques. He wheezed and hacked, wobbling on his feet, his hands at his throat as he slumped and staggered between his father and brother who blinked away his acute distress. Jacques had always been known to overreact to Renee's hugs. Habitually he appeared to be on the brink of death, yet despite the dramatics he had always managed to survive. And the less attention he received, the quicker he snapped out of it.

"It would be better if you came to the lodge provided for me, *Pere*," Nicolas said.

Still staggering around as if he were in his death throes, Jacques crashed into Nicolas's shoulder. Irritated, Nicolas pushed him away, ignoring Jacques's gurgling choking noises.

"You need to be cleaned up, *Pere*," Nicolas continued. "You don't want to frighten her with all that hair on your face."

"I have a nice beard," Renee said as he stroked the flame red whiskers.

Jacques finally stopped staggering around and stood off to the side, bent at the waist as he coughed up phlegm.

"Jacques," Renee blared. "Stop making that noise. You sound like an old woman passing wind."

"Your face looks like a menstruating beaver, *Pere*," Nicolas declared, still oblivious to Jacques's plight. "And you smell."

Renee patted the side of Nicolas's smoothly shaven face. "I'm glad you try to spare your old papa's feelings, my Nicky." He raised one arm and sniffed at his underarm, then rolled his eyes away and lowered his arm. "But I think you're right. I need to wash. I will go with you."

Jacques was puffing almost normally when they turned toward him. "I'm taking *Pere* with me," Nicolas called. "Give me time to clean him up before you bring your woman."

Weakly, Jacques waved farewell as he stumbled off in the opposite direction.

"Your brother has always had a very weak neck," Renee confided to Nicolas as they walked. "I think he gets it from your mother. I hope his son doesn't get it, too."

Rainbow was a most efficient girl. During her brief marriage of convenience with Nicolas, she had become quite the little expert in shaving a man's face, although finely haired Nicolas didn't have one-tenth the beard Renee possessed. While she carefully labored over Renee, Nicolas unpacked his father's belongings and aired a fresh winter shirt, glad to see his mother's fine hand in packing for Renee. Willow had included extra leggings, breechcloth and shoes. She seemed to know Renee would wear the clothing on his back until it rotted away. It very nearly had. It would take many hard scrubbings before the old shirt was wearable once again.

"This is a nice girl, Nicky," Renee said in French. He didn't dare speak Crow. The girl who was shaving him might understand it. "I don't blame you for making yourself comfortable with her. But you do remember you are a married man, eh?"

"It's something I never forget, *Pere*," Nicolas frowned.

"She cries for you, you know that?" Renee said as he eyed Nicolas. His son responded with only a slight shrug and a brief tilt of his head. "You are not impressed with her tears?"

"No," Nicolas grunted. "She cries about everything. She enjoys it."

Renee stopped talking as Rainbow scraped away at his face. Nicolas added more wood to the fire, heating the water his father would use for bathing. "You still don't love her, do you?" he said when Rainbow was finished.

"No," Nicolas answered without hesitation.

"She's much prettier than this girl," Renee ventured. "And she has become very, very sweet."

"I don't care," Nicolas answered. "I only married her because you told me to. I will have children with her because I know you will want them. But never ask me to love her. I owe you my life, but I can't give her my love just because you ask it of me. I promise you that when I am with her, I will be as kind and considerate as I can be. But when I am away from her, I will take other women. Women I choose."

"That's fair," Renee conceded. "But hear this. I will only recognize the children from her body as my grand-children. You can litter the prairies with hundreds more if you feel you must, but never bring them home to me. They will not be mine. You understand that, Nicky?"

"Yes, *Pere*," Nicolas replied, knowing full well Renee was lying. The day Renee turned away one of his grand-children would be the day the family dressed Renee for his burial. In his way, Renee was quietly transparent. His sons saw through his bluster more quickly than anyone else, Willow included.

And it was because Jacques knew his father so well that he had purposely impregnated Charlie.

The Flathead children enjoyed Renee's bath. They stood with hands over their mouths, giggling as Rainbow poured heated water over his head. Renee was completely naked, his body tanned only in certain places, and white in a larger portion of his flesh. He bellowed like a buffalo bull in the mating season as the water touched him and cooled instantly in the frigid air. Nicolas squatted outside the door opening, chuckling as he enjoyed the cigar his father had provided. He winked at the children as Renee tore the drying cloth from Rainbow's hands, drying himself roughly with it.

There was no person on this earth Nicolas loved more than Renee. His heart swelled with pride that this man had chosen him as his son.

Renee caught the wistful look on Nicolas's face. "What are you thinking?" he barked.

Nicolas slowly removed the cigar from his mouth and flipped an ash. "I was only thinking that I want you to live forever, my father."

Renee tied the dry cloth around his waist, waved an

arm, scattering the ogling children, and approached Nicolas. Standing over him, Renee took the cigar away from Nicolas and clamped it between his own teeth. "I will live forever," he said soberly. "You know that, eh? Through Jacques, you and Marie, I am an eternal person. I will always be on this earth as long as one of my children's children survive. That's why I'm not so mad at Jacques. My own immortality grows in the belly of that girl he has taken for a wife. I see myself now in little Cody who crawls around on my floor at home. I live for the day I will see myself in your children as well, Nicky."

Nicolas lowered his eyes. During moments such as these, he hated the fact of his adoption. He especially hated Renee's pretense at fancying to see himself in any of Nicolas's future issue.

"You seem to have forgotten," Renee drawled, reading his son's mind, "that to the Indian, an adopted son or daughter is closer to the parent than a natural child. A son born to you, you can disown. A son you adopt is your son forever, no matter how badly he turns out, or what disgrace he brings to your door." Renee paused, deeply inhaling the cigar smoke. With the cigar clenched between his teeth, he continued. "Your father . . . your natural father, was dying when I found him. You remember that, eh? But even as he died, he thought of you, wanting me to take you as my son. Taking another man's son is a very serious thing and besides, I had a son. I didn't want to adopt a little white boy. But to make him rest easy, I promised, and I kept my promise. You have always been very special to me for that, Nicky. You have grown into a man worthy of your dead father. In your children I will not only see myself and the fine job I have done with you, but my friend who died so well and trusted me so much. I look forward to loving your children with all the same passion I have known for you."

A single tear streaked Nicolas's face. He turned his head, trying to conceal it, but Renee's hand reached out and grabbed his chin, raising his head high with a snap. "Don't be ashamed," he said. "Never be ashamed to mourn a man like that. And always be proud of how, from the grave, he directed your life. You are my son only because of his courage. You are Crow because of him. Both of us will share our eternity through you. And in that place known as the Forever, I will be glad to walk beside him. We will both live on the earth through our shared son, Nicolas DeGeer."

"I love you, *Pere*," Nicolas blubbered.

"I know that," Renee gruffed, pushing Nicolas's face away, his teeth clamping down heavily on the cigar.

Jacques entered the lodge of his brother and stood nervously before his seated father. Renee was clean and refreshed and visibly excited.

"Where is she?"

Jacques inclined his head over his shoulder, indicating that his bride stood respectfully behind him. Renee rose to his feet and crossed the tepee, pushing Jacques aside. Charlie was bundled from head to toe, her face masked by the shadow of the hood pulled over her head.

"She is little," Renee laughed. "Are you sure she is all grown up?"

"She's grown," Jacques beamed with pride. "But remember, she is very pregnant so don't frighten her, *Pere*."

Renee led Charlie by her rabbit-fur gloved hand into the center of the lodge. "What do you think I am? A brute? I wouldn't frighten this tiny person. I only want to kiss her and welcome her into my family." Renee's smile slowly faded as he carefully removed the hood and the blonde hair spilled out. His mouth fell open and he was speechless as he stared at his new daughter-in-law. It was a long painful moment for all of them as Renee battled with the reality.

"She's . . . white," he finally managed in a croaking whisper.

Jacques watched as Renee's expression changed from confused torment to seething anger. He quickly stepped beside Charlie and placed a protective arm around her as his father's temper rose. Renee's face turned an ugly red and his voice thundered like the sound of a dozen cannons.

"She's white!"

Rainbow dove for the doorway, none of the combative principals concerned by her hasty departure.

Nicolas scrambled to his feet. "*Pere,* remember what you said," he pleaded. "You said you would welcome her as long as she wasn't one of our enemies. Well, she isn't. The whites are our friends. You tell us that all the time."

"Shut up, Nicky," Renee bellowed. "I know I say that all the time. I also say the buffalo are our good friends . . . but that doesn't mean I want one of my sons to run off and rut with a female buffalo."

"But I have married her," Jacques said flatly.

Renee gnashed his teeth. For the first time in his life he was tempted to beat his son. He kept his fists at his sides, fighting off the impulse to strike out. His body shook as if he were being held back by some invisible force stronger than he.

"You are not married to her," Renee heaved, his chest expanding and contracting rapidly. "I forbid you to be married to her."

"You cannot forbid something that already is, *Pere,*" Jacques shouted. With that, he drew the cloak away from Charlie's shoulders. He had insisted that Charlie wear the dress that had become too snug for her before presenting her to Renee. The dress was tight across her middle, and her breasts, preparing for the birth of her child, were heavy and swollen. The impact of Charlie's obvious condition was like a bucket of cold water thrown in the face of a drowning man.

Nicolas tried to put an arm around his father's shoulder as Renee turned his back on Jacques and Charlie. Renee roughly shrugged Nicolas off.

"Don't touch me, Nicky," Renee warned. "I might hit you."

Nicolas stepped back as Renee found his place and sat down, his legs too wobbly to hold him up any longer. Nicolas then walked over and stood by his brother. The three young people stood without speaking as Renee came to terms with their presence.

Renee washed his face in his hands, peeking at the three of them every few seconds through his splayed fingers. He tried to rub them out of his eyes but no matter how hard he rubbed, there they stood. Two traitorous sons and one pregnant alien. It was not a sight he ever expected to see.

"This is not going to work, Jacques," Renee said in a reasoning voice. "You cannot keep this woman."

"I have to," Jacques responded. "She's carrying my child."

"I didn't say you couldn't keep the child. The child is ours. I would never send the child away. The whites wouldn't want him anyway because of his Indian blood. But the woman, they will never allow you to keep her."

"But why not?" Jacques cried. "The whites are our friends. Why should they mind my having this one woman of theirs? White men marry our women and we don't mind."

"That is different," Renee shouted.

"Why is it different?" Jacques yelled. "Tell me why it is different."

"Because the whites are not that good at being anyone's friend," Renee boomed. "If they were better at friendship, I might not object to this little girl, but since they cannot be trusted, I have no choice but to refuse her."

The bewildered Charlie, quiet only because Jacques instructed her to be so, and because she didn't understand one word being said, finally caught Renee's eye.

Renee's heart went out to her. She looked so small, so pregnant, so utterly lost in the goings-on around her. Moved by compassion, Renee instructed Jacques to send the girl back to their lodge so that she wouldn't have to stand in her delicate condition amid all the arguing.

Jacques walked her outside, gave her an ardent kiss and told her not to worry, that everything would be all right. It was a lie he forced himself to believe as he tried to convince her. He watched until she was out of sight, then returned to do battle with his father.

It was a strange encounter. Once Charlie was out of the lodge, Renee's spirits seemed to lift. He had brought coffee with him from the Crow Reserve and insisted on making them all a strong pot which they enjoyed along with a round of cigars. Jacques and Nicolas were uneasy, waiting for their father's next tirade. Instead, Renee toasted his unborn grandson with coffee and suggested names for Jacques to consider. Renee said that his favorite name was Antoine and to please his father, Jacques promised that that would be the name of his son. At this juncture, Jacques would have promised Renee anything, so the name Antoine seemed a very small price to pay.

"You will stay with the Flatheads until after the child is born," Renee instructed. "I have never approved of pregnant women traveling, although Indian women do it all the time. This girl seems too dainty for that."

"She is strong, *Pere,*" Jacques replied.

"I don't care," Renee said with a flip of his cigar ash. "It's too great a chance to take. Nicky, you will return home with me. In the season when the leaves turn red on the trees, we will come back for your brother and his family, *oui*?"

"*Oui, Pere,*" Nicolas breathed in relief. The brothers looked at each other with wide smiles. Apparently, the storm was over. Everything would be fine. Jacques was to keep the woman he loved. His planned parenthood had turned the trick.

During the next weeks of life amid the Flatheads, Renee stayed away from Jacques and Charlie. He would only speak to Jacques when Jacques appeared without her. In her company, Renee passed them both as if the pair were strangers he wouldn't trust. This confused and hurt both of them but to keep peace, they let the snubbing pass.

"He'll like me better after I hold out the baby to him," Charlie assured.

"I know," Jacques said, trying to sound convinced and cheerful.

When the snow began to clear, Renee ordered his Crow out of the Flathead camp. Jacques stood watching as they mounted up. Charlie stood behind him. It broke both of their spirits when the Crow rode past them and nobody except Nicolas waved goodbye to them. Charlie felt Jacques stiffen in anger and she wondered: Why does Jock's daddy hate me so much? What did I ever do to him?

CHAPTER TWENTY

The muddy spring thaw made camp life almost unbearable.

"The earth has had enough of us in this place," the Flathead chief announced one day. "It is time to find new ground so that this land can recover from our wintering here."

Jacques and Charlie worked right along with their temporary tribe and moved out with them to higher and dryer country. The Flatheads were glad the young couple stayed among them. The pair were friendly and hard workers and Renee had promised thirty horses as gifts to the tribe for sheltering his son and daughter-in-law. It was more than a fair trade and everyone in the tribe was content with the temporary situation, especially Jacques and Charlie.

With Renee's departure, the strain the couple had endured the past weeks left with him and they once again enjoyed carefree days. Charlie learned how to be a proper Indian wife, spending her days with her willing teachers. During the nights, Jacques took on the task of teaching her French, but in this respect, Charlie was not a willing student. Jacques was on the verge of giving up when one evening he made her mad about something trivial and she fired off in perfect French, her stream of heated Gallic epithets amazing them both.

He grabbed her by the shoulders. "Do you know what you just said?"

"Yes," she gasped. "Yes . . . I knew exactly what I said."

Jacques hugged her swollen body against his. "Oh, Shar-lee, it was perfect. You sounded just like my mother yelling at my father."

"Jock," Charlie squealed. "Jock . . . I speak French."

"Yes you do," he laughed. "Yes you do."

"But when will Jacques come home?" Willow insisted. She watched Renee intently. Everyone seated at the kitchen table watched Renee, especially Nicolas.

"When the leaves turn," Renee grunted.

"But his wife should be here to have her baby," Willow said, unable to tear herself away from the subject. "I want to meet his wife. I want to be the one to help her deliver the child. She shouldn't be with strangers at a time like this, Renee. She needs to be with her new family."

Renee threw Nicolas a meaningful look. Then he passed the same look to Wolf's Tracks who sat on the other side of the table holding baby Cody on his knee. The look was meant to reinforce the charge he had made long before they parted company with their fellows.

"Tell no one about Jacques's wife," he had told them. "No one. There will be big trouble for all of our people if you do. This is a secret that must be kept until I can make things right with the major."

They all swore to leave out the details of Jacques's wife's nationality and report only the basic facts. Jacques had taken a wife. She was carrying his child and unable to

travel until after the baby was born. As if it were a dox-
ology, Renee repeated the same story to Willow.

"She must be carrying the baby badly," Willow mused.

"That's what we think," Renee agreed. "If you had
seen her, you wouldn't have allowed her to travel here
either."

Willow wrapped her arm through Renee's and leaned
her head against his shoulder. "I will be so happy to hold
Jacques's child in my arms." Cody gurgled and slapped the
tabletop with both of his chubby hands. "Oh you,"
Willow laughed. "I'll always want to hold you." When she
looked over at her husband and saw his saddened eyes, she
tried to cheer him up. "Soon, this house will be filled with
grandchildren, Renee. We will have to watch where we
step, there will be so many."

"Something is wrong," Eyes-That-Shine whispered behind
the closed door of their bedroom.

Nicolas ignored her as he tugged his shirt over his head.
She came near him and the touch of her hand against his
bare skin jarred him. He jumped and pulled away. "Leave
me alone. I told you there is nothing wrong."

"I didn't mean there was something was wrong with
you," she laughed. "I meant about Jacques."

"There is nothing wrong with Jacques," Nicolas
growled. He tossed his soiled clothing on the floor and fell
back on the bed. Naked, he lay there looking up at the
ceiling, his hands resting on his chest as he waited for her
to change her clothing, come to bed and put out the light.
He was tired; he was worried about his brother, and he
dearly missed the sweet-faced Rainbow, who had cried
copious tears when he bade her farewell. All in all, he was
in no mood to be cooped up in the same room with a nagging wife.

Eyes-That-Shine tried a new tactic. She grew quiet and
stood as close as she could to him while she slowly
removed her clothing. With her back to him, she heard his
heavy breathing and her heart raced as she imagined he
was becoming aroused. When she turned, she expected
him to be there, desire smoky in his eyes. This would be

the night, she thought, that Nicolas would finally make her his wife and give her the baby she so desperately wanted. She closed her eyes and murmured a prayer, giving thanks that her sweet-tempered ways and matured body were finally tearing down the wall between them. With a small fluttering movement, she turned around and there lay Nicolas. Asleep.

Eyes-That-Shine stood wobble-kneed on her bare feet. This new rejection was a terrible slap in the face and it was more than she could endure. Marie had a baby. Jacques was having a baby, all of her friends had babies, and what did she have? A husband who didn't care about her at all. It isn't fair, her mind raged. It simply isn't fair!

Her benumbed mind floundered as she desperately tried to think of what to do. Tears blinded her as she stared at Nicolas's hateful form. "I should divorce him," she fumed to herself. "Divorce him and find a new husband. One who wants me. One who will give me presents and say sweet things to me. I don't need all this hurt in my life. I don't." Straightening her back, she felt her resolve suffuse her with new strength.

She marched to her side of the bed, put out the lamp and crawled in between the covers. She tried to close her eyes but they kept snapping open, her anger keeping her solidly awake. As she flipped onto her back, she realized that hate, like love, must be shared or it will quickly lead to insanity.

"What?" Nicolas growled at the incessant poking of Eyes-That-Shine's finger. "Don't do that. You're waking me up."

"I only want to tell you one thing and then you can go back to sleep."

"All right, what is it?"

"Tomorrow I am going to live in the lodge of Paints-His-Face-Black. He has asked me to and I think it is best that I do that. Good night."

Nicolas's eyes popped open. He felt her turn over on her side as her words sank in. When they hit home he bolted upright. "You can't do that!"

"What?"

"You know what! You can't leave me."

"Yes I can," she yawned. "Now please, I would like to get some sleep. I have a lot of packing to do in the morning."

Nicolas grabbed her by the back of her hair and pulled her up beside him.

Eyes-That-Shine screamed.

"Stop screaming," he ordered. "You'll wake everybody up."

"I don't care," she fired back. But she did lower her voice before she spoke again. "I want them to know I'm leaving you."

"I order you to stop saying that. You are not leaving me. And you are especially not leaving me for Paints-His-Face-Black. He and I have never been friends and I will not allow him to count this coup on me."

Nicolas's head snapped back as her stinging slap burned his cheek.

"You cannot tell me what to do anymore," she hissed. "I have had enough of you. You think just because you are the most handsome man in the tribe that you can hurt my feelings and treat me any way you want to. Well, you can't, Nicolas. I am a person and I have my pride. Paints-His-Face-Black may not be a friend to you, but he has always been very nice to me and I know he will give me babies and *he* won't pull me by my hair and tell me to shut up."

Nicolas sat there with his mouth hanging wide open. "I'm the most handsome man in the tribe?" he asked stupidly.

"You know you are," she shot back. "That's why you're so mean. All handsome men are mean and *you* are their chief. That's why I'm taking Paints-His-Face-Black. He isn't handsome like you so he will be nice." She flopped back down and pulled the covers up to her chin.

Nicolas turned and looked at her, feeling the terrible silence that had crept into the room. Slowly he eased himself back down and lay facing her.

"Eyes-That-Shine," he said in a soft, urging voice, "I don't want you to leave me. It would cause a lot of trouble if you left. *Pere* has many worries on his mind and I don't think you and I should be the cause for more."

She turned a hate-filled face toward him. Not only could he see her hatred for him in the moonlight filtering in through the window, he could almost touch it. It was like a living presence, snuggling in for the night between the two of them.

"I did not marry your father, Nicky. I married you. If you can't be a husband to me, then I will not stay here and pretend to be a wife when I know only too well that I am not a wife. I am sorry my leaving will cause your father more worries but my life is short and I want to have a nice husband before I am too old to know what to do with one."

"But what can Paints-His-Face-Black give you that I can't give you?"

"A baby," she hissed like a snake.

"How do you know that?" Nicolas demanded. "Has he tried to give you a baby?"

"No," she smirked. "But only a few days ago he offered. He told me that when you got back, I should tell you I wanted to go to him. He said he would give me many presents if I did. He also said he would build me a big house and we would fill it with lots and lots of babies."

"He said that?"

"Yes he did. If you don't believe me, you will after I leave and he takes me as his wife."

"You know he only wants you so that he can embarrass me, don't you?" Nicolas hissed back at her.

The sound of her palm cracking against his face echoed off the walls, and Nicolas's ears rang from the vibrations.

"How dare you say that to me!" she wailed. "You are the most conceited man in the whole world. I tell you I'm leaving you and you worry first about your father and then you worry about being embarrassed. I'm glad I'm leaving you, Nicky, and I hope you die of the embarrassment. I'm just glad you never made love to me because now I can go with purity to my new husband and he will never have to wonder if I still love you and miss you. And one more thing," she huffed. "Paints-His-Face-Black really and truly loves me. He has loved me ever since he saw me bathing. He has been after me ever since that day and never once did he mention your name, except to say that I was too much woman for you."

Nicolas grabbed her shoulders and pulled her into his face. "When did he see you bathing?"

"I don't remember," she fumed. "It was sometime last season when you were gone. But you have always been gone. You can't expect me to remember every single day of your absence."

"I want to know," he growled, shaking her back and forth. "How is it you were with my mother and he saw you bathing?"

"I was with *my* mother," she yelped. She broke free of him and looked at him defiantly. "I went to stay with her for a while and I went bathing with my friends. He and four others followed and spied on us."

"You are a married woman," he raged. "You aren't supposed to go bathing with maidens. Men always follow maidens and spy on them. Jacques and I used to. . . ." his words trailed off guiltily.

"What?" she demanded.

Nicolas turned from her, but Eyes-That-Shine pulled him around to face her.

"You and Jacques?" she fumed. "You used to spy, too. That is what you were going to say. And now you're angry because another spied on your wife, paying you back."

"What I did as a young man is none of your concern. But what you do as my wife is my concern. I should beat you for this dishonor."

"Good," she cried, throwing off the covers and leaping from the bed.

She stood near the window, the moon shining down on her body. When Nicolas saw her soft silhouette, he realized that her body was far lovelier than he remembered.

"You go right ahead and beat me," she challenged. "Then I can show my wounds to your father as proof of what a terrible husband you are and he won't hold it against me that I have chosen another man over his precious son."

Nicolas was angry, yet at the same time he found himself sexually aroused.

"You want babies?" he said in a thick voice that half alarmed her. "I'll give you babies. I'll fill you up with babies."

Suddenly aware of the danger involved in this game she played, she began to quake inside. Her stomach sank to her knees and her heart lodged in her throat. Nicolas slowly left the bed and stood like a menacing stallion, advancing in slow, measured steps as she retreated, her arms folded across her bare chest in a futile effort to conceal herself from his narrowed and keen gaze.

"Nicky," she said in a voice that revealed her panic. "You better stay away from me. Nicky, I mean it!"

"But you said you wouldn't leave me if I gave you a baby," he replied, an evil leer stretching his mouth. "I can't allow you to leave me, so . . . I'm going to have to give you a baby."

"If you touch me, I'll kill you," she warned, her back bumping up against the wall.

Nicolas jumped before she could lunge away, and pinned her against the wall. Eyes-That-Shine began pelting him with her fists, but her blows had little effect delivered at such close range. His mouth covered hers, his tongue probing against her clenched teeth. She wriggled against him, trying to break his hold on her, but her struggles only inflamed him.

"I like that," he breathed against her ear. "You feel good. Wiggle some more."

Eyes-That-Shine's eyes flew open as he pressed himself against her, defying her efforts to push him off. "What's that?" she cried as his hardened phallus crushed against her.

"That's the baby maker," Nicolas rasped in her ear. "I'll show you how it works."

A loud crashing sound roused the household. Renee sat up in bed, grabbing up his rifle. "The Lakota!" he shouted, springing from his bed toward the window. He thrust the rifle barrel through the firing hole as he crouched, trying to sight the enemy. Willow remained in bed as she listened to the strange sounds. After a few seconds she slipped out of the bed and joined her husband, tapping him impatiently on the shoulder.

"It isn't the Lakota."

"Piegan?" Renee tensed, his eyes vainly scanning the darkness.

"No," Willow chuckled. "It's Nicky."

Renee jumped to his feet, facing his wife, who giggled and bit her lower lip. "Nicky?" he exclaimed.

Quickly Willow covered Renee's opened mouth before his baying brought an abrupt end to the honeymoon in progress down the hall. She crooked her index finger and Renee followed her to their bedroom door. She opened it just enough for both of them to pass through and they tiptoed down the darkened hallway. They didn't have to travel far. The noise met them halfway. They stopped and listened.

"Nicky!" Eyes-That-Shine cried. "The bed is breaking."

"I don't care!" their son answered thickly. "Just keep doing what you're doing. It's making me crazy."

Renee and Willow passed discomfited looks as the familiar sounds emitting from the young couple's bedroom reached a mutual peak. Renee and Willow tiptoed back to their room and closed the door.

"Nicky," Eyes-That-Shine gasped as he brought her near to orgasm. Her blood was on fire, her skin was alive and burning as her passion grew, threatening to incinerate her. She had desired him for so long she didn't feel any first-time pain. Her all-consuming lust for him had thrown off any discomfort as she welcomed him, finally, inside her. She wrapped her arms and legs around him as her pelvis rose against him. She wanted to become part of him, share the same heartbeat, breathe with the same lungs. She held him tighter and tighter, losing herself completely, melting into him until the pleasure was almost unendurable.

"Do it," he urged. "Let go. Let go, Shining Woman. Make your love on me."

"Don't leave me, Nicky."

"I won't," he promised. "I won't leave you."

"Nicky . . ." she gasped in a sharp inhalation of breath. "Something's happening."

"That's it," he cried, thrusting himself inside her one final time. He could feel her nails raking his back as he rocked against her. He felt her sharp teeth sink into the flesh of his chest as his undulations became slower. "Harder," he rasped, the mingling of pain and pleasure sending his mind to a new plateau. His head rolled back as he spent his last and heard her cry out as she entered into her own world of pleasure.

They crashed back into their bodies almost as violently as they had left them. Nicolas's arms lost their strength and he fell face forward into the pillows, barely missing the side of his wife's head. He knew he was crushing her but he couldn't move. He was paralyzed from the neck down.

"Nicky?" Eyes-That-Shine mewed after a few bone-crushing moments. "Nicky, you're heavy."

"I'm sorry," he said, his voice muffled against the pillow.

"I think you should get off me now."

"I can't."

"Should I help you?'

"Please. That would be very nice."

Eyes-That-Shine found it wasn't easy pushing off a one hundred and eighty pound man while lying in a slightly downhill position. One corner of the end of the bed had given way. The lower arch of the metal frame remained, but the mangled springs under the mattress had seen their last days of usefulness. The wrought-iron bed was an imploded ruin.

After several unsuccessful tries, Eyes-That-Shine pushed him off and Nicolas rolled over onto his back. A second later, the upper springs began to sing and snap. Nicolas felt the world slip out from under him as his side of the bed gave way completely. He shouted with surprise, sending his wife into a bout of shrill hoots as he landed in an absurd position, his arms and legs extended to the four corners of the earth. He looked over at his convulsing wife as she desperately clung to the remaining upper corner.

"You think this is funny, do you?"

"Yes," she sputtered.

"Fine," he smirked. "Laugh at this." He grabbed her ankle and yanked her toward him. When she landed on top of him, the last of the spring frame and mattress dropped to the floor with a rattling crash.

"What was that?" Renee shouted, popping up in bed.

Willow rolled over unconcerned, snuggling her face against her pillow. "It's only our children enjoying themselves," she drawled.

"If they enjoy themselves much more," Renee fumed, "the whole house will go."

"If it goes, it goes," Willow yawned. "I don't care as long as I get my grandchildren."

"Where is your husband?" Renee asked Marie as she shuffled back and forth between the stove and the cupboard. She found her father a cup and poured him some coffee. Renee accepted it and stood watching his daughter as she turned the bacon that was frying in the skillet.

"He's already out and working on our house," she replied in a flat, exhausted voice. "He said after last night we have to move out if we're ever to know a quiet night's rest."

"Wise man," Renee nodded. "How about them?" His chin went out as he threw his head in the direction of the hallway. "Are they awake?"

"I hope they're dead," Marie scoffed. "They kept Cody awake most of the night and the only way I could keep him quiet was to nurse him. Now my breasts are sore and my head aches. I hate Nicky. I wish you had left him with Jacques."

293

"His wife wanted him home," Renee said, trying to stifle his smile.

"Yes," Marie sighed. "And we all know just how happy she is to have him home again, don't we?"

Renee turned from his daughter before he laughed aloud. His son's nocturnal acrobatics had astonished everyone. During the night Nicolas's antics had been extremely annoying, but in the light of day, Renee couldn't stop chuckling. He sauntered barefoot down the hallway, curious to know if his son had survived his wife's welcome-home present. He opened their door and peeked inside. But even after all the wild racket of the night before, Renee was not prepared for the sight which greeted him. The crippled bed stood in the middle of the room like an open wound, threatening to cave in on itself. Directly underneath the broken frameworks, Nicolas lay on his back snoring the roof down. Eyes-That-Shine lay across him, covering him like a comforter, her head resting on his expanding and contracting chest.

"That boy is one demon of a lover," Renee chuckled proudly. Pride notwithstanding, Renee couldn't abide the fact that the person responsible for keeping the rest of the family awake during the night was now sleeping like a contented bull. He padded into the room, stood over the shell of a bed and emptied his cup of tepid coffee into Nicolas's open mouth.

Nicolas began coughing as soon as the coffee splashed his face and the back of his throat. His arms and legs thrashed as he awoke with a jolt.

"*Pere*," Nicolas hacked and sputtered. Eyes-That-Shine, thrown off of Nicolas, instantly recognized her nakedness and scrambled for refuge. Nicolas grappled with the twisted blankets and threw one over her where she hid underneath like a curled-up mole. "Why did you do that *Pere*?"

"I want you to enjoy the day with the rest of us, my son."

"But I'm tired," Nicolas shouted.

"We all are. And your sister hates you. I don't like you very much myself."

"Why is everyone mad at me?" Nicolas sulked. "What have I done?"

"Do you realize that I thought the Lakota were attacking the house last night? Then I find out, no, it is only my son destroying his bedroom. I'm throwing this bed away. And as long as you both live, you will never have another one."

Eyes-That-Shine tried to smother her laughter but both Nicolas and Renee saw her quaking beneath the blankets. Nicolas gave her fanny a swat as he looked from her to his father. With an embarrassed shrug he said, "That's all right, *Pere*, we didn't like this bed anyway. It was a little weak in the middle."

"Nicky?" Eyes-That-Shine said in a small voice. Nicolas was dressing with his back to her. He glanced over his shoulder and saw her standing with her knuckles against her mouth.

"What's the matter?"

"I think you should wear your shirt today."

"No," he said, irritated. "It's going to be a hot day. Too hot for a shirt."

"People will see your back," she replied softly. "Your hair covers most of it but when you move. . . ." She lowered her eyes in modesty, suddenly too shy to finish what she was saying.

Nicolas paused for a moment, then grabbed his hair in one hand and stretched his head around trying to peer at his own back. He couldn't see all of it but he saw enough. Red welts led from his spine to his hips. Then he looked at his chest and saw the teeth marks just below his clavicle.

"I'll wear my vest instead," he said with a slight smile. "That should cover everything, shouldn't it?"

She nodded bashfully as she fetched it from the chifforobe drawer. He crossed the room and accepted it from her, placing a tender kiss on her mouth. He lifted her chin with a crooked index finger and looked deeply into her large black-brown eyes.

"Shining Woman, if another man ever looks at you again . . . I'll kill him. You are my wife. You will stay with me forever. You understand?"

"Yes, Nicky," she said in breathy happiness. "I am your wife. Forever."

The summer months were like a peaceful dream. The Lakota were raiding to the north, the Blackfeet to the south. The Northern Cheyenne joined with their southern brethren and plundered the Santa Fe Trail along with the Kiowa. Though this was not welcome news for everyone else, the Crow were glad enough about it. They were free to hunt and enjoy the quiet days of an unusually hot summer with only the Shoshone and the Arapahoe to contend with.

Renee's sons, living miles apart, thoroughly enjoyed their lives and their wives. Jacques continually extolled the beauty of poor little bulging Charlie and kept her away from still ponds to avoid her horror at her own reflection. She was pregnant in every available spot beginning with her face and ending at her ankles. She looked so misshapen, the older women, unburdened by children of their own, began doing her chores for her more out of pity than for the reward of the gifts Jacques promised. None of the women could ever recall seeing anyone as pregnant as Charlie. The men laid secret bets that she was carrying a litter of three, possibly four babies.

Nicolas quit the raiding trail. He explained to Medicine Crow that he had been a year away from his wife and Medicine Crow agreed that the couple deserved time together. Their lovemaking grew even more wild and ardent and in order to maintain peace within the household, they discreetly took it outside. They made a love nest a mile away from the house where they loved one another without disturbing anyone except the fellow creatures of the night, who quickly escaped elsewhere, either to search for food or establish new habitats. The couple arrived home in the late mornings or early afternoons, both ravenous and exhausted. They slept the day away on the mat in their room, only to rouse themselves in the early evenings and leave again. They weren't aware until weeks after the fact that Marie and Wolf's Tracks had moved out into their own house.

In mid-June the brothers' separate lives merged, although they were both so far away from each other neither could share with the other their excitement. Nicolas and "Shiny," as he preferred to call Eyes-That-Shine, were waist-deep in the small unnamed river that ran through Renee's holdings. The little no-name river which would one day be called Cody Creek, was only a quarter-mile wide but it ran deceptively deep. Nicolas held on to his wife's hands as she entered the water because she wasn't a confident swimmer. As soon as he scooped her up in his arms preparing to tickle her, she screamed and begged him not to.

"What's the matter?" he asked, somewhat annoyed.

"I don't know," she whined. "I just . . . just don't feel very well. I feel. . . ." She didn't get the last words out. Up came the afternoon's biscuits and jam all over her alarmed husband. Nicolas whirled her around and held her by her waist, his palm bracing her forehead as she spewed vomitus into the fast moving water.

At that exact moment in Jacques and Charlie's tepee, one hundred and eighty miles away, Charlie cried out as her water broke, flooding their bed. Jacques, ever the cool one in battle, leaped to his feet and began screaming for her to stop that.

"I would if I could," Charlie bawled, "but it just keeps coming out."

Jacques raced out of their lodge, yelling for help as he ran through the sleeping village. After Knows Everything joined Charlie and exiled Jacques, the betting began with a renewed zest among the wide-awake men, some wagering as much as their homes on the outcome of the labor. Jacques was kept away from the lodge as Charlie labored all that night.

More and more women rallied to the aid of the new mother. So many, in fact, that they had to roll up the sides of the tepee to admit needed air for the laboring girl. None of the women worried that the men might see inside as Charlie squatted over a fur-lined hole, clinging with both hands to a stake in the ground as she pushed with each contraction. Men couldn't stay far enough away from a lodge where a woman labored. Birthing, while the natural order of life, gave Indian men the shivers and they wanted none of its mystery.

"I don't know what's the matter with me," Eyes-That-Shine wept against her husband's shoulder. "I lost my food on you. I'm so embarrassed. I'm sorry, Nicky."

"It's all right," he soothed, stroking her hair. "See? The water has washed us both clean. You're shaking. Are you cold?"

"No . . . I'm hot. It's so hot? Are you hot?"

"No," he chuckled. "But then I'm not the one with a baby in me."

Eyes-That-Shine pulled back from him, somewhat aghast. "What?"

He kissed the tip of her nose. "A baby, Shiny. You have a baby in you. My baby."

"A baby?" she whimpered. "A real baby? You're not teasing me are you, Nicky?"

"I would never tease you about something so important to both of us." He pulled her back against him and kissed her shoulder blade. "I love you, Shiny. I will never again love anyone else."

"Do you promise?"

"I promise. In front of the Creator Himself . . . I promise."

"Oh," she sobbed. "I have waited half my life to hear you say those words to me. The other half I have spent wanting your child. Now, I have both and I am so foolish . . . all I can do is cry."

"Shoo, shoo," he whispered against her ear. "Never be ashamed of tears that mean happiness. And never be ashamed of anything you do in front of me. You are my life and there is nothing about you I would change even if I could."

That made her laugh. "You used to want to change everything."

"You didn't have breasts then," he grinned impishly.

"What's happening now?" Jacques cried. It was almost dawn and no one was telling him anything. He paced a rut in front of the lodge of men who gambled at a dice game.

"These things take time," one old man ventured. "The women will tell us when it's all over. You should get some sleep."

"Sleep!" he cried. "I can't sleep. My wife is having a baby!"

"So you've said," the old wit returned.

Renee had been gone nearly a month. He returned home to find the house blazing with light. He entered, tired and saddlesore to find a party in progress. Eyes-That-Shine's parents were in attendance as well as half a dozen more of the Whistling Waters Clan. As he entered, his family members clapped him on the back.

"What's happening?" he asked as he glanced around. "Has something happened?" He was propelled toward the suddenly bashful Nicolas who stood with a sheepish grin on his face. "Nicky! What's wrong?"

"Nothing, *Pere,*" Nicolas continued to grin, his eyes darting around the room to the smiling faces of their assembled family. "Everything is right. Eyes-That-Shine is carrying your grandchild."

"She's what?" Renee looked stupefied. He whirled around, searching the room for her. "Shining Girl," he bellowed. "Where is my Shining Daughter?"

"I'm here," Eyes-That-Shine raised her arm as she wormed her way through the crowd toward Renee. Renee grabbed hold of her as if sending her a lifeline. He picked her up and hugged her as her arms went around his neck. "Oh, my girl," he groaned. "My lovely, lovely girl. You have made my life worth something. I thank you for that. I thank you for loving my son."

"And I thank you for forcing him to marry me," she whispered in his ear.

"He would have done that anyway," Renee chortled, kissing both of her eyes. "You are too beautiful to have stayed free of him for long."

He kissed her mouth quickly. "Whatever the child is, boy or girl, it will have all my love and my pride because it comes from you and Nicky."

"Thank you . . . *Pere,*" she sobbed happily.

CHAPTER TWENTY-ONE

The celebration lasted throughout the night. Bleary family members slept wherever they found space for their pallets. Jacques's room was crowded with bodies hugging the floor, while four people crammed his bed. Mrs. Pease would have found it all quite appalling had she been invited. Nicolas and Eyes-That-Shine's room was worse, as there wasn't a bed to hinder sleeping arrangements. Marie's vacated room rivaled her brothers'. Nicolas and Eyes-That-Shine sought refuge in the back garden, sleeping under the stars, Nicolas holding his sleeping wife in his arms. He lay listening to her even breathing. He was tired but his active mind wouldn't permit sleep. The night had been so special for the family and Nicolas missed the far away Jacques so badly he ached.

"Jacques should have been here," Nicolas said to the vast night sky. "Then tonight would have been perfect."

He tried to push away the nagging images which threatened to steal his joy. The images of a jubilant Renee celebrating his love for his daughter-in-law, Eyes-That-Shine. Nicolas tried to will away the guilt he felt as he remembered Renee's adverse reaction toward the pregnancy of Jacques's wife.

"*Pere* should have kissed Shar-lee. He should have said the things to her that he said to my wife. I'm glad Jacques wasn't here. Watching *Pere* would have made Jacques feel very hurt . . . and ashamed. I will never tell Jacques about tonight. Never as long as we both live."

Nicolas heard the back door open and heard footsteps on the back porch steps. Twisting his head, in the half light of the opened kitchen door, he saw Renee leaving the house, walking toward the horse barn. Nicolas raised up and watched as his father disappeared inside the barn, then reemerge a few minutes later carrying something. Carefully, Nicolas slipped out of his wife's sleeping grasp and silently followed his father into the house. He entered the dimly lit kitchen just as Renee placed a new shining rifle into a little-used cupboard.

"Hello *Pere*," Nicolas said.

Renee jumped as if he were a burglar caught in the act. When he saw Nicolas he froze.

"What are you doing still awake?" Nicolas asked, coming closer to Renee. Taken by the excellent craftsmanship of the rifle, Nicolas reached out for it. He was astonished when Renee slapped his hand away.

"No," Renee rasped in a loud whisper as he retreated farther from Nicolas. "This gun is not for you, my Nicky."

"I wasn't trying to claim it," Nicolas replied defensively. "I prefer my bow. But that looks to be a fine weapon and I only want to see it."

"I said no!" Renee barked, shoving the rifle out of sight and quickly shutting the cupboard door. "I don't want you to touch it . . . ever. I never want your hands on that gun. Promise me you will never hold it."

"But *Pere* . . ."

"I said PROMISE!"

The look in Renee's eyes was a trifle wild. Nicolas felt

bewildered, almost like an unwelcome intruder in his own home. Raising his hands in surrender, he began backing out of the kitchen. "I promise *Pere*. If it upsets you so much, I will never touch your gun."

Foam collected in the corners of Renee's mouth as he stared malevolently at Nicolas. "That isn't my gun! I hate the wretched thing. If I could destroy it . . . I would. You must never tell anyone about it, or touch it, Nicky. Now go back to your wife and forget all about this. Wipe the memory of this moment from your mind."

"Yes, *Pere*." Nicolas turned hurriedly and fled the house. He wasn't as careful getting back into the bedding as he had been getting out. His jerking movements stirred Eyes-That-Shine.

"What is it?" she mumbled in a half awake fog.

Nicolas took her in his arms and held on to her as tightly as he could, kissing the crown of her head. "I don't know," he returned in a worried voice. "I don't know."

"Boys!" Knows Everything proudly announced. Instantly a crowd of wagering men gathered around Jacques slapping his back as he stood numb and feeling a bit faint.

"How many?" one of the high-rolling gamblers demanded. Knows Everything held up two fingers showing her hand to the assembled crowd.

"Only two?" a loser lamented. "I wagered on three. Maybe she isn't finished yet! Go back and look again."

"She's finished," Knows Everything scowled.

"How is my wife?" Jacques managed above the din of cheering winners and groaning losers.

"She is sleeping." Knows Everything seized Jacques by the arm and dragged him away from the mob of men. When they were well enough away to speak privately, Knows Everything panted as they walked. "She had a bad time of it but she will be all right. Now I must speak to you about the babies."

Jacques's ragged nerves caused him to speak in clipped words. "What's the matter with my sons?"

The old woman shook her head rapidly as if she didn't have the time or the inclination to deal with his histrionics.

"One is perfect. He's big and has a lusty cry. The other is . . . small. I don't think he got enough food while inside your wife. The big one must have taken nearly all of it leaving just enough for the small one to survive its birth. So, I have given the small one over to my daughter-in-law who has a child still at the breast. My silly soft-hearted daughter-in-law hasn't taken her child off the breast as she should have because she has so much milk and she claims it hurts her when my granddaughter doesn't nurse. But it's disgraceful the way that child walks up to my daughter-in-law and demands to be nursed! It's not healthy for either of them and it shames me as a medicine woman. I'm using your son to break my grandchild from the breast. He needs the milk more than she does. Your bigger son can wait for food until your wife wakes up to nurse him. He is very fat." She paused in their walk and took Jacques's hand. "I'm telling you all of this because the little one may not live. I want you to know I am doing all I can to save him but it may not be enough because he is very weak. He might not even live through the night. Would you like to see him?"

Jacques's throat went dry as his grief mounted. All he could do was manage a slight nod.

"I'll take you to him."

Jacques entered the lodge directly behind Knows Everything. Jacques heard his son before he saw him. The baby made soft mewing plaints as if he were too weak to manage a sound cry. When the old woman moved out of his line of vision he saw the tiny infant which appeared even more miniature next to the abundant exposed breast it nestled against. In the quiet of the lodge Jacques heard the baby sucking madly. As Jacques bashfully neared, he looked down at the baby and saw its eyelids screwed down tight against the light of the fire, its little fist beating at the teat as if fighting for the food he had been denied while inside his mother's body. Jacques squatted down beside the stranger nursing his son. Knows Everything took a seat on the opposite side of the lodge cradling her jealous granddaughter on her lap.

THE GLORY DAYS OF BUFFALO EGBERT

"Thank you," Jacques said to the woman feeding his son. "Thank you for trying to help him."

The woman nodded shyly. Using her thumb and forefinger she pried the baby away from her nipple then held the naked newborn out to Jacques. "He nurses good," she said softly. "I think that is a good sign." The baby began to squall waving its arms and kicking its scrawny legs.

"He's still hungry," Jacques cried. Terror-stricken he pulled back his hands, afraid of the crying baby being offered over to him.

The woman snickered, amused by the warrior father's lack of bravery. "You can hold him while I clean the other breast," she insisted. Carefully, she placed the child in Jacques's shaking hands, her own guiding his as she silently aided the nervous father, helping him to learn the correct way to hold the baby's head with one hand and the little old man's wrinkled bottom with the other. She kept her hands under Jacques's until she was confident Jacques wouldn't drop the fragile baby.

"Antoine," Jacques breathed as he lifted the baby to his face. He gently placed a tender kiss on the baby's forehead and cuddled the child against his cheek as he murmured, "You are Antoine. You are the son of my heart. Please live, my little son. Live because your father loves you. Live because you look so much like your mother and I love her more than my own life. Please, you must try very hard Antoine."

"I'm ready now," the wet nurse said. Reluctantly, Jacques handed back his son. He sat for a moment watching as Antoine, like a blind nuzzling puppy, searched the breast for its nipple, found it, clamped onto it sucking loudly.

"He understood you," Knows Everything choked from the corner. Her little thumbsucking granddaughter stared in wonderment at the tears streaking her Na-ah's broad and deeply lined face.

Renee was his usual self the following day. So much so Nicolas began to believe the episode in the kitchen had been nothing more than a strange dream. As if to prove

305

this early afternoon theory, he bided his time, waiting until there was no one remaining in the house. The moment came when the entire clan gathered outside in the yard surrounding the house. More than half of the women and children had gone off to collect firewood while men readied the little-used barbecue pit and prepared the buffalo carcass for the spit and grill.

While Eyes-That-Shine basked as the petted center of attention, Nicolas excused himself, walking away from the house toward the stand of trees. He tried to tell himself he imagined the feel of Renee's eyes on his back. He walked a straight line disappearing amid the trunks and limbs of trees. Hidden, he watched his father until he felt certain Renee had forgotten about him.

Nicolas raced through the little forest until he was behind the outbuildings of the house. Using these various sheds for cover he darted between them, flattening his spine against the third and last. It was an extremely hot afternoon. Sweat glistened on his taut body as his eyes scanned the back of his parents' home and measured the distance. He knew that during the final sprint he would be fully exposed. If Renee were to see him it would be during these last few yards.

Nicolas was an excellent runner, but he knew his running would draw attention. Instead he began sauntering casually toward the back door, his mind busy fabricating excuses should he be challenged.

"I need to tie my hair back, it's uncomfortable on my neck."

"I have to get a fan for Eyes-That-Shine. She's getting too warm in the sun."

All of his excuses sounded reasonable and perfectly innocent.

"But why do I have to have excuses? It's my home! I have every right to go inside my own house!"

But to make his drummed-up excuses a reality, he first went directly to his room and grabbed the leather thong to tie back his hair and the fan for Eyes-That-Shine.

Reentering the kitchen he stopped and watched through the window. His father seemed to be enjoying the company of their brothers. He stood watching long enough to see the men in the backyard groan as they heaved the gutted carcass impaled on a thick metal rod and suspended it between the waiting tripods over the snapping fire. A second later, Nicolas ducked away from the window. Renee, turning toward the house with his arms folded against his chest, and laughing, just missed the sight of Nicolas spying on him from the window.

Nicolas sprinted over to the cupboard and opened the door slightly. The noon light filtered inside the darkened closet. The bright sunlight flashed a blinding glimmer off the flamboyantly etched silver stock and barrel. If Nicolas had seen the devil himself, he couldn't have slammed that cupboard door any faster. Standing with his back against the door, his blood racing in his ears, Nicolas now knew without a hope of a doubt that the previous night's occurrence had not been a bizarre, hallucinative dream. The gun was real. The unnerving encounter with Renee had been real. As Nicolas stood trying to absorb it all, a cloud high in the sky moved between the earth and the sun. The interior of the kitchen during that brief moment went very dark.

Four days after the birth of his sons Jacques cooed and made silly faces at his fat son, holding the pudgy infant exactly the same way he had learned to hold Antoine, except that with this baby there was so much more to hold. The newborn filled Jacques's hands. Unlike the continually crying Antoine, this baby was content and owned an agreeable personality.

"Francoise," Jacques announced. "This is Francoise." Full of pride, Jacques pressed his lips against the fat belly and bubbled a loud kiss.

From her bed Charlie watched her husband with their child. "Do you think your father will like him?"

Jacques threw her a wide grin. "Yes! He will love him. And our little Antoine as well. They are wonderful babies Shar-lee."

Raising herself onto the backs of her arms, she asked, "When will Knows Everything bring Antoine home?"

Jacques stopped kissing Francoise's tummy, stared

at her. "Perhaps tomorrow," he hedged. "Or the day after."

His flimsy reply worked against him. Charlie threw back the covers and left her bed. "Not good enough, Jock," she growled as she passed her horrified husband.

"Shar-lee!" Jacques cried after her. "No Shar-lee!" Finding himself encumbered by the wriggling baby, he was in a quandary. Francoise, sensing his father's fear and indecision, began crying and thrashing. But Charlie ignored her lusty son and her pleading husband as she marched off like a mother cougar in search of her missing cub. It didn't take her very long to find him. The wet nurse had become the main center of attraction as nearly all of the Flathead women surrounded her lodge. She and Antoine were the tribal curiosities. Charlie pushed a cluster of women aside and entered the lodge uninvited. The women inside made room for her as she walked over, taking a seat beside the woman holding Antoine to her breast. Charlie held out her arms saying simply, "Give me." A moment later the engorged Antoine lay in her arms, milk on his rosy cheeks, his closed eyes relaxed in blissful slumber.

"Oh, he's beautiful!" Charlie exclaimed. "He's so beautiful. He looks like Jock. Exactly like Jock." She ran a tender hand over the dark downy crown. She pulled back the soft doeskin blanket to further examine her baby. His fists were clenched as if ready for a fight. His tiny toes were curled under but splayed out as she ran a finger against the bright pink soles of his feet. His puckered mouth began sucking silently. Judging from the roundness of his bloated belly and seeing the pale haggard face of the woman who had been tending him, Antoine had been nursing steadily all through the night. Charlie lifted him closer to her face and inhaled his scent. He smelled clean and fresh and new. The odor of death was nowhere near him. He might be small, but he was healthy . . . and he was hers.

"Thank you," she said respectfully. "You saved his life for me. I will always love you for what you have done for my son." She kissed the woman's cheek, rewrapped her baby and took him home.

THE GLORY DAYS OF BUFFALO EGBERT

Jacques stood outside their lodge in a frenzied state, a naked screaming Francoise in one arm, an indescribable smear all over Jacques's arms and midriff that matched the blackish slime covering Francoise's bottom exactly. "Shar-lee!" he yelled in relief as he caught sight of his wayward wife. "Shar-lee help me! There so much . . . Stuff is coming out of him!"

Charlie knew next to nothing about the care and feeding of newborns but, faced with Jacques's terror, she forced herself to remain calm and appear confident. Moments after entering their lodge she had both father and son cleaned, Jacques quieted, Antoine snuggled in the bed and Francoise at her breast. When the sounds of Francoise's robust nursing woke Antoine, Jacques sat back in awe of his wife as she managed both sons at her breasts expertly.

"Nothing to it!" she chirped.

It was a pronouncement Charlie wasn't to hold for long. Three days later Charlie waved the white flag and Jacques found himself out of his home as both the wet nurse and Knows Everything moved in, holing up inside the lodge with Charlie until her milk supply was able to meet the needs of both greedy children. Without the comfortable hubbub of his family, Jacques was like a lost puppy wandering from tepee to tepee gratefully accepting shelter and companionship when he wasn't out hunting to repay all the favors done on his and Charlie's behalf. He wasn't happy that whenever he went near his own tepee, Knows Everything stood on guard shooing him away like a stray dog begging scraps. Charlie was either feeding their sons or napping and while she was thus engaged he was not allowed inside his own home.

CHAPTER TWENTY-TWO

During the first six weeks of his grandsons' lives, Renee was absent from the DeGeer stronghold. He had departed the second time four days after the family celebration. When Nicolas questioned his mother, Willow shrugged off Renee's sudden departure saying he was scouting again for the fort. Fostering a nagging suspicion, Nicolas rode over to the fort and chatted with the other Crow scouts. He didn't know why, but he was relieved to the marrow to find Renee's story to Willow proved true. The new commander of Fort Ellis, Captain Tippleton, had arranged a parlay with the Northern Cheyenne. The Santa Fe Trail was in a strangle-hold with the Southern and Northern Cheyenne in league with the Kiowa. Their allied raids were taking a toll on the pilgrims foolhardy enough to use the trail during this particularly disastrous summer. The westward pioneers were undergoing a severe trouncing.

And the Indians were also hitting the American government where it lived—in the pocketbook.

Innocent lives aside, the results of the summer raids were exorbitant. In stolen mules alone, the Indians were profiting in the thousands of dollars. The tribes were stealing army mules and then selling them back to various forts at bargain rates. The Indians could afford the low offers because they quickly stole the mules back again, peddling them elsewhere.

One mule with a telltale white star on its left jaw was recorded as being purchased by the army no less than forty-seven times at different posts in Colorado, Oklahoma, and East Texas. Each purchase of the starred mule cost the army the allotted amount of twenty-five dollars of assorted dry goods and ammunition. After the forty-eighth abduction the yo-yo mule reappeared in New Mexico as the property of a Mexican farmer. Infuriated, the army took legal steps and an informal hearing was held by the exasperated army officials. At the impromptu trial the farmer readily swore on two Bibles that he had raised the animal from a colt. Luckily, fifteen Kiowa were on hand to back up the farmer's story as they had enjoyed a long acquaintance with the accused Mexican.

The horrific summer wore doggedly on. The Comanche sacked and pilfered the beleaguered Texas, a state still destitute and impoverished from having been on the losing side of the Civil War. The Arapaho laid siege to Denver and countless civilians died of starvation and disease while the governor of Colorado begged for help. The Santa Fe Trail, because of the unity of the Cheyenne and Kiowa, had to be closed to pilgrims as the waning manpower of the army proved unable to defend it. The Lakota freely ranged wherever their allies needed them most. The Blackfeet blazed new paths of destruction into Old Mexico, seeming to have decided on an exotic holiday in tropical climes. The Mexican government screamed for Washington to do something before they were forced to declare war on America. The threat wasn't taken seriously since it was apparent Mexico was unable to fend off the Blackfeet successfully. But to save the face of the "good neighbor" to the south, Washington did its best through diplomatic channels to still the clinking of well-rusted sabers.

Captain Tippleton first arrived at the Crow Reserve in the early spring, arrogant and self-important with his gleaming brass and tailored uniform. He was an impressive young man both in appearance and bearing. A graduate of West Point, he could recite army regulations in his sleep.

During the first weeks of Tippleton's command of Fort Ellis, Renee sat back and watched the young officer fall victim to the commission of all the time-honored errors. Renee thoroughly enjoyed new officers. He saw every one of them as comical. During the inexperienced officer's first days, Renee enjoyed Tippleton enormously. When Tippleton's authority and prestige began to crumble around him and he grasped that his career was hanging by a thread, he showed a flash of good sense. He hastily sent for Renee.

Tippleton's superior ego again almost proved his ruin. During their first face-to-face meeting, he had the audacity to try to intimidate Renee. He intentionally kept Renee waiting in the outer office for over an hour. Then, when he elected to spare the lead scout a moment of his valuable time, he added more fuel to the insult by commanding Renee to stand at attention while inside his office. Had there been a chair available, Renee would have taken it. As the only chair obtainable obliged Tippleton, Renee instead leaned lazily against a wall as he insolently lit a cigar.

Tippleton's fair-complected face went purple in fury. "I understand you're a renegade," Tippleton scoffed sarcastically.

"Ah, *oui*," Renee agreed readily with an aloof nod. "And I understand you're an idiot."

"What?"

"I believe I have repeated the gossip of the fort plainly *mon capitaine*. Everyone, especially my Indian brothers, say, 'Don't work for that man, Renee. He is worse than a sun-mad fool. If you leave him alone, he will be gone from here very quick.'"

The blood drained from Tippleton's arrogant face. He would have thrown Renee out on his ear had it not been for the fact that Renee was his only hope of surviving this

312

command and both men knew it. The morale of his regular army enlistees was desperately low. The numbers of the summertime reserves were ebbing away as many of the change-of-heart volunteers deserted in the night to return to their farms or strike out for the gold fields. Even reliable Crow scouts were becoming harder to find. The Crow were "hunting" more than anyone ever remembered them needing to.

"But *why* do the Crow need to hunt animals that are moving like brown valleys through the countryside?" Tippleton raged at his second-in-command. "Buffalo are everywhere! Every day I receive fresh complaints of buffalo trampling farm crops and kitchen gardens all over Absaroke. Why can't the Crow shoot the buffalo closer to home?"

Renee's drawling voice brought Tippleton back to the moment. "Don't take life so hard *mon capitaine.*" Renee smiled as if he had read the other man's thoughts. "There are only two things in this life a man ever truly owns. One is the love he feels in his heart. The other . . . the mistakes he makes. Everything else is on loan. *Comprenez-vous?*"

"Yes," Tippleton replied weakly. He turned his face away and with one hand motioned toward a closed door at the far end of the office. "You'll find an extra chair in that storage closet."

"*Merci, mon ami.*"

They began their two-year acquaintance on this somewhat shaky ground. The young captain quickly learned to respect Renee's opinions as well as trust them. Renee advised and directed the younger man with a fatherly concern. As well as they learned to work with one another, neither entertained the notion of inviting one or the other into his home. The boundaries of their friendship had, from the beginning, been clearly drawn. Renee was an "Indian-man." The Captain was an officer and a gentleman. For the captain to invite Renee into the private splendor of his living quarters he would run the risk of censure from his fellow officers. And for Renee to welcome the captain into his home meant he would have to call the man his "brother." Renee had long ago abandoned all hope of being a brother to another white man. The only whites he had known to be worthy of the title were long dead. For those long-buried frontiersmen had been the old breed of white men. They had been white men actually seeking to be brothers with the Indian. The new white men among them only saw the Indians as a "problem." The captain was one of the latter whether the young man chose to admit it or not. Therefore, there was no room for Captain Tippleton at Renee's table. Renee's only reason for aiding any officer of the fort, especially the commander, was his original aim, to guide the Crow allies in the direction most beneficial to the Crow people. He really didn't care a whit that his instructions led to the promotion and reassignment of the officers he tutored. They were quickly replaced with new officers in need of his wisdom and cunning. In Washington's distorted Indian policies, Renee had found job security.

"What the hell are we going to do about the Northern Cheyenne, Renee?" Tippleton ranted. "That potato-faced Sherman is yelling at me because, *my* Cheyenne, as he so fittingly phrases it, are running riot with *his*!" Tippleton slammed an opened palm down on his desk top. "*My* Cheyenne!" he repeated like a curse. "As if I personally owned an entire nation of Indians for God's sake! And then he sends me this letter full of woe about the Kiowa sending him over the brink! That sonofabitch inoculated the Kiowa against the pox! Now that they're all healthy and on the rampage he wants *me* to feel sorry for *him*!"

Renee leaned back in his chair, bit off the butt end of a fresh cigar and lit it. "Have you ever thought of money?"

"What?"

"Money," Renee repeated, mouthing each syllable.

"Money!" Tippleton roared. "God's eyes, Renee! Have you gone stark raving mad? What the hell has money got to do with anything? Indians don't want money!"

"Whoever told you that has his head so far up his back end he breathes through his belly hole." When Tippleton continued to stare silently, his disbelief still evident, Renee sighed heavily. "Indians love money. They kill for it every day. But, is that not what all wars have ever been about, *mon ami*? Money? White men came to the Indian and taught them what money was and what it could do. Now, they like it."

Tippleton fish-eyed Renee for a long moment. Then he opened his cigar box, took out a cigar, extravagantly bit off the end tip, spat it to the floor. He lit the tobacco, poured two glasses of brandy, shoving one glass across the polished table in Renee's direction. Both men lifted their glasses in a half salute. "Convince me," said Tippleton.

Renee savored the brandy, rolling it on his tongue before swallowing it. He knew he would have to chew fresh blades of grass before going home to prevent Willow from smelling the alcohol on his breath. If she suspected he had been drinking there would be hell to pay. His Crow brethren would have a few well-chosen words to add as well. The Crow had always been violently opposed to alcohol and punishment was always swift in the offing for any of their number caught with whiskey. Those caught dallying with crazy-water were bound and gagged, then left in the center of the village to be ridiculed for twenty-four hours. Following this humiliation the criminals were lashed between two trees and publicly beaten. The severe punishment proved to be a working deterrent, for there wasn't a Crow alive and proud of his status as a warrior who was tempted by the dubious delights of John Barleycorn.

"There is a particular Kiowa chief your general writes in complaint of. Have you guessed why this man is more bothersome than the rest?"

Tippleton shook his head.

"This man is named Satanta. He has been described to me as a big man who is loud. Very loud. I am also told he's the richest of the Kiowa. Satanta seems to me to be a man who knows the value of a dollar. And the value of white women. While I have never met this man I believe I know how he works his game against the whites. First he catches white women. According to reports he found out some time ago that women are easier to chase down than mules and worth more in trade. He keeps the women for a little bit, but," Renee warned, wagging a finger at Tippleton, "never assume the women are for his pleasure. He never touches them. They would lose most of their value if he slept with them . . . so he leaves them alone. When they are ragged and half-starved he takes them to a fort to sell them off. Just before he gets to the fort he stops a little way off and he makes obscene gestures, tricking the women into believing he is going to rape them after all. When they are suitably crazy with fear, he then takes them into the fort where the women cry and beg the soldiers to buy them from the chief before they are forced to suffer the 'fate worse than death.' Satanta sometimes gets as much as three hundred dollars for one scrawny white woman. Now . . . tell me again that Indians don't like money."

"You sound as if you half admire him," Tippleton replied, taking a harder look at Renee.

"I do," Renee quipped, flashing a smirk. "Were it not for the fine paying jobs the army give my Crow brothers, I would point them in that direction myself. As I say, white women are easy to catch, and they are worth more than mules."

"So I should offer the Cheyenne money," Tippleton mused, swinging his swivel chair off to the right, his cigar poised in one hand as he considered the notion.

"Ah, *oui*. You pay them to come home and they will be back to fast we will choke on their dust."

The suggestion became more and more appealing as Tippleton pondered it. He puffed on his cigar turning the air around his head a dingy blue-gray. Absently fanning away some of the smoke he asked, "How much should we offer them?"

"Ten thousand."

Tippleton bolted upright in his chair coughing and hacking, his eyes wet with tears. In a wheeze he managed, "Ten thousand?"

"*Oui*. Is a small price when you think your government has lost twice that already and the summer is still hot. The Cheyenne still have plenty of time to do more than ten thousand dollars' worth of damage before the leaves change and they wander home. But if you don't get them back before that time *mon capitaine*, you are a finished man. Your general will throw you out himself, eh?"

Without another moment's hesitation Tippleton snapped, "Make the arrangements, Renee."

"Bon." Renee left that same afternoon, returning two weeks later to enjoy the family celebration held in honor of Eyes-That-Shine's pregnancy.

Nicolas mounted his horse after his whiling away the afternoon visiting with the lay-about Crow scouts. All of the off-duty scouts seemed rather cheerful regarding Renee's current mission. They laid wagers that the Cheyenne chiefs would drag their feet during the negotiations with the army while their braves continued to plunder the countryside. Then the Cheyenne chiefs would accept the peacemoney, only a week or two before their own scheduled departure. In doing so, the Cheyenne could maintain they had come home early as agreed, pocketing the government's money fairly.

Nicolas laughed with his brothers, believing the charade as comical as the rest. He shook his head slowly as he looked from atop his horse toward the south where his father bargained with the Cheyenne.

A seated, army-hatted Crow shook his head saying, "Renee's a good talker, but even he can't out talk the Cheyenne. No one can argue with the Cheyenne. They're all crazy. A man will go farther in life turning around and arguing with his own behind. It's better just to leave the Cheyenne alone, like we Crow, only bother them after they have bothered us first."

"You're right," Nicolas agreed. "But still, *Pere* has to do something. The Cheyenne are bothering the southern whites."

That statement produced a large round of guffaws. Another scout waved an expansive arm southward. "The whites down that way are just as crazy as the Cheyenne. I say go ahead and let them all fight. No one needs any of them. The world would be a better place if they would all just get off of it."

Nicolas walked into the kitchen where his mother and wife stood shoulder-to-shoulder preparing the evening meal. Before pausing to greet either of them he marched straight toward the dreaded closet, opened it and found the mysterious gun missing. Surprising both women, Nicolas began laughing loudly at his own private joke.

"Nicky?" Eyes-That-Shine called. "What is it?"

"*Pere!*" he boomed. "I know now how *Pere* is really talking to the principal Cheyenne chief!"

"Oh, him," Willow shrugged, going back to her task of peeling an onion. Nicolas crept up behind her and wrapped his long arms around his mother, burying his face in her neck.

"Do you know that *Pere* is the smartest man in the world?"

"I know he says he is," she smiled, enjoying Nicolas's affection. "What has he done now?"

"I can't tell you," Nicolas said quickly, kissing Willow's neck. "It's a secret. But the next time *Pere* tells you how smart he is, Mother, believe him."

"I'll try," Willow sighed.

Antoine miraculously gained weight. As his face and tiny arms and legs filled out it became blazingly clear that the babies were identical twins. Both of them were exceptionally bright, alert to their surroundings and eternally hungry. After four weeks of life, they could lift their heads while lying on their bellies, focus their eyes, smile and drool small hiccuping laughs.

After the babies settled into a manageable feeding schedule Jacques was finally allowed to move back in with his family. A happier man never lived on this earth. He tried to teach each son his own particular name but with little success. They both answered to anything, especially the sounds of one or the other nursing. The zeal which they employed against Charlie's breasts appalled the slightly jealous Jacques.

"You know when they are able to walk they are going to attack you, don't you."

"They're attacking me now," she moped. "But I'm dreading the day they're able to set traps for me and wrestle me to the ground."

THE GLORY DAYS OF BUFFALO EGBERT

.　　.　　.

Renee returned from his second meeting with the Cheyenne after an absence of four weeks, reporting that the Cheyenne were homeward bound and still in the mood for mischief. The Crow Nation geared itself against that event, somewhat despondent that their peaceful summer days were drawing to an end. If, as Renee reported, the Cheyenne were still in the raiding mood, the Crow would become their primary target. The Cheyenne fixedly believed the Crow to be enormously wealthy after so many seasons of close association with the whites. It was to be expected that the Cheyenne would set their sights on that wealth. General Sherman, though he did not communicate further with the commander of Fort Ellis, began to feel the relief of the Northern Cheyenne's absence. Captain Tippleton, now under pressure, wasted not a moment in stabilizing his defenses against their presence.

Renee's homecoming was to be brief. "We have to go get Jacques," he announced at the supper table his first night home. "And we must go quickly while it is still reasonably safe to travel. Wolf's Tracks voiced his agreement and volunteered to go along. Nicolas, too, volunteered eagerly.

"*Bon,*" Renee gruffed. "I'll get five more men to ride as escort and three strong boys to herd the horses I promised the Flatheads." Looking about the table, Renee finalized the planning. "We will leave day after tomorrow. Woman," he said, absentmindedly rubbing the curvature of Willow's spine, "pack well. Pack lots of food. Don't slow me down with extra clothing because if you do, I'll only throw it away. We have to be light if we are to make good time and protect the infant from harm."

"Do you think the child is old enough to survive such hard travel?" she asked, working her fingers in a rapid counting off of the months.

"I wouldn't go if I believed the journey home would endanger the child," Renee assured her.

The following day the DeGeer kitchen teemed with activity. The three DeGeer women labored all day

preparing the food containers. Willow was in a happy
dither knowing that in a few weeks she would have her
son, his wife and their child under her roof. She drove her
two daughters relentlessly. Marie and Eyes-That-Shine
exchanged wary looks as Willow vocalized the list of
things that would have to be done to prepare for Jacques's
homecoming.

"She's going to work us like slaves," Marie muttered.

"I know," Eyes-That-Shine whispered in turn. "But this
is so important to her. We must work our hardest and try
not to complain. She has missed Jacques terribly."

Marie looked at her sister-in-law with a new-found
respect. "You know, you really are a very sweet and considerate little person."

Eyes-That-Shine blushed at the compliment. "I . . . I
just love my family. I am proud to be part of it."

The next morning the men sat on their horses waiting
impatiently for Nicolas to finish kissing his wife goodbye.
As the rising sun crested the horizon, Nicolas gave his last
instructions to his teary-eyed wife.

"You must be careful about yourself," he warned.

"I will," she promised.

"And no visiting your mother."

"Yes, Nicolas."

"When you feel tired, you must rest no matter how
much work needs to be done."

"Nicolas!" Renee thundered. "Either mount your horse
or I will drag you out of here by your hair!"

"Yes *Pere*," Nicolas called back. Embracing Eyes-That-
Shine one last time he murmured, "I love you Shiny. I will
miss you very much."

Eyes-That-Shine nodded quietly, her tears speaking for
her. She watched her beloved husband as he ran toward
his horse and executed a perfect leap onto the animal's
back. She waved farewell, standing with Willow and
Marie. Together they stood and watched until the men
and horses were small dark images against the full red of
the giant rising orb ascending from its sleeping place at the
center of the earth.

"Nicky seems worried about Paints-His-Face-Black,"
Willow confided in a curious tone. "He told me to shoot

320

him if he comes around here. He acts as if you might be stolen while he is away."

Eyes-That-Shine sputtered uncontrollable giggles. The other two women watched her in bewilderment as she threw back her head, her body quivering with laughter. "Paints-His-Face-Black doesn't even know I'm alive!"

Willow instantly caught on to the joke though Marie remained quite clearly in the dark. "You are a little monster," Willow teased her nearly hysterical daughter-in-law.

Eyes-That-Shine gasped sharply, sending a worried look to her mother-in-law. "Oh! You won't ever tell Nicky, will you?"

"Never," Willow chuckled, giving her daughter-in-law a slight squeeze. "Worrying about another man seems to do him a lot of good."

"Antoine is rolling too much," Jacques complained. "Isn't he supposed to crawl on his knees?"

"Not yet," Knows Everything chuckled. "He is still too young. He really seems to enjoy the rolling doesn't he?"

"I wish Francoise would roll," Charlie complained. "He just lays there getting fatter and fatter. Sometimes he will kick his legs, but mostly he just smiles and waits for his next meal."

The lodge had grown too hot to live in during the Indian summer afternoons. Jacques had fashioned an opened shelter of poles and thatched roof. The family inhabited the wildwood gazebo during the hottest part of the day with the babies lying naked on soft blankets enjoying the shade and wafting cooling breezes. The curious little family was on display for any and all who wished to sit in the shade and pass the time with them.

The children of the village adored Francoise. He rarely complained and didn't cry when they passed him back and forth or carted him around like a living doll. Antoine wasn't that obliging. He only allowed his mother or his father to hold him and even then only when necessary. He favored his own activity. He was happiest on his stomach lying on his blanket where he airplaned his arms and made bubbling sounds or found something strange to stick into his mouth for an exploratory taste. Though he shared the same face with his older brother, the babies were still easy to tell apart, as fat didn't seem to stay with the hyperactive Antoine the way it adhered itself to the tranquil Francoise.

"May we play with Francoise?" a group of little girls asked timidly.

Both Jacques and Charlie readily agreed and the happy girls scooped up the pudgy baby, the eldest girl expertly hoisting him onto her hip, balancing him easily as off they went to play house in their miniature tepee with their live baby to mother. Jacques and Charlie enjoyed an afternoon of relaxation and peace ... until the Crow came thundering in.

Jacques jumped to his feet and raced toward the approaching Crow, waving both of his arms over his head and jumping up and down excitedly. Nicolas leaped from his horse and the brothers collided, hugging one another, turning each other around crazily as they embraced. The rest of the Crow dismounted, each warrior beaming as he took his turn hugging Jacques. Charlie saw her husband's face stream with happy tears as he welcomed his kinsmen.

"You got a hug for your father?" Renee growled as he approached the group of men.

"*Pere!*" Jacques exclaimed, throwing himself into Renee's opened arms. "Oh *Pere*, I have missed you so."

"What did you think? That I would leave you to become a Flathead?" Renee challenged, holding his son tighter. "I said I would come to bring you home and I have." Pushing Jacques back just enough to look at his son's beautiful face, Renee asked in a graveled voice, "Where is my grandchild?"

Jacques wiggled out of his father's arms and excitedly took Renee's hand, dragging him away from the group. "Come." Then he called to the rest of his brethren, "Come. I want you all to meet my family."

Charlie retreated from the advancing procession, a steady dread growing in her heart. "Why did he have to come back?" she asked herself. "Why couldn't he have just left us alone?" She almost hated Jacques for the look of sheer happiness on his face as he led his father toward her. "I want them to all go away! All of them!" her soul screamed. "Even Nicky! I want to stay with the Flathead people. They love and accept us. Why do we have to go and be with the Crow? Jock's afraid of his father! I know he is. Go away! Go Away!"

But she knew Renee would never go away. And she knew that they would leave the security they had known and go with the Crow because Jacques wanted to go. He would never feel completely whole without his family or his people no matter how much he loved her or his sons. He needed the rest of his family with an intensity she knew she would never understand. And she loved him so much she never allowed him to see her pain when he talked of "going home."

Her apprehensions and fears mounted with each step the approaching group took. She recognized the Crow as the same men who had come the first time. She didn't know their names but their immobile faces had been burned into her memory. Their cool manner toward her was still unchanged though Jacques seemed oblivious to it. She stood to one side in the shelter as they clustered around the baby on the blanket. Renee, grudgingly, managed a curt nod in her direction. It was much the same gesture he might use against a cur dog to warn the stray off. Charlie retreated another step, standing outside the circle of men and hoping against vain hope.

Renee lifted the baby high in the air holding the infant over his head and laughing as Antoine yowled. "He is wonderful!" Renee shouted. "Antoine! My beautiful Antoine! I am your *Pa-Pere*! I have come to take you home little baby man!"

"Shar-lee," Jacques said to his wife in French. "Go get Francoise for *Pere*."

Renee looked at Jacques with puzzlement as he tucked the crying Antoine in one arm.

"You see, *Pere*!" Jacques glowed with pride as Charlie scooted off. "I have taught my wife to speak the language of our family. And she speaks a little of the Flathead tongue and some Crow as well. She's a good cook, too. You will eat with us tonight. Shar-lee will fix everything."

"Who is Francoise?" Renee asked, cutting through the boasting of his son.

"Your other grandson," Jacques laughed.

"There are two of them?" Renee asked as if stricken.

Jacques continued to laugh as he held up two fingers, nodding enthusiastically. "Two. Antoine and Francoise. *Pere!* I made for you your own tribe."

Renee grabbed on to the back of Jacques's head, hugging Jacques's face against his own. He planted kisses on Jacques's eyes. *"Mon Dieu,"* Renee breathed.

Jacques and Charlie's lodge was filled to overflowing. The sides of the tepee were rolled up, the cool twilight air circulating and refreshing the seated Crow as Charlie and her two women assistants darted in and out, serving an elaborate evening meal. Renee's platter sat untouched before him. He wouldn't let go of his grandsons, not even to eat. The scowling Antoine had stopped crying, seeming to have abandoned all hope that this strange man would ever release him. Francoise loved the attention and gurgled happily while his brother sat sullen on Renee's other leg.

"I want to hold one of them *Pere!*" Nicolas demanded. "You've had them all day! I am their uncle."

"All right," Renee growled, surrendering Francoise. "Take this one. The little one is just getting use to me. I don't want you to spoil our growing friendship."

Jacques twisted his head around giving his passing wife a wink as if to say, "See how well everything is going?" She ignored him as she refilled Medicine Crow's platter and moved out through the doorway.

"Francoise, Francoise," Nicolas gurgled into his nephew's face, holding the baby nose-to-nose. "You are a beautiful little person." Turning to his brother he asked in a lower tone, "But isn't he just a little . . . fat?"

Jacques snorted, wiping his mouth with the back of his hand. "He was born that way, Brother. Though I admit he is getting worse."

"He can be our secret weapon," Medicine Crow remarked in his dry way. "When he's two seasons older we can roll him downhill toward our enemies and scare them to death."

Charlie, tending the stewpot, turned her head toward

the laughter erupting inside the tepee full of men. One of the women brushing melted fat on the roasting meat said to her, "Isn't it something the way men always take the credit for their children? It's as if our sex had nothing to do with any of it. We're out here working and they are in there congratulating each other. Sometimes I wish their penises would fall off."

"And just what would we do with men with no penises?" the other woman chortled. "They would be even more useless to us than they already are."

"Cody is walking and talking," Wolf's Tracks proudly told Jacques. "You won't know him when you see him. His hair is to his shoulders and he can pee by himself, though Marie still has a hard time about him peeing in the house. He said he doesn't like to pee outside because bugs land on his penis."

"When are you and Marie going to have another baby?" Jacques asked with a laugh.

"We don't know," Wolf's Tracks shrugged. "We've been trying but so far we haven't been lucky."

Jacques clapped his brother-in-law on the shoulder. "I know the best way to make babies. An old woman here told me just how to do it. First you have to . . ." Jacques broke his stride when Charlie and the other two women reentered, carrying bowls of the prepared stew. "We'll talk later," he whispered. "The meal is excellent, Sweetheart." He nodded to Charlie. "*Pere* brought coffee. Could we have some please?"

Charlie lifted Renee's untouched platter. "It's over there," Renee said to her, inclining his head toward one of the pouches lying in the corner. He went back to playing with Antoine as if she no longer existed. Charlie felt strongly tempted to dump the uneaten meal on top of his head and then beat him unconscious with the platter. Charlie got away from Renee quickly before temptation became a reality.

She swallowed her temper and suffered her father-in-law's rudeness only for the sake of her husband. As she made toward the pouches, Nicolas reached out a hand and touched her arm.

"I like the babies," he smiled up at her. "My wife and I are going to have a baby. Our children will play together as Jacques and I played together. This is a wonderful thing you've done, Shar-lee."

"Thank you, Nicolas," she muttered, fleeing the tepee before her hateful father-in-law could see her crying.

"She speaks French very well, Jacques," Nicolas said in admiration. "You have done a remarkable job with Shar-lee. She's respectful, obedient and a good breeder. I hardly recognize her from the girl we first found."

Jacques swelled with pride, enjoying his brother's compliments. "It was a lot of hard work," he said, all but physically patting himself on the back. "But she's a good wife and well worth all the effort." He was careful to make the statement in Crow. Charlie might appear tamed but she was still more than capable of raising a knot the size of the Dakota Territory on the side of his head.

CHAPTER TWENTY-THREE

Renee's attitude seemed to change with the dawning. He appeared at his son's lodge after Jacques had gone off to make his goodbyes to the elder Flathead chiefs, quietly helping Charlie pack up her household goods and strap the belongings to the pack horse. He left her without a word. She wanted to thank him but he had gone off to say his own goodbyes and shake hands with the chiefs. The Flathead chiefs were vocal and loud with their thanks for the horses and gifts Renee had presented the tribe.

"You come visit us soon. We will give a big party for you," Renee said, shaking hands with all of them in turn. "A big party. Plenty of food and many presents because you are our good and honored friends. I will look for you when the leaves bloom on the trees after the winter season."

"We will be there," the chiefs readily agreed.

"But do me one last favor," Renee said, rubbing his chin. "The girl Rainbow. Find her a husband quick. My son Nicolas has a wife who carries his child. I don't want her upset by the knowledge that her husband once had a sweetheart among the Flatheads. It would be bad for my son's marriage. She's a very jealous woman."

"We understand," Shot-His-Horse's-Foot nodded. "Women can be fussy about such things. We will arrange a marriage for the girl quickly."

Renee hugged the older man, his hands clapping the chief's back. He left them and made for Charlie, who was busy balancing her sons' cradle boards on either side of her horse.

"No! No!" he yelled waving his arms at her. "That's wrong!" Charlie stood aside as Renee tugged at the tight rawhide knots. "They will eat dust in this position. They must ride high or they will choke to death."

"But I can't manage that," Charlie said, helpless against Renee's take-charge brusqueness. "I don't have room for both of them on my back. The women told me this was the best way to travel with them."

"Women!" Renee spat. "Their brains are too small to think of better ideas. I will take care of my grandsons' comfort." He cast her an apprizing look. "You are really too small to carry either one of them." After a moment's deliberation he said firmly, "Jacques will carry one on his back, and I will take the other. I'll take Antoine. Let Jacques break his spine with Francoise, eh?"

Charlie actually found herself smiling at Renee's joke, missing the sad light that flickered through Renee's dark eyes. "You know," he grunted as if further conversation pained him, "I have never thanked you for the love you have given my son or the fine grandsons you have given me. I thank you now, Shar-lee. From the bottom of my heart I thank you."

"You are very welcome," she said, her chin beginning to quiver. Afraid to ask, but daring to anyway, she ventured, "Does this mean you accept me as your daughter-in-law?"

Renee tenderly placed an arm about her quaking shoulders. In a thick gritty voice almost on the verge of a sob he said, "For the sake of my son ... there is nothing I wouldn't do."

Charlie was laughing and in relieved spirits as Jacques helped her onto her horse. Renee watched them together as their excitement in going home began to infect the rest of the Crow party. The days of hard travel were made easier by the couple's good humor. Charlie's happy little face shone like the noon sun. It was the way everyone would remember her.

For, nine days later and forty miles outside the safety of the Crow Reserve, Charlie was dead.

The group of thirty Cheyenne stormed down on them with complete surprise as if they had been lying in wait for the Crow. Their firing rifles as they charged the hapless Crow sounded only like harmless little popping noises, the deadliness of the weapons dwarfed under the immense, endless blue sky. Charlie was struck in the chest before she could scramble from her horse and find safety. Of all the Crow, she was the only casualty. Renee reached her first, picking her up in his arms and running with her limp body toward a gully, while bullets zinged by his head. Antoine, strapped to Renee's back, screamed in terror as he was jostled in the cradle board. Renee took refuge behind a fallen tree on the lip of the gully, and ripped open the front of Charlie's dress.

"Forgive me," he blubbered, unable to control his tears as his hands tried to staunch the appalling flow of blood. "Please forgive me."

Charlie, past all pain and concern, looked at him in silent wonder as her eyes misted with the frost of death. "For what?" she asked flatly. Before he could answer, her head slumped and rested against his arm as her spirit left her.

"For everything!" Renee wailed. He held her body against him, his copious tears mingling with her blood. "For everything *ma petite*," he sobbed, "for *everything*, my little precious girl!" Renee collapsed, sobbing against her bloodied chest.

The Cheyenne withdrew under the heavy return fire of the Crow. Their leader waved a rifle of shining silver and

329

florid design over his head. The expensive weapon reflected the sunlight back into the eyes of the Crow as the Cheyenne war chief signaled the retreat. At the sound of the enemy's horses drumming away, the Crow stood firing after them while Jacques ran for all he was worth toward Charlie. He arrived by her side too late to even kiss her goodbye.

"Noooooo!" he screamed, wrenching Charlie's empty shell away from Renee. "Shar-lee!!" He continued screaming as he shook her, her loose head wobbling back and forth. "Shar-lee! Don't be dead! Shar-lee! I command you not to be dead! Wake up! I am your husband and you have to obey me Shar-lee!"

Nicolas stood behind his brother, frozen by the horrible sight. Jacques was in a frenzy. Renee's face was a sea of drying blood crusting in the lines around his eyes.

"Nicky!" Renee barked, causing Nicolas to jump. "Take Antoine! And get Francoise off your brother's back before Jacques accidently kills him."

Nicolas moved into the fray, having to fight against Jacques's superhuman strength. Renee was helpless to offer any assistance. He was pinned down both by Charlie's dead weight and Jacques. Without the immediate aid of Medicine Crow and Wolf's Tracks, Nicolas never would have managed to free either screaming baby. Both babies were blue with hysteria as if they, too, were mourning the mother taken from them.

Renee assisted as much as he was able in the removal of Antoine from his own back. When he was certain the twin boys were out of harm's way he wrapped his arms around Jacques and the lifeless form of Charlie and grieved with his son.

"Build a travois," Renee quietly instructed Wolf's Tracks. Wolf's Tracks, dismayed, stood watching and listening as Renee rinsed himself of Charlie's blood and put forth his intentions. "We will take her home and bury her on our land."

"But we are still too far away for that," Wolf's Tracks gasped in horror. "Her body will stink from the sun before we get can her home. Renee, this isn't a decent way to treat the dead. They have to be buried quickly so that they can have peace."

"I will not leave the mother of my grandsons in this lonely place!" Renee shouted. "Build a travois! We will travel with her as fast as we can."

They traveled on without stopping, except for one or two hours a day to relieve the horses. Jacques stayed behind the main group guiding the horse hauling the body of his precious wife. Jacques felt cold inside and out. He appeared to be in a wild dream state, unable to see or hear anything other than his continual pain. He hadn't spoken a word nor shed another tear after covering Charlie's remains and lashing her down securely on the travois. He left the care of his sons to his father and brother. His ears were deaf to their crying. He was only conscious of the life torn out of him and lying motionless on the dragging travois. Hatred slowly replaced the love his withering heart had once known. The hatred not only changed his heart but his countenance as well. His handsome features hardened into a mask of stony rage. He was a fearsome sight for all who looked on him riding quietly to the rear of the party leading his dead wife homeward.

A wet nurse was found immediately for the starving babies. Medicine Crow himself brought her to Renee's home. Willow was frantic by the time the young woman arrived, helping the surrogate to disrobe and attaching the weakening babies to her breast. Jacques seemed unaware of the peril his sons faced as he remained outside the house, cutting down and stripping trees, constructing the sky grave for Charlie, whom, despite the odor of her corrupting flesh, he kept near him, talking to her as if she were still alive and attentive.

"This is a good place for you Shar-lee. There are many trees and you can hear the river from here. It will sing to you while you are sleeping, precious one. And I will come and bring you flowers and sing to you as well. I wish you

hadn't left me Shar-lee." He sat down and placed his
hands in his face, weeping in his palms. "I hate it that you
left me Shar-lee. I hate it. I wanted you to grow old with
me. You were my 'Sit Beside Me Woman.' So special to
me. So very special. I will never love anyone the way I love
you, Shar-lee. Never as long as I live this hateful life
without you."

Renee ventured near, silently placing a hand on his
son's sobbing shoulders. "May I help you with her grave
my son?"

Dumbly, Jacques waved a vague hand.

"Thank you," Renee said faintly.

The entire clan of the People of the Whistling Waters gathered as Charlotte DeGeer was hoisted up and onto her sky
grave. They sang a death song for her. They sang her
praises of being a good wife and mother. They sang their
thanks to the Creator who now held her in His arms for
allowing her into their lives, though only a few had actually known her while she lived. Jacques used his knife and
cut off his hair to shoulder length, placing the bunched
grief offering on top of her chest before she was covered
over for the final burial. As they covered her, Jacques
stepped back and again used the knife, cutting a diagonal
line across his chest, his blood weeping down his body
while he sang in a tremulous voice of his unbearable grief.
Willow and Eyes-That-Shine, each holding one of his sons,
turned their faces away. The sight of Jacques's mourning
was too much for either woman to endure. Wolf's Tracks
held Marie against him, crying into her hair. Crying, for
he knew were he in Jacques's place he would pray for his
own death rather than face life without the woman so necessary for his life's purpose. Nicolas was stricken. Even
more so than his brother, despite Jacques's terrible loss.
Nicolas was curled up, down on his knees, his face against
the hardpan soil, his tears turning the dust to mud as he
grieved for his brother. Because Nicolas knew. Yet he
fought against the inner glimmering, too devastating to
acknowledge.

Renee stood alone in the distance, away from the burial party, spiritually unable to fully attend the ceremony. He stood with his hands held behind his back, his voice a husky whisper as he wept, "*Au revoir, ma chere petite.*"

After two weeks, Willow realized she was going to have to work out an alternative plan with the wet nurse. The little girl-woman had her own child and a husband who needed her and the strain of living between two separate households was beginning to tell on the girl's good nature. After the twins' morning feed, Willow plunked herself and the girl into the wagon, taking the grateful girl home for the last time. Then she went on to the trading station and bought a milk cow. Mrs. Pease waylaid Willow inside the station, coming to the rescue with a new contraption she called a "bottle."

"You will have to boil the bottles in water before each use," Mrs. Pease grandly dictated. "The nipples too. It's very important to do that, Mrs. DeGeer, or the babies will get sick from ... 'germs.' " She elongated the word so firmly Willow's eyes flashed in alarm.

"What is that?"

"Tiny things you can't see with your eyes no matter how hard you squint. But they are there, nonetheless, and they cause fever. The only way to kill these creatures is to use soap and boiling water."

"I will remember," Willow promised fervently.

"You must have nappies, too." Mrs. Pease glowed, pleased at being in full charge of Willow once again.

"Can I see nappies if I squint?" Willow asked in a little voice.

Mrs. Pease slapped her girdled thighs with her hands. *Will my work never be finished with this ignorant Indian?* she thought, her chest heaving in dismay. She flounced herself over toward a shelf at the back of the store burdened with assorted cloths. She took a bolt of the white cloth and placed it on the counter to be tallied in along with the cow and bottles. "She'll have this also." She waved majestically to the young male Crow store clerk. "And large pins. A box of those if you please." Crooking her index finger toward Willow she said, "Come here, Mrs. DeGeer, I'll teach you about nappies."

Once again the agent's wife was in her element. She was a natural teacher and busybody and Willow was her favorite victim/pupil. Mrs. Pease talked nonstop as Willow worked at getting the knack of folding and pinning diapers. According to Mrs. Pease, all civilized babies wore nappies, as this article of clothing saved work for mothers. Modern women no longer had to run about mopping up behind untrained children, though with the instructions on laundering and drying the diapers in the sun, Willow honestly couldn't see how the diapers saved anything other than a child's parent's lap from the occasional soaking.

Armed with her new gadgets and milk cow, Willow returned home and took charge of her grandsons' care and feeding. Renee had spent his days building two cradles which he moved into Jacques's room, ignoring Willow's waspish remarks that the babies should sleep in their bedroom within her easy reach.

"They are Jacques's sons," Renee said tightly. "He must assume responsibility of them."

"He won't do it!" she shouted, a diapered baby slung on each hip as she followed him while he carried the cradles down the hallway. "He just sits out there by that grave night and day. He doesn't eat. He ignores anyone who comes near him, or worse, yells for us to go away. We've all tried with him, Renee. He doesn't care about anything anymore."

Willow lowered her graying head and began to weep pitifully. "It's like he died with her."

"I've had enough of this," Renee growled, as the cradles crashed to the floor. He snatched the babies from his wife and stormed out of the house.

"Jacques!"

"Go away *Pere*," Jacques replied in a dead voice.

"I will," Renee huffed. "I only came to give you something."

"I'm not hungry," Jacques said, refusing to turn his eyes from Charlie's grave.

"I don't care," Renee gruffed, placing himself in

Jacques's line of vision toward the tall grave. "But if you're going to join her, she will ask you about your children, so you might as well let your sons starve along with you. Because the moment you join that little girl in the Beyond she will ask you about her sons. If they're with you she will be happy, but if you come alone she will pester you about them. And what would you say to her my Jacques? 'Oh! I forgot'?" Renee squatted down and thrust each baby into Jacques's unwilling arms. "Women are funny creatures, my stupid son. They bring children into the world and their welfare consumes them. They worry more about their babies than they do their own well-being. Not like the selfish *Pa-Peres,* eh? We men only know our own needs and to hell with our own flesh."

"That isn't true," Jacques gasped, juggling his wriggling sons. "I worry about my sons."

"But not enough to live for them, eh? Or to see to it that they live either, true? They would be dead now if they had been left to their father's care."

"Mother has taken care of them," Jacques replied sullenly, his dark eyes burning.

"Your mother is tired of them. They are her grandsons, not her own babies. They are your babies and so you must take care of them or kill them quickly to spare their suffering. But whatever you do, Jacques, it must be your decision because the rest of us are tired of trying to make life easy for you. You want to die? Fine! Die! But don't forget your sons. Have that much mercy on the rest of us you leave behind to mourn you."

Renee hastily abandoned Jacques and the wiggling babies. Jacques thinly called after his father but Renee ignored his pleading and kept on walking. As he entered the house, he called Willow away from the window where she kept vigil.

After an hour of pacing in the kitchen, Willow whimpered. "The babies need to be fed. They're crying, Renee. I can hear them and I can't stand it!"

Renee, seated at the table, barked for coffee and shouted, "They are Jacques's worry, Woman. If he wants them to be fed he will bring them inside and feed them himself."

Willow didn't bring Renee a cup of coffee as she sat
down at the table and chewed her fingernails down to the
nub. The back door banged open and Jacques stumbled
into the kitchen, nearly losing his hold on his bawling
sons. Willow jumped up from the table and rushed to him,
despite the warning looks Renee directed at her. Jacques
looked so gaunt and heartsick, but he was at last inside the
house.

If Willow hadn't known Jacques to be her son she
would have passed him in the road as some pitiable down
and out derelict of some unknown tribe. A defeated warrior bereft of any hope for the future. His chopped-off hair
was a tangled mess filled with dirt and debris. His chest
was filthy from the blood-caked wound he hadn't tended.
And he reeked like carrion. He was clearly in no fit condition to take care of his sons. He needed mothering more
than they did.

"Eyes-That-Shine!" Willow shrilled. Her daughter-in-
law's footfalls pounded softly as she scurried down the
hallway. When she stood in the kitchen entrance Willow
pointed to the back door. "Go get your sister. I need both
of you to help me." To her seated husband, she barked,
"Renee ... get the washing tub outside and build a fire
under it."

When Renee sat there blinking at her, she raised her
voice another octave.

"Move!"

Within minutes, the household was in a healthy tur-
moil, the DeGeers finally on the path to a semblance of
recovery.

"Mother?" Jacques called in the darkness toward his parents' bed. Willow raised up, letting him know she was
awake. "Could you help me, please—just one more time? I
can't fight the two of them by myself."

Willow entered the kitchen five minutes after Jacques
summoned her finding it a disaster. Jacques had tried to fill
bottles only to have them spill when he couldn't get the
tight-fitting nipples pulled on. Patiently, he had decided
the spillage had been the bottle's fault and had tried again

336

with a fresh one. Meanwhile, the babies were crying louder and louder, worming on their bellies all around the kitchen floor.

Antoine was under the table on his flattened belly, his arms and legs stuck out to the sides as he bawled until he was red in the face. Francoise, having believed his traveling brother was on the track of food, had followed, managing to wedge himself under one of the benches, his head against the foot of the bench, which wouldn't budge, no matter how hard he pushed. His little mouth was puckered in defeat as he weakly wailed his plight. Both brothers were soaked, their soggy poorly-fitted nappies loosely draping their bottoms. The abandoned pallet was soaked from their urine and bunched in an acrid, malodorous wad.

Eyes-That-Shine sat in the bed, chewing the inside of her cheek as she listened to the furor coming from the kitchen. "The babies are really screaming," she said to the dozing Nicolas.

Nicolas grumbled incoherently as he drew her back down beside him. Lying on the pillow next to him, Eyes-That-Shine stared at her husband's reposing face. Feeling her stare, Nicolas tiredly opened his eyes as he declared, "*Pere* says Jacques has to do it. You can't go out there."

"But, Nicky . . ."

"Go to sleep," Nicolas ordered.

Willow cleaned up the countertops and the bottles while Jacques fished out his sons. He put them back on the soddened pallet and went to fetch more diapers and a dry blanket. Returning, he sat on the floor as he stripped them both down and washed them under the watchful eye of his mother.

"Have you been up with them all night?" she asked, her voice edged with pity.

"Yes," he sighed. "I don't remember them being this much trouble before."

"You don't remember, because you slept through it

while your wife tended them," Willow said, as she tenderly stroked the back of Jacques's head.

Jacques lowered his head sadly as he thought of Charlie. It went against Crow custom to say her name out loud now that she was buried.

"I didn't realize how she made my life so comfortable."

"She must have been very nice," Willow half-choked in her determination not to cry.

"She was, Mother. She was very . . . nice to me." In a strangled voice, he rasped, "I miss her so much."

Willow cradled his head against her waist as Jacques wept. "Cry it out my son," she urged softly. "Cry for her as long as you need to. I understand your pain. I am your mother and I hurt with you."

"I'm going to get the Cheyenne for this," he sobbed.

"Good," she said in a hardening voice. "And kill one for each of your sons. They need their revenge as much as you need yours."

Deep in the heart of the Cheyenne village a sub-chief known as Walks Tall polished his prized rifle. It had been a profitable summer for him. His three wives were happy with all the booty he had pillaged for them. But the gun was the new joy of his life. He raised the stock to his cheek and sighted down the barrel. In pantomime, he repeated his actions in shooting the fatal round that had taken Charlie's life, mouthing the sound, "Bang." And the little white woman had died quickly, as promised. Now he could use the gun against the Crow in all fairness. This had been a very good summer indeed.

"Snow," Renee laughed, holding Antoine in his arms. His little grandson bubbled a laugh as the flakes fell on his chubby face. "This is snow. When you are older I will show you how to play in it. Later, when you are a big boy I will teach you how to survive in it just the way I taught your PaPa."

"Renee!" Willow called out the door. "Get that baby in here before you make him sick."

"Women don't like the snow," Renee confided. "Never forget that. I will have to teach you about women, too. But not in front of your *Ma-Mere*, eh? She won't like what I have to say."

CHAPTER TWENTY-FOUR

Renee walked back to the house, stomping the snow off of his boots on the top step. On the kitchen floor, little Francoise sat on a blanket gnawing on a piece of hardened biscuit, gooey slobber running down his arm.

"You are a crazy man taking that baby out in this weather," Willow chided, as she prepared the evening meal. She paused in front of the window, watching the silent snow descending. The early winter season created a fresh concern about Jacques.

"He's out there somewhere," she said softly as she watched the snow drift past the window. "Out there hunting Cheyenne." It worried her endlessly that Jacques had refused Nicolas's offer to accompany his band of warriors.

"You have to be here for your child's birth," Jacques had said evenly. "This is my war. I don't know when I will be back."

THE GLORY DAYS OF BUFFALO EGBERT

That had been three weeks ago. Surely, Willow reasoned, he must be on his way home. "The others who went with him will insist on coming home now that it is snowing. He will be here tomorrow," she assured herself as she prepared the meal.

Jacques, his face painted half-black and half-red, rode straight through the Cheyenne lesser village, his Crow warriors behind him. He threw a torch at a lodge. As it caught fire and the male inhabitants ran out, he gunned them down mercilessly. His followers, inspired by his bold tactics, acted out the same pattern. Within a half hour, the little village of thirty tepees was a crimson and ocher blaze against the inky sky. Women and children were ignored as they fled for safety, but few of the men escaped.

When Jacques's rifle ran out of bullets, he raced around on his charging horse, stabbing the life out of the defending men with his lance. Many Cheyenne fired at him, some at point-blank range, but they all missed. It was as if his medicine of unadulterated hatred had erected an invisible barrier between himself and the rifles fired against him. Jacques laughed at their failed efforts. And laughed as he killed them. This one raid alone would have been more than enough to satisfy the revenge need of an average warrior. But for Jacques, the dying Cheyenne didn't have enough blood to wash away his foul loathing.

"Tear everything up!" he yelled to his comrades.

He threw a lasso over the top pole of a burning lodge. He kicked his horse into action and pulled the lodge to the ground.

When the Crow finished their attack, the village was a charred, smoking ruin. The survivors staggered out of their hiding places long after the Crow had ridden away. Pitifully, they dug around in the debris searching for shoes, blankets, anything that might help them survive the weather. But there was nothing left. Jacques had been very thorough and there was nothing the homeless refugees could do except try for the safe confines of the secondary camp many miles away.

During the four-day trek, a few Cheyenne died en route,

either from their wounds, or from the lack of protection against the bitter cold. But enough staggered into the larger village to spread the word of the terrible wrong the Crow had done them.

"They fought like white men," a near-frozen woman reported. Of all the survivors who were bundled in blankets and given shelter in the overcrowded lodge, she was the only one strong enough to make a sensible report of the recent calamity.

The chiefs and sub-chiefs who listened to her gave her more hot coffee to ease the clattering of her teeth as she told them of the horrors. As she talked, the coughing and wheezing of her fellow evacuees filled the ears of the attentive men.

"They attacked us in our sleep and burned our homes," she gasped, passing the cup back for more of the hot liquid. "Just like white men. The Crow have gone as crazy as their white brothers."

"We'll get them for this," Walks Tall promised the woman. The other chiefs voiced their agreement.

Instead of their words pacifying her, she seemed to grow more frantic. She clawed at Walks Tall's shirt with her cold, blue hand.

"You can't," she rasped. "They have a leader who won't die. No bullets touched him, though everyone shot at him. His medicine is so strong, you can feel it with your hands."

"What did this man look like, so I will know who to kill?"

"Half of his face is black," the woman said. "The other half is red. His hair is short, and he is very big. And he laughs when human beings die. The death of our brave men gave him pleasure. His laughter was worse than anything I have ever heard. He will come back. He will come for all of us. I know he will."

"Then I will wait for him," Walks Tall vowed. "And when he meets me, his laughter will be heard no more."

"I'm telling you, we will not go back home!" Jacques shouted to his men.

342

"But we are cold and we are almost out of food," one warrior reasoned.

"I know that," Jacques scoffed, sounding exactly like his father. "We are going north to a cave I know of. There, our brothers will meet us. They will bring all the things we need. Our number will be twice what it is when we again strike the Cheyenne. That little village was just to let them know we are coming."

"Couldn't we attack them again in the warm season?" another asked.

"No!" Jacques thundered. "They will expect us in the warm season. They will be ready for us then. Now, they sit by their fires and talk against us. We will show them that it takes more than talk to stop us. My medicine is stronger now than it will be in the warm season. Do you understand?"

Jacques waited while the Crow voted among themselves. Finally, a spokesman was chosen.

"We will follow you, Jacques. Your medicine is very strong. Stronger than the cold of this winter season. Tell us what to do and we will do it."

Four days later, after the woman made her damning report to the Cheyenne chiefs, sixty Crow arrived at the cave designated beforehand by Jacques. They brought the much-needed horses, extra ammunition and food supplies. Jacques allowed his men to rest as he and two other scouts went in search of their primary target. This was also the same day Willow stood at her kitchen window, falsely prophesying her son's imminent return.

"That's a big village," one scout commented. He whistled between his teeth as they studied the Cheyenne citadel.

"We can take it," Jacques assured him. "Somewhere down there is the dog who shot my wife. I know I'll never know who he is, but I'll take enough of them out so that he will know me, should he accidentaly survive. Let's go back for our brothers."

They raced back toward their hidden horses and as the snow fell, they rode like shadowy specters for the cave.

• • •

Walks Tall was making love to his favorite wife in an effort to blank his mind against the Crow war chief, whom the Cheyenne now spoke of in hushed tones. The Crow with the black and red face. The Crow who couldn't be killed.

Walks Tall was irritated that none of his people believed he could kill the Crow devil. "I have a magic gun," he ranted to anyone who would pause long enough to listen. "My magic gun never misses. Only magic puts an end to magic. When the warm season comes, the devil Crow will feel Walks Tall's magic."

Holding on to this happy thought, he neared orgasm, only to be interrupted by the screams outside the thick walls of his lodge.

The woman who had braved so much and had walked so far, surviving the flames of her original village and the cold of the long trek, fainted dead away when she saw the black and red face galloping like an evil spirit through a stand of tepees. She collapsed under the realization that no one and no place would ever be safe from this hate-filled man.

Jacques's horse jumped over her, throwing snow back onto her prone body as he wreaked his havoc yet again.

The tactics he engaged dissolved the Cheyenne, who were totally unprepared for this late-night assault. The village had guards but the guards were lying dead in the snow, their throats slashed before they could sound the alarm.

Prior to the bellicose plunge through the village, Jacques ordered his men to first go for the herd of horses. They were to scatter the herd so that the Cheyenne, formidable on horseback, would be forced to defend themselves on foot against a mounted enemy. There wasn't an American general more thorough than Jacques. But even Custer, first engaged to the south in a valley on the Washita and then preoccupied with fathering a son and heir on the body of a captured Southern Cheyenne girl,

THE GLORY DAYS OF BUFFALO EGBERT

didn't possess the abhorrence of this enemy which Jacques harbored. Custer, a self-serving grandiose individual, merely sought glory and an exalted page in the history book. Jacques knew a higher calling. He hadn't time for the lesser passions which stirred the souls of secondary men.

Naked, and in a muddled flap, Walks Tall ran out of his lodge, cock aloft and magic rifle in hand. His penis fell as he raised his rifle to his shoulder and fired at the Crow racing by him on horseback. The charging Crow screamed fiercely as they tossed flaming torches into the doorways of lodges.

Walks Tall fired and brought down one attacker. Something knocked his shoulder and as he looked up, a Crow rode by. Quickly, Walks Tall looked at his left shoulder and saw blood pouring from a wound. Enraged, he fired at the enemy who had dared to use a battle-ax against him. He let go a victory cry as the Crow slumped and fell from his horse. His fatal mistake was in dashing over to look at the painted markings on his victims' face.

As he leaned over the dead Crow, disappointment bitter in his mouth because the paint markings weren't those he sought, he felt his back rip in half. His mouth flew open in petrified surprise. He turned slowly. His last sight was the black and red face of the mounted warrior who held on to the lance that penetrated his body. There, in the glow of his dying village, he recognized the face of the devil Crow. Then he heard that strange mocking laughter the woman had warned him of. Feebly, he tried to raise his magic rifle and fire, but as he gasped a final breath, he witnessed the enemy's hand closing around the powerless barrel as the maniacal Crow leered and mocked the dying Walks Tall.

"You want to give me your nice gun, eh?" Jacques laughed sardonically. "Thank you very much. I'll have it, if it pleases you." He wrested the rifle from Walks Tall's slackening grasp. Like a giant pine, Walks Tall fell sideways into the snow that glowed a golden amber from the many fires consuming the village.

Jacques drove the lance farther into Walks Tall's spine, gave it a twist and snapped it out cleanly, then rode off in search of livelier Cheyenne game. He used his new rifle against them. As Walks Tall had believed, the repeater was magic. The sights on it were perfect. It never missed, but then this very special weapon had been painstakingly crafted with the sole intent that it not miss.

Winter months saw few, if any, public celebrations. Jacques's return with such an astonishing victory and with only a few men missing, was cause for celebration, despite the frigid temperatures. After a few days of mourning the lost young men, a scalp dance was held.

Renee heard about the activity in the distant village from a young man Medicine Crow had sent over with the news. By the time Renee and Nicolas mounted up and made for the main camp some twenty miles down Elk River, the festivities were already winding down.

Jacques, wearing fresh warpaint and full-feathered regalia, danced in the center of honor. Renee and Nicolas had to shove their way forward in order to see him.

Nicolas wore a wide proud smile as he saw his brother dancing fierce and tall in the honored position. Jacques's right arm was aloft as he danced and shrilled out his piercing war whoop, all the while waving the prized rifle he had taken directly from an enemy's hands. Walks Tall's scalp dangled from the end of a leather strap tied just below the barrel sight.

Horrified, and with heart thumping wildly, Renee recognized the rifle. Panicked, he glanced over his shoulder back toward Nicolas. The excitement and noise of the scalp dance was intense. Men shouted and whooped. The high soprano voices of the women tremoloed. The drums were deafening. The firelight cast a peculiar light amidst the falling snow. He felt a twinge of relief that Nicolas, so caught up in the moment, hadn't yet recognized that rifle.

Renee knew he would have to act quickly. Time was not his friend. But his insides churned, repulsed that that hated weapon was now in the hand of his precious son. He allowed himself that one second of emotion before he pushed himself back into the crowd, grabbed Nicky's arm and pulled him outside the fringes of the celebration.

"Go home. Tell your mother your brother is safe."

"But she knows that *Pere*!"

"NO! She doesn't. Your mother is a nervous person. She doesn't believe anything anyone outside the family tells her. I have no one else to send with this news, so do as I say. Go!"

Moments later Renee watched as a stony-faced Nicolas, in the throes of seething anger, mounted his horse and without so much as a goodbye, left. Renee stood, a solitary figure, watching as the darkness swallowed Nicolas.

He silently raged against fate. That hateful gun had come back to haunt his soul. Not that he needed additional haunting. Her face was never far from his mind. Her last words repeated endlessly until they were no longer a question but an accusation. "For what!"

What indeed. What a terrible price both Renee and that little girl paid for her one crime . . . the wrong skin coloration. A white girl was not allowed to be in love with his son.

Neither Jacques nor the girl would have survived the ugliness resulting as the natural consequences of their disastrous union. Blindly in love, neither would have been persuaded to see reason, that life was not the bliss they had shared inside the safe environs of the obliging Flatheads. In the real world, Jacques faced being shunned by his own people. Then too, there was the high probability that Jacques would have been hung by the whites for having dared to take a white woman to his bed. And what for the girl? A life as a whore after having freely bedded an Indian?

Left with no other option, Renee had made a deal with the devil.

Nicolas slogged home alone. Wolf's Tracks waylaid him before Nicolas reached the midway point, reining up furiously on the snow-covered pony.

"I was coming to get you," Wolf's Tracks' breath huffed white against the onyx of night. "It's her time! Eyes-That-Shine is having your baby."

Nicolas no longer dawdled. He kicked his horse and rode with his brother-in-law as fast as their horses could manage in the deepening snow. Marie met them at the back door of the family home, Cody standing silently as he clung to the fringe of her heavy dress, the twin boys straddling each hip.

'You can't come in now," Marie snapped impatiently. "Her laboring is in the last stage. Mother says you are to take all of the children and keep them at my house."

Nicolas heard his wife cry out one long pain-agonized moan. Despite Marie blocking the entrance, Nicolas took a step to move past her. "Shiny," he whimpered.

Wolf's Tracks grabbed the back of Nicolas's arm and yanked him. "This is no place for us," he hissed.

Marie thrust Francoise into her brother's limp arms. "Get out of here," she ordered. "I'll come to you when she's finished." After giving the children to the two men and sending them on their way, Marie raced back to the bedroom where Eyes-That-Shine labored.

"We are all very proud of this fine young chief," Never-Changes-His-Mind proclaimed as he passed the pipe to the next major chief. "He needed his revenge on the Cheyenne for the fearful wrong they did him, and he got it with few losses to our side. He struck two villages, Renee," the chief gleamed. "One was destroyed completely. The second received a big wound. The Cheyenne will long remember this victory of the Crow. They will continue to talk about it after we are all long dead. The Cheyenne have learned to fear us because of Jacques, the way the Piegan learned because of the men they lost at Nicolas's hands. You have raised two fierce sons, Renee. We are all very proud of you."

"Thank you," Renee said, unable to tear his eyes away from the rifle settled atop Jacques's crossed legs. "I have to take him home now. His sons have missed their father. He should be with them."

"That is proper," Never-Changes-His-Mind nodded. "It was as much their revenge as it was Jacques's. It's a terrible thing for young boys to lose their mother. Terrible."

"Jacques," Renee called to his son. "We go now."

Before Jacques rose, he lifted up the rifle in his two

hands. "First," he said, "I would like to present the enemy's rifle to. . . ."

"No!" Renee shouted, cutting Jacques off. "There is only one person who deserves that gun."

"Who?" the assembled men asked. Many of the chiefs had been eyeing the weapon and leaned in toward Renee, eager to know the name of the lucky recipient.

Renee looked directly into Jacques's eyes, locking and holding the contact made with his son.

"She no longer has a name," Renee said so softly they all had to strain to hear. "She lies in the sky and waits to hear that her murder has been avenged. That gun of the Cheyenne," he said, pointing directly at the hated rifle, "with Cheyenne hair hanging from it, will be my son's last farewell to the mother of his children."

The gathered men were all a trifle staggered by the magnitude of the gift to be offered to the dead and thus, lost forever to the living. When Jacques slowly agreed that his father was right, the disappointed chiefs' hands were tied. The fate of the coveted rifle was sealed. The weapon, so beautiful and so historic to the Crow people, would never be seen or used again. For once it was placed inside the grave, it could never be retrieved. The chiefs quietly lamented that such a magnificent weapon was doomed to go to rust and ruin in the arms of a dead woman.

"I don't want you to have to look at her," Renee said to Jacques as they faced the weathered grave from their mounts. "It will spoil your memories of her as she was. I'll put the gun in her hands."

Renee snatched the gun quickly, before Jacques could argue. Maneuvering himself to stand precariously on his saddle, Renee loosed the grave coverings and raised them just enough to slip the rifle inside and then threw the stiff coverings back into place, tying the ropes lashing the corpse with frantic, sweating hands.

"Here is part of your victory, Little One," Renee whispered, the words so soft that only he could hear them. "Your final victory will be my own death, I know, but please wait a little longer. Your husband and your sons need me. Think of that before you strike me down. I don't ask because I am afraid to die. I ask only because of them."

Easing his shaking legs back into the stirrups, Renee turned to Jacques. "*Bon*. It is finished."

"Hiya!" Nicolas waved both arms and jumped up and down, attracting the attention of his father and brother as they stabled their horses. "Come this way after you shelter your ponies. You can't go to the house."

Jacques's face appeared grotesque as he smiled behind the split-faced war paint. "Nicky is becoming a papa!"

Willow sent Marie over with extra blankets and hot food to the holed-up men playing babysitter to the three children. Renee made more coffee while Jacques bathed, washing the war trail off of his face and body.

After his bath, Jacques dressed in clothing provided by his ever-thoughtful mother and then walked quietly into Cody's room where he found his sons sleeping peacefully on the mat Wolf's Tracks had made for them. He had only been away for six weeks and yet his sons seemed to have doubled in size. Antoine stirred as Jacques stroked the back of his little head, spikey with dark brown hair. He placed tender kisses on each of his sons' rosy cheeks and then left them as quietly as he had come in.

"You didn't wake them up, did you?" Nicolas growled. "It took both of us to get them to sleep." He motioned toward Wolf's Tracks, who slumped on the couch that he had built himself. It had been an attempt to copy one of the settees in his father-in-law's house, though his efforts had fallen miserably short of the mark. The end product was a thing too short to be a bed, and too wide to be a proper couch. But it suited Wolf's Tracks and Marie, so it was duly installed as one of their first pieces of furniture.

Jacques joined Wolf's Tracks on the couch, his adrenaline waning, fatigue beginning to set in. He wanted dearly to join his sons in sleep, but he knew that was out of the question. Nicolas was pacing and fretting. The last thing anyone would enjoy while Nicolas was in this state was sleep.

"One more push," Willow encouraged.

"I can't," Eyes-That-Shine sobbed. "I'm so tired."

"Shining Girl," Willow said gently, but firmly, "I can see the baby's head. Your work is almost over. Now I want you to use all of your strength and push one last time as hard as you can."

Marie held her sister-in-law's white knuckled hands tightly. Eyes-That-Shine, in her Herculean efforts to expel the child, pulled against Marie, rising up on the bed as she pushed, locking a deep breath in her throat.

If she had passed a watermelon from her anus, Eyes-That-Shine couldn't have felt more relieved as the baby slipped out of her. The infant cried loudly as it entered the world. Willow laughed and cried as she held the baby, glistening and as slippery as an eel in her two hands.

"It's a girl," Willow announced as she held the baby, who was still attached to her mother by the umbilical cord. Weary, Eyes-That-Shine was all smiles as she lay back on the bedding. Willow held the newborn up high so Eyes-That-Shine could view her tiny daughter.

"Marie," Willow beamed, "run tell Nicky. I can do the rest of this by myself."

"You have a daughter!" Marie cried as she burst into the room. "She's beautiful. She looks just like her mother."

Nicolas stood stunned. Renee shouted a whoop. Wolf's Tracks and Jacques swarmed over the dazed Nicolas, clapping his back and pumping his hands.

"A little girl," Nicolas repeated in wonder. "I have a little girl. My very own little girl." He turned to Renee who was busy stabbing cigars in each of his sons' mouths. "*Pere* . . . I'm a . . . father."

"Ah *oui*," Renee agreed, lighting up two cigars and then jamming one of them into Nicolas's slack mouth. "You're a father. And now that you know how it is done, I expect to see more from you. What do you think of the name Margueritte? That was my mother's name. Margueritte DeGeer. I know she would be proud for this little one to have her name. Do you like it?"

"Very much," Nicolas said, puffing proudly on his cigar. "Shiny will like it, too." The thought of his wife caused him to turn on his sister. "How is Shiny? Is she all right?"

"She's fine," Marie said, waving her sister-in-law's accomplishment aside with an impatient hand. "She only had a baby. We women do that all the time."

"How would you know?" Wolf's Tracks teased. "I've only been able to get one baby out of you."

Marie gave Wolf's Tracks a small punch to the midsection. "In the spring, I dare you to say that to me again."

All eyes turned in her direction.

"Marie, are you. . . ?" Renee breathed.

Wolf's Tracks bent double to look his wife in the eyes, his expression a giant question mark.

"Yes," she giggled.

Wolf's Tracks blinked rapidly as he whispered to her. "You thought I knew again, didn't you?"

Winter was normally a peaceful season after hectic summer months. But in this strange year, the Crow calendar ran in reverse. Theirs had been an idyllic summer to be followed by a hellish winter of raids and counter-raids.

In the month prior to spring, Cheyenne and Lakota emissaries appeared at Fort Ellis, demanding to speak with Tippleton. To his face, the Cheyenne listed their grievances against the Crow and declared open war, not only against the Crow, but against their white allies as well. The Lakota, never wishing to be left out of a fight, threw in their lot with their Cheyenne brothers. The visiting Indians declared that the war was to take place in the first months of spring. If the Crow and the army didn't meet them on the designated battlefield, they promised to burn the fort down around Tippleton's ears.

In a push for compromise, Tippleton invited the Indians into the fort, installing them in the best quarters, and sent for Renee and the dominant Crow chiefs. It was Tippleton's frail hope that at the council, the Indians would shout out their differences around a conference table, avoiding further bloodshed.

"I didn't realize you were bringing your sons," Tippleton said, eyeing the three menacing young men who followed close on Renee's heels.

Tippleton had stopped the Crow delegation at the door of the grand ballroom, now employed as the conference room because it was the only room large enough to accommodate the gathering of antagonistic chiefs. The ballroom had been constructed strictly for the officers and their ladies for weekend fetes of dining and dancing, to relieve the ladies of their incessant boredom of plains life. The cultured ladies had designed and furnished the ballroom themselves with bishop-sleeved drapes for the windows and round, mahogany tea tables, around which were clustered Queen Anne tapestry-upholstered chairs. The huge male Indians who filled the delicate armless chairs looked utterly ridiculous, but there was nothing Tippleton could do at this late date to alter the seating arrangements.

"My sons go where I go," Renee said. "If this distresses you, my sons and our chiefs will trouble you no further. You can deal with the Cheyenne and the Lakota in your own way."

Tippleton didn't attempt a reply as he opened the door and led the DeGeers and the seven Crow chiefs inside.

"That's him!" one burly Cheyenne shouted, rising from his chair and pointing directly at Jacques. "His paint is gone, but I recognize him by his hair. He is the chief who led that coward's attack against us in our sleep."

Jacques's arms folded against his bare chest, smiled broadly. "You must have seen me from your hiding place, because if you had been in the fight, I would have gotten you, too."

The insulted Cheyenne made a lunge for Jacques.

His brothers grabbed his arms and held him back. "Not here, not here," they said to him, trying to cool his fury. The warrior shook free and returned to his seat, his smoldering black eyes burning holes into Jacques.

Bear Ribs stood on wobbling legs, unable to accept the

sight of his long-lost nephew in the room and the fact that
he was standing with the Crow. In a shaking voice, he
addressed Wolf's Tracks. "Are you riding ... with the
Crow?"

"I am," Wolf's Tracks nodded curtly.

"You left us for the . . . Crow?"

"I did."

"You don't miss your own people?"

"Sometimes," Wolf's Tracks snorted. "But I never miss
the knife you planned for my back, Uncle. Now that I am
a Crow, you are free to hate me to my face."

Precious little was left to be said after that public
denouncement. Bear Ribs resumed his seat, no longer able
to look in the direction of his nephew, although Wolf's
Tracks had absolutely no repentance as he stared directly
at Bear Ribs. Wolf's Tracks had become a Crow only
because of the strife initiated by his uncle. After he became
a Crow, he bore the tribal mark proudly and with his head
held high as he made a new home for himself among
strangers. He felt his long-overdue vindication when he
saw Bear Ribs sitting quietly defeated with his head lowered, surrounded by the comfort and security of family
and friends—all of the things Bear Ribs had sought to steal
from Wolf's Tracks. Because of this unexpected encounter
with his lost nephew, and the witnessed rebuke, as a man
and as a chief, Bear Ribs was finished. In plain view of
everyone, Bear Ribs shriveled. Only one of the Lakota,
and he a distant cousin belonging to the Oglala, acted
halfway friendly toward Wolf's Tracks. Wolf's Tracks and
the slightly younger man attempted forlorn smiles to one
another along with dispirited waves. Prior to the arrival of
the Crow, the Lakota delegation had introduced this
young chief to Captain Tippleton as Crazy Horse.

Tippleton, edgy from the various outbursts, ushered the
Crow to their seats and signaled his armed troopers lining
the walls of the hall to be ready to open fire should he give
the word. He took his own place by his interpreter, the
two of them standing in the center of the room. Through
the neutral white man, a member of the Shoshone Nation
by marriage, he said, "I want to hear from one Cheyenne

and one Crow, one at a time, so that I understand clearly in my mind the cause of this war."

Medicine Crow stood immediately. "I will speak first for all the Crow Nation. I have a sad story to tell and it is time the Cheyenne heard it." Placing a hand on Jacques's shoulder, he began. "This is my little brother. I have known him since his birth. He has always been a good person, full of life and hope."

He paused and looked around. Every man in the room was staring at him.

"Over two seasons ago, he found a little girl," Medicine Crow continued. "She was very beautiful and he loved her. She bore him two sons . . . twins. This was done while they wintered with the Flatheads. My brother was bringing his family home to the Crow when he was attacked by the Cheyenne and his wife was killed. With her went the life and hope I have always known this young man to have. He warred against the Cheyenne to avenge the terrible crime brought against him and his baby sons. He attacked the Cheyenne in a shameful way to repay the Cheyenne for their dishonorable killing of a young mother who was unarmed and unable to protect herself. But, unlike the Cheyenne, he killed no women and no children. If there is any truth in the mouths of the Cheyenne, they will have to confess that only their men suffered wounds."

The Cheyenne chief leaped to his feet. "He burned our winter homes!" he charged. "Our women and children went hungry and were cold because of him."

"But he didn't shoot them," Medicine Crow said in a final tone. "Homes can be rebuilt. Food can be hunted. But the life of a dead wife cannot be returned to her husband."

Captain Tippleton was surprised and disgusted by the charges he heard. Without giving pause for thought, he blurted out the most damaging statement made during the entire council. "All of this is about a *woman*?" he said, amazed. "You people buy and sell women all the time. Why didn't someone just sell him another wife?"

The discomfited interpreter tried to play down Tippleton's asinine statements, but Jacques, Nicolas, Renee and Wolf's Tracks understood every word the Captain had uttered. They shouted down the anxious interpreter, repeating word-for-word the statements made by the white man in their midst.

A near riot ensued as the Indians bolted from their seats, chairs falling over behind them with splintering crashes. The Cheyenne, the Lakota and the Crow sprang to the center of the room and surrounded the army captain, all of them yelling at once.

"You think we have no feeling for our women?" one Cheyenne spat, shoving Tippleton roughly.

"Our women are the most beautiful women in the world!" a Lakota shouted. "That's why we can't keep white men away from them."

"If any man ever dared to shoot my wife," another angry Cheyenne screamed, "I would rip his heart out of his chest with my bare hands!"

Jacques pushed his way close to Tippleton. "What do you mean, I could just get another wife?" he shouted, forgetting to speak English. "My wife was my heart. If my heart stopped beating, could I just get a new one of those? You are a crazy man. I should shoot you!"

"I left my people because of my love for my wife," Wolf's Tracks thundered. "Would you leave your people for your wife?"

"I surrender," Tippleton yelled, raising his hands high. "Renee! Damn it! Tell them I'm sorry."

Renee pushed into the middle of the circle, arriving nose-to-nose with Tippleton.

"I should let them have you," he growled. "I never believed you thought so little of these men. Only dogs go from female to female without feeling. If you can believe that of these men, then you are worse than a fool. I am quit with you."

"Your son has started a bloody war, Renee!" Tippleton raged, his face mottled in fury. "Either you do something to stop it or I will personally hold the rope that hangs you, and your son."

Pressed tightly against each other amid the crushing bodies of the wrathful Indians, the two adversaries seethed, neither of them blinking as their eyes held.

Renee's voice was full of contempt when he offered the captain one last bit of common sense. "If you want to stop them from warring against your people, *mon capitaine,* you must begin by offering your brotherhood."

"How the blue hell do I do that?"

"Fix them a big meal and then give them all the presents their arms can hold. Then their war will be back where it belongs. With the Crow."

Renee pushed away from Tippleton, the Crow delegation following him out of the grand hall. Tippleton never saw Renee again.

CHAPTER TWENTY-FIVE

Though Tippleton tried, he was unable to call the Crow back. But using Renee's last piece of advice, he ordered the camp cooks to prepare a grand meal fit for visiting dignitaries. Again, Renee's logic proved to be as sound as a silver dollar. The Indians found it difficult to utter threatening rhetoric while their mouths were filled with delicious foods. The normally sedate dining hall almost played witness to another war when the army cooks brought out the dessert trolleys. Captain Tippleton was to learn another crucial fact about Indians: that they loved sugar.

When the Creator blessed humanity with the sweet tooth, He proved He loved the Indian best when He gave each of them no less than four apiece. The guest Cheyenne and Lakota forgot their manners, jumping up from their various tables, rushing the confectionery carts, grabbing handfuls of cake and gooey berry pies. Captain Tippleton and his junior officers panicked and bolted from the dining room. The Indians failed to notice as they climbed over one another in their efforts to win their fair share, clawing, gobbling, shoving and pushing. The aghast cooks, unaccustomed to rave reviews for their culinary abilities, raced back into the kitchen and barred the door.

As the shouting slowly died away and the last of the remaining Indians drifted out of the dining hall, the four cooks ventured timidly out to assess the damage. To their dismay they found chairs overturned, tablecloths strewn helter-skelter or sagging from a few righted tables. The polished floor was smeared and embedded with food scraps. Whipped cream that had decorated the cakes, along with staining berry pie filling, coagulated or dripped from the walls and ceiling. The dessert lunge had been a proper battle and the dining hall had been left like a shattered and forsaken field. The sight proved too much for one of the younger cooks. He keeled over in a dead faint.

It required two weeks of hard labor before the dining hall again met army specifications, but the meal and the gifts from the sutler's store, hand-in-hand with Medicine Crow's oratory, had put an end to a major confrontation for at least a year. War would come, but happily for Tippleton, not until long after he was relieved of command from Fort Ellis and transferred to Washington, D.C. to serve as an advisor to the Indian Affairs department. But until the all-out declaration, there continued a series of minor incidents.

During the winter and summer of 1875, the Lakota and Cheyenne rampaged virtually unchecked. Their primary targets were Crow hunting parties but they hit out at any whites foolish enough to venture out without armed protection. The thriving township of Absaroke became another prime objective. The town that had remained unscathed during previous conflicts found itself suddenly harried, burned and pillaged as a scheduled monthly event. The new city fathers, men who had no patience with the "old timey days" when whites and Indians freely mingled, lived to regret their past snubbing of the Crow

Nation for now that the life of the town was threatened, the Crow looked after their own concerns and offered their neighboring whites no help whatsoever.

During one of these attacks against the town, the former Mrs. Cooksey and all her beleaguered brood were murdered. Mr. Aldershot, the redoubtable second husband and stepfather hid in a storm shelter while his wife and stepchildren were being butchered, and escaped unharmed. Briskly burying his wife and her children, he then quickly packed up his remaining wealth and left the failing town with a small wagon train, sharing his wagon with Mr. and Mrs. Russell, Charlie's parents. They headed off to Oregon, Charlie's original destination. Like their daughter, the Russells never reached their objective. Midway in their flight out of the Montana Territory, the small clump of wagons was attacked. All five wagons were annihilated along with their occupants. The Russells' wagon was one of the first to catch fire. As Mr. Russell whipped the team of horses into a lathering gallop, the wagon pitched, then rolled over on its side in a flaming inferno. The three people inside were killed instantly.

The Crow didn't blame Jacques for any of the current troubles. The Lakota and the Cheyenne had always been their natural enemies and were a constant threat to them. The Crow were used to warring with these destructive tribes. They had suffered the two tribes for decades and, as far as anyone could remember, except for the previous peaceful summer when the Lakota and Cheyenne were off in the south, the pattern of life had always been the same. The Lakota or Cheyenne attacked, the Crow retaliated. The uncertain way of life had settled into the natural order of life on the plains. But during this crucial season, as more and more army troops moved into the territory, one name among the Lakota seemed to be repeated again and again.

Crazy Horse.

The young Oglala Chief had finally come in to his own, usurping the waning powers of Red Cloud. Red Cloud had been a powerful leader until the day he accepted the invitation to visit the capital, Washington, D.C., to parlay with the white leaders. Viewing firsthand the bustling life

THE GLORY DAYS OF BUFFALO EGBERT

of the whites and overawed by their industry and numbers, Red Cloud's hope for his people was crushed more thoroughly than by any other weapon used against him. When he returned, he retired to his tepee, a hollow of a man, broken both spiritually and physically.

"We can't win against them," he reported to his other chiefs. "There are simply too many of them and too few of us. We are a small island of red in a great sea of white."

With his abdication, the prairie crown passed to Crazy Horse. A born leader and shrewd tactician, Crazy Horse was destined to lead the Lakota into the zenith of their glory. His rise to power not only proposed problems for the Crow, but for the DeGeers personally. The first salvo was fired when Wolf's Tracks resigned as an army scout.

"I won't track my brother for white men," he told Renee flatly.

"But you are with the Crow now and Crazy Horse is killing Crow!"

"That may be," Wolf's Tracks sighed wearily, "but when we were young, he and I were brothers. I knew him as 'Curly.' That was his name then. This Crazy Horse name, I never knew it. But whatever his name may be now, I still love him in the same way I love Jacques and Nicolas. When I saw him at that meeting, my heart lifted with joy. I knew then that however long I live with the Crow, I will always love and miss Curly. Knowing this, Renee, would you ever understand my tracking down this most special brother?"

Renee stood quietly as Wolf's Tracks studied Renee's aging profile.

"I couldn't do it, Renee," Wolf's Tracks said solemnly. "I couldn't lead my Crow brothers against Curly, any more than I can lead him against the whites and the Crow. I can't be in this fight," he sighed heavily. "I just can't."

"I respect you for this, Wolf's Tracks," Renee replied somberly. "I'm glad you have spoken your heart. You are a good man. I am proud to call you my son. But what will you do now to support your family?"

"Hunt," Wolf's Tracks said with a simple shrug.

And so it was that Wolf's Tracks went his lonely way, hunting and trapping to feed his wife and two sons—

Marie, Cody and baby Jean. His youngest son's name would later be anglicized to John, both his sons being listed on the Crow census of 1880 as Cody and John Wolfson.

Wolf's Tracks' divided loyalties destroyed him in the end. In the fall of 1875, while checking his traps farther along the Yellowstone River than he should have been as a lone hunter wearing Crow markings, a party of Lakota attacked and killed him before they realized who he was.

When Wolf's Tracks failed to return home, Jacques, Nicolas and seven other Crow went out searching for him. They found his remains atop a sky grave the Lakota call a *Woja*. After his Lakota assailants realized their error, they gave their wayward brother a Lakota warrior's burial. Two horses, with slit throats, lay on their sides, their bridles tethered to the base of the grave. The spirits of the dead animals would prevent their former brother from entering the other world on foot as a beggar.

Jacques and Nicolas, overcome with grief, adorned the grave with their own special offerings. Nicolas placed his favored bow and quiver of new arrows at the base of the high burial site. Jacques gave up his war shield. Frontiersmen with years of experience among the Indians would find the grave and quickly appreciate that here had been a man of two worlds and in death enjoyed the honor of both.

A week later, another Lakota party led by Crazy Horse watched respectfully from a distant hill as the DeGeer family escorted the bereaved Marie to her husband's resting place. The Lakota made no movement as they sat astride their horses. A tear traveled down Crazy Horse's cheek as he watched a sobbing Marie cut off her hair and secure the long tresses to her husband's grave. As the DeGeers prepared to leave, Renee raised an arm to Crazy Horse, who returned the salute to the infamous Renee. It was the last peaceful greeting one would ever show the other.

"You cannot stay in this house unprotected!" Renee shouted at his stubborn daughter.

THE GLORY DAYS OF BUFFALO EGBERT

"My husband built this house," Marie said evenly. "He made all the furniture with his two hands. This is my home. This is where I will raise his sons. That is my final word, *Pere*."

"But these are dangerous times," Renee said as he followed her around in her small kitchen. "Your brothers . . . they have their blood up. They are always gone now. I am an old man, my hair is white and no one wants me on the trail anymore, but I can still see and I can still shoot. It is up to me to protect the women of the family, but I can't do that if my women are spread all over the place. You all have to be under one roof if I am to take care of you." He took her into his arms and stroked her bobbed hair as she wept against her father's chest. "See reason, little one. I'm not asking you to give up your home. I only want you to stay with your mother and me for a little while. When the Lakota are driven back to their own lands and the army can keep them there, then you can come back and raise your sons in peace. Your husband would want you to do this, Marie. He would be the first to tell you to do it."

"All right, *Pere*," she whispered after a great deal of tears and long silent thought. "I'll go with you. But just for a little while."

"*Tres bon*. I will help you pack."

The DeGeer household in the chilling winter was alive with children. Little Cody developed a crush on baby Margueritte that was to last a lifetime. Though technically cousins, they were not blood related and little Cody seemed to sense this. Had they been adults during this period, Cody's love for Margueritte would have been in vain. But with the advent of boarding schools ten years in the future and the slow dissolution of the clans, as a man in the early 1900s, Cody stood a good chance of winning Margueritte's favor. He contented himself in the meantime by playing with her and fetching toys she cast aside. Margueritte, armed with a pair of astonishing deep green eyes, was an exceptionally beautiful one-year-old, whereas the poor six-year-old Cody was saddled with his father's coarse looks.

Jacques's sons were a plague. Jacques came home spo-
radically and when he was home, he spoiled his sons, then
blithely left, abandoning the rest of the family to cope with
the legacy of his actions. Antoine remained an inch shorter
than Francoise, as well as six pounds lighter. In temperament, he was his mother all over again. Antoine was
always on the move and nothing escaped his attention.
The DeGeers developed a new war cry. Whenever finding
anything broken, overturned or missing altogether, the
same cry could be heard rattling the window panes.

"Antoine!"

Yet when Francoise was found up to mischief, the
family sighed rather than scolded. All knew only too well
that Francoise's misadventure had been Antoine-inspired,
-planned and -executed. For it was Francoise, always the
slower-moving felon, invariably caught with the goods.
Antoine, quick as a hummingbird, habitually deserted his
older brother to suffer the consequences, as was the case
on the morning Francoise was found sitting in a kitchen
cupboard, holding an emptied jam jar in his chubby
hands. Antoine was found sitting in the living room, hum-
ming to himself as he rocked in a cushioned rocker, the
flawless picture of innocence except for the blueberry jam
staining his cherubic little face. Indian parents rarely
administered corporal punishment and Willow, absolutely
never. As a result, Antoine got away with unadulterated
murder and held the household in a grip of terror from the
moment he awoke until he literally passed out from
exhaustion.

He was well past two years old when the family made
yet another frightening discovery. Antoine could climb. At
two years and four months, Antoine became half-spider
after mastering toe holds in the log walls. For a time
Willow thought the top shelves of her cupboards safe from
him, but with the tempting array just beyond his reach, he
honed his new skill and she was soon sighing in tired,
though patient, disillusionment.

Renee, disgusted with chasing Antoine from one
trouble spot to the next, came up with what to him seemed
the perfect solution.

"I think he should be tied."

"You don't tie up babies!" Willow gasped.

"Antoine is not a baby," Renee decreed. "Antoine is a disaster."

Willow, her head bowed and her hand against her mouth, said softly,"But you love him best. Of all of our grandchildren, you love Antoine the most."

"Yes, I do," Renee admitted grimly. "But why, I don't know. I just do.'

A few weeks prior to Christmas, Nicolas and Jacques breezed back into the homestead as if they had just been out on a playful romp and not heavily involved with a war with the Lakota. Renee was torn between relief at their safety and anger at their having been away for so many weeks, worrying him a deeper gray. He swallowed his temper as his sons had brought home with them a well-muscled virile looking youth from the Greasy In The Mouth Clan by the name of Extra Horses. The young warrior had earned his name because he usually took along three, sometimes four, extra horses on raids with him. It was his habit to ride one mount until it dropped, then transfer mid-ride to a fresher one, continuing his escape. His was an excellent strategy. No one ever caught him, and many a Lakota had tried.

Extra Horses was tall and extraordinarily good looking, even for a Crow. The hard physical work required in the constant training of horses had built up the muscles in his chest, arms, and legs. He was envied by his peers as their bodies were lean and stringy, typical of Indian males who disdained lifting and carrying anything heavier than their weapons and shields. He was painfully shy with women and Jacques suspected he was still a virgin.

Jacques confided those suspicions to Nicolas one day. "He has to be virgin, Nicky. Watch him around women. He can't talk. He won't even look them in the face. I once saw him trip over his own feet trying to get away from a flirting girl. And he's so well built and pretty in the face that all the young girls desire him. But if a girl threw herself naked on top of him, I really don't believe he would know what to do."

"Sad," Nicolas said with a shake of his head. Their

glances slid toward one another and they smiled slyly. "I think we should take him home."

"My thought exactly, Brother," Jacques grinned.

The self-effacing and timid Extra Horses felt lost and over-awed by the normal clamor of the DeGeer household. He had never been inside a house, so trying to relax in what felt to him more a prison fortress than a home, was his first hurdle to overcome. But the introduction to Marie threw him into a stumbling, mumbling dither. Marie was just as shy and self-conscious, because of her stubbed, shoulder-length hair. She didn't feel pretty without her hair cascading behind her. Then, too, her figure worried her. Her hips had been widened by the birth of her sons and she failed to notice that they swayed seductively when she walked, or that Extra Horses stared after her with a look of yearning in his eyes. His worst moments came when the match-making family contrived to have the unsuspecting couple "accidentally" sit beside each other on the trestle bench at the kitchen table during meals. Everyone at the table, Marie included, ate and chatted merrily. But Extra Horses couldn't eat with Marie so close beside him, nor could he speak. His hands shook, causing him to spill bowls of food passed his way. He was so mortified by his own awkwardness that he began plotting polite ways of escaping the houseful of rambunctious DeGeers, but particularly Marie. The constant noise of the household gave him headaches and he didn't care for the way the boy-child they called Antoine studied him. Antoine's fixed stare made him feel like a piece of walking fresh meat.

After the second day of Extra Horses' visit, Renee treed his sons. "Are you sure this young man is all right in the head? He acts strange."

"He's just very shy, *Pere*," Jacques said. "But you should see him work with horses. He's a master at breaking and training them. And against the enemy, he's fierce and cunning. But around women, he's a little . . . well, useless."

"Ha!" Renee snorted. "That's because he can hang on

to a bucking horse and use a gun to kill the enemy. Women have to be handled a little differently." Scratching his chin idly, Renee pondered out loud. "Marie seems to have noticed him. Perhaps this odd duck might be good medicine for her."

"We thought so, too," Nicolas nodded.

Marie was in the kitchen helping her mother wash and dry the dishes. "I feel so sorry for Jacques's and Nicolas's friend," Marie said as she stood at the sink. "He acts so afraid of everything."

Willow, too, had noticed her daughter looking favorably more than once at their young houseguest. As she washed and Marie dried, Willow decided to help push her daughter toward the ungainly Extra Horses. Marie, Willow determined, was far too young to be a widow, especially with two children to raise. Marie needed a strong young husband to provide for her and protect her.

Willow quickly pushed away the notion that Jacques might need a wife as well. Jacques was a man and so his needs were vastly different. He could take a woman for pleasure whenever he needed one. And Willow wasn't at all anxious for Jacques to have a wife because a new wife would mean a new mother for the twins. As big a job as the twins were, Willow wasn't ready to relinquish their care to another woman. Especially a woman who might not want them at all, but cared for them simply as a means to hold Jacques as a husband. No, Willow decided, Jacques was different. But Marie. . . .

"Do you know what I've heard about shy men?" Willow asked, leaning her head close to Marie's and whispering in her ear.

"No. What?"

"That they make the best lovers."

"That's just an old woman's story," Marie laughed.

"No, it isn't," Willow deadpanned. "I've heard it said by too many women too many times for it to be just a story. That Extra Horses . . . he is really shy and with a body like his, I'll bet you he's the best lover of them all. And that pretty face." Willow's expression turned dreamy as she placed a sudsy hand to her heart, as if she were suffering palpitations. "If I were a younger woman and your father wasn't around, I'd grab Extra Horses. I would throw him to the ground and find out for myself if that old story was true or not."

"Mother!" Marie shrieked, slapping Willow's backside with the dry cloth.

"Well, I would," Willow said, going on about her washing. "And I wouldn't feel guilty about it either. A beautiful man doesn't walk into a woman's life everyday. It's my bad luck that he's walked into mine when I'm too old to catch him."

"Mother!" Marie squealed. "You are a scandal!"

"I know," Willow agreed. "But I can't help it. I keep imagining those big arms around me, and then I feel faint."

The little woman-to-woman chat in the kitchen needled Marie. Her gaze roamed in Extra Horses' direction involuntarily and just as involuntarily she found herself next to him whenever they shared the same room. A widow for only seven months, she suffered guilt pangs as she tossed alone at night in her bed. She was torn between grief and loyalty toward her deceased husband and her overpowering physical craving for the young man under her father's roof. Her dreams were a torment. They were of Extra Horses—his smoldering eyes half-closed in desire as his face neared to kiss her yearning mouth. Marie awoke with a gasping start from one such dream, bathed in sweat. She tried to go back to sleep, but for the rest of the night she stared blankly at the ceiling.

Willow passed Renee a knowing wink as the weary and disheveled Marie staggered into the kitchen for her morning coffee. Willow, a passionate woman by nature, knew all the signs of another passionate woman in heat. It hardly mattered anymore if Extra Horses were a good lover or the world's worst. Marie had to have him or go mad. Watching her daughter, Willow knew Marie was ready for the *coup de grace*. Willow gave her husband the silent sign that the time had come to prime Extra Horses.

Renee finished his coffee and went off to awaken his sons. Entrapping the backward Extra Horses would require all of his skill, cunning, and out-and-out deception. Were Renee to leave the young stallion to his own devices, he knew Extra Horses would bolt for freedom, as his name so readily implied.

"Talking won't do it," Jacques frowned. His brother and father sat on his bed, Antoine on Renee's lap, the child listening intently as if he, too, were in on the secret planning. Francoise had toddled off to the kitchen where *Ma-Mere* prepared breakfast.

"Jacques is right," Nicolas agreed. "If we even hint that we want him to marry Marie, he'll steal away in the dead of night and we won't ever find him again."

"Then we're going to have to get them alone together and let nature take its own course," Renee grunted.

"*Pere,*" Jacques started to shout. Then, heeding Renee's shushing, he lowered his voice to a snake's whisper. "This is Marie we're talking about. I don't want her to act the wanton."

"Don't worry," Renee assured. "No one will ever accuse your sister of that. I'll put a gun to Extra Horses' head and force him to marry her if he takes advantage of her and then tries to run."

"This is a terrible thing to do to a man," Nicolas said sadly.

"What's so terrible?" Renee snapped. "Is it terrible for a man to have a beautiful wife and a family of boys to father? There are a lot of men in the world wanting to have that. Extra Horses will thank us later for what we're doing to him now. You'll see, Nicky. That is a very lucky young man in the next room. We just have to give his luck a little push."

"How are we going to do it?" Jacques breathed.

"Easy." Renee summoned them in closer. "Listen to your old *Pere.*"

The next morning all of the DeGeers disappeared. Extra Horses was treated to an extra morning's sleep without Antoine pulling open his eyelids to wake him up. He lay in blissful slumber on his mat in the living room, the house completely quiet.

Marie was tired that morning from a restless night. In her bemused state, she hadn't noticed the lack of noise as she prepared for the day, locked up in her room, brushing and re-brushing her hair, encouraging it to grow. Her mother had come in early and collected the children, allowing Marie a leisurely morning.

Marie dressed and then left her bedroom and entered the kitchen. "Mother?" Silence. Unnerving silence. She ventured out into the formal dining room and passed on into the living room, her eyes searching for her family, her ears pricked at the dead quiet of the house. She found Extra Horses sleeping on his stomach on his mat, his arms framing the sides of his head. She sat down beside him and poked his shoulder with her fingers.

"What is it?" he muffled.

"Extra Horses?"

The sound of Marie's voice brought him fully awake. He turned and looked at her, one eye peering a half inch above his arm. His heart began its rib-threatening thumping at the excitement of having her so near. He tried to breathe evenly and had to force himself to concentrate on the words she spoke.

"Did my family tell you where they were going?" Marie asked.

"A-are they all gone?" he stammered.

"Yes," she cried. "All of them. Even the children. I don't understand this. I can't believe they would just leave without telling me."

"Maybe they're all outside," he gulped. He began to shake. Marie was sitting too close. Much too close.

Marie took hold of his bare arm, her hands scalding his flesh as she tugged at him. "Come help me look for them."

"Now?" he cried. "You mean . . . now?"

"Yes, I mean now," she fumed. "Don't you want to help me?"

"I—I want to help you. But. . . ." His shyness made him tongue-tied. "You have to . . . leave the . . . room first."

"Oh," she teetered. "I forgot. You're not dressed, are you?" She rose and walked away. "I'll make coffee and wait for you in the kitchen," she called back over her shoulder.

Extra Horses slowly closed his eyes and lowered his head, uttered an audible moan. He had been dreaming about her all night long. Hot passionate dreams that made him feel ashamed. She was a recent widow and a sister to his two friends. "It isn't decent to feel this way about her," he chided himself. "And now . . . I am alone with her." He broke out into a clammy sweat. "Her father must trust me very much to leave us alone together." He tried to dwell on Renee's trust as he lay on his back, his quilt a phallic tent.

Extra Horses entered the kitchen cautiously, as if he were expecting the Lakota to be lying in wait for him on the other side of the doorway.

Marie smiled as she set a platter of fried bacon on the table and went back to the stove to pour a cup of coffee for him. When she turned with the cup in her hand, she saw that he continued to huddle in the doorway like a trembling puppy.

"Please come in and sit down," she coaxed. She buried her smile as he skulked in and almost fell over the trestle bench trying to take a seat. This might be . . . fun, she thought devilishly and suddenly was very glad they were alone.

Marie made straight for him, sitting down beside him as close as she dared. She placed the cup on the table, wise enough not to place the cup in his shaking hands.

"I think I know where they have all gone," she said in a breathy voice while placing a hand on his arm as if unaware of her familiarity.

Extra Horses, though wearing a thick winter shirt, felt the burning heat of her casual hand through the heavy leather of his sleeve.

"W-w-where?" he stuttered, unable to tear his eyes from her offending hand.

"Probably down to the trading store."

"All of them?"

"It looks that way," she sighed. "I didn't see anyone out in the yard but there are wagon tracks in the snow."

"T-they should have taken us with them," he said,

lowering his head and concentrating on placing his hands around the tin cup of hot coffee. Extra Horses was a man who dealt with life like a clock. One tick at a time. His normally clear mind faded as he sat there shaking and perspiring, the ticks of his internal clock sounding all at once. Just drink the coffee, he commanded himself while lifting the cup to his mouth with both hands. If she would only move away, even a little bit, his inner voice pained. But she didn't. Marie moved closer and bumped against him, causing him to slosh coffee all over himself.

"Oh my goodness," Marie laughed. "You've spilled again. You are so funny."

She left the table and Extra Horses tried to wipe away the hot liquid from his leggings.

"Here, I can help you," Marie said when she returned with a towel.

Extra Horses sat quietly, suffering all the pains of those damned to hell, as she used the towel to wipe away the spill, her hands lightly running all over his body. He knew he couldn't stand it anymore as his senses turned traitor on him, enjoying her intimacy, her touch, her woman's scent. As his loins heated, he realized he was enjoying it much too much. He grabbed the towel away from her with a jerk.

"Stop that," he said in a firm tone. He couldn't look at her as he finished the task himself.

"Have I offended you?" she asked timidly.

Hearing the worry and concern in her voice, he looked up at her and read the misgivings in her beautiful liquid eyes. His heart caught in his throat. He tried to speak, but couldn't.

Marie arched one brow, realizing that she had him squarely in the palm of her hand. She sat down beside him, mesmerizing him like a snake hypnotizing a grounded bird. "I wouldn't offend you on purpose." He was frozen with terror as she inched nearer and spoke in a breathy whisper. "I think you are nice."

"You do?" he croaked in falsetto.

"Hum-humm," she purred. "I'm glad my brothers brought you to visit with us. Are you glad?"

THE GLORY DAYS OF BUFFALO EGBERT

Extra Horses answered with a rapid nod as the hypnotic Marie pulled him further into her spell.

"I wish you would prove to me that you're glad." Her full mouth parted as she brought her face to within inches of his. "I'll prove to you how glad I am."

A small pitiful cry escaped his throat as Marie placed her mouth against his. His heart was beating as fast as a trapped rabbit's. He couldn't breathe. His whole body burned white hot, sweat trickling down his spine. But he didn't push her away. He couldn't. He slowly became absorbed by her tender kiss.

"Marie...." he whispered as she withdrew slightly. "Do that some more, please."

Marie smiled slyly as her arms went around his neck. A few seconds later his arms encircled her, pulling her in closer. Both of them moaned in their throats as the timorous kissing gave way to full-blown passion. Extra Horses held her tighter and tighter, their heads twisting as they devoured each other. After a kiss that lasted five minutes, Marie felt a slight wave of alarm as his kiss became urgent and demanding. She placed her hands against his shoulders, trying to push him away, but had little success because of his strength. After three more failed attempts, she finally managed to twist free, only to have his mouth crash back down on hers. Half frantic, Marie balled her fists and pelted his shoulders. He was so solidly built her battering only fazed him enough to bring him back into a semblance of reality.

"We can't kiss ... this ... good," Marie panted. She was slightly benumbed by how true the old women's tale concerning shy men was proving itself. "This is my father's house. He wouldn't be happy with what we are doing."

"He isn't here," Extra Horses gulped. "Please, can't we kiss just a little more, Marie? Please?"

She sat perfectly still, allowing him to again enfold her in his arms, enjoying his eagerness. "Would you like to touch me as well?" she said softly.

He nodded his head so violently she was afraid he might injure his brain.

"All right," she purred. "Here," she said, placing one of

MARDI OAKLEY MEDAWAR

his large hands against the roundness of her breast. "You may touch me here but no other place. All right?"

Extra Horses caressed her as if her breast were a precious treasure known only to him. A little cry escaped his throat as his desire welled up.

Marie placed her mouth on his, relishing his gentle kiss and his respectful caress, her nipple growing hard as excitement stirred and raced like mercury through her veins. Her hand traveled his chest muscles that rippled as she stroked him.

Extra Horses let go a frightened cry, breaking away from her as Marie's hand lightly touched the bulge between his legs. Sheepishly he glanced at her, his eyes sparkling with fear.

"Touching is all right," Marie cooed. "We have all of our clothing on."

Surrendering to her persisting hand, Extra Horses closed his eyes. His shoulders rolled forward as he placed one of his own hands on top of hers, pressing her fondling hand harder against him as Marie kissed his neck and traced his extended jugular vein with her tongue. He was almost at the point of orgasm when Marie murmured in his ear.

"You are huge," she whispered.

Without any warning, Extra Horses pushed her away with such force she nearly slid off the bench. He quickly scooted to the other end, propping his elbows on the table, and hiding his shamed face in his hands.

Shaken but undaunted, Marie now believed she knew the real cause of Extra Horses' shyness. Totally enamored of him, she stubbornly refused his rejection.

"Extra Horses," she said softly, moving back beside him. "Extra Horses, talk to me."

"Go away, Marie," he said into his hands. "Please . . . just go away."

Angrily, Marie clawed his hands away from his face, her own expression puckered as if she were about to do combat with one or both of her brothers.

"I will not go away!" she ranted. "I'm going to stay here until you talk to me."

"All right," he shouted, his face contorted in pain.

"You want me to talk, I'll talk. I'm no good for women, Marie. It's not because I don't like them. It's because . . . I was born . . . there's too much. . . ." His speaking abilities lessened as embarrassment crept back in and he wasn't able to finish his confession.

"Are you trying to tell me you think you are too big?" she asked.

He answered with a chagrined nod.

"Someone told you that, didn't they?"

Again the nod.

"Was it a woman?"

A small shake of his head.

"Male friends?"

His gaze crept slowly toward her as he nodded. He was nonplussed as Marie placed her forehead against his shoulder and began to shake with silent laughter.

"It isn't funny, Marie," he growled.

"Yes, it is," she hooted. She took his troubled face in her hands and forced him to look at her. "Did you never think your friends might be teasing you because they were jealous of your size?"

Extra Horses' eyes went blank as he answered in an alarmed voice. "No! They are my brothers. Brothers don't lie to each other."

She let go of his face as she doubled over, helpless against the silent laughter holding her mouth widely open.

"You mean . . . they lied?" he said, a surprised look on his face.

"Yes," she bleated, sound now accompanying the spasmodic laughter.

The revelation was almost too much to be borne as Extra Horses, a plain and simple man despite his handsome looks, thought back over all the years of self-inflicted celibacy. What had been meant only as a joke, he, in his self-conscious way, had taken as absolute gospel.

"Marie," he said defensively, "I would really appreciate it if you could stop laughing at me."

But Marie couldn't stop because she was at the snorting stage, helpless as tears rolled down her cheeks.

"I really did believe them," he said quietly.

She looked at him for a fraction of a second, holding her breath as she did so, then buckled at the waist.

"They said I was built for buffalo, not human women."

"Stop!" she shrieked. "You're killing me."

CHAPTER TWENTY-SIX

"Remember what I told you," Renee instructed the family as their wagon lumbered homeward. "We must all stay between them and keep them apart now that they've enjoyed getting acquainted. If we're successful, Extra Horses will be out of his head in a week."

Renee's secret weapon was his astute knowledge of men. In the following days, Extra Horses tried his best to sit by Marie at the table, but someone always pushed in between them, forcing him to sit far away from her. He tried many times to steal her off by herself but one or both of her brothers always appeared as if by magic, spoiling the moment. Extra Horses had to content himself with a brief, chaste kiss. Now that the ice had been broken with Marie and she didn't consider him a freak of nature, his blood came to a boil and simmered in his veins like molten lava.

Within three days he ached for her so badly he chewed his pillow in his sleep.

Renee maintained a steady watch over his prospective son-in-law and when he knew the time was ripe, he pushed Extra Horses one last subtle time so that the hesitant young man could find the gumption to ask for Marie's hand.

"Come on, Cody," Renee said in a robust, playful voice. "You are going to sleep with *Pa-Pere* and *Ma-Mere* tonight." His loud voice carried into the living room and was plainly heard by Extra Horses who was lying in his bed.

"May I really sleep with you, *Pa-Pere?*" Cody squealed, his little feet thumping the hard wooden floor of the hallway.

"Yes, you may, little baby-man," Renee said, leading Cody by the hand. "Your *Grandmere* misses her Cody. We will all snuggle against the cold, eh? Just like when you were a tiny baby."

For the impatient Extra Horses, it took an eternity for the house to settle. He could hear Jacques in his room, battling with his lively sons. Their racket went on and on.

Trying not to be the ruin of his father's scheme, as a last resort, Jacques allowed Antoine and Francoise in his bed with him. He hated sleeping with the twins. The boys were only half toilet-trained, hence they were notorious bedwetters. For Marie's sake, Jacques resigned himself to suffering a very soggy night.

Nicolas and Eyes-That-Shine giggled like children under their blankets, knowing the trap was set and that soon the unsuspecting Extra Horses would blunder in headfirst.

"Maybe he won't go in there," Nicolas rasped, voicing the unthinkable.

"Oh, but he will," Eyes-That-Shine returned. "He wants Marie so badly he's slobbering on himself."

As it neared midnight, everyone in the house lay wide awake and with ears sharp. Finally, with the first whine of the creaking floor, the scheming family smiled. Extra Horses had finally summoned the nerve to creep toward Marie's closed door.

Renee nudged Willow when he heard the quiet footfalls

in the hallway. "Get ready for your part, Wife. I'll tell you when."

Extra Horses opened Marie's door and closed it quickly and silently behind him. Marie lay curled in a little ball in the center of her bed as he tiptoed toward her. When he placed a trembling hand on her shoulder, Marie pretended to awaken with his touch.

"Marie," he said in a loud mumble. "It's me. I have to talk to you."

She moved over in the bed and raised the quilt. "It's too cold out there. Talk to me in here."

Extra Horses didn't need a second invitation. He all but leaped into the bed. A second later his mouth was on hers, kissing her, unleashing all of his pent-up passion and desire, and pushing her down into the bed as he moved on top of her.

"Marie . . . I have to have you," he strangled. "I can't stand this anymore. Please, Marie. Give me your loving. Touch me again the way you did too long ago." He shuddered as Marie's hand closed around his erect penis. He ground his teeth in the agony and pleasure her touchings gave him. "Marie," he rasped. "Take your clothes off. I want to touch you, too."

"I can't," she sobbed softly. "Not in my father's house. I'm not married to you. He would die with shame if he knew we were even doing this!"

"I'm going crazy," Extra Horses muffled into the pillow beside her head.

Marie's hand ran the length of his enormous member to the base as she breathed heavily. "I would love to feel this inside me. I ache to feel you inside me."

Extra Horses heaved himself up onto his arms. "Enough to marry me?"

"I don't know," Marie hedged.

"Is it because of your dead husband?" he pressed.

"No," she drawled, turning her face from him. "Because . . . you've never said you care for me. Only that you want me. If you don't care for me . . . then I don't want you for my husband."

"I care, Marie!" he shouted, forgetting for a moment

where he was. "I care, I care, I care! Now will you marry me?"

"Marie?" Willow called through the closed door.

Extra Horses jumped off of Marie and fell on the floor, landing on his back.

Willow heard the heavy thud and bit down hard on her lower lip. Composing herself, she opened the door to finish her part in the three-act farce.

"Marie? Are you all right?" Willow asked. "Your father and I thought we heard you crying. And what was that noise? It sounded like you fell out of your bed."

Renee was hot on his wife's heels, hoisting a lighted coal-oil lamp over his head. "How is she? Is she hurt?"

Nicolas took his cue the second he heard his father's voice and left a writhing Eyes-That-Shine who smothered her laughter into their pillow.

"What's the matter, *Pere*?" Nicolas gruffed loudly, joining the crowd at Marie's opened door.

Jacques wasn't able to move quite as quickly as his co-conspirators. He had to haul both of his sons along with him. He appeared behind Nicolas, both of his arms full, his sleeping shirt soaked from his sons' urine.

"Are we under attack?" Jacques cried.

"No," Renee barked, sounding impatient. "It's just your sister. She cried out in her sleep."

"Will everyone please leave me alone?" Marie pleaded. "I'm all right!"

Renee entered her room, holding the lamp out in front of him. As the lamp illuminated the room, Extra Horses was clearly seen trying to hide underneath Marie's bed. Renee roared like a bull. Both he and his sons charged forward, Jacques pausing a second to thrust his sons into his mother's waiting arms. Nicolas and Jacques dragged the kicking Extra Horses out from under the bed, loudly threatening him with physical abuse for his terrible breach of manners toward his hosts.

Marie stood in the center of her bed, screaming like a banshee, waking baby Jean in his cradle. Jean's crying set off Antoine and Francoise.

"Jacques! Nicolas!" Marie screamed even louder. "Let him go!"

They ignored their sister as they pulled Extra Horses back and forth between them.

"We should kill you!" Jacques raged.

"You've insulted our sister and in our father's own house!" Nicolas roared into Extra Horses' anxious face.

"He did not! He did not," Marie bawled. "He only came in here to ask me to marry him."

"What?" all three DeGeer men thundered in unison.

Renee pushed between his sons and stood close to Extra Horses who, in the light of the lamp Renee held between them, looked ashen with fright. "Is that true?" he demanded. "Is what my daughter says the truth?"

"Yes," Extra Horses choked. "I had to speak to her before I spoke to you, Renee. It would have hurt me too much if you said it was all right but she refused me."

"You're right," Renee growled. "A woman's rejection can be very humiliating for a man. And because I understand a man's pride, I forgive you your bad manners. But I have to ask you one question that gnaws my mind. Do you think it's proper to discuss marriage with a woman when you are naked?"

Willow fled the room. It had all become too much for her to brazen through. Behind the closed door of her bedroom, she let go her wild laughter as her grandsons screamed, their noise cloaking her hilarity.

The couple married nine days later. The wedding was kept small and brief, for they were expecting a blizzard. Only stalwart members of Extra Horses' clan braved the weather to attend the services. Five days before the wedding, the DeGeer men, which now included Extra Horses who, to honor his father-in-law, adopted the family name, cleared Marie's house of anything and everything that might remind her of Wolf's Tracks, and threaten the happiness of her new marriage. It was the Indian's down-to-earth belief that there could be no home for the present if the past was not solidly laid to rest. Marie had had a good life with Wolf's Tracks. He had been a devoted husband

and father, a fine son to Renee and a loyal brother to Jacques and Nicolas. But he was gone and nothing could ever bring him back. Marie had to go forward with her young life. A life that would revolve around the love and needs of a living husband. But before that could happen, the ghost of Wolf's Tracks had to be exorcised.

Marie stayed in her room. She held her sons and watched out the window as her father, brothers and intended husband built a large bonfire and set alight all the furniture Wolf's Tracks had struggled to build with his big clumsy hands. Watching the flames, she nursed baby Jean and cuddled Cody.

"As long as you two live," she said to Cody, "your father lives. Always remember, he was my first love. No matter how many brothers and sisters come after you, you will always be the most special to me. But never say that to your new father. It would hurt his feelings. He is a most sensitive man."

"Yes MaMa," Cody promised.

If it had not been for his slavish devotion to Margueritte, Cody would have felt very left out of family life during the wedding and honeymooning of his mother. Happily, he tended the baby girl while Eyes-That-Shine helped Willow with the wedding dress and the furnishing of the empty house where Marie and Extra Horses would share conjugal bliss. With all the bottles still in the DeGeer house, leftovers from the twins, the feeding of baby Jean proved no problem. Marie and Extra Horses could honeymoon until they crippled one another if it pleased them. Willow had everything else well under control. And that pleased her.

"Watch Cody," Eyes-That-Shine whispered to Willow as they sat on the living room couch. Willow was bottle-feeding baby Jean. Cody was on the floor, lying on his stomach next to Margueritte. They were playing a game of peek-a-boo, Margueritte's favorite pastime.

Cody put a blanket over Margueritte's head and called, "Where am I Margie? Where am I?" When Margueritte pulled the blanket back and laughed, Cody laughed, too. "Here I am," he sang. "Here's Margie's Cody."

Cody's head shot up as he heard his grandfather calling him from the kitchen. He jumped up to run for Renee until Margueritte wailed a complaint at being abandoned. Cody showed to whom he felt the most loyalty as he dashed back to Margueritte and squatted down in front of her. "I won't be far away," he crooned. "I will come back to you. I promise Margie. Don't cry. I will come back." He scooted off and Margueritte's eyes stayed on the doorway as she waited for him to make good his word.

"He is so good with her," Eyes-That-Shine mused. "He looks so rough, but with Margueritte, he is so gentle."

"Cody has always been a good little boy," Willow said proudly. "He gets his looks from the other one." She was referring to Wolf's Tracks, but his name could no longer be mentioned, even in casual passing. "That one had a gentle spirit, too. Even though he had terrible features, I am glad he fathered Cody. The world could do with more men like him, no matter how unlovely they look. My only hope for Cody is that he finds a good woman to love him. One who won't care that he isn't handsome. A woman like his mother, who never saw the other one as being ugly in the face. But," she sighed, "I'm glad she has a pretty husband this time. Together they will make beautiful babies. I only hope their spirits are as nice as their faces."

Eyes-That-Shine put a resounding amen to that comment. "What we do not need is more like Antoine! I know Jacques would kill me for even saying it, but some days I would like to drown Antoine in the river."

"It wouldn't work," Willow chuckled. "If he didn't pop back up to the surface, the men would all jump in and drag him out. Babies like Antoine appeal to men. We women favor the sweet ones. But men . . . they prefer children with daring and Antoine has a lot of daring."

The harsh storms of winter kept the Lakota and Cheyenne temporarily at bay. The foul weather blessed the Crow with time to prepare for a trouble-filled summer. Jacques stayed home with his children, taking them out on occasional hunts. Francoise didn't appreciate the father-son outings. He hated going out as much as Antoine hated coming back. They looked like tiny little Eskimos dressed in their furred winter garb and snowshoes. Francoise plodded along in the gut-strung rigging, awkward and dour, while Antoine scampered like a jackrabbit, barely noticing the webbed contraptions strapped to his feet.

Jacques had No Talker make bows and arrows to fit his sons. No Talker, his voice a rough whisper due to the cancer in his throat from years of inhaling dust and stone chippings, used the opportunity to wheeze out a warning to Jacques to return to the bow himself before he met his doom. Jacques promised he would, but both he and the old man knew he was only being polite. Jacques had just purchased a fine new repeater, almost a carbon copy of the one placed inside Charlie's grave.

Francoise was very careful with his bow. The family mourned that the same couldn't be said for Antoine. Antoine aimed and fired at anything that came within his small range. He put out two window panes, ended the life of one of Willow's fancy living room lamps and missed Renee's derriere by inches as Renee bent to chuck baby Jean under the chin. An armed Antoine was more than Marie could endure. She cut short her honeymoon and retrieved her sons.

Marie needn't have worried. After the near miss of his posterior, Renee took the bow away from Antoine and Francoise, hiding the lethal weapons in his bedroom. He presented the twins with two ponies to end their incessant crying and to make up for the loss of their bows. Happily for all concerned, the ponies seemed to satisfy the lively boys. Not to be outdone, Extra Horses found a beautiful pinto for Cody, presenting the small horse with all the pomp of a stepfather anxious to win over a new son.

Cody took to his horse like a born rider. He amazed even Renee with his skill and the hours of care he lavished on his pony. But as much as Cody loved the pony, the brown and white pinto did not usurp his feelings for little Margueritte. Nothing in Cody's life was more important than his favorite cousin. Margueritte learned to walk holding on to Cody's hands. He fed her special tidbits of

whatever sweet treats came his way. He rarely accepted
the special treats for himself. He squirreled them away in a
piece of calico cloth for Margie. He gave them to her when
they were left alone together, his heart filling with joy as
she ate trustingly out of his hand.

As for Antoine, he had special feelings for his girl
cousin as well. He enjoyed terrorizing her. As Margueritte
toddled about the house, legs wide, arms bent at the
elbows as she mastered her new craft, Antoine jumped out
from behind doors or furniture screaming a war whoop
and plop, down she would go, smacking her baby's
bottom on the hardwood flooring, squawling until her
face turned beet-red. When enough became too much,
Eyes-That-Shine took Jacques to task over the sins of
his son.

"Jacques, if you don't spank Antoine, I will."

Calmly, Jacques pursed his lips, his eyebrows meeting
at the bridge of his nose. "Little Sister, I love you very
much, but if you spank my son, I promise, I will spank
you. Margueritte isn't hurt. She's only mad. In fact, she
reminds me of you when you were little and Nicky made
you mad. And you see how well you and Nicky turned
out."

"There is just no talking to you," she huffed, storming
off with her baby girl in tow.

Before Eyes-That-Shine's complaints could inflame the
rest of the family, Jacques took his sons out again, dragging along a small tepee. He and his boys stayed out until
mid-February. When they finally returned, everyone was
glad to see them, including Eyes-That-Shine, who grudgingly admitted that life had grown almost dull without
Antoine to keep the household enlivened.

"I shot two rabbits, *Ma-Mere*," Antoine proudly
reported as Willow unwrapped his heavy clothing. The
entire family had gathered in the large kitchen to greet
their missing members.

"You did, baby-man?" Willow exclaimed as she kissed
his rosy cheeks. "Where are the rabbits?"

"Francoise ate them," Antoine accused as the culprit
Francoise stood shamefaced. "But we still have the skins,"
he chirped. "*Pere*. Show *Ma-Mere* and *Pa-Pere* the skins."

Jacques opened a bag and produced two hacked rabbits' skins. "He skinned them himself," Jacques grinned.

"Oh, no!" Marie howled, clutching little Jean. "He's finally done it. He's given him a knife!"

"All boys need a knife, Marie," Jacques frowned. "Cody should have a bow and a knife. It's past his time. You overprotect your sons, girl. Extra Horses should wean Cody from your breast so he can grow his man teeth."

Extra Horses looked down at the little boy standing quietly beside him. "Son, would you like to have a bow and a knife?"

Cody looked shyly up at his stepfather. "Yes, please."

"No!" Marie blared.

"Woman," Extra Horses said calmly but firmly. "He's my son. He will have a bow and a knife and I will teach him to use them."

"Well said, Brother," Jacques smirked.

"Shut up, Jacques," Marie sulked, stomping out of the kitchen.

"So much for the happy homecoming," Francoise said in his typical dry tone. The DeGeers doubled with laughter.

Early March saw an end to family jocularity. The Lakota stormed three Crow homes, burned them to the ground and slaughtered the inhabitants. Tippleton joyously received his transfer orders from General Sherman. Brigadier General George Crook was sent into the Montana Territory to advise Sherman as to the extent of the growing hostilities between the Crow and Lakota. Crook burned up the telegraph wires between Montana and Oklahoma, advising Sherman of the "severe seriousness of the Sioux's spring campaigns." In April of 1876, Colonel John Gibbon was ordered to march from Fort Ellis to meet with the gathered Crow on the Yellowstone River. Nicolas, Jacques and Extra Horses left two weeks before Gibbon, joining up with their brothers, eager to be in on the big fight everyone knew was coming.

THE GLORY DAYS OF BUFFALO EGBERT

Before Jacques left, he counseled with his sons. "I want you both to try and be better little persons for your *Granmere*. She's a sweet woman but you two try her nerves. And, Antoine, I mean it. Do you understand me?"

"*Oui,* PaPa," Antoine grumbled, his rosebud mouth twisted to one side.

Francoise began to cry. Tears rolled down his pudgy cheeks and splashed onto his shirt. "I don't want you to go, PaPa. I am afraid for you to go."

"PaPa is a warrior," Antoine said proudly, his small spine stiffening as he folded his arms across his puffed out chest.

Jacques pulled in both of his sons, hugging them tightly as he kissed each of them on their faces. "Your PaPa is so proud of his boys. So very proud. Your mother would be so pleased if she could see how well you are growing up. When the flowers bloom I want you to remember to take some to her grave as often as you can. Tell her they are from her husband and sons who miss her. Will you do that for your sentimental PaPa?"

"Yes," they said together.

"*Bon,*" Jacques said as he rose from his kneeling position. "It is time for me to go. Your uncles are waiting."

Colonel John Gibbon was a slight, springy man of thirty-seven. His mustache was so glazed with wax it shone like glass in the bright morning light of the early spring. Standing five feet eight, he wasn't tall by Crow standards. The Crow, prideful of their stature, typically paid little heed to shorter men, believing them to be lesser than themselves. Yet Gibbon held them spellbound. Paying the Crow his highest compliment, he wore his fancy dress uniform for the Council. The Crow sat on the ground and watched, transfixed, as this spry man paced his little prancing walk back and forth in front of them, his Crow interpreter following at his heel half-tempted to try the jaunty stride himself. Colonel Gibbon felt the eyes of all the Crow on him and his ego doubled, believing they held him in reverent awe. Had he been able to read their minds, he would have been mortified, for a great many of

them sat wondering if his strange gait was the result of
hemorrhoids developed after too many days in the saddle.
But, eccentric strut aside, he did reach them with his
words.

"Crow Brothers. The Sioux are your enemy and ours.
For a long time they have been killing white men and
Crow. I am going to punish them. If the Crow want to
make war upon the Sioux, now is their time. If the Crow
want to prevent the Sioux from sending war parties into
Crow country to murder more Crow, now is the time. If
the Crow want to get revenge for their brothers who have
already fallen, now is the time."

Jacques, Nicolas and Extra Horses were sitting on the
front row, a scant two feet from the prancing army
colonel. The three of them began beating their war clubs
against the ground. The action was soon taken up by the
rest of the Crow, the earth responding to the rhythm,
vibrating steadily beneath the Colonel's highly polished
boots. The three DeGeers and twenty-seven others left
with Gibbon immediately. The rest of the Crow warriors
promised to meet General Crook in two months' time.

On June 14, 1876, nearly two hundred Crow, under the
leadership of Medicine Crow, Old Crow and Good Heart,
met General Crook on the banks of the Tongue River, a
river which wound its way along the Montana-Wyoming
border. General Crook had been a busy man while waiting
for the Crow. He had established a base camp and supply
post along Goose Creek. His actions had not gone unno-
ticed by Crazy Horse. Crazy Horse sent five riders to warn
Crook off with his message: "Cross the Tongue when you
are ready to die."

Crazy Horse wasn't fooled for one moment by the soldiers
who seemed to heed this warning and settle into a permanent campsite, making no movement whatsoever toward
the barrier river. His warriors, however, were elated,
believing they had frightened the white army to a standstill. But Crazy Horse knew a waiting man when he saw

one. He immediately sent for more warriors, instructing his couriers to be careful and slip by Crook's Crow scouts. When he was given word several days later that his extra warriors had arrived, Crazy Horse cunningly kept his extra hundreds hidden in the hills.

Somehow, and no one could talk him out of it, Crook came up with the notion that Crazy Horse was protecting a village. Time and again he sent his Crow to search for the supposed village, Nicolas and Jacques leading the scouts every time a party was sent out. And after each reconnoiter, Jacques and Nicolas stood in the general's personal tent with the same report.

"*Monsieur* General, there is no village. There are only men. Lots and lots of men."

The DeGeers were dismissed, Crook no more convinced of the truth than he had ever been.

"Those two Frenchy-Crow didn't look hard enough," he growled. "There's a village out there all right. I can feel it. I can almost smell the women cooking their putrid foods. I haven't met a half-breed yet who wasn't a coward at heart. It wouldn't surprise me to learn that those two hid from the Sioux. I'd bet my last dollar that they didn't look for anything, much less a village."

Jacques and Nicolas left the officers' area, happy to be away from the glowering general. "Are all white men crazy?" Jacques asked his brother.

"Yes," Nicolas grunted.

The exhausted brothers collapsed in the Crow encampment, but sleep wasn't to be their reward after so many days and nights deprived of it. The ground rumbled with the sound of hundreds of horses. Nicolas and Jacques jumped from their beds and raced out of their tepee, running with the rest of the Crow, armed against what they believed was an attack. They came to stand alongside Medicine Crow, all of the watching Crow astonished by the sight coming toward them. It was the Shoshone. Hundreds of them, dressed in their finest and under the command of Chief Washakie, an old dog of a man, well past his years of combat, but girded for it none the less.

The arriving Shoshone put on quite a show of their equestrian abilities, riding in tight-knit groups, each group moving around the other in such precision it boggled the minds of the watching soldiers. Admiring their impressive entrance, Medicine Crow rumbled a deep chesty laugh. With an over-the-head wave of his arm, he signaled his Crow to mount up. The Crow, never ones to stand idle while others of their kind showed their feathers, displayed some fancy riding of their own, some standing in their saddles, arms extended, others choosing to lie pressed against the sides of their horses as they all galloped circles around the parading Shoshone. The men of the regular army cheered the spectacle, waving their hats in the air. The officers were agog over the parade. "There isn't a man on God's earth who can outride an Indian," said one shavetail lieutenant.

That evening the Crow and the Shoshone, longtime enemies but at present allies, conducted separate ceremonies. The soldiers who meandered back and forth between the Indian encampments to ogle the proceedings, were fascinated when they discovered that the ceremonies were identical. The Indians beat their drums and sang songs, preparing themselves for the battle to come.

In the meantime, Washakie and Medicine Crow held council with General Crook and his staff of officers. Of all the men present, Medicine Crow was the most tender in years, but his ability to listen and digest all that he heard made him the greatest leader of all the assembled men. This ability, combined with his warrior's skills, had catapulted him early into the rank of a major chief. He listened attentively to Washakie's brash statements of quick victory and Crook's rambling insistences of a Lakota village which they must seek out and destroy.

Feeling uneasy in his heart, Medicine Crow elicited from Crook the assurance that the Indians would participate in the battle in their own fashion and only under the command of their chosen chiefs. At first Crook refused, but when he became fearful that Medicine Crow would leave and take his Crow with him, he grudgingly yielded to Medicine Crow's terms and the meeting was called to a close.

Leaving the general's tent in the company of his old

nemesis, Medicine Crow turned to Washakie. "Don't hold that man's hand too tightly. I am afraid of him."

Before dawn on June 16th, Crook crossed the Tongue River, turning northwest in the direction of the ground held by the Sioux. He sent out Indian scouts of which Nicolas DeGeer was one. The scouts reported back in the late afternoon that the hills, "move with Lakota." Crook sent Nicolas and his men out again as he camped with his army on the edge of Rosebud Creek. Medicine Crow doubled his Crow guards, growing more and more uneasy as the long night passed. But the more Medicine Crow worried over his younger brother's report, the more confident Crook seemed to become. Crook was simply unable to comprehend that when his Crow scouts reported that the hills were full of the enemy, they meant exactly that. The Crow scouts saw about fifteen hundred men of the combined Lakota Nations who were with Crazy Horse. And going on their Indian instincts, the scouts knew that Crazy Horse had more than twenty-five hundred more men that they hadn't seen. Crook was steadily placing all of his men, red and white, in serious jeopardy and there was no getting through to Crook his strategic error.

The allied army mounted up the following morning, advancing still further against the biding Crazy Horse. On the morning of June 17th, Crook initiated the biggest gaffe of his military career. While the morning dew clung to the wild roses growing in profusion around the creek and in the valley which had inspired the name of this fateful place, Rosebud Creek, Crook allowed his men to bisect the stream, unsaddle their horses and relax as they made their morning coffee and breakfast. Even the ardent devotee of the white man, Washakie, was incapable of understanding this foolhardy behavior.

Quickly, the old Shoshone chief counseled with Medicine Crow. Together they stood on a small hill studying the terrain, turning in small circles as they surveyed the larger hills surrounding them. The valley was like an amphitheater. Crazy Horse himself couldn't have chosen a better battlefield or positioned the enemy army at a greater disadvantage. Crook's soldiers were in a valley and divided by the creek. The valley was surrounded by hills and bluffs. Crook's men had no inkling of the danger they were in as they took their leisure. Medicine Crow and Washakie exchanged dark looks.

"Now you understand what I said of this man?" Medicine Crow asked.

Washakie nodded.

"We must take our men into the hills far away from this place," Medicine Crow seethed.

The Crow and the Shoshone quickly made for higher ground while the soldiers idled, smelling the roses and savoring their coffee.

From his lofty perch above the cursed valley, Medicine Crow heard the first volley of shots. He saw his Crow scouts racing for safety, one horse in tow with a body slung over it. The Sioux were in hot pursuit of the fleeing Crow. Medicine Crow and a following of his men galloped down the side of the bluff and intervened, saving the scouts who rushed into Crook's encampment yelling, "Lakota! Lakota!"

The limp body on the trailing horse slid to the ground. It was Nicolas. He had been shot in the head.

Crook yelled at his men to mount up and ordered the surgeon to tend to the fallen half-breed. Nicolas was still alive but just barely.

Orderlies raced over and grabbed Nicolas by his arms and legs and tossed him none too gently into a wagon. As the doctor kneeled over Nicolas, the wagon groaned as it left the valley at breakneck speed. Out of the thick of it, the doctor quickly established a first-aid tent and within an hour, it was overflowing with the dying and wounded. Because Nicolas was first in line for treatment, he received better care than a quick prayer and a bandage.

"His mother did a fine piece of work brewing him," the doctor muttered, as he checked Nicolas. "She blessed him with a skull of cast iron. I can get the bullet," he told his aide, "but he's gonna bleed like a sonofabitch when I take it out. So get ready for it." The doctor, Captain Jefferson, extracted the chunk of metal as if it were an abscessed tooth and his aide, Private Daniels, instantly applied the compresses. Nicolas would live, though he wouldn't regain consciousness for five days. For Nicolas, the Battle of Rosebud Creek was over.

For Jacques, it had only begun.

Two factors saved Crook on that fateful spring morning. One was his alert Crow and Shoshone. The second was his crazed conviction over the nonexistent village. The Crow and the Shoshone withstood the brunt of the assault as wave after wave of Lakota poured down from the hills, filling the picturesque valley with the sounds of gunfire and the groans of men fighting in hand-to-hand combat. The fabled valley of roses would not see its annual crop of bright orange rose hips for the autumn harvest, a great wintertime fare, tangy and nutritious. The rosebushes were crushed under the pounding hooves of horses and bloodied by dying bodies.

The Crow and Shoshone fought so bravely Crazy Horse called for more assistance, signaling his waiting hundreds. It was then that Crook's insanity inadvertently saved the day.

General Crook, giving up on his Crow scouts to tell him the truth about the village and still fixated with the idea, sent Captain Anson Mills and his cavalry company up the Rosebud canyon with the mission of finding the village and destroying it. A burning village, Crook reasoned, would throw off Crazy Horse's attention from the valley where Crazy Horse was establishing a sound victory.

Crazy Horse saw the detachment of army leave, but he refused to follow after them. This valley was a good place to fight and Crazy Horse wasn't about to change the battlefield.

Crook realized his mistake finally, and at last, as Crazy Horse continued to hammer away at the divided army, the allied Indians held the breach Crook's breakfasting had produced. Quickly, Crook sent a man after Mills, ordering Mills' return.

Jacques slowed his horse when he fired his rifle. While

he was at a standstill, he felt a stab to his left leg. A mounted Lakota had maneuvered in close to him and was hacking away at Jacques's leg, the Lakota's battle-ax rising and falling and dripping with Jacques's blood. Calmly, Jacques shot the offending Lakota squarely in the chest, then paused a moment, and then looked down and saw that his left leg was wounded deeply—his leggings soggy and thick with his own blood. He felt mildly curious about the lack of pain and with his right leg he kicked his horse into a canter, riding into the center of the battle. He kept riding and shooting until his blood loss was so severe he blacked out and fell off his horse backwards.

Medicine Crow saw his brother's slow-motion fall. He saw Jacques's favorite horse escaping the battleground. On foot, Medicine Crow raced to Jacques and stood over him, firing his repeating rifle to defend Jacques's body from the Lakotas anxious to get at it. Ironically, several Shoshone came to Medicine Crow's aid and stood with him in a semicircle, defending the fallen Crow. They would have all been murdered if Crook's stupidity hadn't provided a savior who rushed in and saved them.

Mills was reached in time and he was as canny a man as his commander was inadequate. Mills found himself behind the Lakota reinforcements Crazy Horse had sent for. Charging after them and firing, the Lakota galloping toward the battlefield were surprised by the hard-riding army closing on their flank. Panic-stricken, they erred in the assumption that the returning Mills was an army such as themselves, extra men called out of reserve. The reinforcement band of Lakota broke before reaching the battleground, scattering back to the safe confines of the hills. Mills didn't bother to chase them. He kept up his charge straight into the active battlefield. Crazy Horse's strategy, which would have proven fatal for his enemies under normal circumstances, was now lost to him as Mills was moving in fast on Crazy Horse's rear guard. Before his valuable men were killed, Crazy Horse signaled the retreat. The Lakota left the valley, Crook the winner of the battle by an unmitigated bungle. It wasn't a victory Crook would ever enjoy.

Lieutenant Cravis, an accountant by nature, a soldier

by parental design, was Crook's ruination. Notebook in hand, Cravis penned a clear and damning accounting of the littered battleground. Twenty-five thousand rounds of ammunition used, thirteen Lakota dead on the ground. Twenty-eight soldiers dead, another fifty-six severely wounded. Cravis didn't bother tallying the numbers of the dead and wounded suffered by the Indian allies. Their numbers were too vast even for him. He hid his notebook from Crook as the battered and limping army straggled the miles back to the main base at Goose Creek.

The barely-touched Lakota had ridden off to fight another day. One week later Crazy Horse and his men converged on another valley and another General— Custer—at the Little Bighorn River. Having noted his one mistake with Crook, Crazy Horse didn't repeat it with Custer. And the Crow, too, had learned a hard lesson. After the Rosebud defeat, the Crow went back to their original edict set down years before by Renee and Major Pease. The Crow would act as scouts but the army couldn't force them to join in any of the fighting. None of the Crow scouts leading Custer participated in the Little Bighorn except for Mitch Boyer. And Mitch rode out against his own kind only because of the insults Custer hurled at him.

If Custer had one talent, that talent was in knowing how to goad an Indian. He taunted Mitch unmercifully about being a Frenchy-Sioux and not a true Crow at all. Mitch was so embarrassed in front of his fellow scouts, he allowed his wounded pride to place him in the middle of a slaughter and become a victim of the most stinging defeat the U.S. Army ever suffered.

Custer's Cheyenne wife, a young girl of startling beauty, was a captive he had chosen from among the frightened remnants of one of his most nefarious campaigns. In the winter of 1868 Custer rode against the Southern Cheyenne, attacking the winter village of the peace chief known as Black Kettle in a surprise assault on the sleeping village nestled on the Washita River. It was a massacre Custer heralded as a resounding victory.

The young girl he chose was named Monahsitah, a name noticeably absent in the white Mrs. Custer's highly publicized journals. Journals she supposedly penned while at her husband's side and braving the raw frontier. The absence of the Cheyenne girl's name was later to be seen as proof that the journals, coupled with several photographs taken of Colonel and Mrs. Custer on prairie picnics, while all the rave of Washington after Custer's death, were primarily fiction, the white Mrs. Custer having braved more years on the frontiers of Washington, D.C. than with her husband on the frontier. But to give the woman her due, the politicians of Washington were far and away more savage than the Indians she supposedly met. The Cheyenne girl held no love for Custer but, due to her strict moral upbringing, remained loyal to him until she was certain the father of her son was truly dead. After the report was confirmed beyond all shadow of doubt, Monahsitah lost no time in remarrying one of her own kind. Custer's son, shielded and raised by the Cheyenne people, was named Yellow Swallow.

Jacques drifted in and out of consciousness as Medicine Crow supervised his transport toward medical attention. Captain Jefferson had his hands full as he scurried from one wounded man to the next. The doctor paused long enough at Jacques's side to tell Medicine Crow, through an interpreter, that although Jacques had lost a lot of blood, his life could be saved. However, the nearly severed leg would have to be amputated.

Medicine Crow watched silently as the doctor raced off to inspect the other wounded being brought in. He crouched down beside Jacques and lightly slapped his face, bringing Jacques around.

"Little Brother, precious to my heart," Medicine Crow said somberly. "That medicine man says you will live. But only if he takes your leg away. Little Brother, hear me. I need to know if you wish to live out your life as a one-legged man, or die now and enter the next world with both."

Jacques's whole being throbbed with pain, his eyes were glazed with it. His rasping voice was barely audible over the cries and moans of the other wounded.

"Would you have me live out my life in shame? To

crawl on my belly and be as a beggar feeding on scraps and . . . pitied . . . by my sons?"

"No," Medicine Crow choked. He turned his face away as a single tear tracked his face. After a long moment he stood and spoke tenderly. "Close your eyes, Little Brother."

Jacques slowly complied, only faintly feeling the muzzle of Medicine Crow's rifle against his temple. "I love you," he heard Medicine Crow sob.

All heads turned as the shot sounded. Captain Jefferson was kneeling over three wounded men, just a scant seven yards away from Jacques when the shot was fired. He looked back over his shoulder at a lifeless Jacques, then stared in utter horror at Medicine Crow.

"Dear God in heaven!" Jefferson cried. "He shot him! He shot and killed his own man!"

CHAPTER TWENTY-SEVEN

Antoine murkily remembered his father. Over the passing years, Jacques had become a tall, shadowy, featureless figure lurking in the back of his mind. Nicolas was *Pere*. *Mere* was Eyes-That-Shine. *Pa-Pere* Renee was an old and senile man who sat for hours on the front porch in his rocking chair. Renee's mind never fully recovered after Willow's sudden passing two years prior, in 1883. The DeGeers no longer buried their own in the sky. A family cemetery was located on the site of Charlie's original grave, her body reburied next to Jacques, Willow at rest on the other side of her son. Nicolas and Eyes-That-Shine had another child, a son, whom they named Jack, honoring their lost brother.

The face of the Crow reserve was slowly changing as more whites moved on to the agency, taking over Crow jobs and listing themselves eligible for Crow entitlements. The whites wanted to Americanize everything and began first with a census, a census which lumbered the Crow with Christian names. On these rolls, Extra Horses was known as Henri DeGeer. He and Marie had three more children, two girls, Susanne and Isablee, and one boy named Marc. Eyes-That-Shine, renamed Anne, never received her own house which Nicolas had promised her. But it didn't worry her because she had all she could cope with as mother to four children and as a stand-in for Willow, managing the large house left to her.

Cattle foraged on the DeGeer range as buffalo meat became an almost unheard-of luxury during the last two decades of the 1800s. Nicolas and Henri raised the mongrel cattle for family consumption and for sale to the army. During his half-lucid moments, when Renee espied the grazing beasts placidly wandering the open range, he loudly complained about the "buffalo in the yard," and yelled for Jacques to shoot them. Renee always yelled for Jacques when he wasn't yelling for Willow. He no longer recognized Nicolas, which Nicolas shrugged off to his worrying wife.

"Why should he?" Nicolas asked. "I don't look like myself anymore. He probably believes I'm the one who died, not Jacques."

Nicolas's reasoning was plausible in that he kept his hair tied back in a single ponytail, attired himself in thick denim jeans covered by leather chaps, went about in clogging boots and a black western hat on his head. Renee only saw a white man as Nicolas climbed the steps to the porch. Renee's cataract-filmed eyes darted toward the intruder and challenged, "Were you invited here?"

"Yes, I was," Nicolas replied patiently.

"Are you staying to eat?"

"Yes, I am."

"Then you must be a friend to my son Jacques."

"*Pere* . . . I'm Nicolas."

"Nicolas?" Renee went back to his steady rocking as he thought about Nicolas. Then, with an impatient wave,

Renee gruffed, "Nicolas is in the house, too. You may go in."

There was a new movement afoot which, if Renee had had the wit left to understand its subtlety, would from somewhere have found the strength for one last fight. The movement was called "Friends to the Indians." It began in splinter groups, later to converge in historic Lake Mohonk, New York, as a single powerful lobby to pressure Washington to their way of viewing the Indian situation. Their goal was a simple one, to exterminate the Indian tribal way of life and assimilate the Indian into the American way of life. Tribal habit of share-and-share-alike was abhorred and viewed as communistic. Tribal languages were regarded as an unnecessary barrier between Indians and their white neighbors.

The "Friends" decided to launch their high-minded campaign against Indian children, proclaiming the Indian adult generation a lost cause. Missionaries were the next flood of white pilgrims the Indians were unable to fend off. Quakers took over the schools, churches and social orders. Indian agents were also replaced by Quakers. The Crow language was duly outlawed as a public form of address.

Antoine's bare feet raised dust as he ran at breakneck speed away from the hated school. The schoolmistress stood on the porch of the schoolhouse screaming after him.

"Antoine! Antoine DeGeer. You come right back this minute."

Antoine paused momentarily, dropped his trousers, flashed her his rounded bottom, then raced on, heading for home. Breathless, he found Nicolas in the barn unsaddling a work horse.

"Pere," Antoine wheezed, "she did it again."

Nicolas dropped the saddle and made for his heavily breathing son. He dropped to one knee, taking Antoine's small shoulders in his hands as his eyes searched the boy's sweaty face.

"You told her never to do that, but she did it anyway, *Pere*." Antoine paused to gulp in a load of air. "She beat Cody's hands with that stick. She almost made him cry this time, *Pere*."

Martha Carpenter heard the sound of horses' hooves outside. She paled, one hand trembling. Those slight movements were all that revealed her frayed nerves. She stood straight and tall as she reminded herself that she had locked the door of the schoolroom. Mr. DeGeer might be angry, but he would have to keep his emotions where they belonged—outside. She was the authority and she was determined to drive that point home. What she hadn't counted on was Nicolas's booted foot. The door splintered under his impact and she almost swooned as Nicolas, followed by an even angrier Henri, strode in as if they owned the classroom. She collected herself, not missing for a moment the darting smiles of the children as the men marched through the evenly rowed desks toward her.

"Mr. DeGeer," she began in her most authoritative voice. "You are out of order. Your presence is most unwelcome. . . ."

"Let me see your hands, Cody," Henri interrupted, standing next to his son. From under his desktop, the shy adolescent Cody extracted his big clumsy hands. They were mottled and welted. Henri nodded to Nicolas, his eyes flickering fury.

Wordlessly, Nicolas picked up the punishing ruler. "Hold out your hands," he fumed.

Martha Carpenter took two steps backwards. "I will certainly do no such thing!" she gasped.

"Then I will help you."

Quaker Agent Williams was taking his afternoon constitutional as was his wont, his pudgy hands clasped behind his back, his bowler hat perched atop his balding head, at peace with himself and his mission in life. Things were going swimmingly. Quaker Williams basked in the applause the "Friends" awarded him in regard to "his Crow." The accomplishments of the five civilized tribes in the East were the targeted goals Agent Williams held for his plains charges. So far, the Crow were a shining example of what could be accomplished among the nomads. The Crow were settled on allotments of lands, the surplus land, treaties never standing, deeded back to the government. The Crow country was now cut by half. In another twenty years it would be halved again.

The children were in compulsory school. The adults were farming and raising cattle. There were still the pesky problems of chiefs, tribal customs and heathen religion, but Quaker Williams knew there was time enough to eradicate these trouble spots. Yes, there was time. The next generation of Crow would be English-speaking Christians, mingling and interacting with their white cousins.

The piercing screams from the schoolhouse brought him up short. Astonished, he saw the children flying out of the schoolhouse, breaking like a swarm of flies, heading off in various directions.

"Oh, those little scamps," he chortled. "Another snake in the schoolroom, is it? Well, I'd best go to the rescue of Sister Carpenter."

He was even more surprised when he met Nicolas standing at the top of the stairs. Henri DeGeer was mounted on his horse with the DeGeer children in front and behind him on the horse. The DeGeers were a quarrel-some family and though Agent Williams was loath to admit it, he didn't care for any of them.

"What seems to be the trouble here?" Williams blustered.

"That woman!" Nicolas fired. "That woman is the trouble. She won't stop hitting our children. So I hit her. The same way she hit our Cody. And if she ever hits another child, I'll be back."

"Now see here!" Williams shouted after Nicolas. "You just can't come in here and hit teachers!"

402

THE GLORY DAYS OF BUFFALO EGBERT

Nicolas heaved himself up into the saddle and fetched Francoise up after him. Francoise in turn helped up Margie. "And you white people can't come on to Crow land and hit Crow children. You should remember you are only guests here. Nothing more! If you can't behave correctly as guests, then you should get off our lands forever!" Nicolas whirled his horse around and the DeGeers left the waffling agent in the dust.

The quaking Quaker rushed into the schoolroom to find Sister Carpenter sobbing, her head down on her desk. "My hands," she moaned. Agent Williams carefully lifted her hands and examined them. Ugly red welts pulsated in her palms. The offending ruler lay in two pieces on the floor.

"Oh God!" she cried. "Give me strength to love these heathen!"

Renee DeGeer died on the front porch in his rocking chair September 23, 1886. Stepping on to the porch and removing his hat, Nicolas realized his father was dying when Renee failed to challenge his presence in the too-familiar pattern.

"*Pere?*" Nicolas breathed.

Renee's eyes, strangely clear, regarded his son.

Nicolas raced toward Renee, skidding into a crouch in front of the rocking chair. "*Pere?*"

"Don't shout," Renee grumbled. "I can hear you, Nicky."

Nicolas took Renee's cold hands in his. They felt bloodless. Renee's body was dying but his mind flickered one final gleam of life.

"I killed her, you know."

"Who, *Pere?*" Nicolas sobbed. "Who did you kill?"

"Jacques's little girl wife," Renee sighed heavily, glad at last to be free of his dreadful secret.

"I know," Nicolas said in a voice too soft for Renee to hear. He lowered his head, rocking slightly as he strangled the sob, "I've always known."

Renee hadn't heard Nicky's words and his mind seemed to dull again to the present as he pleaded, "Don't ever tell him what I've just told you Nicky. I don't want your brother to hate me. But . . . she was . . . white. I know she wouldn't have meant to, but her being white would have torn this family apart. If I had sent her away, Jacques would have gone with her. I couldn't have that. I could not face life without either of my sons." He leaned his weary head back against the rocker and slowly closed his eyes. "For so many years . . . I wished . . . I wished she had been Cheyenne." Renee slumped and was gone.

Renee was laid to rest beside his wife in the DeGeer burial ground. Nicolas stood beside the grave long after all the other mourners and the preaching-man had drifted away. His heart was broken by the sight of the four graves, especially the fresh one. For with the burial of Renee DeGeer, Renee took with him the best part of Nicolas's life. The glory days of warriors and roaming hunters. All that had been but would never be again.

Except for the legal change of name, he was once again Egbert Higgins. And standing alone in his wool suit, he was dressed for the part.

Tears streaming his face, Nicolas, in a soft voice, said aloud, "If I could have just one more morning. Just one more day, with all of you. But I am alone now, with barely a shadow. Why am I alone?"

Nicolas looked back at his waiting horse. A thought flashed through his benumbed mind. Because of the customs of Christian burial—"We bring nothing into this world—we take nothing out"—Renee did not have a horse. Nicolas stared incredulously at his own horse, the saddled pinto standing fifty yards from the grave site, waiting patiently for him.

"No," he seethed in a whisper. "I will not allow this. My father will not walk into the Forever a poor and pitied man. NOT—MY—FATHER. Not Renee DeGeer! His enemies will not mock him."

Purpose firing his heart, Nicolas walked toward the animal, removed the rifle from the saddle holster, raised the rifle and, pausing a moment to wipe a blurring tear from his eye, shot the horse through the brain. The horse hit the ground in a wave of dust and flying dirt. Standing over the dead animal, Nicolas untied his hair, threw back his head, stretched his arms out wide, his fist clenching the rifle and, honoring his father as well as his former life, he emitted a final piercing war cry.

Coming Soon!

REMEMBERING
THE
OSAGE KID

MARDI OAKLEY MEDAWAR
author of *The Glory Days of Buffalo Egbert*

**A sweeping novel of the Native American
experience as seen by a powerful and
controversial member of the Osage nation**

Filled with the color and spirit of Oklahoma
history—from the life and lore of the Osage
nation to the hardscrabble frontier days
of marauding outlaws to the prosperity
of the 1950s—here is the stirring tale of
two very different men linked by
a fierce pride and a tragic secret.

**For more information
visit:** www.SpeakingVolumes.us

On Sale Now!

A SHERIFF LANSING MYSTERY
Book 2

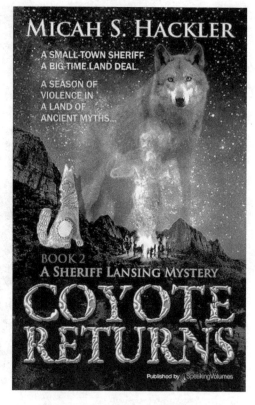

For more information
visit: www.SpeakingVolumes.us

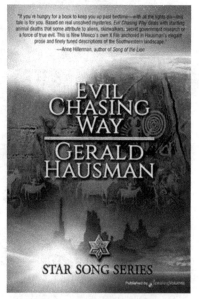

CPSIA information can be obtained
at www.ICGtesting.com
Printed in the USA
LVHW081046020123
736268LV00035B/1491